TURNING POINT

TURNING POINT

Book Three in The Kathleen Turner Series

Tiffany Snow

Published by Amazon Publishing
P.O. Box 400818 Las Vegas, NV 89140
ISBN-13: 9781611099836
ISBN-10: 1611099838

For Nikki.

I couldn't have done this without you.

Thank you for letting these characters become as real to you as they are to me.

CHAPTER ONE

Someone was following me.

The streets of downtown Indianapolis were busy this Friday night. Even though it was the second week of February, after two months of nothing but cold, snow, and ice, a spell of unseasonably warm weather had brought the residents of Indy and the surrounding suburbs out in droves.

Laughter and gaiety surrounded me as I hurried through the crowds oozing down Capitol Avenue. My pulse beat quicker and the hair on the back of my neck stood up. I chanced a quick glance behind me, but saw no one paying the least bit of attention to me.

I knew he was back there. Just because I couldn't see him didn't mean he couldn't see me.

He'd been following me for several blocks, always staying just out of sight when I turned around, and I'd caught only glimpses of an arm, a shoulder. But he was getting closer. I could feel it.

A group of men were strolling in front of me. An idea struck and I eased my way in front of them. My height—or lack thereof—had its advantages, I thought, as I slipped past them into an alley. Hopefully, they'd concealed my movements long enough to lose the man following me.

Unable to withstand the temptation, I stopped and peered behind me. When no figure stepped into the alley, I slumped against the brick wall at my back, releasing a pent-up breath.

"Nice move, princess. You almost lost me."

I gasped, jerking around.

"Damn it, Kade! You scared me to death!"

Kade Dennon, former FBI agent and current gun-for-hire, was completely unfazed by my outburst, the smirk I knew all too well curving his lips.

"It was a good thought." He crossed his arms and leisurely leaned one shoulder against the wall. "Use your weaknesses to your advantage. Being short doesn't have to be a detriment."

"I'm not short," I groused. "I'm"—I searched for a more palatable word—"petite."

"Whatever," he said with a snort. "Let's try again. I'll give you a sixty-second head start. Go." He looked down at his watch, timing me.

"Wait." I held up my hand. "It's getting late and I have a date with Blane tonight. Can we call it good for now?"

Blue eyes framed in lush, dark lashes and topped by wickedly arched brows peered at me. It didn't matter how often I saw him, Kade's dark beauty never failed to take my breath away. His square jaw, roughened with a day or two's growth of stubble, tightened. Black hair—which I knew from experience was soft to the touch—fell over his brow. I likened him to a fallen angel, and the description had never been more apt, clad as he was in his customary dark jeans, black shirt, and black leather jacket. I also knew a gun was holstered at his hip, and somewhere on his person was concealed another, as well as a wickedly sharp knife.

"Fine," he finally said, the word clipped. "But your wake-up call tomorrow is six a.m."

"On a Saturday?" I protested.

"And no coffee beforehand," he ordered. "I don't want you puking on me."

I didn't have a chance to reply before he was gone. With an ease I envied, he'd slipped into the crowd and disappeared.

I sighed in defeat as I trudged to my car parked a few blocks away, wondering if this was ever going to work.

Kade had shown up at my door a couple of weeks ago, declaring that if I was going to be of any worth as an investigator, I needed to be trained.

Well, that's putting it more delicately. His exact words had been, "You need to be trained before you really fuck something up, end up dead, or both."

How could I say no?

In truth, I'd been excited and nervous about my new job as investigator for the law firm of Kirk and Trent. I'd worked there as a runner, delivering documents, until Kade had given me an abrupt promotion right before Christmas. I guess you could call him a silent partner in the firm.

So far, the training had included time at the firing range with my new gun (courtesy of Kade), daily early morning runs (also courtesy of Kade), self-defense classes with a Marine, and these impromptu lessons that had no name. I ached all over from hitting the mat too many times in the self-defense lessons, dreaded the morning runs like a condemned man awaiting execution, and had only done so-so on what I privately thought of as the "cloak-and-dagger" training. The only place I'd held my own was the firing range.

Not for the first time I wondered if this was a job I could actually do.

I unlocked the door and climbed inside my black Lexus SUV, a company car paid for by the firm. Twenty minutes later, I was back at my apartment.

I lived on the top floor of a two-story apartment building near downtown, in a neighborhood where people didn't walk their dogs after dark, at least not alone. When I'd first moved to Indianapolis almost a year ago, this had been the best I could afford. Even then I'd had to work two jobs just to make rent and pay the bills—I was a runner for the law firm during the day and bartender at night at The Drop. Luckily, my new promotion meant an increase in salary and I'd been able to quit the bartending gig.

I hurriedly showered, pinning my long strawberry blonde hair up so it wouldn't get wet. There wasn't enough time for me to blow it dry before Blane arrived.

My heart beat a little faster as I thought of Blane, anticipation making my stomach flutter. Blane Kirk: high-powered lawyer, former Navy SEAL, rich playboy, my ex-boy-friend. One of those labels didn't seem to fit with the others. Our introduction had been less than what romance novels were made of, consisting as it had of my tripping and falling face-first into his lap during a client meeting. I still cringed when I thought about it.

We'd broken up before Christmas, after I'd found him in a clutch with his former girlfriend, Kandi-with-an-i. What I hadn't known then—what Blane didn't tell me until later—was that he'd suspected her of being the leak behind repeated attempts on my life. He'd thought that by breaking up with me and dating her, he'd be able to keep me safe. That hadn't worked out so well.

Since then, Blane had been "courting" me, for lack of a better word, in an attempt to win me back. I'd been leery of jumping back into a relationship, even though I knew I was in love with him. His list of ex-girlfriends was as long as my arm—both my arms, actually—and I had no interest in having my heart broken a second time.

Yet those reservations hadn't stopped me from going out with him, spending time with him, kissing him. It seemed no matter my resolve, I was helpless when it came to Blane.

My phone rang just as I was checking the clock; Blane was a few minutes late, which was unlike him.

"Hello?"

"Kat, it's me," Blane said.

Kat. That's me. At least, that's what Blane calls me. My full name is Kathleen Turner and, yes, I was named that on purpose. My father, Ted Turner, and my grandmother, Tina Turner, were only too happy to pass on the family tradition of naming a kid after a famous Turner. Since I had no brothers, it was up to my only cousin to carry on the dubious honor. Not that I knew if he would, since I hadn't heard from him in years.

"Hey," I said, sinking down onto my leather couch. If he was calling rather than knocking at my door, it couldn't be good news.

"I'm sorry, Kat, but I'm going to have to cancel our date."

I held in a sigh. "That's okay," I replied, keeping my tone light. No need for him to know how disappointed I was.

"I have to leave town for a few days. Something's come up."

A slight stiffness to his words made me frown, a hint of worry creeping in.

"Is everything all right?"

"Absolutely," he said easily. "I'll call you, okay?"

"Yeah, sure," I said, wondering if I had imagined something that wasn't there.

A few moments later, we'd disconnected, and I was left thinking about what would make Blane leave town on a Friday night. I'd been too taken aback to ask where he was going, and now I mentally kicked myself.

I changed into an old T-shirt, baked a frozen cheese pizza, and ate it while watching the latest episode I'd recorded of *Dancing with the Stars*. Not exactly the evening I'd planned.

Finding some rocky road ice cream buried in the back of my freezer, I scraped the carton clean, absentmindedly licking the spoon as I thought about Blane. I'd moved out of his house and back into my apartment two weeks after Christmas. My excuse for temporarily living with him—the fact that I'd been shot in the leg by a psychopath—was no longer viable. The physical and emotional wounds had healed well enough by then.

But I hadn't wanted to leave.

It was nice, living with Blane. I loved that he was the first and last person I saw every day. He was true to his word, giving me space and not pressuring me, though he had no compunction against using the explosive chemistry between us to tease and torture me. Each night he would kiss me before leaving me alone in my bedroom, and his kisses weren't chaste and sweet. They were hot, skilled, and demanding—always leaving me wanting more—which, of course, was his intention.

It was during one of these heated encounters that I had abruptly decided I needed to go back home. I couldn't think around Blane. Everything I wanted and felt was confused when his arms were around me, when he was touching me, kissing me. What did it mean, this pseudo-relationship and my living with him?

"Wait . . . stop," I'd said breathlessly, wrenching my lips from his.

That didn't deter him. His mouth trailed a scorching path across my jaw and down my neck.

"Blane—"

Blane kissed his name from my lips. I became lost in his touch again for who knows how long.

"I should go back home," I blurted.

Blane's entire body went still. I could feel his heartbeat racing as he pressed against me. Or maybe that was mine. He raised his head, his green eyes glittering in the semidarkness of the bedroom.

"You want to go back to your apartment." It didn't come out as a question, but rather a statement.

Nervous butterflies danced in my stomach. "It's not that I want to," I stammered. "But maybe it would be for the best."

Blane didn't say anything for a moment, and the silence seemed oppressive. I couldn't hold his penetrating gaze, so I stared at the white linen of his shirt.

"I'll take you home in the morning," he finally said.

When I looked back up, I couldn't read anything from his face. Before I'd even realized what was happening, he'd placed a kiss on my forehead and disappeared out the door.

I lay in bed, staring at the ceiling for a long time. I didn't know what had happened, what Blane wanted from me. Had he expected that I'd just continue living with him?

That just wasn't me.

Then I heard the sound of the piano downstairs.

Glancing at the clock, I pulled on a matching white robe to cover my nightgown. It was after one. Padding downstairs on bare feet, I followed the sound to the library. Inside, there wasn't a single lamp burning. The only light was filtering through the windows from the streetlamps outside.

Blane sat at the piano with his back to me, his hands moving furiously over the keys. Music filled the room as though it were a living thing. I watched in silent awe. I'd never seen him play like this before. His careful control was gone; only passion remained.

I don't know how much time passed before he suddenly stopped and turned around, startling me. I'd moved closer without even realizing, so engrossed in the music had I been. Now I stood mere feet from him.

He was disheveled, his dark-blond hair tousled, the neck of his shirt open, and his sleeves carelessly pushed up. Blane was almost always impeccably dressed, every inch of him screaming "powerful attorney." Seeing him with his armor off and guard down was a rare thing.

The overwhelming silence in the library and Blane's seemingly accusing look made me feel as though I'd rudely intruded on a private moment.

"I'm so sorry," I said softly, taking a step back. "I heard music . . ."

"That's all right," he replied, his voice a soft rasp. "I didn't mean to keep you up."

Since he didn't seem angry, I halted my retreat. Cautiously, I asked, "What were you playing?"

"Rachmaninoff."

I nodded as if that meant something to me, though I would have been hard-pressed to even repeat the name he'd just said.

"It was beautiful," I said sincerely. "But why are you playing at this time of night, Blane? What's wrong?"

He didn't answer for several moments and I held my breath. Finally, he glanced away. "Nothing's wrong, Kat. Let me help you back upstairs."

My breath came out in a huff as frustration reared inside me. I pressed my lips firmly together to keep from saying the words on the tip of my tongue. It seemed a recurring theme: Just when I thought Blane might open up to me, really open up, he pushed me away.

The next morning, he took me home.

For all that we'd been through together, Blane kept an emotional distance from me. He'd done so much—even put himself in mortal danger for me—but I didn't know if it was because of me, or simply because that's who he was. And he'd never said.

Since I'd moved out, we'd been dating. It was a combination of nice, sweet, and frustrating all at the same time. We were getting to know each other better, but it still seemed like Blane kept me at arm's length. Except when he was kissing me.

I fell asleep thinking about him and wondering where he'd gone, what he hadn't told me, and when he'd call.

∾

The covers were ripped from my body and I jerked upright, barely stifling a shriek. Kade was standing in my bedroom, the corner of my blanket in his hand.

"You're late," he said.

I flopped back onto the mattress with a groan, turning so my back was to him, and buried my head in the pillow. "Go away," I mumbled. "It's still dark outside."

He didn't respond, and for a blessed moment, I thought perhaps he'd heeded me.

"Black's my favorite color. How'd you know?"

It took a moment for my sleep-fogged brain to process what he had just said. The cold air brushing my backside brought things abruptly into focus.

"Kade!"

I shot up and yanked down the T-shirt that had ridden up to my waist overnight, exposing the black lace of my underwear.

His eyes drifted slowly over me, from my sleep-tousled hair, down my chest to my bare thighs.

"Five minutes," he said, abruptly turning and leaving the room. The door shut behind him.

I blew out a breath and pushed a hand through my hair, calming my suddenly pounding heart. Kade and I hadn't spoken of what lay between us, not since he'd told me that he cared about me. I'd hurt him that night. Not that I'd wanted to, but there'd been nothing I could say that wouldn't drive a wedge between him and Blane—his half brother.

I just knew I liked seeing him turn up on my doorstep, even if that meant getting up at the crack of dawn to go running through the streets of downtown Indianapolis.

Dragging myself from the warm confines of the bed, I hurried into the bathroom. Ten minutes later I was dressed in layers, with my hair pulled back in a ponytail.

"Ready," I said as I laced up my shoes. Kade was waiting impatiently with arms crossed in my living room.

"It's about time," he grumbled, heading for the door. I stuck my tongue out at his back.

"I saw that," he said warningly, his back still turned. He held the door open for me.

"You did not," I said with a laugh, smacking him on the arm as I passed by.

"Ah, so you did mock me," he said, following me down the stairs. "You should practice lying, princess. You don't have a deceitful bone in your body."

Kade started running as soon as we hit the pavement. He went at a pace I could keep up with, at least for a little while.

"I can lie," I protested, my breath coming out in puffs of cold as we ran.

"Please." Kade rolled his eyes. He wasn't even breathing hard. "I don't think I'll be taking you to Vegas anytime soon."

"Why do I have to lie anyway?"

"It comes in handy," he said. "Being able to make someone believe a lie can save your life."

I was turning this over in my mind when he added with a wicked grin, "And get you laid."

I went to smack him on the arm again, but he moved out of my reach.

"I'm the bad guy, princess. Catch me."

And just like that, he took off.

"Shit," I muttered miserably before putting on a burst of speed myself.

I ran as fast as I could through the streets, now starting to glow with the light of dawn. I knew I was never going to catch him, his legs were too long and he was just too fast. He rounded a corner up ahead and I abruptly changed direction, heading off to my right.

I ran harder, cutting through empty yards and a parking lot. Tearing around the edge of a building, I raced down an alleyway, only to find a chain-link fence blocking the end.

I quickly spotted a Dumpster shoved into the corner. Wrinkling my nose in distaste, I climbed up on top of it, hunched down, and waited.

Sure enough, about five seconds later, Kade came running down the street. He had slowed down quite a bit and was looking over his shoulder, no doubt wondering where I'd gone. I waited . . .

Now!

I jumped, hurtling through the air. He looked up, but not in time to get out of the way. The breath rushed out of his lungs when I tackled him, and we both went crashing to the ground.

Pressing my advantage of surprise, I climbed on top of him, grinning in glee at my victory.

"Caught you!" I said. "Betcha thought I couldn't do it, right?"

In a flash, Kade had flipped me over onto my back, straddling me and holding my wrists prisoner above my head.

"And what exactly were you planning to do with me once you'd caught me?" he asked, his voice a sibilant whisper in my ear.

I heard the words but couldn't concentrate enough to reply. I could smell the musky aroma of his sweat and feel the press of his thighs against my hips. His face was inches away, his blue eyes locked on mine. My breath was coming in pants, my chest heaving, and time seemed to stand still. His gaze drifted down to my mouth.

"What the hell? What's going on here? Get off her!"

The shouting broke my trance and I jerked my head around to see a heavyset middle-aged man hurrying toward us. He was carrying a bat. I squirmed frantically and Kade leisurely got to his feet.

"I'm okay." I forestalled the would-be rescuer, jumping up. "I'm fine."

The man halted. "Are you sure?"

I nodded. "Absolutely. I just . . . fell . . . and he was helping me."

The man snorted in disbelief, but turned and walked back in the direction he'd come from.

I could feel Kade's eyes on me, but I avoided looking at him. I nervously readjusted my ponytail, which had come loose in our tussle.

"Let's go," Kade said, and he broke into an easy jog.

I hurried to catch up to him and we ran back to my apartment in silence.

"Meet me at the gym at six o'clock tonight," Kade said, glancing at his watch. His breathing was deep and controlled, whereas the sound of my sucking air into my lungs would have embarrassed me if I hadn't felt like I was going to throw up any minute. I clutched at a stitch in my side.

Kade lifted an eyebrow, his mouth twisting in amusement. My eyes narrowed, daring him to say a word.

"Six o'clock," he said again.

I nodded to show I'd gotten the message and watched as he slid into his black Mercedes. In a few moments, he was gone.

Lugging my aching body back into my apartment, I collapsed flat out on the floor and groaned. Tigger seemed to think that was an invitation to cuddle. He was stretched out next to me in short order, his loud purr vibrating against my side. I halfheartedly patted his marmalade fur, too exhausted to raise my arm for a proper petting.

The only thing that got me off the floor was the thought of a hot shower and coffee.

I whiled away the afternoon doing laundry, making lunch, and trying to pick a practice lock Kade had given me. It was a difficult task and I grew frustrated quickly. When the lock finally tumbled and opened, I crowed with delight.

"Only took"—I glanced at the clock above my television—"an hour and a half."

I sighed. Well, Kade had never said this would be an easy job.

Speaking of which, it was time to go to the gym. When I'd imagined a gym before, it was with vague thoughts of a place filled with exercise machines, maybe a pool, weights, stuff like that. That wasn't the kind of gym Kade sent me to.

This dingy place wasn't in a great part of town, and considering where I lived, that was saying something. The fading sign over the door outside read Danny's Gym. Inside, the usual smell of sweat and linoleum hit me, though it wasn't entirely unpleasant; the gym was kept immaculately clean. There were free weights and weight sets over in one corner, and heavy punching bags along the wall. The center of the room was dominated by a large boxing ring.

Today, the gym was nearly empty save for the owner, Danny, the Marine who had been training me. A head taller than me and sporting a crew cut, he stood with his arms crossed over his massive T-shirt-clad chest, watching two people in the ring.

I frowned as I got closer, studying the figures. Then my eyes flew open wide in surprise.

Kade and Branna were sparring.

They circled each other, Kade barefoot and dressed only in gray sweatpants that clung to his hips and thighs. His hands were taped as though he'd been boxing.

Branna was wearing formfitting black yoga pants and a black tank top. Her long, nearly black hair was tied back in a French braid. I felt dowdy in my shorts and T-shirt, my hair in a ponytail.

I hadn't seen Branna since Chicago, when Kade and I had infiltrated a data center and she had hacked into the security cameras. Kade had told me that he and Branna had shared a foster home, that she had been abused as a child and he had done what he could to stop it.

I didn't want to feel anything for her—she barely tolerated me. I'd known the moment she first looked at Kade in Chicago that she was in love with him. But the knowledge of her past raised a reluctant sympathy in me, though she would hate me even more if she knew those thoughts were going through my head.

Kade made his move. He was fast and I held my breath. Branna was a small, delicate-looking woman, but she dodged him, pivoting on her toes. He snagged her arm, but she easily twisted away, doing something to his hand that made him wince. They moved again, grappling, and I was sure he was going to hurt her. Then suddenly Branna grasped his arm, used his momentum to twist him . . . and a moment later, Kade was flat on his back. My jaw dropped in astonishment.

Beside me, Danny clapped. "Nice one," he said.

Kade groaned, accepting Branna's outstretched hand as he got to his feet. "I'm getting too old for this," he groused.

She laughed lightly. "Don't be ridiculous." I could hear the slight trace of her Irish accent. "I'm just better than you are."

He rolled his eyes at this, then spotted me. "Perfect timing," he called out.

Branna turned to see who Kade was talking to, and I could almost feel the temperature drop ten degrees when she saw me.

"What's she doing here?" Her voice held none of the warmth from when she'd teased Kade. It seemed she was no fonder of me now than she had been in Chicago.

Kade gave her a sharp glance. "She's here to train."

He climbed out of the ring and made his way over to Danny and me. Branna remained where she was.

"Make sure you lock up when you're done," Danny said, glancing at his watch. "I'm meeting a buddy, so I'm outta here."

"Will do," Kade replied. He turned to me as Danny left.

I tried and failed to not ogle his bare chest, carved in planes of muscle and glistening with sweat. Kade wasn't a huge guy, but the lean sinew of his body was honed to perfection.

"So how'd your date go last night?" The question seemed innocuous on the surface, but the sarcasm in his voice gave it a whole other meaning.

I shifted uneasily. Blane's and my relationship was a touchy subject with Kade, ever since he'd seen me fall apart after witnessing Blane and Kandi together.

"Blane had to cancel," I said.

Kade lifted a single eyebrow in silent question.

I shrugged. "He said he had to leave town for a few days," I explained, frowning. "Didn't he tell you?" Blane and Kade kept rough tabs on each other, from what I knew of their relationship.

"I'm not his keeper," Kade said, then abruptly changed the subject. "Today I want you to train with Branna."

"What? You must be joking," I stammered in surprise. "I've been training with Danny. Why Branna?"

"She's closer to your size and a woman. She has a better understanding of how to train you than Danny does, though he's been great at showing you the basics."

Before I could protest further, he took me by the arm, leading me over to the ring, where Branna still stood, glaring at us.

"You didn't tell me I'd be having to train the bartender," Branna said, her voice rife with condescension, ignoring me completely as she glared at Kade.

"You get paid no matter what," Kade said indifferently, handing me into the ring.

I reluctantly took off my shoes, eyeing Branna's malicious gaze.

"You don't have to turn her into a ninja, just show her some moves, defense techniques. Danny's been working with her, but you're going to be able to show her things he can't."

The ringing of a cell phone preempted anything Branna might have said, and Kade dug into a duffel bag stowed alongside the wall. "I have to take this," he said as he glanced at the number. "Be right back."

He walked to the back, where Danny's office was. When he was out of sight, I returned my attention to Branna.

For a moment, neither of us spoke. I could again appreciate how beautiful she was, even with her lip curled in distaste. Black hair, green eyes, and near-porcelain skin had a dramatic effect. She was small but curvaceous, and I envied the narrowness of her waist. Kade was correct, she and I were about the same height. But that's where the similarities ended.

"Danny's been training you," she stated rather than asked.

I nodded. "A bit." Which was a nice way of saying I ended up on the mat a fraction less often than I would have a month ago.

"Well, then," she replied with a smile I wasn't sure I liked. "Let's see what you've got, shall we?" Her accent made the words sound innocent, but the gleam in her eyes said otherwise.

All kinds of alarm bells were going off inside my head as I watched her assume a fighting stance. I desperately wanted to get out of the ring, but I didn't know how to do so without looking like a coward. Her disdain and contempt made me angry, and I wished I had the skills to put her in her place. Unfortunately, I could see how this was going to go. I grimly hoped none of my bones would be broken before Kade reappeared.

Branna moved and I watched her warily, caution making me keep my distance. We circled slowly, each observing the other for a sign, whether of weakness or opportunity I couldn't say. When she did come at me, I was unprepared, taking a blow to my stomach. My legs were swept out from under me and I hit the mat hard.

Branna's tinkling laugh made my hands curl into fists as I coughed, trying to get my breath back. My stomach burned from her hit, but I gamely got back to my feet. Branna looked simply delighted now. Gone was the irritation at having this chore handed to her by Kade. I guessed the prospect of kicking my ass was an agreeable one to her.

The next few minutes were a blur of pain and sweat. Branna toyed with me like a cat with a mouse, and I knew I was going to be sporting black-and-blue marks all over later. I kept a tight grip on my temper, though I was furious. Branna was a bully.

I was on all fours, sweat dripping down my nose onto the vinyl, wondering how much more my body could take, when I decided I'd had enough.

"I don't think Kade's going to appreciate your training methods," I wheezed, painfully sitting back on my haunches.

"Then he should have thought of that before," Branna replied haughtily. Not even her hair was mussed from the tight braid. I hadn't been able to lay a finger on her.

"Does he know you're in love with him?" I asked. "Because you don't strike me as his type."

Branna's eyes narrowed.

"I hear he likes blondes." I smiled.

At that, she came at me as I'd known she would, but this time I was prepared. Still on my knees, my hands shot out to catch her calf as she kicked out at me. I gave it a hard twist and yank. She grunted in pain as she hit the mat. I launched myself to my feet, sure I was going to pay for that, and I wasn't wrong. Her rage at being bested, even if only fleetingly, was scary. In seconds, I was facedown on the mat with blood dripping from my nose, and this time, Branna was giving me no time to recover, yanking me by my hair until I was on my knees.

"Branna! What the fuck is going on?"

The pressure on my hair suddenly eased and I collapsed back down on the mat, groaning. Kade had finally returned, and if I hadn't been so relieved to hear his voice, I would have gladly killed him for leaving me alone with the Terminator.

"I told you to train her, not kill her!"

"It's not my fault your little protégé can't hold her own in a fight," Branna defended herself.

The vinyl felt blessedly cool against my cheek, and I wouldn't have moved for quite a while if Kade hadn't gently turned me onto my back. As I blinked blearily up at him, the look of dismay on his face as he surveyed me was replaced by cold anger.

"Jesus Christ!" he exploded, the anger in his voice making me jump. "Why do you always have to make it personal, Branna?" Kade asked in disgust. "I needed you to do a job, not release your inner bitch."

I thought that Branna's "bitch" wasn't so much "inner."

"If you don't like the way I do things, then you shouldn't have called me," Branna shot back, though I noticed that her fair skin had turned a shade of crimson at Kade's words.

"Get out," Kade said.

He returned his attention to me and helped me sit up. The pain in my stomach made me catch my breath. I gritted my teeth, not wanting to give Branna the satisfaction of hearing me make a sound.

"Fine," Branna bit out, grabbing her bag from along the wall. "But do your own damn training from now on."

"No shit," Kade replied, barely glancing her way as she slammed out the door.

"I don't like her very much," I managed to say while using the hem of my T-shirt to swipe at the blood accumulating beneath my nose.

"At the moment, neither do I," he said. "Can you stand?"

I nodded and tried to rise, but Kade had to help me. I maintained a tight grip on his shoulder as his arm curved around my waist. The strength in his muscles and the feel of his skin beneath my fingers distracted me from my aches and pains.

He helped me to a bench and I gratefully sat, resting my head against the wall and releasing a sigh. Kade got up, returning a few moments later with a wet cloth.

"I'm sorry, princess," he said quietly as he gently wiped the blood from my face. "I wouldn't have left you alone with her if I'd known she would do that to you."

I didn't mind the nickname Kade had coined for me. Though it had begun as something disparaging, it had turned into a type of endearment. He'd begun using it after watching me do a karaoke performance of my beloved pop princess Britney Spears. I wasn't good at a lot of things, but I could do a dead-on Britney impression.

"It's all right," I dismissed his apology. "It wasn't your fault." I left unsaid, "That Branna's such a bitch."

"Come on," he said, getting to his feet. "I know what'll help."

I stood slowly, wincing, and followed him to the back. I glanced around curiously at lockers and shower stalls lining the walls. Kade pushed his way through another door, which he held open for me.

As I stepped inside a small wood-paneled room, I was immediately assailed by humidity and the smell of chlorine. A bubbling hot tub sat in the middle of the room.

"Get in," Kade said, nodding toward the tub. "It'll help with the ache."

I glanced down at my attire uncertainly. I hadn't brought an extra change of clothing.

"I won't look," Kade snorted, then smirked. "I've seen it before anyway."

I blushed at the reminder. Kade had seen me naked before, that was true. He'd helped save me from being turned into a cinder when my car had been blown up. The damage to my clothes had been irreparable, and he'd taken care of that, though I'd been unconscious at the time.

I still hesitated and Kade heaved a long-suffering sigh. "I'll be back in fifteen."

He left the room and I could no longer resist the allure of steaming water. Stripping down to my plain white cotton underwear and bra, I eased into the water. It was blissful, and I could feel the coiled tension in my muscles loosening up. Sinking down to my neck, I rested my head against the side and closed my eyes. It felt heavenly.

I had nearly fallen asleep, so I was surprised when the door opened and Kade stepped back inside. I groggily lifted my head. He'd changed into jeans and pulled on a T-shirt. I briefly mourned the loss of the view of his naked chest.

"Time's up, princess," he said, holding out a towel for me. He turned away to shut off the hot tub, then left the room again.

I stripped off my wet bra and underwear, pulling my T-shirt and shorts on over my bare skin. It felt weird, but I was only going home. Holding my dripping clothes, I emerged from the room to find Kade by the doors, staring out at the darkening streets. When he heard me approach, he turned, taking in my appearance, including the small bundle I held.

"You going to be all right?" he asked.

I shrugged. "A few bruises. Nothing I can't handle."

He gave a short nod.

When he said nothing further, I smiled nervously. "Well, I guess I'll see you tomorrow."

"Let's grab some dinner," he suggested. "I'm starving."

I blanched. "I can't go somewhere like this," I protested. "I'm not wearing any—" I abruptly cut off, my face heating.

Kade looked briefly pained. "Wear this," he said, digging inside his duffel bag and tossing me a hoodie. "And don't remind me about what you're not wearing."

I shrugged into the hoodie and zipped it up. It smelled of Kade. Whereas Blane always wore cologne, Kade rarely used the stuff. The aroma drifting from the cotton was a mix of leather, spice, and warm musk—nothing that could be captured in a bottle, and all uniquely Kade.

"I'll drive," he said, and I didn't argue as I followed him out the door.

The Mercedes was an expensive car, and I enjoyed riding in it. I surreptitiously watched Kade's hand deftly handle the gearshift. If I allowed myself to think about it, I could almost imagine I was Kade's girlfriend rather than his employee. Sitting in his car, wearing his clothes—it was not an altogether unwelcome notion. I knew that few, if any, women had been allowed this close to Kade.

The image of Blane abruptly intruded, and guilt hit me hard. I shouldn't be thinking about these things. It was classless and tacky to entertain thoughts of Kade like that when I was dating Blane. The sexual tension between Kade and me was thick enough to cut with a knife, but that didn't mean I had to act on it.

I deliberately looked away, turning to stare unseeing out the window.

A few minutes later, Kade stopped the car. We were parked on the street near a building marked simply Tavern. I raised my eyebrows in silent question at Kade.

"What?" he asked innocently. "They've got great burgers."

I followed him inside. It was a busy Saturday night, and the tables, booths, and barstools were full of people. Kade slipped into the crowd and I grabbed a fistful of his shirt hem so I wouldn't lose him. Reaching behind his back, he unfastened my hand from the cloth and laced my fingers through his. A warm sensation flowed through my veins at the gesture and the feel of his thumb brushing across the top of my hand.

A moment later, we slid into an empty booth in a far corner. I sat with my back to the room while Kade's was to the wall.

A waitress whose nametag proclaimed her to be Cindy handed us menus. Kade ordered a beer and so did I.

I began perusing the menu, waiting. I didn't have to wait long.

"What did you see?"

It was the standard question Kade had begun asking. This was my observation lesson, and I'd been practicing. I put down my menu and looked at him as I answered.

"There are two exits, the front and the one at the rear past the bathrooms. Five waitresses and two bartenders, plus two cooks. They must have trouble relatively often, because the phone number for the cops was taped to the wall near the phone. A possible problem tonight will be the five men at the bar arguing over the basketball game—IU versus Purdue. IU is winning in the second half, but the Purdue fans appear drunker."

The corner of Kade's mouth twitched in approval, and the warm feeling from earlier spread.

"Oh, and there's a hooker reeling in a john at the other end of the bar," I added.

"Nice job. Though I think you forgot the two guys who checked out your ass on the way in," Kade said with a smirk.

"Likewise I didn't mention the three women who watched you walk across the room like you were sex on a stick," I retorted.

I'd wanted to scratch their eyes out.

Kade's grin widened. "Sex on a stick?"

I didn't give him the satisfaction of replying.

"Any helpers?" he asked, getting back to business.

I nodded. "Two guys at the table in the southeast corner. One of them's wearing an IFD T-shirt." Kade had taught me to look for anyone who might be in the police, military, or fire department, as they'd be most likely to help a complete stranger in trouble, especially a woman.

The waitress came back with our beers and took our order.

"Address?" he asked once she was gone.

I told him where we were.

"Nearest cross street?"

I told him that, too.

"Why'd you move out?" he asked out of the blue.

I stared at him in confusion. "Move out of where?"

"Blane's."

Oh. I took a nervous sip of my beer. "I was just staying there until I healed."

"And he let you go?"

I bristled. "Let me? I wasn't aware I had to wait for him to 'let' me do anything."

"Don't get your panties in a twist," Kade said. "Oh wait, I forgot." He leaned across the table. "You're not wearing any."

He took another swallow of his beer, his eyes glittering with mischief as he watched me.

"Thought I wasn't supposed to remind you about that," I said archly.

Kade shrugged. "Doesn't matter. It's all I can think about anyway."

I swallowed. "Kade, I'm dating Blane. You know that."

Kade's jaw tightened and he finished off his beer without replying. The waitress appeared with another, as well as our food, which she set before us on the weathered wooden table surface.

"Are you sleeping with him?"

I choked on my beer. "I can't believe you just asked me that," I spluttered, my cheeks burning.

"That means you're not," he said, and there was no mistaking the satisfaction in his voice. "It's been six weeks. If Blane hasn't sealed the deal by now, it's open season."

I was almost afraid to ask. "Open season on what?"

The look in his eyes made my breath catch. "On you."

CHAPTER TWO

As I drove back to my apartment, I thought about what Kade had said. He'd deftly changed the subject after his declaration. Perhaps my dismay had clued him in. I could think of nothing worse than Blane and Kade fighting.

Nothing worse except them fighting over me.

I snorted in derision. I was so not worth coming between them. Not that I thought I wasn't a decent catch—I was pretty enough, and intelligent. I could sort of cook, and I wanted to have kids someday. But Blane and Kade were in a whole different league, not only in looks, but in careers, education, and success. I was just a bartender who had been given a job that I had serious doubts I could pull off.

I showered and pulled on a T-shirt, my back aching from Branna's so-called lesson. I'd just turned off the lights and climbed into bed when my cell phone rang. I glanced at the caller ID, and my heart skipped a beat.

Blane.

"Hello," I answered, settling down under the covers.

"Kat."

The sound of Blane's voice made me smile.

"Did I wake you?"

"No. I wasn't asleep yet."

"Are you in bed?"

"Yes."

"What are you wearing?"

I laughed. "A very sexy T-shirt."

"You look sexy in anything," Blane said. "What did you do today?"

I sighed. "Well, Kade dragged me out of bed at the crack of dawn—"

"Kade?"

I stopped speaking. Blane's voice had registered surprise and warning.

"What was Kade doing in your apartment?"

I swallowed, suddenly deeply uneasy. "He's training me," I answered. "He got back in town a couple of weeks ago."

Silence.

"Didn't he tell you?"

"He did not."

Never had three words conveyed quite so much. I didn't know what to say, so I said nothing.

"How is he training you?"

Uh-oh. Blane had his courtroom interrogator voice on.

"He . . . um . . . makes me run . . . in the morning"—I nervously twisted the corner of the blanket in my fingers—"and started me in a self-defense class." No need to tell him how Branna had beat me up today. "I have to go to the shooting range and practice, too."

I stopped, unsure if I should mention anything about the cloak-and-dagger lessons.

The other end of the line was ominously quiet.

"Blane? Are you still there?"

"Yes."

The controlled anger in his voice made me cringe.

"I'm sorry," I apologized. "I assumed you knew, that he had told you."

"There's nothing for you to be sorry about," he said. "I'll take it up with Kade. Don't worry about it."

I briefly wondered what that conversation would be like, then decided I really didn't want to know.

I changed the subject. "When are you coming back?"

Blane sighed tiredly. "I don't know. I'd hoped to be back in a day or two, but that might not work out."

Lightning flashed outside. A storm was brewing. I watched as I listened to Blane speak, something in his voice causing a sense of foreboding to creep over me.

"Listen, Kat." His voice lowered, became more grave. "The Navy . . . I had a meeting today."

Lightning again, this time closer.

"Kat . . . they want me to reenlist. They have a need for a specialized liaison between the JAG Corps and Special Ops, due to the secrecy and sensitive nature of what they do. They want me to take that position."

My stomach twisted painfully and I clutched the phone to my ear. "What does that mean?" The words felt stiff and foreign on my tongue.

"It means I'd go back to active duty for a while—six months probably—before assuming the responsibilities of the job."

The lightning seemed to be right outside my window now, and I couldn't blink, no matter how my eyes were burning.

"Where would they send you?"

He paused before answering. "Iraq, probably. Maybe Afghanistan."

I couldn't speak. Couldn't breathe. Active duty meant combat. Danger. Possibly death.

"Kat?"

My eyes still wouldn't blink, and now things were blurring. The lightning streaks became flashes of light, which seemed like bomb blasts.

"Kathleen? Talk to me."

"Yeah." My voice was a hoarse whisper.

"I haven't decided, Kat." His tone was softer now. "I haven't given them an answer, and I don't need to for a while. I have some time."

"Okay." I could think of nothing else to say.

"I miss you," he said.

My eyes finally closed. "I miss you, too."

"Good."

I smiled weakly. That was such a Blane thing to say.

"I'll talk to you soon," he said. "Sleep tight."

"Night, Blane."

"Good night, Kat."

I lay the phone on my bedside table before turning onto my back. I stared at the ceiling, briefly illuminated every few minutes from the lightning flashes outside.

Blane might leave. Go back to being a full-time SEAL. I'd hardly see him, talk to him.

He might die.

When I finally slept, my dreams were filled with images of Blane dying on a battlefield a long way away, and far from me.

∽

"Rise and shine, princess."

Bright light invaded my eyelids and I jerked awake, sitting bolt upright.

Kade was rummaging through my dresser drawers, pulling clothes out and tossing them into a nearby suitcase.

"What are you doing?" I asked, rubbing the sleep from my tired eyes. I looked at the clock. It wasn't yet four thirty. "Why the hell are you in my apartment at this hour?"

"Road trip," Kade crisply replied, not even glancing my way.

He dangled a lacy pair of underwear from one finger.

"Kade!" I exclaimed, vaulting out of bed and snatching them from his hand. My cheeks burned, but he only smirked at me. "What do you mean, 'road trip'?"

He began grabbing jeans and shirts from my closet, tossing them toward the suitcase. "Ryan Sheffield. Remember him?"

How could I not? An ex–CIA agent given the task of doing whatever had to be done to ensure the outcome of a case Blane had tried—even if it included killing me. We hadn't found out who he'd been working for, and now my interest was piqued.

"Yeah. What about him?"

Kade turned toward me. "Well, I found out where he'd been living, prior to his untimely demise."

The self-congratulation practically oozed off him, and I had to bite my lip to keep from grinning. The last thing Kade needed was more inflating of his ego.

"And where is that?" I asked.

"Denver."

"You're going to Denver?"

Kade was still pawing through my closet, grimacing in distaste at some of my clothes. "*We* are going to Denver," he corrected.

"We?"

He glanced at me. "You're my employee. I pay your salary. Yes. *We* are going to Denver." He tossed some clothes at me and I reflexively caught them. "Get dressed. We leave in ten." Then my bedroom door was closing behind him.

I dashed into the bathroom. Fifteen minutes later, I was hauling my suitcase into the living room.

"About time," Kade grumbled, handing me my coat. I pulled it on over my jeans and long-sleeved button-down shirt. I'd layered the navy shirt over a cream-colored tank, not knowing if I'd be warm or cold on the plane.

"Wait," I said. "What about Tigger?"

We both turned to look at the lump of feline in the corner of my couch.

"Can't you just leave out some food and water?" Kade asked.

I just looked at him.

"What?" he said.

I rolled my eyes. "Let me take him to Alisha. She owes me one."

Alisha was my next-door neighbor. She had left her dog, Bacon Bits, with me for several days when she'd gone to take care of her sick grandmother. I figured now would be a good time for her to return the favor.

Fifteen minutes and several lectures on the dangers of travel in the middle of the night later (my neighbor was obsessive-compulsive about everyone else's business), we were finally on our way to the airport.

I was quiet while Kade drove, my eyes turned toward the window and the darkened scenery flashing by. I couldn't get the conversation with Blane out of my mind and it was making my stomach churn with dread. What if he decided to reenlist—to go back to active duty? Honestly, I didn't think I had it in me to wait, day after day, for a call that might or might not come. I wasn't that strong.

We boarded the plane with little ceremony. Only once we were ensconced in our seats watching the sun rise over the wing did Kade speak.

"What's the matter?"

I turned to him. He was gazing intently at me, his blue eyes seeming to penetrate my thoughts. I looked away.

"Nothing," I said. "Just tired."

"Bullshit," he shot back. "If you're going to be with me on this, I need you to actually be here. Not lost in dreamland. So if you're not up for it, tell me now. I don't want my life in the hands of someone who's too busy staring out the window to notice what's going on around them."

Anger flared immediately. "I'm not distracted," I said. "And I wasn't aware your life was in danger while we're sitting on a flipping airplane." My sarcasm was thick.

I changed the subject. "So tell me what you found."

He looked at me as though he knew perfectly well what I was doing, but he went along with it. "Ryan Sheffield was CIA," he said. "You knew that."

I nodded.

"What we didn't know, and didn't find out before your buddy Frankie took him out"—I flinched at that. Frankie had most definitely not been my buddy; he had planned to torture and kill me—"was who Sheffield was working for. I've spent the past few weeks tracking down every lead I could find on him. Eventually, they led to Denver."

"Why Denver?" I asked.

"Why not?"

I sighed and looked out the window again.

If you didn't count the flight to Chicago with Kade—which I didn't since it had been in what had felt like a flying limousine—it had been a long time since I'd flown anywhere. Mom and Dad had taken me to Disney World when I was ten—that had been the only other time I'd ever flown. I hadn't enjoyed the experience overly much then, and it wasn't any different now. My fingernails bit into the armrests as the plane taxied down the runway, picking up speed.

"Afraid of flying?" Kade asked dryly, eyeing my death grip on the chair.

"Of course not." I slid the window shade down. If we plunged to a fiery death, I didn't need to see. "I'm afraid of crashing, not flying."

Kade snorted and I shot him a glare.

A few tense (for me) minutes later and we were airborne. When it seemed we weren't going to make an unexpected landing, I relaxed somewhat. Something bad could still happen, but most crashes occurred at takeoff and landing. I had a couple of hours before I had to worry again.

The flight attendants served drinks and I was grateful to get my hands on some coffee. My eyes narrowed as the cute, pert brunette lingered over Kade, chatting quietly with him and laughing at something he said in an undertone. Her hand rested on his arm as she handed him something. She smiled and finally moved on to the next row.

"Did you get her number?" I asked, my tone bitchy. "Maybe you'll have time for a booty call in Denver."

"Put the claws away, princess." Kade handed me the slightly warm package. "I got you some breakfast. For free, I might add."

He smirked as I unwrapped a cinnamon roll.

"You have to learn to use every advantage you have to get what you want. You're a beautiful woman, Kathleen. Use it. A smile and a touch can sometimes get you further than the threat or use of force."

I flushed as I tore off a piece of the bun and put it in my mouth; it was sticky and sweet. I lingered over it, eating slowly.

Kade thought I was beautiful. Blane had said so before as well. I didn't think I was. "Beautiful" was a word reserved for models and movie stars. I didn't feel beautiful.

"So I thought you weren't going to come back to Indy before summer," I said. Not that I was complaining. I'd heard nothing from Kade since he'd left late Christmas night, and I'd worried, knowing that his job was dangerous—and most likely highly illegal.

Kade shrugged. "Had some downtime. Thought I'd give you a hand in your new job, since I'm guessing Blane didn't give you a lot to do."

I shook my head ruefully. "No, not really. Background checks, paperwork, that kind of stuff. That's about all."

I'd had the distinct impression Blane hadn't approved of my promotion, though whether it was because he felt I wasn't qualified for the job or if he thought it was too dangerous, I didn't know.

"Boring," Kade decreed.

I shot him a grin in agreement.

Kade leaned toward me. "Stick with me, princess," he said conspiratorially. "I'm a lot of things, but I'm never boring."

We landed without incident (thank God), and soon were driving toward downtown Denver in a rented SUV. I'd never seen mountains and I stared in wonder at the snow-capped Rockies off in the distance.

"You ever been here before?" Kade asked, watching me gaze out the window.

"I've never been anywhere before," I answered truthfully.

"No vacations as a kid?"

"Disney World once. A cop's salary wasn't the stuff dreams are made of, so we didn't go many places."

"Who's your favorite princess, princess?"

I laughed at his question, my mood lightening. "Belle, of course."

"Why 'of course'?"

"She's smart, loyal to her dad and the Beast, clever, brave, kind, warmhearted." I ticked off the many attributes of Princess Belle on my fingers. "And she loves to read."

"I thought Cinderella would be every little girl's favorite."

I grimaced. "No way. She was a complete doormat for her stepmom and stepsisters. Though she does get all the press."

Kade laughed, a sound I rarely heard him make. It was good to hear.

"You obviously have given this a great deal more thought than I have," he said.

"Belle's awesome," I continued, extolling her virtues. "She was able to see past the curse on the Beast to what he was—who he could be—on the inside. He became a better person because she loved him and he loved her." I sighed. "It's a great love story."

Kade's voice had an edge to it as he glanced my way. "So are you Belle? A woman who could love a beast?"

Our eyes met and I drew a sharp breath, just now realizing the subtext of our conversation. Suddenly the light banter about Disney princesses, of all things, was rife with deeper meaning.

"Life's not a fairy tale," I said, avoiding the question. "If it were, I'd get to wear a ball gown every day."

Kade chuckled again and the tension was broken.

"Sorry I missed your birthday," Kade said after a while.

Surprised, I said, "It's okay. I didn't expect you to remember it."

My birthday had been a couple of weeks ago, on January 21. I was now officially twenty-five years old.

"What did you do to celebrate?"

"Blane took me out to dinner," I said. "It was nice. He bought me a purse."

I didn't say that he'd not bought me just any purse, but a brand that I knew cost over a thousand dollars. I'd been terrified to use it—afraid I'd get something on it or mess it up. It still sat in the pretty bag it had come in, on the top shelf in my closet.

Talking about Blane reminded me of the conversation we'd had last night, and my stomach twisted.

"What's going on?" Kade asked, glancing my way. "You look like I just told you Belle's a fictional character."

I smiled halfheartedly. "Blane called last night." I hesitated, unsure if I should tell Kade what Blane had said. Surely Blane wouldn't mind; they were brothers, after all. "He said... he said that he was thinking of reenlisting."

I looked at Kade, whose hands had tightened on the steering wheel.

"Why the fuck would he do something so stupid?" Kade gritted out.

I shook my head. "He said something about a special liaison position, but that first he'd go back on active duty for six months. Back to Iraq, or Afghanistan."

I could feel the tension rolling off Kade in waves, and it seemed neither of us had anything to say after that. It grew quiet, both of us lost in our own thoughts.

Downtown Denver was busy this Sunday morning, and traffic was thick. As we drove through the city, the buildings became increasingly older and more dilapidated. Car and foot traffic thinned to a trickle, and then Kade turned down a side street. It was an odd mix of residential and industrial, with a few scattered brick warehouses among small run-down homes.

A couple of kids were playing in the front yard of one house, and my eyes were drawn to them: two boys, about nine or ten years old, running around with a dog as scraggly as they were. One of the boys threw a stick and the dog bounded gamely after it.

After another block, Kade pulled the car to the side of the street and stopped. We were in front of one of those brick warehouses.

"This is where Ryan Sheffield lived?" I asked, skeptical.

"Home sweet home," Kade replied. "Let's go check it out." He pulled the gun from the holster at his hip and made sure it was loaded, then glanced meaningfully at me.

"I have it," I groused, hooking the long strap of my purse over my head and across my chest. The small gun he'd bought me lay inside. I refused to wear it in a holster like Kade. I just wasn't comfortable enough with the firearm to do that.

"Gee, I feel so safe knowing my partner has a gun . . . buried inside her purse," Kade said sarcastically.

I rolled my eyes. "Are we going or not?"

In reply, Kade got out of the car.

It was warmer than I'd expected, so I shucked my coat and left it in the front seat of the car. Kade discarded his leather jacket as well. The thin cotton of his black button-down shirt fit him closely. He'd rolled back the cuffs, and the top buttons were undone, exposing the skin of his throat. Unlike Blane, he didn't wear a T-shirt underneath.

I realized I was staring and jerked my gaze away before Kade could notice and make some smart-ass comment.

I followed as Kade crossed the street and rounded the building to the west side. We passed boarded-up windows, and some that were broken, their tinted glass shards reflecting bits of sunlight back at me. They almost seemed like eyes watching me go by. I shuddered.

"How'd you find this place again?" I asked. By now we'd reached the back. Kade paused in front of a staircase that led down to a steel door.

"I hacked into the CIA," he said casually before starting down the stairs.

My jaw dropped. "You what?" I squeaked. "You can't do that!"

I hurried after him, appalled, and latched on to his arm so he would look at me. "They put people in prison for that, Kade."

One corner of his mouth twisted upward. "Only if you get caught."

He pulled a lockpick from his pocket and crouched down. Quicker than I wanted to believe, the door clicked open.

"How do you do that so fast?" I groused quietly, remembering how long it had taken me to pick a lock while sitting in the comfort of my living room.

"Because I'm good," Kade replied, just as softly, easing open the door and leading the way inside.

It was dark and musty. The meager light filtering in through the dirt-crusted windows wasn't enough to illuminate the space. Kade stood for a moment, listening, and I did, too, unsure what exactly we were listening for. There seemed to be no one else there.

Kade started forward, his gun in his hand, and I fell into step behind him. I disliked being in the back, but I didn't want to lead, either. It felt uncomfortably reminiscent of going through a haunted house—a surprise might be around the corner up ahead, but it was just as likely someone was waiting to pounce on you when your back was turned.

Kade moved so silently I felt clumsy in his wake. Even my breathing sounded loud in my ears.

We crept down a long hallway to a set of stairs going up. At the top was a hallway that stretched in both directions.

"You go left, I'll go right," Kade said. "Yell if you find something."

Right.

I reached into my purse and reluctantly pulled out my gun. The heavy weight of it in my hand was somewhat comforting as Kade disappeared around a corner.

"Yell if I find something," I muttered to myself. "You can bet your ass I'll be yelling." Screaming bloody murder, more like it.

I walked down the hallway, opening the first two doors I found, and peered into empty, abandoned rooms. My heart was pounding so fast I felt light-headed. I tried to slow my breathing.

"It's all right. Nothing's going to jump out and grab me," I reassured myself.

Yeah, right.

One door remained. I held my gun steady as I eased it open, then breathed a sigh of relief. Another empty room. I stepped inside.

Suddenly there was a whoosh of air and something hurtling at my head. I screamed, terror spiking hard in my veins. Instinctively, I threw up my arms to cover my head. A gunshot sounded, loud and harsh, and I screamed again.

"Kathleen!"

I heard Kade before I saw him come charging in, gun drawn. He took in the room with a quick glance before focusing on me, cowering in a corner and shaking all over.

"What was that all about?" he asked, his brows drawn in confusion. "Was someone in here?"

I really didn't want to tell him. Really, really. But I took a deep breath and blurted, "There was a bat."

Kade just looked at me. "A bat."

"It was big," I protested.

"So . . . you shot it?"

I glanced down at the gun in my hand. "Um . . . yeah . . . I guess so. It flew at me . . . and I was already jumpy . . . and thinking of Freddy and Chucky and Jason." I named the horror-movie villains that had terrorized me in my childhood, whose faces had run through my mind in that split second of fear.

Kade snorted in derision. "You watch too many movies."

He held his hand out to me. "Come on. I found something, and it's not a flying rodent."

I put my gun away and took his hand. My palm was still sweat-slicked from my adrenaline rush, but his hand was warm and dry.

We went up one more flight of stairs to the top floor. This level was remarkably different from the others. Clean, for one thing. Someone had transformed it into a living space complete with carpet and furniture. With its exposed brick walls, it looked like an expensive loft you'd find in a nice apartment building in downtown Indy.

I followed Kade through the apartment to a far corner, which had been set up as an office workspace. Kade sat down in front of the computer and motioned to the two filing cabinets that stood nearby.

"Take a look through those," he said, tapping the space bar on the keyboard. The monitor flickered to life and he began typing.

I started at the top of the cabinets, the first drawer sliding out easily. It was full of manila file folders. Thinking I'd found something, I rifled through them. But although there were lots of folders, they were all empty. Same thing with the drawer below it.

How odd. I searched all the drawers, but there was nothing inside any of them.

"There's nothing here," I finally said, turning back to Kade, who was still typing furiously.

He didn't respond.

"Did you find anything?" I asked.

Spinning in his chair, he pinned me with a look. "Nothing. Everything's been wiped clean."

A loud *boom!* sounded from below us, and I jumped, startled. The whole building shook. My wide eyes met Kade's.

"Well, fuck," he said.

My reaction wasn't quite as calm. My mouth went dry and, for a moment, I was frozen.

Kade leapt to his feet, grabbed my arm, and yanked me with him, running for the stairs. Immediately we saw that we'd have to turn around. Flames licked up the walls, eagerly consuming the wooden steps. I could feel the heat in waves.

"That's unfortunate," Kade said dryly.

"You think?" Panic made my voice shrill.

"Don't be bitchy," Kade chastened me.

I ground my teeth.

We ran back into the loft, Kade scanning the room—for what, I didn't know. I started looking, too. Something caught my eye—a scrap of a Post-it peeking from underneath the couch. I grabbed it just as I heard the shattering of glass. Kade had thrown a chair through a window.

"We can't jump!" I cried. "It's at least fifty feet down!"

"Wasn't planning on it, princess," Kade said. "What did you see when we came inside?"

"You're quizzing me *now*?" I couldn't believe it.

He dragged me to the window. Dropping from this height was enough to kill us.

"I'll give you a boost," he said. "Grab onto the window frame and climb up to the roof."

"Why are we going up?" I protested. "We need to be going down."

"Just do it," he ordered in a tone I dared not disobey.

Trying not to look down, I angled my body out the window. Kade grabbed my waist, hoisting me up so I could grab on to the concrete above the window. His hands moved to my rear, pushing until I popped up high enough to scrabble onto the roof. A few seconds later, he appeared next to me.

"Come on," he said, grabbing my hand.

We ran to the opposite corner of the roof, and I saw it. A fire escape ladder hooked to the side. Kade must have spotted it before we'd entered. He jumped down to land on the platform, then held his arms open for me. An explosion sounded behind me, and the roof above the office collapsed.

I jumped.

"Always have an escape plan, princess," Kade said when I landed. "No time to climb down." He grabbed me around the waist and yanked me to him. "Hold on."

I obediently wrapped my arms around his neck.

He stepped out onto the ladder, grasped the edge, and pulled. We began sliding downward at a dizzying speed, the rusted metal groaning and clanking as the ladder unraveled after years of nonuse.

We came to a bone-jarring halt ten feet from the ground.

"Slide down," Kade ordered. "That'll get you closer."

"What about you?"

"I'm tougher than you are."

Okay, no arguing with that.

I released my death grip on his neck and began a clumsy slide down his body. His shirt was slippery and I lost my grip, yelping in dismay as it tore. I caught hold of his waist and looked up. Kade was hanging by both hands now, the muscles in his arms straining under our combined weight.

"You're heavier than you look," he ground out.

He was so going to pay for that remark.

I shimmied the rest of the way down, holding on to his ankle before I let myself drop the remaining few feet to the ground. Barely had I regained my balance than Kade was next to me. We ran. Moments later, Kade was flooring the SUV and we were racing away, leaving destruction in our wake.

After the complete chaos and panic of the last few minutes, the silence inside the car seemed bizarre. I looked over at Kade, who caught my eye.

"That was fun," he said.

"That's not the word I'd use to describe it," I said when I finally caught my breath. "What happened?"

His grin faded and he looked back at the road. "It was a trap. A setup. Whoever went looking for information on Sheffield was going to get roasted alive. Everything was wiped clean."

"Not completely," I said, digging in my pocket. I unearthed the crumpled Post-it, looked it over, and handed it to Kade. "Saw that under the couch."

"Rob," Kade read. "And a phone number. Looks like you're more than just eye candy, princess. Good catch."

I closed my eyes, leaning my head back against the seat. Suddenly, I was exhausted.

We came to a stop a short while later and I opened my eyes. We were in a parking lot. I looked around. It was a cheap motel in the middle of downtown Denver.

"Don't you know any nicer places?" I asked.

"You're too good for a place like this?"

I shot him a look. "Absolutely."

Kade's lips twisted as he turned off the engine and pocketed the keys. "I'll keep that in mind."

I waited while he rented a room, coming back with a key and grabbing our bags. Following him, I was relieved to see that he'd gotten a room with two beds, though I would have preferred separate rooms altogether.

"Why are we sticking around?" I asked, sitting down on one of the beds.

"I have a contact nearby," Kade said, unbuttoning and shedding his torn shirt. "He may know more about what happened today."

My eyes widened as his hands moved to his belt. "What are you doing?"

"Thought I'd grab a shower," Kade said with a smirk. Care to join me?"

I jerked my gaze away, ignoring him. I heard him chuckle softly before disappearing into the bathroom.

I flopped back on the bed with a sigh, exhausted. My eyes slipped shut.

~

It was darker in the room when I woke, and quiet. The sun must be setting, I thought drowsily. At some point, Kade must have covered me with a blanket, the cozy warmth of my cocoon making it difficult to fully awaken.

My eyes grew accustomed to the darkness and I realized Kade was sitting in a chair by the window. He had dressed but neglected to button his shirt. He was drinking from one of the motel's plastic cups, a bottle filled with an amber liquid at his elbow.

I watched in silence as he lifted the cup to his lips. Condensation had formed on the plastic and a drop fell to land on his bare skin. He leaned back in the chair with a sigh.

My gaze too avidly followed the droplet as it lazily trailed down his chest and disappeared under the denim waistband of his jeans.

Kade's still-damp hair curled gently over the collar of his shirt. He lifted the cup again. I watched the movement of his throat as he swallowed.

When I looked up, I found his blue eyes staring intently at me. The pull between us was nearly tangible now in the quiet of the motel room.

Kade set his drink down, got up, and crossed to the bed. Silently, he stretched out facing me, so close I could feel the faint brush of his breath against my cheek and smell the slight tang of soap from his shower.

Reaching out, Kade combed his fingers gently through my hair, pushing it over my shoulder. His touch was soft against my jaw. Our eyes met and held.

I grasped his hand in mine, pulling it away from my face and resting it between us.

"Don't," I whispered.

"Why not?" His thumb caressed the back of my hand, and my skin seemed to tingle from his touch.

"You, me . . . us . . . isn't going to happen."

His blue eyes seemed to see more than I wanted him to, but I couldn't look away.

"You know that, right?" I continued.

"I know that you like me, you care about me, you're attracted to me."

"But I love Blane." The words fell out of my mouth without any forethought. Yet I knew they were true. Regardless of the attraction I felt or the strength of the temptation of Kade, I loved Blane.

Kade's eyes had turned cold. "Will you love him when he leaves you to head to Iraq?"

"Do you think he'll go?" I couldn't keep the anguish from my voice.

The hardness of Kade's face softened, and I thought I detected a hint of pity when he said, "Probably."

CHAPTER THREE

I stood under the hot spray of the shower, Kade's words echoing inside my head. I couldn't pretend that the idea of Blane going back into the Navy didn't terrify me. Not only for his safety, but for what that would mean for anything the future might hold for us.

I remembered Adriana Waters—the ex-wife of Navy SEAL Kyle Waters. She had been devastated when he'd re-enlisted, despite knowing she was pregnant. She'd miscarried shortly into his deployment and divorced him a few months after that.

"Be sure to fall in love with someone who loves you more than you love them," she had told me. I could still recall the bitterness in her voice and the disillusionment in her eyes.

I loved Blane, but did he love me? And if so, would he love me enough not to reenlist? And did I love him enough to stick around waiting for the very real possibility that he'd die in combat?

Should I get out now, before it was too late? Or was it already too late?

I couldn't answer any of these questions.

When I came out of the bathroom dressed in fresh clothes, Kade was just getting off his cell phone.

"My contact just called." He glanced over at me. "I need to go meet with him."

"Okay." I said, pulling my hair back into a ponytail. "Let me grab my purse."

Kade gave a snort. "You can't go."

"Why not?"

Kade sauntered closer. "Because where I'm going"—he twisted my ponytail around his finger and gave a gentle tug—"isn't the kind of place for a girl like you, princess."

"But who'll have your back?" I asked.

"I've been doing this alone for a long time," he smirked. "I think I can go one night without backup."

I pulled my ponytail out of his grasp and huffed in exasperation as he walked out the door. How was I supposed to do my job if he left me behind?

Making an instant decision, I shoved my feet into my running shoes. Grabbing my purse and the extra room key, I headed out the door—just in time to watch Kade cross the street a block up.

Trying to remember everything he'd taught me about surveillance, I followed him at a distance, close enough to keep him in sight but not draw his attention. There were just enough people out downtown to camouflage my pursuit.

A crowd filled the sidewalk up ahead and Kade disappeared into it. I stepped up my pace.

As I pushed my way into the mix of people, I realized I'd lost him. Looking up, I saw stairs leading into a nightclub. The sign overhead proclaimed it to be Bar Sinister.

Well, that didn't sound ominous or anything.

I maneuvered my way to the front of the line, where a huge guy was manning the door. Even with the temperature around forty-five degrees, he wore a short-sleeved T-shirt stretched tightly across his massive arms and shoulders. Tattoos covered his arms and I could see more on his neck that disappeared under his collar. He wore silver earrings in each ear, and his head was shaved.

When I got to the door, he stepped in front of me. Looking me up and down, he said, "I don't think so."

Surprised, I glanced up, then up some more. He towered above me.

I swallowed heavily. "My friend is in there," I said, digging inside my purse. "How much for the cover?"

"It's not the cover, sweetheart. This ain't no place for a sorority chick like you." He gave me another derisive once-over and snorted.

I looked down at my clothes, then at the people around me.

Hmm. Okay, maybe he had a point.

While my jeans, cami, and pullover sweater might seem fine to me, compared to the leather, lace, and stilettos around me, I looked like the proverbial fish out of water. Even if I did get in, I'd stand out. Bad idea.

I backed away and pushed to the edge of the crowd, ignoring a few leers and aspersions on my sexual predilections cast my way.

I chewed my lip, trying to think over my options. Kade was in there without backup, and while I wasn't under any delusions about how much actual help I'd be should the need arise, some was better than none, at least to my way of thinking. Kade obviously held a differing opinion.

Movement caught my eye and I looked down the narrow alley next to the building. Two women had emerged from a side door and were stumbling away, teetering precariously on their high heels. Making a quick decision, I jogged down the alley toward them.

They seemed to find their own unsteadiness amusing, as they were laughing and clutching each other to stay on their feet. I could smell alcohol, cigarette smoke, and stale perfume. One was a tall blonde. The other was about my height with hair a shade of red I was sure was not found in nature. Scrutinizing her for a moment, I realized she would do nicely.

"Excuse me," I said.

Neither one responded, still giggling as they stumbled away.

"Excuse me," I repeated more loudly.

That finally got the redhead's attention and she turned toward me. I could tell immediately from her eyes that she was stoned or drunk, maybe both.

"What do you want?" she slurred.

"Want to make twenty bucks?" I asked.

She looked me up and down. "Sure, honey, but if you want a threesome, it'll cost you fifty."

My face grew hot, but I tried to ignore my embarrassment at her assumption. "That's not quite what I meant."

I explained what I needed. She grinned at me.

"Sure thing, honey."

A few minutes later, I stepped inside the dimly lit bar. The bouncer had let me in without batting an eye. I don't think he'd even recognized me.

It had taken fifty bucks to swap my clothes for the redhead's. I was now wearing something that would have made my mother faint on the spot.

A black leather miniskirt was glued to my skin, starting beneath my belly button and ending so it just covered my ass. If I even thought about bending over, I'd be displaying my entire . . . well, everything. Up top I had on a leopard-print tube top, my breasts straining against the thin satin fabric. I'd have to make sure I didn't raise my arms at the same time or the girls would be popping out like twin jack-in-the-boxes.

A spiked leather band around my neck, leopard-print stilettos (which were killing my feet already), and black lipstick completed my outfit. I'd taken my hair down and tousled it as wildly as I could without the benefit of hairspray.

The inside of the bar was packed with people. Surprisingly, the temperature was cool and goose bumps erupted on my bare arms. A DJ was playing heavy metal; the loud grinding of the guitar and shrill voice of the singer assaulted my ears. The bass was turned up enough for me to feel the pulse in my body. The predominant lighting was red mixed with black light, the better to showcase the graffiti on the walls, glowing eerily in the semidarkness.

When my eyes adjusted, I started moving through the maze of bodies, scanning the crowd for Kade.

"Tell me that collar comes with a leash and I'll say I've died and gone to heaven."

I turned to see a guy, tall and thin, leering at me. He had numerous piercings in his face and giant plugs through his earlobes that looked really painful.

I forced a smile. "Sorry. I'm not on the market to be someone's pet." I slipped into the crowd before he could say anything else and, purely by chance, saw Kade.

He was at a corner table, with another man sitting on a stool across from him. Each had a glass on the table, though neither was drinking. Taking a deep breath, I made my way toward them. I didn't know if the other guy was friend or foe, so decided it would be best not to tip my hand.

"Looking for a date tonight, tall-dark-and-dangerous?" I smiled seductively, sliding my hand over Kade's shoulder.

"Not tonight—"

Whatever else Kade had been about to say died on his lips when he turned to look at me, a flash of startled recognition crossing his face. I smiled prettily and batted my eyelashes. The look of surprise was quickly wiped away and his eyes narrowed.

"On second thought, I'd like nothing more than a night with you." Snagging me around the waist, he pulled me between his knees, turning me so I faced the other guy. Kade's hands rested possessively on the bare skin of my midriff, my back pressed against his chest.

Now that I was close enough to get a good look at his companion, I could see he was in his early thirties, with brown eyes and brown hair. While attractive enough, he wouldn't stand out in a crowd. If I passed him on the street and then had to describe him, I'd be hard-pressed to do so. I thought perhaps that might be by design.

"You were saying?" Kade prompted the man.

The guy looked me over and rolled his eyes. "Really?" he asked Kade, quirking an eyebrow.

"I'm not dead yet," Kade countered.

"You will be, you keep barking up this tree."

I stiffened. What did he mean, Kade would be dead?

"Have a drink, princess." Kade held his glass up for me and I automatically took it, swallowing a mouthful of ice-cold vodka and tonic.

"You find out anything more on Sheffield?"

The guy shook his head, taking a sip of his own drink. "Nah, man, only that the dude was into some fucked-up shit. The people pulling his strings are impossible to find, much less fight."

"Any word on who rigged the building to blow?"

"Nope. I asked around, but no one's talking. But it was a good move. Anybody got close enough to find that guy's place wouldn't live to tell the tale."

"Did he have any friends? Partners?"

"Only name I came across was Parker. Supposedly they'd hang together at that club down on Fifth."

"I'll check it out. Thanks."

"Seriously, man," he said. "I'd leave it alone, drop it now, while you can. You get on these guys' radar and you're dead. They'll smoke you before you even know what hit you."

"I'll take that chance," Kade said. "Thanks for the warning, Garrett."

I took note of the name as Garrett downed the rest of his drink, nodded at Kade, and disappeared into the crowd.

"Interesting disguise," Kade said, his lips by my ear. His hands caressed my abdomen, the pads of his thumbs drifting to the skin at the bottom edge of the tube top. I watched the crowd, a shiver running through me. I told myself it was from the chill in the air.

"You left me behind," I said stiffly. "I had little choice."

"I left you behind for a reason."

I felt him move my hair to the side, then the lightest brush of his lips on my shoulder.

I abruptly turned so we were facing each other. With him sitting on a stool and me wearing heels, we were roughly eye to eye. "I can hold my own," I said evenly. "So don't leave me behind again."

He studied me, then gave a slight nod. "Understood."

His gaze drifted down to my mouth and he frowned. Reaching behind me, he dabbed his cocktail napkin into his drink, then swiped it across my lips, removing the thick black lipstick.

Surprised, I didn't move as he worked assiduously.

My lips felt a bit raw when he was done; the cheap lipstick had chapped the tender skin. My tongue darted out, licking the residual sheen of vodka left behind. Kade was rapt as he watched my mouth. His hands had drifted down and now stroked the backs of my thighs. Trapped as I was between his knees with the table at my back, I couldn't move away.

"Don't," I warned, afraid he was going to kiss me.

"What is it with you and the barely-there clothes?" His voice was bitter. "I'm a man, Kathleen. What do you expect?"

"I expect you not to do something you'd regret," I said stiffly, stung at the veiled accusation that I was deliberately tempting him.

"I'm the wrong brother for those kind of expectations."

Before I could retort, he'd risen to his feet and grabbed my hand. "Let's go."

"Where are we going?"

"To find Parker."

I followed him through the club out into the street. It was a relief to be in the fresh air, and I gratefully filled my lungs. The next moment, I wished I were back in the bar as a gust of icy wind hit me and I began shivering.

"So where exactly did you come by the clothes?" Kade asked, removing his leather jacket and swinging it over my shoulders.

"I can't divulge my sources," I replied, pushing my arms into the sleeves.

Kade's lips twitched.

I jumped when he let out a piercing whistle. A taxi pulled to the curb, and Kade held the door while I got in. He slid onto the seat next to me, giving the driver the name of another bar.

I settled back in the seat, noticing that though the jacket helped cover me up top, now that I was sitting, the skirt left almost nothing to the imagination. I tried to tug it down, to no avail. The backs of my thighs and more were bare to cold vinyl.

"Problems?"

I glanced up to see Kade's blue eyes watching me, a smirk playing about his lips.

"I'm fine," I said archly. His gaze traveled down to my thighs, pale against the dark seat and pressed tightly together. "Don't look at me like that."

"If I can't touch, then I sure as hell am going to look," Kade replied matter-of-factly.

I averted my eyes, though I could feel the weight of his stare. I restlessly shifted in my seat. I nearly jumped out of my skin when Kade suddenly touched my leg, hooking his hand underneath my knee and drawing it up until my foot rested on his lap.

"Killer shoes," he observed, ignoring my scramble for modesty as I pulled his jacket down as far as it would go. Removing my shoe, he began massaging my foot, his strong fingers digging into my instep. It felt so good I bit back a moan, tentatively relaxing back against the car door.

"Who was that guy?" I asked.

"Garrett."

I rolled my eyes. "Yeah, that much I got. Who is he to you?"

"Garrett and I go back a ways. Met him at the Academy."

"The FBI Academy?"

Kade gave me his that's-a-dumb-question look. "He left the FBI before I did. Saved my life once, and I've returned the favor. We help each other out occasionally. He has good street contacts in a lot of places."

Tucking my foot between his body and the seat, Kade reached for my other leg, removing the shoe and giving my aching arch the same treatment. I tried to tug my other foot loose so I wouldn't be sitting with my legs spread, but Kade kept it wedged tightly.

"Wish it wasn't so dark in here," Kade mused. His eyes glittered in the passing streetlights.

The feel of his calloused fingers on my skin, even in this fashion, felt like seduction. He massaged the ball of my foot, easing the nerves knotted there, before cupping my heel in his palm. I'd never considered a foot massage as sexual, but then again, I'd never before been on the receiving end of one of Kade's foot massages.

I leaned my head against the seat, closed my eyes, and tried to pretend what I was doing was okay. But even I couldn't ignore Kade's hand moving from my foot to my calf.

"Kade," I warned, trying unsuccessfully to pull my leg out of his grip.

He slid closer to me, his fingers brushing the tender skin behind my knee, the rough pad of his thumb sliding up the inside of my thigh.

The touch sent a spiral of lust into my veins, making me gasp. Kade watched me, his gaze unrelenting.

Ruthlessly, I tamped down my desire, a bitter note of shame welling inside as I thought of Blane. He and I were trying to patch up our relationship, build something again, and here I was thinking impure thoughts about his brother. It made me embarrassed, angry at myself, and angry at Kade.

"Knock it off, Kade!" My tone was sharp as I pushed away his wandering hand.

"Tell me you don't want me," he demanded. "Look me in the eye and say you don't feel the heat between us. Do that, and I'll stop."

"It has nothing to do with that and you know it," I retorted. "Even if Blane and I don't work out, and I'm not saying we won't, that doesn't mean I'm going to hop into bed with you."

"I never said anything about a bed."

I rolled my eyes. This time he let go of my limb when I tugged, and I righted myself in the seat, turning toward the window so I wouldn't have to look at him.

"Blane excels at making women fall in love with him. Now ask me how many times he's been in love."

His words stung, hitting me in my most vulnerable spot—doubt in what Blane truly felt for me. I turned and asked, "And you're a much better option than Blane?"

"I never said I was a better option, just an alternate one. One you should consider."

"And how do you think Blane would feel about you offering to be plan B?" I asked derisively.

Kade's lips thinned and I knew I'd hit my mark. "Neither Blane nor I are your happily-ever-after, princess. Blane will break your heart, and I'm the guy your mom warned you about. Don't kid yourself about that."

I couldn't have spoken even if I'd known what to say.

Fortunately, the cab slowed to a stop just then. Kade sat up and passed some money to the front while I scrambled to find my shoes and my equilibrium. I had one stiletto on and was searching for the other when Kade grabbed my ankle and slipped the shoe on my foot. Then he was hauling me out of the cab and onto the sidewalk. His jacket reached farther down my thighs than the skirt, but not by much.

We stood in front of another bar, though this one looked smaller than Bar Sinister and if I hadn't known what it was, I would have passed it up. I could hear music from where we stood. Kade headed inside and I hurried after him.

Kade handed the man at the door a fifty for the cover charge. I snagged a finger through one of Kade's belt loops so I wouldn't lose him, a shot of nerves hitting me as we snaked our way through the crowd.

We stopped at the bar, and Kade motioned me to an empty stool. I scowled, but my hostility toward stools was lost on him and I had no choice but to squirm onto the thing.

Kade ordered drinks, and when the bartender set them in front of us, Kade slid out a hundred-dollar bill.

"I'm looking for a guy called Parker," he said.

The bartender smoothly pocketed the money before saying, "Might be in the back room. Blond hair. Scar on his left cheek. Likes to watch." He moved away.

Kade turned toward me, resting his back against the bar. "You should stay here."

I glanced around. The patrons of this place had a different vibe, and I could feel eyes on me. I wet my lips nervously. "Please don't leave me," I said in an undertone, hating the fact that I was afraid.

Kade leaned closer. "What's back there isn't pretty, Kathleen, and I'm positive it's nothing you've ever experienced before. Listen to me. Stay out here or go back to the motel."

I hesitated, then shook my head. "I'm coming with you." Being with Kade, no matter the situation, was preferable at the moment than being on my own.

Kade sighed. "Fine. Finish your drink. And do what I say. No questions."

I picked up the cold glass, taking several healthy swallows before sliding off the stool. Kade took a firm grip on my hand and we headed toward the back of the club.

We reached a long, darkened hallway guarded by another bouncer. Kade slipped him some money, and the two spoke quietly, then we were allowed to pass.

The hallway turned sharply and our way was blocked by red velvet curtains. Kade pushed them aside and we stepped through. What I saw made me stumble in shock. Kade had to grab me to keep me from falling.

The room was set up to focus on a stage, music pulsing in the background. There were two rows of chairs, the top row set on a raised platform. The chairs themselves were red velvet, large and plush, set several feet apart. About half of them were occupied, but it was difficult to make out faces in the darkness, which contrasted sharply with the well-lit stage. That was where everyone was looking and that was what had shocked me.

On stage, behind glass, were two men and one woman. The woman was completely naked except for a chain hanging between her breasts, held in place with clamps on her nipples. Her wrists were bound and hanging from a hook above her head. One of the men, dressed in leather pants, held a crop. His wrist flicked and I heard the slap of the leather against the woman's buttocks. Judging by the red marks on her skin, that wasn't the first time he'd struck her. She moaned, but she didn't seem to be in pain. Or perhaps if she was, she liked it.

The other man wore leather chaps, and that was all. He stroked himself while he watched, fully aroused.

I was too stunned and appalled to move. Kade's firm grip on my waist pulled me forward, jerking my attention away from the show. He carefully looked over the room, then chose an empty chair. I remained standing, wondering what I was supposed to do.

"Kneel down," he hissed quietly.

I hesitated, then let out a tiny cry as he yanked me down, my knees hitting the floor hard. I glanced reproachfully at him.

Leaning down, he whispered in my ear, "Look around."

So I looked around, and understood.

The people I hadn't been able to see clearly earlier were more visible now that my eyes had adjusted, and I saw that most of them weren't alone. A few seats down was a woman with a man at her feet. Squinting, I saw an actual leash attached to his neck, the other end held in her hand. So the guy earlier hadn't been joking about the leash thing.

I looked farther into the darkness. In the far corner, a woman was kneeling in front of a man, her head bobbing up and down between his legs. Flushing red, I hastily averted my gaze, only to see a man masturbating in the front row.

My eyes were drawn unwillingly back to the stage. Again, I was stunned at what I saw. The woman was now unbound, but on her knees. The man with the whip stood in front of her, though the whip had been discarded and she was giving him a blow job. He held her head in place while he thrust into her mouth, a grimace of pleasure and pain on his face.

That in and of itself was shocking enough without seeing the man in chaps fucking her from behind.

It was like passing an accident on the highway—I knew I should look away, I just couldn't. I was horrified at the casual display of such intimacy in front of strangers, not to mention the fact that two men were enjoying one woman at the same time. I wasn't naive enough not to know people did stuff like that, but I'd never dreamed I'd see a live version of it.

I tore my gaze away, my face so hot I knew I had to be six shades of red. I was clutching Kade's pant leg as though I were going to be torn away from him at any moment. While I wanted to look up at him, I was so mortified that I literally could not. Now I knew what he'd meant when he'd tried to make me stay in the bar. If only I'd listened.

A man walked up then, taking the seat on the other side of Kade. I was grateful to see that he was alone.

"I was told you're looking for me?"

I looked up in surprise to see that the man was addressing Kade.

"Thought you might like a . . . private show," Kade replied. His hand moved to my head and he began playing with my hair, his fingers running leisurely through the strands.

"How much?" the man who had to be Parker asked.

"Two hundred."

Parker turned his attention to me, and I hastily looked down.

"Is she trained?"

"She'll do whatever I tell her to do." Kade gave a sharp tug on my hair—not enough to hurt, but enough to jerk my head back and make me gasp in surprise. His face was strange, cold and hard, and though I knew he was acting, it bothered me to see him that way.

"Show me first."

Alarmed, I sucked in my breath, but Kade shot back, "No freebies."

Still looking at me, Parker asked, "Fine. How much to participate?"

I unconsciously dug my nails into Kade's denim-clad leg. To his credit, he didn't bat an eye when he answered. "Five hundred."

"Does that include you?"

My eyes widened, but Kade's lips just twisted in a humorless smile.

"Sounds like a party."

"Meet me in room thirteen," Parker said. He got up and left the room.

Kade immediately released his hold on my hair and I sucked in a huge gulp of air, realizing just then that I'd been holding my breath. I felt demoralized. A hand beneath my chin turned my head, and I was forced to look at Kade.

"Are you all right?"

I didn't speak, just gave a minute shake of my head to indicate that no, I certainly was not "all right."

Kade immediately stood, pulling me up with him. I kept my eyes away from the stage, where the threesome was still going at it, as Kade wrapped an arm around my waist and hustled me across the room and through another door. He moved fast, nearly carrying me, so that my toes barely brushed the ground.

When we stopped, I didn't want to look up, so I kept my face buried against his chest.

"Hey, it's all right," he crooned softly. "Come on, princess. Look at me. Nothing's going to happen to you. Nobody here but you and me."

I cleared my throat, told myself to get a grip, and stepped back. Avoiding Kade's eyes, I glanced around and saw he'd taken us into a fancy bathroom with red velvet wallpaper and burnished brass fixtures. A mirror surrounded in lights was nearby and I stepped to it, nervously smoothing my hair. The familiarity of the gesture comforted me. What I'd witnessed was dark and seedy, a travesty of everything I'd known about sex until now. And part of me hurt that Kade was no longer shocked by the cruelties of the world he lived in.

Kade's reflection caught my eye and I hastily looked away from his penetrating blue gaze.

"I forget sometimes," he murmured.

"Forget what?" I asked, turning on the water to wash my hands. God knows what all had been on the floor back there.

"Forget how innocent you are."

My eyes jerked to his in the mirror and I turned around. "I'm not—"

"Innocent?" he interrupted. "Really?"

"I've just never seen anything . . ." My voice trailed off and I waved my hand uselessly to indicate the room we'd just left.

"Like that," Kade finished.

He didn't require an answer and I didn't give one.

With a sigh, he rubbed a hand across his face. "Sorry, princess. I should've stuck you in a cab back to the motel. I don't know what possessed me to bring you here."

The nickname stung, and I regretted not better controlling my reaction to this place. "It's okay," I said. "I need to toughen up if I'm going to do this job. We are here to do a job, right?"

"Yeah."

"Besides, how would you have gotten him without me?"

Kade just looked at me until realization dawned. All I could think to say was "Oh."

"If he knows more about Sheffield, we need him."

"Then let's grab him and get the hell out of here," I said.

Kade scrutinized me before accepting that with a curt nod. Taking my hand, he led me out of the bathroom and through a maze of corridors and doorways. We stopped in front of a door with an elaborate 13 written on it.

Putting his lips to my ear, Kade whispered, "I won't let anything happen to you. I promise."

The anxiety inside my chest eased. He leaned back to look at me, his blue eyes intent on mine. As strange as it was, I still trusted him to keep me safe. I nodded.

He opened the door and we stepped inside.

The room was dimly lit and filled with things I had no name for. I couldn't even determine a purpose for some, not that I wanted to know. What I didn't see was Parker.

He leapt out from the shadows and I saw the glint of a knife in his hand. Before I could react, Kade gave me a hard shove and I fell sideways to the floor and out of Parker's path.

Kade threw up an arm to block the knife, grabbing Parker's wrists and twisting. The knife clattered to the floor.

The men were a blur of movement, the silence of the room punctuated by grunts of pain and exertion as they fought. I winced at the sound of flesh hitting bone. Blood erupted on Kade's face.

I couldn't think what to do, how to help. Just like the heroines on television that I criticized for idly standing by in times of crisis, it seemed I was afflicted with the same paralysis.

My heart leapt when Kade seemed to get the upper hand, pummeling Parker. I saw it too late—Parker grabbed something made of wood and cracked it against Kade's skull. It happened so fast and Kade fell to the floor.

I stared in dismay at Kade's motionless body. A scream was building inside me, clawing its way up my chest. Hysteria and panic beat with the rhythm of my heart.

Parker turned toward me, wiping blood from his mouth with his sleeve. "Your turn, bitch."

CHAPTER FOUR

Adrenaline surged and I lurched to my feet, scrambling away from Parker's reach. But he was too quick and there was nowhere to go. He pushed me hard into the wall, locking his hands around my throat and starting to squeeze.

My flailing hand caught the edge of my purse, and I shoved it inside, searching while spots danced in front of my eyes. I couldn't breathe . . . and it hurt . . . and I couldn't find my gun . . .

Suddenly, the pressure eased. Parker's face showed surprise, then he collapsed at my feet. Only then did I see the knife lodged in his back. Kade was half-lying, half-sitting on the floor across the room. He had thrown Parker's knife.

I gasped for breath, greedily gulping in air. My throat felt raw and I lapsed into a coughing fit. I bent, with my hands on my knees, as I tried to recover. Kade was already on his feet, though blood dripped sluggishly from a cut at his temple.

"Kade . . ." I didn't know what else to say. I'd thought for sure that Parker had killed him. My relief was so profound that tears sprang to my eyes. My initial impulse was to throw myself in his arms and hug him.

"Are you all right?" he asked, examining the curve of my neck. His fingers softly brushed the abused skin.

"I'm fine," I said, blinking rapidly to dispel the wetness in my eyes. "Let's get out of here."

With a nod, Kade stooped down, taking Parker's wallet and cell phone. Then he pulled me behind him before cracking the door and peering into the hallway.

The coast must have been clear, because Kade pulled me out of the room. His arm slid around my waist, holding me tightly as we walked through the maze. I didn't know how Kade knew where we were going and I didn't ask. I was just grateful we were stepping out a rear exit a few moments later.

We didn't speak while Kade hailed a taxi and we drove back to the motel. It wasn't until we were back in the room that the full impact hit me. My knees buckled and I sat heavily on the bed, my arms wrapped around myself. I was shaking uncontrollably.

Kade sat down next to me and I went willingly when he pulled me into his arms, cradling my head to his chest. My arms seemed to move of their own volition, creeping around his waist to hold him tight.

"I thought you were dead tonight," I finally managed to squeeze out past the lump clogging my throat. "He nearly killed you."

Kade's hand lightly stroked my hair. "I'm nearly killed a lot."

A shudder went through me.

"You're cold," Kade said, disengaging himself from my grip. He stood, grabbing an extra blanket from the closet.

I didn't resist when he slipped his jacket off my shoulders and down my arms. The chilled air in the room hit my exposed skin, and goose bumps erupted.

"I could really get used to that outfit," Kade said with a sigh before wrapping the blanket around me.

That brought a reluctant smile to my lips.

"Come on. You need to get some rest." Crouching down, he slipped off my shoes, and I obeyed his urging, curling up on the bed with my head on the remarkably flat and unyielding pillow. He adjusted the blanket around me, then stood.

"Where are you going?" I asked apprehensively.

"Nowhere," he replied. "Just need to take a look at that guy's phone and wallet." He placed a chaste kiss on my forehead. "Go to sleep."

I watched him disappear into the bathroom, then heard the sound of the water running. A shower sounded good, but I was just too tired.

~

I was back in that room from the club tonight, only rather than observing the stage, I was on the stage. I was naked, my wrists bound and caught above my head. Scared, I pulled and yanked, but I couldn't release my hands. Finally, I gave up, looking around instead. No one was in the audience. I appeared to be alone.

Then I saw him.

Kade stood in the shadows, staring at me. When our eyes met, he stepped forward into the light. It shone down from above, casting his eyes into shadow.

My breath caught in my lungs. He was barefoot, clad only in his jeans. Greedily, I absorbed the view of his muscled chest and arms, planes and angles that I knew were hard to the touch.

The hungry look I knew so well scanned my body. Kade took his time examining me, and I flushed hotly under his scrutiny. When his eyes once again met mine, they seemed to burn.

Kade prowled toward me with an easy grace—a work of art in motion. His dark beauty was edged with a dangerous, otherworldly quality.

My heart was racing when he moved close enough to touch me, and I couldn't tear my gaze from his.

My alarm had morphed into a different kind of fear. He reached out, a lone finger trailing up my side, then brushing over my collarbone to trace a tantalizing path between my breasts down to my navel.

"You want this," he said, his voice low and sensuous, like warmed brandy flowing through my veins. "You just won't admit it."

I couldn't move, bound as I was, couldn't get away.

Kade's hand slipped between my thighs. I whimpered in the back of my throat at the intimate touch.

It wasn't true. I didn't want Kade.

His eyes delved into mine, a knowing twist to his lips as I refused to speak. The wetness beneath his hand didn't lie. I squeezed my eyes tightly closed, horrified at my body's reaction.

"Your turn, bitch."

My eyes flew open, only it was no longer Kade touching me, but Parker.

I screamed, thrashing, unable to get away. I screamed again, a raw sound tearing out of my throat.

"Kathleen! Wake up!"

Kade's voice penetrated the horror of my nightmare and I jerked awake to find I was tangled in the blanket. Still caught in a web of fear, I frantically pushed it off, sitting up and drawing my knees to my chest.

Kade sat next to me, his hand tightly gripping my arm. The pressure produced an acute sensation to my already overly heightened nervous system. "Are you all right?"

I nodded shakily. "Just a bad dream."

Well, it had ended that way, though that's certainly not how it had begun. My body remembered, too, arousal and shame still pulsing through my veins.

Kade eased me back down on the bed, where he lay spooning me, one arm draped casually over my waist. "Go back to sleep. You're all right."

I wanted to push him away, not have him touch me, but I just gritted my teeth and stayed quite still. My whole body cringed at the picture my traitorous subconscious had painted.

The bare skin of my back above and below the tube top pressed against his chest. I could feel the slight abrasion from the hair on his arm as it lay in the curve of my waist. The brush of his warm breath tickled my shoulder.

"Relax," Kade soothed. "You're strung as tight as a bow." He pressed the palm of his hand against my abdomen, his thumb brushing lightly over my skin.

That wasn't helping.

I squeezed my eyes shut. "I just need . . . some space," I said.

Kade's hand froze. Without saying a word, he pulled away to lie on his back, bending his arms behind his head. I could practically feel the anger and tension rolling off him in waves.

I turned over so I was facing him, then hesitated. I didn't want to hurt him, but neither did I want to encourage him. "I just . . . need some boundaries," I tried to explain.

He didn't say anything, so I tried again. "I care about you, but we're just friends, Kade. I belong with Blane."

"Who are you trying to convince?" he asked. "Me? Or yourself?"

When I didn't answer, he abruptly stood. "I'll be back," he said, shrugging on a shirt and grabbing his gun and jacket. He didn't even bother buttoning his shirt before he was out the door and gone.

I couldn't sleep after that, so I took a shower. Kade still hadn't returned by the time I got out and had pulled on a T-shirt and sweatpants. I checked my cell phone and saw that it was really late, and I had three missed calls, all from Blane.

Feeling guilty for missing his calls, and for a great many other things, I set my cell back down on the table. I thought about Kade's parting shot to me and shook my head. He was wrong.

The door opened and Kade stepped inside. He shot me an unreadable glance.

"We have to go," he said. He began throwing my things into the suitcase.

"Right now? Why?" It was barely after four in the morning.

"The guy—Parker—knew I was coming."

I digested this as I searched for shoes. "How do you know?"

"His phone. I checked it. He got a text." Kade zipped the suitcase. "He was told to kill me."

"By who?" I grabbed my purse, shoving my cell phone inside.

"I don't know, but someone knows I'm in town, and by now I'm guessing they've figured out I'm still alive."

"But why?" I was alarmed. Kade was moving fast, and that more than anything else told me there was definitely something to worry about. "Why would they try to kill you?"

"Because I'm getting too close. Too close to finding out who was pulling Sheffield's strings, trying to get Blane to lose that case." He set the suitcase beside the door. "I've booked you on a flight back to Indy. It leaves in two hours."

"What about you?"

"I'll lead them a different direction." He peered carefully through a slit in the side of the curtains.

My stomach wound itself into knots at his words. "Why can't you come with me?"

"They know who I am, they're looking for me," Kade said flatly. "Getting on a plane would lead them right to me, and to you. I shouldn't have brought you here."

I couldn't think, couldn't process all he was saying. "But... but . . . how? How do they know about you?"

Finally, he turned to look at me, and the ice in his gaze chilled me. "Only a handful of people knew what I was looking for. Someone betrayed me, and they're going to wish they hadn't."

Fear lapped at me. I couldn't decide if Kade thought he was invincible, or if he just didn't care whether he lived or died.

"You can't take them on alone," I protested. "Let me stay. I can help."

"Forget it, princess," he said, looking back out the window. "And it looks like we're going to have to travel light and exit out the back."

Leaving the suitcase, he grabbed my arm and hauled me toward the bathroom, where he opened the window and popped the screen onto the concrete outside.

"And this is why I stay in cheap motels," he said, boosting me up into the window.

I dropped onto the concrete in a crouch, remaining that way until Kade landed silently beside me, his gun in his hand. He took my hand in his and we crept along the back of the building.

It was dark and sinister at this hour of the night. The motel was near a residential neighborhood of old, run-down houses separated from us by a rusty chain-link fence. A lonely streetlamp cast a weak pool of light nearby and I heard the distant sound of cats fighting, their yowls giving an eerie quality to the scene.

"Stay here," Kade whispered to me, dropping my hand and moving away.

I grabbed a handful of his jacket. "Where are you going?" I couldn't keep the fear from my voice.

"Two guys were in the parking lot. I want to know who sent them." He gently but relentlessly unclenched my fist from the soft leather. "Don't worry. Stay put."

I watched him disappear soundlessly into the darkness.

I waited, my heart beating a staccato rhythm while my palms grew damp. The air was cold, but I barely felt it, so focused was I on listening for Kade's return. Reaching inside my purse, I searched blindly for my gun before my fingers closed around its cold metal. I pulled it out and flicked off the safety, cradling the butt in both hands.

A gunshot made me jump, my nerves already on a razor's edge. I sprang to my feet and ran, praying Kade was all right.

Rounding the corner of the building, I took in the scene at a glance.

A man lay motionless on the ground, a pool of blood spreading beneath him, while another grappled with Kade. I drew closer, trying to see if I could get a shot in, but they were moving too fast and I was afraid I might hit Kade.

In one sudden maneuver, Kade had the man in a headlock. He gave the man's head a vicious twist, I heard a sickening crack, and the man dropped lifeless to the ground.

"Point that gun somewhere else, would you?" Kade ordered, breathing hard.

Stunned, I numbly obeyed. "I thought you were going to talk to them, not kill them," I said, my voice cracking.

"They weren't feeling chatty," Kade said sharply. "I've learned it's better to be the one left standing." His eyes narrowed as he looked at me. "And I thought I told you to stay put."

Distant sirens drawing closer saved me from having to reply.

"Let's go," Kade said, grabbing my hand.

We hurried down the street, turning a corner and going several more blocks until the sirens faded away. The sun was beginning to peek over the horizon, giving everything the pale gray cast of early dawn. I shivered in the cold morning air.

"Put this on." Kade handed me his jacket.

I shook my head. "It's cold. You need it."

Kade abruptly stopped walking, took the jacket, and placed it over my shoulders. "Don't give me any shit. The least I can do is keep you warm."

I reluctantly pushed my arms into the sleeves.

He turned away, looked down the street, and let out the same piercing whistle he had last night. A moment later, a yellow taxi pulled to the curb.

"Time for you to go," he announced, taking my elbow.

"No," I said, planting my feet. "I'm not going to just leave you on your own, Kade."

The very idea had me rebelling. How could I just get in the taxi and leave him behind? An unknown entity was tracking him down, bent on killing him. The thought made my stomach roll, nausea rising like bile.

"You are going," Kade insisted, dragging me to the car and ignoring my struggles to free myself from his grip.

The driver rolled down his window.

"No matter what she says, or what she threatens, take her directly to the airport. Understand?" He handed the man three hundred-dollar bills.

"Yeah, I got it," the driver said. His watery brown eyes peered interestedly at us while his work-worn fingers took the money and pocketed it.

Kade opened the back door. "Get in."

"No."

"I said, get in."

"And I said no!"

Kade's eyes took on a dangerous glint that made me quake inside, but I stubbornly stood my ground. If there was anything I could do to help ensure his survival, then by

God I was going to stay and do it, and he would just have to deal with it.

He moved closer to me, and I retreated until my back hit the cold steel of the taxi. I kept my eyes warily on his, my pulse leaping, though I couldn't say if it was from fear or his proximity.

"You choose to stay with me, then I'm going to fuck you."

My jaw dropped. "What?"

"You heard me. That's the only reason I keep you around. I mean, come on, princess," he continued derisively, "you're more of a liability than an asset in this line of work. But having an easy lay within reach is convenient. It's just a matter of time before you spread your legs for me."

The blood drained from my face as I stared at him. It had been awhile since he had wounded me so precisely with his words. I'd thought he had come to like me, respect me, care about me. I'd let down my guard, and his words had a devastating effect. The little voice inside my head sighed a sad "I told you so."

"Blane doesn't have to know," he said, his hand cupping my breast through my thin T-shirt. "I'll fuck you, then you can go back to him, and only you and I will know he got my sloppy seconds."

The crack of my palm against his cheek was deafening in the quiet of the empty street.

"Go to hell," I gritted out, furiously blinking back tears. I pushed him away from me and scrambled inside the taxi, anxious to get away from him and lick my wounds.

"Go," Kade commanded the driver, who wasted no time in stepping on the gas.

Twisting in the seat, I looked out the back window. Kade still stood in the street, watching. The wind ruffled his hair and, though I knew he had to be cold, he didn't move. His face was an unreadable mask, the condescending smirk was gone, and realization slapped me upside the head.

"Wait!" I cried out. "Go back! Turn around! I need you to go back!"

"No can do," the driver said flatly. "You're going to the airport. He already paid."

I gripped the back of his seat. "You have to take me back!"

The driver shook his head, resolutely ignoring me. I shifted back around, but Kade was no longer there, only empty space where he had stood watching me leave.

I should have known, should have seen through it, that Kade would have said or done anything to get me into the taxi, even if it hurt me. He'd rather I believe his lies and think the worst than have me subjected to whatever danger hunted him.

If only it hadn't taken me those precious seconds to realize that.

I managed to pull myself together enough to get back to Indy. I dumped my gun in a trash can, since the case I had to get it through security was back in the motel room. The flight was a blur, as was the cab ride back to my apartment.

After collecting Tigger from Alisha, I collapsed on my bed, numb. I stared at the ceiling, Kade's grim expression as he watched me leave replaying in my mind until I fell asleep.

~

When I woke, it was late in the afternoon and my head felt like a mariachi band had set up shop there on Cinco de Mayo. I dragged myself into the bathroom and felt better after showering and brushing my teeth. I figured since I'd nearly been killed twice in the last twenty-four hours, no one had better gripe about me taking the day off.

I heated up a TV dinner in the microwave and sat on the sofa to eat it. Tigger curled up behind my head next to the window. Flipping on the TV, I sat back to watch the news. I'd decided I wasn't going to think about Kade, or the worrying would drive me insane. There was nothing I could do.

The food stuck in my throat, and I had to swallow heavily to get it down. Resolutely, I took another bite and tried to focus on what the blonde news anchorette was saying.

"The nephew of famous billionaire philanthropist David Summers is pleading not guilty to charges that he raped a local woman. The trial will take place here in Indianapolis." The footage showed a well-dressed guy, maybe twenty-five, being led away in handcuffs to a police car. He seemed remarkably at ease, even flashing a grin to the press.

The picture changed, showing a man whose face I knew very well.

"Our sources tell us that Indianapolis attorney Blane Kirk has taken the case. It has long been rumored that Kirk may be interested in running for political office. He may cement his political future if he successfully defends Matt Summers, whose uncle—David Summers—is known to take a very active role in the political action committee Improving America Now."

I choked on my food. What the hell was this? I got that the people Blane defended weren't always rainbows and unicorns, but really? Did he take the case because of the connections this Summers guy had?

The fact that the defendant was accused of rape hit too close to home. Blane didn't know the details, but he did know I'd had a close call a few months back. Only Kade's presence had prevented me from becoming another statistic. I knew that everyone was innocent until proven guilty, but I couldn't dislodge the sour feeling in my stomach.

My appetite gone, I dumped my food into the trash. I couldn't imagine Blane defending someone guilty of rape, even if they did have connections that could help his political career. Even I had heard about David Summers, and I knew next to nothing about politics. I had little to no interest in the machinations of Republicans versus Democrats. I voted once every four years for president and that was it, something I'd never divulged to Blane. I had a sneaking suspicion he would take a dim view of my lackadaisical attitude toward the governance of our country.

My cell phone rang, and my heart leapt.

I didn't stop to examine the sinking sensation I felt when I saw that it was Blane.

"Hello?"

"Where have you been?" Blane's voice was strung tight.

"I'm sorry I missed your calls last night," I apologized. "Kade and I were investigating this guy in Denver."

"He took you with him?"

I bristled at the incredulity in his tone. "Yes, he did. He's training me, remember?"

"And how many close calls did you have while you were in Denver?"

I flinched. "Two, maybe three." My voice was small.

Blane cursed and I could mentally see him running a hand through his hair in frustration. "Listen, I'm heading back on the last flight tonight. I'll see you in a few hours. We need to talk."

I went on offense. "Good, because I really want to discuss your latest case with you."

Silence.

"Has it already made the news there?"

"Yep."

"We'll talk when I get there," he said. "I have to go."

"Bye."

My feelings were in turmoil. I was frustrated at our relationship, which seemed to be caught in a stalemate. It seemed very obvious that Blane disapproved of my new job at the firm. Did he believe in me at all? Or was I just another pretty face?

It was several hours before Blane would be here, and I fidgeted, not knowing what to do with myself. I was too on edge to sleep, so I watched TV. Reruns of old episodes of *Simon & Simon* were on and I thought the blond brother reminded me a little of Blane.

The sound of the door opening woke me, my tired eyes slitting open to see Blane's form weakly illuminated by the light from the muted television. I watched as he set down his suitcase, garment bag, and laptop case, settling them quietly on the floor. He locked the door behind him, removed his coat, then stooped to give Tigger—who had jumped from his perch to welcome him—a scratch behind the ears.

The emotions I felt at seeing Blane were so overwhelming I could only lie there and observe him as they washed over me. I hadn't realized how very much I'd missed him, or how much I needed him. My reasons for holding him at arm's length suddenly seemed silly and naive. He was mine for the moment, and after my tumultuous time with Kade, Blane's solid, steady presence was a welcome respite.

Although bigger than his brother, Blane moved just as silently, and soon he was crouched in front of me.

"Kat?" he whispered, his fingers lightly brushing my hair.

I loved Blane. Sometimes it really was as simple as that.

Without speaking, I reached my hand around the back of his neck and pulled his head down to mine.

Blane needed no urging, his lips relearning the contours of mine. He kissed me as if we had all the time in the world, with slow, deliberate sweeps of his tongue against mine. Heat and desire gradually built between us.

I broke our kiss off long enough to sit up on the couch and pull my T-shirt over my head. His mouth found the sensitive skin of my shoulder while my hands worked at the buttons of his shirt. I wasn't wearing a bra and gasped when the rough pads of his fingers touched my breasts, cupping their weight, his thumbs lightly brushing the tips.

Finally done with the seemingly endless series of buttons, I pushed Blane's dress shirt aside, only to be met with the barrier of his T-shirt. I made a noise of frustration that would have been a curse word if my mouth hadn't been otherwise occupied with Blane's. He laughed, a soft chuckle in the back of his throat that warmed me from the inside out.

"Let me help you with that," he teased, pulling away enough to strip off the offending cloth.

"You wear too many layers," I complained, then couldn't think much of anything anymore. The sight of his broad chest and shoulders made my mouth go dry, and I had the insane urge to rub my skin against his and purr as though I were Tigger.

Blane didn't work out because he was vain and wanted a body women drooled over, though he wasn't unaware of his physical appeal. He kept his body in as good a condition as possible because that's what he'd been trained to do as a SEAL. The better shape he was in, the better his chances of survival, and that was that. Some lessons can't be unlearned.

I thought again of his possible reenlistment, but I shoved it to the back of my mind.

Blane's hands returned to caress my breasts, now achingly aroused and sensitive to the slightest touch.

My fingers traced the contours of his chest and biceps, the firm muscles still fascinating and impressive to me. Our eyes caught and held. We didn't speak, just looked into each other's eyes as he touched me and I touched him.

Capturing his roughened jaw in my palm, I leaned forward and pressed my lips to his for a sweet, tender kiss that I hoped conveyed what I didn't have the courage say.

It must have worked, because his arms slid around my waist to pull me close, our bodies colliding, skin against skin. I wrapped my arms around his neck and my legs around his waist, eagerly deepening the kiss.

Before I knew it, Blane had stood, with my arms and legs still wrapped tightly around him like a koala bear clinging to a tree.

"Impressive," I murmured against his mouth.

"You haven't seen anything yet," he replied. His voice had that deep roughness to it that never failed to send a thrill of desire through me.

Somehow we made it into my moonlight-dappled bedroom—my attention was on other things, like his lips, his neck, and his jaw—and Blane laid me down on the bed. I pulled him down with me, cradling his body between my thighs. Distantly, I heard his shoes hit the floor.

His kisses were like a drug, and I couldn't get enough. I started to push my flannel pajama pants down, but Blane stopped me.

"Let me," he said. Sitting back, he eased down the fabric, taking the panties I had on with it. When I was naked, he just looked at me.

I squirmed a bit under his steady gaze, moving my arms to cross over my exposed chest, but he caught my wrists and held them.

"Don't cover yourself," he implored softly. "You're beautiful. Your skin glows like ivory in the moonlight, your hair a cascade of silver. You take my breath away, Kat."

Well, when you put it *that* way . . .

Taking my hand in his, he lifted it to his face and gently pressed his lips to my palm. From my palm, his mouth traveled to the inside of my wrist, then the tender skin inside my elbow, all the way to the curve of my shoulder, pressing warm, wet kisses along the way.

Blane slid his arms under my back to wrap around me, nuzzling my neck. The stubble on his jaw was a gentle scrape against my skin and I twined my arms around him, tilting my head to the side to give him better access. I heard him inhale deeply through his nose.

"Do I smell bad?" I asked, suddenly worried.

"You smell like home," he replied, his voice a rough whisper in my ear.

His words sank deep inside me, nestling somewhere near my heart.

He kissed me, a melding of his mouth to mine that was as thorough as it was unhurried. It seemed more than sexual, more than lust, more than what it had ever been before.

Blane lifted his head and I could see his eyes, glinting silver in the moonlight. He moved so he was braced on his elbows above me, both palms cradling my face as his thumbs brushed my cheekbones. His gaze was intense and I couldn't look away. A moment passed.

"What is it?" I asked, a sense of foreboding creeping over me. He seemed very grave, and I wondered if he had bad news to tell me.

"No matter what," Blane said quietly, "I want you to know that I love you."

My heart seemed to stutter in my chest as I stared at him, shock warring with joy inside me. Blane didn't move, merely watching my reaction, his expression as serious as if he'd just told me he had only a week to live.

"You do?" The question fell out, and I flushed as I realized how insecure it made me sound.

Blane's lips twitched a little before he replied. "I do."

A few seconds passed before I could make my mouth move again, to form the words I hadn't spoken to anyone in a very long time.

"I love you, too." My voice broke on the last word, and I was embarrassed at the tears I had to blink back.

Then his lips were again on mine, and I kissed him, holding nothing back. But soon, it wasn't enough, and I fumbled at his belt before he removed my hands and undid it himself. I waited impatiently while he shed his remaining clothes and rejoined me in bed. The desire I had to give myself to Blane after what had just happened between us was overwhelming, almost like a need to confirm our words with actions.

As much as I wanted to hurry, Blane wanted to take it slow, savoring each moment of our lovemaking. When he finally slid inside me, stretching and filling me, I let out a deep sigh of contentment.

Then he was moving, his body, hard and powerful, surrounding me, pushing me closer to the edge. He loved me with his mouth and his hands, my sighs and gasps filling the room while he repeated words of love in my ear. And when I couldn't take any more, when he urged me to let go for him, we fell over the edge together.

CHAPTER FIVE

Blane's breathing was deep and even as I watched him sleep, the moonlight providing enough illumination for me to see him clearly. His square jaw was dark with stubble, and lines of fatigue were etched around his eyes. I wondered what else had been going on while he'd been away, what other problems he was dealing with. Would he tell me when he woke? Or would he keep it to himself, wanting to protect me from anything unpleasant?

That thought quite effectively pierced the happy bubble in which I'd been blissfully floating.

I slid out of bed, taking care to not wake Blane. Grabbing his shirt, I slipped it on before closing the bedroom door quietly behind me. I made a pot of coffee and took a steaming cup into the living room. My sleep schedule was all off, and I was now wide awake, even though it was barely after five in the morning.

I grabbed a blanket and sat cross-legged on the couch sipping my coffee. Tigger leapt up beside me, settling half on and half off my lap. I absently stroked his fur, lost in thought.

What would change between Blane and me after what we'd said last night? I didn't take the phrase "I love you" lightly, and I didn't think Blane did either. I was nervous to see him when he woke, but contented, too. Blane's feelings for me were no longer a mysterious unknown quantity. He'd put a name to them, and so had I.

I couldn't help the stupid grin on my face.

A buzzing noise distracted me. It sounded like my phone, but it wasn't the culprit. Getting to my feet and following the sound led me to Blane's cell phone, in the pocket of his coat. A glance at the screen had my breath catching in my chest.

Kade.

I debated not answering. It was Blane he was trying to reach, after all. But what if something was wrong? What if he needed Blane right away? I decided to answer the call.

"Hello?" My voice was tentative.

"Whoever you are, you shouldn't be answering Blane's phone. Now be a good girl and put him on," Kade responded briskly.

"Kade, it's me. It's Kathleen."

Silence.

"I see you made it back to Indy in one piece," he finally said stiffly.

I nodded stupidly, before remembering that he couldn't see me.

"Yeah." I didn't know what else to say. "I see you're still alive, too."

"I'm hard to kill," he said. More awkward silence.

"I know you didn't mean it," I blurted, unable to hold back. "I know you just said those things to get me into the car."

A pause. "You needed to leave," he replied, his voice flat. "It was a dumb move, bringing you with me. I nearly got you killed."

"I'm sorry I believed you, if only for a moment."

Sorry didn't feel adequate enough to convey the regret I felt at my own stupidity, for immediately putting him back into the category of a ruthless bastard who cared about no one but himself.

"It's easier that way, isn't it?" he finally asked, his voice rough.

I didn't know what to say, didn't want to look at the meaning behind that question.

"And I'm guessing Blane is in your bed," he continued when I was silent.

Again I didn't reply.

Kade cursed and I winced. "Put him on the phone," he said. "I need to talk to him." His tone cut off any argument I might have made.

"All right," I said. "Hold on."

I went back into the bedroom, but paused inside the doorway. Blane seemed to be caught up in the middle of a bad dream, moving restlessly on the bed and mumbling.

"Just a sec," I said to Kade. "He's having some kind of nightmare. I need to wake him."

"No, Kathleen, wait—"

But I'd already leaned over the bed and grasped Blane's shoulder.

"Blane, wake—"

Blane exploded upward, his fist flying toward me and catching me on the jaw. It was a glancing blow, but enough to send me hurtling backward. My head connected with the wall, and I let out a startled cry of pain before collapsing to the floor.

"Oh my God, Kat!"

Blane leapt from the bed, fully awake now and at my side in an instant. "God, I'm so sorry. Are you all right?"

He helped me up to a sitting position, and my vision swam. I closed my eyes and cradled my aching head. My jaw throbbed and my whole body was shaking.

"Christ, I'm so sorry, Kathleen." Blane touched my back as gently as if I were made of glass, which at the moment, I felt like I was.

"I'm okay," I managed. "Just . . . get the phone. It's Kade."

I motioned to where the phone had fallen out of my grasp. I could hear the tinny sound of Kade's voice, calling my name.

Blane grabbed the phone. "What?" he barked.

He listened for a moment.

"Yeah," he said grimly to something Kade had asked, glancing guiltily at me, then away again. "No, I didn't," he gritted out. "No shit. I will. Listen, I'll call you back, all right?"

Blane disappeared into the kitchen. I heard the sound of ice clattering.

Getting off the floor seemed like a good idea, so I eased my way onto the bed. I'd been hit before, but this had taken me by surprise. Even though it had been an accident, it was taking my emotions a bit longer to catch up with logic.

Blane reappeared with a makeshift ice pack, a dish towel wrapped around some ice cubes.

"Here," he said, sinking onto the bed beside me. "Hold this to your jaw. It'll keep the swelling down."

I did as he said and watched as he pulled on his pants, then went into the bathroom. This time he came back with a glass of water and two painkillers.

"Take these," he said. I traded him the ice pack. "How do you feel?"

"I'll be fine," I said once I'd swallowed the pills. "Just took me off guard. I wasn't expecting . . ." I waved my hand vaguely to indicate . . . whatever had just happened.

Blane heaved a sigh, shoving a hand through his hair. "I'm sorry. I should have told you before."

"Told me what?"

"It hasn't happened in a long time," he replied. "But sometimes I get nightmares, the kind I had all the time when I first got back from being deployed. And it's best to not touch me in order to wake me. Better to just call my name."

"But why now?" I asked. "We've slept together before and this hasn't happened."

Blane looked at me, and I knew I wasn't going to like what he had to say.

"The position they offered me, Kat," he said. "It's an opportunity unlike anything else. I could make a difference, really help other SEALs. It just has me thinking. Considering. Remembering."

"You'd have to be deployed again," I said.

He nodded. "But only for six months."

Six months. It sounded like a long time when someone you loved would be in harm's way. I reached for the ice pack and held it against my jaw so I wouldn't have to look at Blane.

"I haven't decided what I'm going to do yet," he said quietly.

"Why not?"

He didn't answer, so I glanced at him. Our eyes caught and held. He reached out, brushing his fingers through my hair.

"Because of you."

Blane's answer, so simply and honestly given, made relief swell inside me. So I was a consideration in his decision after all. I leaned against his chest. His arms wrapped around me, his chin resting on top of my head.

When I knew I could speak without my voice breaking, I asked, "So when do you have to decide?"

His shoulders lifted slightly in a small shrug. "A few weeks. I have to get through this case first."

I stiffened, drawing back out of his arms. "This guy you're defending. He's innocent, right?"

Something shifted in Blane's eyes as I looked at him, waiting for my answer. Finally, he shook his head. "No. He's not."

Appalled, I pulled myself out of his grasp. "You've got to be joking! Why would you defend a rapist? I get that you're a defense attorney, but to defend the guy when you know he's guilty?"

Blane's jaw tightened. "Sometimes I have to do things I don't necessarily want, or like, to do. That includes defending people who are guilty, and this is one of those times."

I jumped to my feet, putting some distance between us. "Why this guy?" I rounded on him. "Is it because of his uncle? That rich guy with all the political connections?"

Blane hesitated. "Partly," he admitted.

"You'd defend a rapist just to further your political career?" My anger waned in the face of my dismay.

Blane stood, approaching me. "I didn't say it was to help my career," he said carefully.

"Then why?" I hoped his explanation would make all the difference.

The words seemed hard for Blane to get out, but finally he said, "I . . . can't tell you."

My jaw dropped in surprise before anger and frustration surged. "What do you mean, you can't tell me? Can't or won't?"

"Won't. You just have to trust me, Kat."

"That's rich," I said. "You're telling me that I just have to trust you with something you won't even tell me? Trust is a two-way street."

"So you're telling me that you don't trust me?" he bit out.

"I'm only dishing back what you're handing out, Blane," I shot back. "In case you've forgotten, we broke up because of something you didn't tell me, and now you're doing it again!"

"This isn't the same thing at all," he denied angrily. He turned away, stalking to the window and looking outside, his arms crossed over his chest.

I had the feeling he was trying to take a break, to ratchet down the escalating tension between us. It worked. I took a breath, then another. Going over to him, I slid my arms around his waist, pressing a kiss to his back and leaning into him.

"I don't want to fight," I said quietly.

Blane turned, settling his hands on my waist. The lines of strain I'd seen around his eyes while he was sleeping were even more pronounced now that he was awake. My stomach clenched with worry. It was obvious Blane was going through something, and arguing with me could only make things harder for him. I decided to bide my time, approach him again after we'd both cooled off.

Our eyes met and his hand moved up to cup my jaw. I tilted my head into his touch, the rough pads of his fingers skimming my cheek. He looked down at me, to the open neckline of the shirt I wore, and he grasped the gold locket resting between my breasts.

Kade had given me the locket for Christmas. It contained a tiny picture of my parents. I'd been overwhelmed with the gift, and rarely took it off. Blane had asked me where I'd gotten it, and hadn't made any comment when I'd told him.

"I'm not going to ask you," he began carefully, still looking at the locket, "what happened in Denver. Whatever his faults, I trust Kade to keep you safe. I always have. But I wonder about this job he's given you, if it's really something you want to do." His gaze finally rose to meet mine.

I hesitated before answering. "I'm not sure," I said honestly. "Before, it felt like my life was happening to me, rather than the other way around. Now it feels like I have a chance to fix that."

"There are other things you could do, Kat."

"Like what?" I asked, wondering what he would say.

"I think you should consider what you want," Blane said. "What do you want to be when you grow up, Kat?" He smiled softly and dropped the necklace, returning his hand to my waist and pulling me closer.

I gave a small huff of laughter. "Once upon a time, I wanted to be you," I said, resting my palms against his chest.

"Me?" Blane asked, his brows knitting in confusion.

"A lawyer," I explained. "But after seeing you, watching how it works, I don't think I'd want to do that." I thought for a minute. "I guess when I pictured it, my life, I always assumed I'd have a job of some sort, but I mostly looked forward to the day when—"

I stopped, realizing what I'd been about to say. Heat rose in my cheeks and I looked away.

"When what?" Blane asked.

I shook my head. It would sound really pathetic to say it aloud.

"Come on, tell me," he gently persisted. "Please, Kat," he said when I still remained silent.

"The day when I wouldn't be alone," I blurted. "Visions of my future always seemed to revolve around having a family, not so much a job. I never had brothers or sisters, so I dreamed of a big family, lot of kids, laughter and a messy house and people to love." I felt stripped bare in front of him, having confessed thoughts I tried not to dwell on.

"Why wouldn't you want to tell me that?" he asked gently, tipping my chin up so I was forced to look at him.

"Because it's embarrassing," I explained. "So trite and cliché. That's not the kind of thing liberated, independent women are supposed to think. I'm supposed to want a career and climb the corporate ladder and bust through the glass ceiling and all that. Not dream of soccer games and tea parties, piano lessons and PTA meetings, peanut-butter sandwiches and training wheels."

Blane leaned down, pressing a hard kiss to my mouth. When he raised his head, he said, "Thank you for telling me that. And for the record, you're one of the strongest, most independent women I know. It's not a crime to want a family of your own."

My embarrassment faded in the face of his sincerity, and I reached up to pull him down for another kiss.

It was getting late and we both had to be at work, so we took turns in the shower (despite the fact that Blane argued we would save time by showering together). I did my hair and makeup while Blane shaved. It was a novel experience, getting ready side by side. We hadn't been this physically intimate in weeks, this much in each other's space, and I found it made me happy.

I was pouring another cup of coffee for myself when Blane emerged from the bedroom, shrugging on his suit jacket.

"How do I look?" he teased, stepping into my personal space.

Amazing, that's how he looked. He wore a black single-breasted soft wool suit, a crisp white shirt, and a sharp-looking silver-gray silk tie in a black paisley print. His dark-blond hair was still slightly damp from his shower, and I caught a whiff of his cologne mixed with the scent of his aftershave.

I made a small noise of appreciation, then reached up to twine my arms around his neck, standing on my toes to kiss him. Blane tasted of mint, and the feel of his freshly shaven skin was like an aphrodisiac. I loved him like this. He looked powerful, gorgeous, and masculine. A dangerous man under the cool veneer of civility. I couldn't get enough.

While I may have entertained the thought that I was in control of our kiss, he quickly disabused me of the notion, and soon I was gasping for air, my pulse racing.

"You make me not care that I'm going to be late," Blane muttered against the skin of my neck. His hands had moved to cup my rear, holding me against his body. I could feel the effects of our impromptu make-out session pressing hard against my abdomen.

Reluctantly, I stepped out of his grasp. His eyes glittered with a predatory light, and I shivered.

"Save it for later, counselor," I said breathlessly, yearning to rip his clothes off and have my wicked way with him.

"Promise?" he teased.

"Absolutely." I'd be counting the hours.

He glanced at his watch, frowning. "We have a new lawyer starting today," he said, putting his cell phone and wallet in his pockets.

"Really?" I asked, only sort of interested. While Derrick Trent and Blane were the partners, they also employed about a dozen other lawyers in the firm. I'd once rarely interacted with them, but lately a few had asked me to do some investigating for them.

"Yes. They'll be helping me with this case."

Blane dug out a hard case from his luggage, unlocking it to reveal the gun he always carried. Indiana was a conceal state and Blane had a license to carry. I thought he was never fully comfortable until his Glock was wedged comfortably in the holster he wore at his hip.

The Matt Summers case was what Blane meant. I bit my tongue against what I wanted to say. Our argument hadn't really been resolved, just postponed. I didn't want to end our time together on a negative note, so I remained silent.

"Dinner tonight?" Blane asked, grabbing his coat, briefcase, and keys.

I nodded. "Sure."

"Okay. I'll call you later." One more quick kiss and he was out the door.

He jogged down the stairs to his black Range Rover—the Jaguar remained in the garage for the winter months. He drove out of the lot before I closed the door on the frigid February morning air.

I had to get moving or I'd be late, too. Dumping my coffee into my travel mug, I fed Tigger, grabbed my coat and purse, and headed to work.

The law firm of Kirk and Trent wasn't in downtown Indy proper, but nestled in a suburb on the north side of the city. It was about thirty minutes from my apartment, if you counted traffic, but I didn't mind the drive. Since I now drove a company-owned Lexus SUV, I enjoyed the time spent commuting. Kade had gotten it for me after my car had been blown up—nearly with me inside.

I was humming softly to myself as I walked into the firm. Although the argument with Blane and my qualms about his case still lingered, I thought we'd taken a huge step in our relationship last night. And this morning, when I'd told him I wanted a family and kids, he hadn't run for the hills like so many men would have.

Putting my purse in the drawer of my desk and shedding my coat, I thought with a snort of what Kade's reaction would have been if I'd said the same thing to him.

Kade.

Oh no. I'd completely forgotten to remind Blane to call him back. With everything that had happened this morning between us and everything else Blane had going on today, he might not remember to call Kade.

Taking the elevator to the top floor, I stepped out into the foyer. A large grandfather clock ticked away the minutes. I could see Clarice, Blane's secretary, working at her desk.

"Good morning," I said brightly.

"Same to you," Clarice said with a smile. "How have you been? I haven't seen you in a few days."

Quick images of the building exploding in Denver, sliding down the fire escape, Parker and the guy Kade had killed with his bare hands went through my mind.

"Busy," I replied. "You?"

"Fantastic!" She beamed at me, then held up her left hand. A diamond sparkled on her ring finger.

"You got engaged! Clarice, that's wonderful!" I rounded the desk to give her a hug. "I'm so happy for you!"

"Me, too," she said, gazing at her ring. "It was sweet. Jack was so nervous."

"Tell me all about it," I said, pulling up a chair.

"Well," she began, obviously delighted to share her story. "He took me to the Eagle's Nest at the Hyatt. I wasn't expecting it at all. But he'd made reservations ahead of time and there was a beautiful bouquet of flowers on the table. I thought it was an early Valentine's Day dinner or something. Then the waiter brought out champagne, and there it was. The ring was inside the glass."

I grinned as she got all teary-eyed.

"And then he got down on one knee and asked me."

"That's a great story, Clarice," I said. "Have you told the kids yet?"

She nodded, pressing a tissue delicately to her eyes. "They're so excited."

"I bet. Jack is a really great guy. He's going to make a fantastic stepdad."

We chatted a little bit longer and I admired her ring again. They hadn't set a date yet, but were thinking perhaps July.

"Would you be my bridesmaid?" she asked tentatively.

I hugged her again. "Absolutely. I'm so thrilled for you."

I glanced at Blane's closed door. "Is Blane in his office?"

She nodded. "Yes, he's meeting with that new lawyer he and Derrick just hired."

"Do you think he'd mind if I popped in real quick?"

"Don't be silly," she said. "You're probably the one person he wishes would interrupt him more." She winked.

Clarice had been privy to many of Blane's dating escapades. The duty of a farewell gift usually fell to her. But she was a die-hard romantic, and I thought she was hoping Blane and I were going to be a long-term thing.

So was I.

I tapped lightly on the door to Blane's office. When he called out to come in, I pushed open the heavy wooden door.

Blane sat behind his paper-strewn desk talking to the new hire. What I hadn't even considered was that the lawyer sitting opposite him would be a woman. I didn't know why I had assumed it would be a man, I just had. They both turned to look at me.

"I'm sorry to interrupt," I said, recovering from my surprise.

"It's fine," Blane said. "I'm glad you stopped by. Kathleen, this is our newest attorney, Charlotte Page." He motioned to the woman. "Charlotte, this is Kathleen Turner, one of the firm's investigators."

Charlotte stood, stretching her hand toward me with a smile. I shook it, forcing my lips into an answering smile.

She was really pretty. Not that pretty was the best way to describe her. More like striking. She had jet-black hair and olive skin, deep-brown eyes, and full, inviting lips. Clad in a navy pinstripe suit and skirt with a white silk blouse and heels, she topped me by several inches. Her figure made my stomach sink. Perfectly hourglass, her narrow waist rounded into hips that tapered to sculpted legs.

Well, at least I was better endowed, I thought snottily.

Then she spoke.

"Kathleen, it's a pleasure to meet you."

She had an accent—Spanish maybe. Combined with her exotic looks, it was the proverbial icing.

"Nice to meet you, too," I lied. My self-esteem wasn't such that I could gladly welcome her working side by side with Blane.

"Charlotte graduated top of her class at Columbia," Blane elaborated. "She clerked for Justice Thomas."

"That's really great," I said. She was the personification of everything I'd wanted to be when I was eighteen.

"Mr. Kirk exaggerates my accomplishments," Charlotte said modestly.

"It's Blane, not Mr. Kirk, and I'm not. If anything, I'm underrepresenting your outstanding record, Charlotte." He gave her a genuine smile.

If people actually turned green with jealousy, I knew I had to be rivaling the Hulk in skin tone. While my logical side knew I was being irrational, it was pointless to try to tell that to my emotional side.

"Well, I'll just leave you two alone, shall I?" I tried hard for a pleasant tone but must not have wholly succeeded. Blane gave me a slightly quizzical look.

"Did you need anything else?" he asked me as Charlotte resumed her seat.

"Oh, yes." I'd nearly forgotten Kade. Again. I directed my words at Blane. "I wanted to remind you to call Kade."

Blane's expression shuttered. "Of course. Thank you." He looked back down at his desk, effectively dismissing me.

Wondering what that was about, and with a last nod to Charlotte, I left the room. I stood outside the door, lost in thought, and more than a little depressed.

"What's wrong?" Clarice asked.

I flopped down in the chair by her desk. "Why didn't you tell me he'd hired Penélope Cruz?"

She grinned. "You mean Charlotte?"

I rolled my eyes.

"She's really nice," Clarice said, "and has excellent qualifications."

"And she's drop-dead gorgeous," I said sourly.

"Kathleen, you have to stop this." Clarice sounded exasperated. "Blane loves you. I'm sure of it. You can't go thinking that every woman that walks by is going to be the one to take your place."

I thought about what she said. She was right. Blane did love me. My initial reaction to Charlotte wasn't something I could control, but I didn't have to let her presence throw me into a tailspin.

"You're right," I said with a sigh. "It's just sometimes I realize how mismatched we are, and I wonder when Blane's going to realize it, too"

"Mismatched how?"

"Well, let's see. Blane is successful, rich, gorgeous, smart." I ticked the accolades off on my fingers. "Whereas I'm . . ." My voice trailed off.

"You are the one he's chosen," Clarice said firmly. "Everything else is just stuff that doesn't really matter. It's how you feel about each other that counts."

I could hear in her voice the hope and joy of someone in the throes of love, still on the high of her engagement. I certainly didn't want to burst her bubble.

"Forget I said anything, Clarice," I said with a wave of my hand. "I'm probably just PMSing or something. So are the kids going to be in the wedding? And what colors have you chosen, because I look awful in yellow."

I distracted her with wedding talk for a while before heading back to my cube. I had a stack of files waiting for background checks and two requests to follow a supposedly cheating spouse to catch him in the act. With a sigh, I got to work.

It wasn't until late afternoon that something out of the ordinary happened. I got a phone call from Charlotte's secretary requesting my presence.

I went up to the third floor, where half the firm's lawyers had their offices. Every two lawyers shared a secretary, but I was unfamiliar with Charlotte's. Maybe she was new as well. She was young, with oversized glasses that made her eyes seem quite large for her thin and narrow face.

"Hi," I said to her. "I'm Kathleen."

"Oh, hi," she replied, shuffling a stack of papers into a pile. "I'm Jessie. You can go on in."

I approached Charlotte's open office door, hesitantly poking my head in. It was a bit of a shambles, and I could tell she hadn't fully moved in. Stacks of file boxes stood in the corner, and she'd discarded her jacket on an elegant Princess Anne chair.

"You called for me?" I said by way of greeting.

Charlotte looked up from where she'd been bent over a box. Her shirt was sleeveless, showcasing her toned arms, and her hair was pulled up into the kind of messy bun I could never master.

"Thank you for coming so quickly," she said, again with the friendly smile. Standing, she put some of the books she'd unearthed from the box onto a nearby bookshelf. They looked like weighty tomes of knowledge. I wondered if she'd actually read them.

"Sure," I replied. "What can I do for you?"

With a small sigh, she moved to sit behind her desk and motioned me to the chair opposite her. "Have a seat. Please."

Obediently I perched on the edge of the chair and waited for her to speak. She eyed me for a moment.

"Blane mentioned you might have some suggestions on apartments, places I might be able to rent for a while, until I get settled," she said. "I'm living in a rent-by-the-week hotel at the moment, and am anxious to get a place of my own."

Good Lord, why in the world would Blane have her ask me, of all people? The thought of Charlotte living in an apartment complex like mine was laughable. Kade's upper-class loft apartment came to mind, then I immediately dismissed the thought. I didn't want her anywhere near Kade.

"Um, I'm probably not the best person to ask," I finally said. "I live in a small place close to downtown. Not the greatest of neighborhoods. There are lots of nice places close to here, though. Maybe you should look in Carmel."

"Okay," she said. "I'll do that. Thank you."

"No problem." I forced a stiff smile and made to rise.

"Wait. One more thing."

I sank back into my chair, looking expectantly at her.

"I have the feeling," she began, "that you don't like me much." A small smile played about her lips, but her eyes were serious.

"That's not true," I said, though I was taken aback at her insight. "I don't even know you. How could I possibly know whether or not I like you?"

"Exactly."

I pressed my lips together tightly, waiting for her to make the next move. I grudgingly admitted to myself that she'd made her point.

"I don't have many female friends," Charlotte said. "Women tend to find me . . . threatening."

Really? I couldn't imagine why.

"I'd really like it if you and I could be friends," she continued.

I had no idea what to say. Now I felt all kinds of bad for immediately hating her. She'd been nothing but nice to me so far and I hadn't really given her a chance.

"Um . . . yeah . . . sure . . . okay," I stammered.

She beamed a dazzling smile at me. Being with Blane had done wonders for my self-esteem. I knew I was pretty, even really pretty given the right clothes and makeup, but Charlotte was simply stunning. The kind of woman who could wear overalls and no makeup, and men would still stop to stare.

I returned her smile with a weak one of my own.

"If you don't mind"—she grabbed a folder from one of the piles on her desk—"since you're one of the investigators for the firm, I'd like you to look through this."

I flipped open the folder and gasped, not expecting the lurid photos inside.

Charlotte grimaced. "I know. Those are the photos of the victim. Her name is Julie Vale."

I slowly paged through the photos. The girl was lovely. Long blonde hair. Petite with a curvy figure. I looked closer. A figure marred and disfigured with bruises and lacerations.

"Are these rope burns?" I asked, pointing to her wrists and ankles.

Charlotte nodded. "It's not a pretty sight. Whoever raped her was a sadistic bastard."

I swallowed, closing the folder and looking up at Charlotte. "So what do you want me to do?"

"As ugly as it is," she said with a sigh, "we need to know more about her. I thought you could look into it, maybe go by her work, talk to people. See what you can find out."

"And this is to help get Matt Summers off," I retorted. "The bastard deserves to go to jail."

"It's our job to defend, not play judge and jury," Charlotte replied evenly.

I nodded, getting to my feet. "I'll see what I can do."

Charlotte thanked me and I left her office, taking the folder to my desk and studying the girl who'd done nothing to deserve what had happened to her.

That night, Blane took me to dinner at the restaurant we'd come to view as our usual place. It was where he'd taken me the night my car had broken down. The first time there I'd just had soup, but tonight Blane ordered the shrimp cocktail for us to share, then ordered me the special.

"So," I said once the waiter had cleared our plates. "Charlotte seems very . . . capable."

"She's perfect for this case," Blane said, taking another drink of the cabernet he'd ordered. "On a rape case, it's essential to have a female lawyer in front of the jury."

His words made the food in my stomach turn sour. I knew he was just doing his job, being pragmatic about trying the case, but I still hated the thought of him getting a rapist off.

When I didn't say anything, Blane reached over and took my hand. "I know how you feel, Kat, and I'm sorry. But I have to try this case. Please trust me."

It seemed I didn't really have any choice in the matter. He wouldn't tell me his reasons and he wasn't going to drop the case, no matter my objections.

"Let's talk about something else," I said, easing my hand out from under his. "Did you call Kade?"

I'd been worrying in the back of my mind about Kade. He was quite capable of taking care of himself, but it would only take a moment of not being quick enough, not seeing the danger, and it would be over.

Blane stiffened, his expression turning unreadable. "I did" was all he said.

"And?" I prompted. "Is he all right? What did he want?"

"You seem awfully concerned with Kade's well-being," Blane noted.

"Of course I am, he's your brother. Why wouldn't I be?"

"He's fine," Blane said curtly. "Had some business to discuss. That's all."

Blane's easy dismissal made me angry. "Did he tell you that someone's trying to kill him?" I asked.

Blane's eyes snapped to mine. "What are you talking about?"

Looks like he hadn't. "Kade said he was close to finding out who was pulling the strings on Sheffield, so we went to Denver to investigate. But somebody knew he was coming. They sent two guys to kill us, and I'm sure Kade's still on their hit list."

Blane's expression had grown more forbidding with each word out of my mouth. "What happened to the guys?" he asked.

I swallowed, remembering the sickening crack of the man's neck. "Kade got to them first."

"And where were you while this was going on?"

"Watching."

Blane cursed, tossed some money on the table to cover the bill, took me by the elbow, and led me to his car. When we were on the road, he hit the Bluetooth button on his cell. After a moment, I could hear ringing over the car speakers.

It rang a few times, then a familiar voice answered. "Yeah," Kade said.

The relief I felt at hearing him, knowing he was alive, rushed through me. I bowed my head to keep my composure, taken aback at the strength of my feelings.

"You didn't tell me that someone's trying to kill you over this Sheffield thing," Blane accused.

"Someone's been chatty," Kade replied, unaffected by Blane's anger.

"Of course Kat told me. Why wouldn't she? What I want to know is why you didn't."

"It's not related to Summers, it was a lead I was pursuing on my own. Nothing you needed to know about."

"I told you to let the Sheffield thing go. It's not worth it. You not only ignored that, you pulled Kathleen into the mess, too."

That got a reaction. "Don't go there, Blane," Kade shot back. "Kathleen was never in any danger. I sent her home once I knew what was going on."

"I don't want her involved in this."

I felt like the worst sort of voyeur, listening to their conversation when I knew Kade didn't have a clue that I was there. And I really didn't like the rising level of tension between Blane and Kade as they continued to argue.

"Blane, stop," I said loudly, unable to take any more.

They both abruptly stopped talking. Blane glanced my way.

"Kathleen?" Kade asked.

I took a deep breath. "Yeah, I'm here."

"Nice of Blane to mention that small detail." Kade's voice was thickly laden with sarcasm.

"I didn't realize it was necessary," Blane said. "I don't hide things from Kathleen. Can you say the same?"

"Stop it, both of you," I interjected. "I'm not a child to be dealt with and coddled. I went with Kade of my own volition, Blane. He's not to blame for my choices. And may I remind you that even now you're working a case for reasons I can't fathom and you won't divulge."

"You haven't told her?" Kade said, an edge to his voice.

Blane grimaced. "We'll talk later." He ended the call.

I remained quiet until we pulled into my parking lot. He had just turned off the car when his phone rang.

"Kirk," he answered sharply. He listened for a moment. "I'll be right there."

My heart sank.

"I've got to go. Summers got himself in a mess and I can't have it leaking to the press," he said.

"It's fine," I said. "I understand."

Our eyes met and held. Blane leaned toward me, moving slowly until his lips brushed mine. Then he was kissing me with a hunger and desperation that left me breathless. I clung to his shoulders, overwhelmed.

When he lifted his head, he cradled my jaw in his large palm, his eyes intent on mine. I couldn't look away.

"You're like water," he murmured, "slipping through my fingers." He pressed a kiss to my forehead and looked again into my eyes. "We're going to get through this," he said firmly. "Just trust me, Kat. That's all I'm asking."

My emotions were in turmoil. I wanted to trust him, but I didn't like that he wasn't being fully honest with me. Yet I couldn't deny him. I nodded. "Okay."

A brief flash of something like relief crossed his face. "I'll be back as soon as I can," he assured me.

"All right. Be careful." I got out of the car and watched as he drove away.

As I got ready for bed, I dwelled on Blane's uncharacteristically emotional declaration. I didn't understand what he meant or why he would say such a thing. I fell asleep on the couch waiting for him.

Loud knocking on the door woke me, and I struggled to gain my bearings. It took a moment to remember why I was on the couch and that Blane wasn't yet here. I blearily focused on the flickering light of the television.

The knock came again and I jumped up, thinking Blane must have forgotten his key.

I opened the door and bit back a shriek.

A man stood in the shadow of the open doorway. Tall and unshaven, he wore jeans, a T-shirt and a jacket. His lips twisted he surveyed me.

I quickly flipped on the light switch, illuminating the darkness.

"Chance?" I asked in disbelief.

CHAPTER SIX

H ey, Strawbs. Let me in?"
His words were casual and the old nickname familiar, but his voice was strained. Jerking myself out of my
shock-induced immobility, I stepped back.

"Yeah, come inside," I said.

Chance glanced over his shoulder at the darkened parking lot before quickly moving past me.

I locked the door behind him. "What in the world are
you doing here?"

He snorted. "Nice to see you, too."

"I haven't seen or heard from you since Mom's funeral,"
I said stiffly. I crossed my arms over my chest. "How do you
expect me to react to you showing up at my apartment un-
announced in the middle of the night?"

"I thought you'd be glad to see family," he said, reaching
for me. "God, it's good to see you" He hugged me tightly.

The familiar feel of his arms around me cracked my icy
reserve.

As Chance shrugged off his leather jacket, my eyes
widened at the gun stuffed into the back of his jeans. He
glanced curiously around my apartment, then made himself

at home on the couch, sinking into the leather cushions with a tired sigh.

My cousin and I didn't much resemble one another. Where I was fair, he was a dark brunette, his hair naturally wavy and thick. He was taller than me by several inches, and it seemed he'd spent time in a gym since I'd last seen him, the muscles in his chest and arms straining the thin cotton of his dark-gray T-shirt. The only thing we shared was the same blue eyes.

Chance was only a couple of years older than me and we'd been close as children; he was the big brother I'd never had. Always fascinated with the color of my hair, he had dubbed me "Strawberry," which had shortened to "Strawbs" over the years. When his parents divorced, he'd moved with his dad to Atlanta. After that, we'd seen each other only rarely. The last time had been at my mother's funeral three years ago. I hadn't heard from him since.

"So are you going to tell me what brings you here?" I asked, sinking down beside him, my legs curled beneath me. "It's a little late for a social visit, even for family."

"I was in the neighborhood," Chance replied, glancing away from me.

"Are you here from Atlanta? On business or"—I remembered the gun—"something?"

"On business," he said, looking uncomfortable. "Listen, I probably shouldn't have come by. It was a bad idea. I should go." He rose from the couch.

"No, wait!" I grabbed his arm as he stood. "You can't just leave, you just got here!"

He looked uncertain, so I pressed. "Please stay. Talk to me. I . . . I've missed you."

Chance crushed me in another hug and I held on tight. "I've missed you, too," he said, his voice thick. "So much. You have no idea."

We stood like that, emotion clogging my throat, for the better part of a minute before I drew back.

I cleared my throat, blinking back the tears that had threatened. "Can I get you something to drink?" I asked. "Water? Pepsi?"

"Got anything stronger?"

I went to the kitchen and returned with a bottle of beer. Chance accepted it, downing a long swallow.

"How've you been?" he asked. "When did you move here?"

"Almost a year ago. I would have told you, but I didn't know how to reach you." I tried to not sound bitter.

Chance had been the one to hold my hand when I'd buried my mom. Even though miles had separated us, we'd never lost that closeness of childhood and I'd been grateful to lean on him during those rough days. When he'd left to go back to Atlanta, it hadn't occurred to me that it would be the last I'd see or speak to him in a very long time.

Chance had the grace to look abashed. "Listen, I would've been in touch . . . wanted to be. Things just happened . . . and before I knew it, it was too late."

"What are you talking about?" I was confused. "What things happened?"

Chance swiped a tired hand across his face. "Can I borrow your shower first?" he asked with a sigh. "Then we'll talk."

I waited, perched on the edge of the couch, while Chance took a shower. I'd refrained from making any comment when he'd discarded his gun on my coffee table.

I didn't know why he was here now or why he'd been so conspicuously absent for so long. I'd tried a few times to get in touch with him after Mom's funeral, but I'd eventually given up. It was obvious that he'd grown out of our childhood attachment. It had hurt me, but I figured people grow and change, and maybe I just hadn't meant as much to him as he'd meant to me.

Chance came out of the bathroom, wearing the same clothes but now with damp hair. Sitting back down beside me, he gave my hair a stroke the way he always had, his fingers tangling in the long locks.

"Thanks," he said.

I nodded, unable to speak. The familiar gesture had robbed me of my strained composure.

"Hey," Chance said gently, catching my chin with his fingers and turning me toward him. "What's the matter?"

I swiped at my eyes. "You," I choked out. "I can't believe you're here after all this time. You're the only family I have left. I could have really used you over the past few years." I tried to conceal my hurt, but I could still hear it in my voice.

A pained look crossed his face. He brushed the tears off my wet cheeks, then took my hand in his. "I'm so sorry," he said. "I can't tell you how sorry I am. I've thought about you so many times. Believe me, if there had been a way for me to be around, I would have. I swear to you."

I knew Chance. I could read his face as well as my own, and knew he was telling me the truth, could tell he'd felt the pain of our separation as much as I had. The hurt I'd carried around for three years finally eased, like a dam breaking, and I didn't resist when he pulled me into his arms again.

We sat like that for a while. He asked me why I'd moved to Indy and how I liked my job. Tigger had jumped on my lap and I absently petted him as I talked. Wanting to keep things light, I didn't go into detail about Blane or Kade or the things that had happened in the past few months. Chance leaned his head back against the couch as I quietly spoke.

I had no idea what time it was when I was finally talked out. We sat in companionable silence for a while before I asked, "So are you in town for long?"

"Maybe a little while," he said.

"Will I see you again?"

"I'll try really hard." Chance pulled away, turning to look at me intensely. "It's important, very important, that you don't tell anyone about me. Not my name, not that I'm here, nothing."

"Why?"

He hesitated. "I can't tell you. Just please, trust me. I probably shouldn't have even come here tonight. I just . . . I just really needed to see you again."

My eyes stung again and I nodded, agreeing to keep his secret.

Chance had meant everything to me as a kid. I'd trusted him to watch out for me, keep me safe, take care of me— and he had. I still didn't know what had happened after Mom's funeral, but I trusted that he had a reason for staying away, and it hadn't been because he'd wanted to. He was my only family, and if he wanted me to keep a secret, then that's what I would do, no matter what.

He glanced at his watch, then stood. "I need to get going," he said, tucking his gun behind his waist and shrugging into his jacket.

"But it's the middle of the night!" I protested.

"Best to slip out when it's darkest, right before the dawn."

I followed him to the door, anxiously wanting to do or say something that would keep him there a bit longer. When he opened the door, the cold air seeped inside and I crossed my arms over my chest, wishing I had something more on that a T-shirt and shorts.

"I'll be back when I can, I promise," he assured me, pausing outside to pull me into a tight hug.

I looped my arms around his neck and squeezed. "Be careful."

"I will. Night, Strawbs."

With a peck on my forehead, he was gone, fading into the darkness enveloping the stairs down to the parking lot. I waited for a moment, then saw a motorcycle drive away, Chance on its back. The image blurred and I swiped a hand across my eyes.

"Strawbs?"

The voice startled a shriek from me, and I spun to face the shadows by Alisha's door.

Blane stepped forward, his eyes on mine.

"Who was that, Kat?"

I gaped at him, at a complete loss for words. I hadn't expected him there and I certainly hadn't expected to have to explain Chance's presence. The words "He's my cousin" sprang to my tongue, but I bit them back just as quickly.

Chance had been emphatic about me not telling anyone who he was. I wouldn't betray him. Not even to Blane.

"A . . . friend," I said lamely.

Blane's eyes narrowed and he stepped closer, looming over me. "What kind of friend?"

I swallowed. "I've known him for a long time. He was just . . . in town and thought he'd stop by." All of which was true.

I turned and went back into my apartment.

Blane followed me. "He kissed you," he said. "That seems like a very good friend. What's his name?"

Panic flared. There was no way I could hold up under a full-blown Blane interrogation, so I went on offense. "What is this, the Inquisition? He's a friend, that's all."

It was only then that I took a good look at Blane. He looked exhausted, though his gaze was sharp. The shadow on his jaw proclaimed it had been awhile since he'd shaved. He was wearing the same clothes he'd had on when I'd last seen him—a suit with a white shirt, his tie now discarded.

Blane stalked me while I slowly retreated. "It's almost dawn, Kat." He spoke in that calmly reasonable lawyer tone of his that usually always boded ill for whatever argument I was making. "I come to my girlfriend's apartment to find her in an embrace with a mysterious unknown man. Why wouldn't I ask these questions?"

I sidled beyond his reach. "Are you jealous?" I asked in disbelief, watching as he removed his jacket without once breaking eye contact.

It seemed incomprehensible to me that Blane could possibly be jealous of anyone. My entire apartment seemed filled with his presence, his charisma and electricity drawing me into him as though I were a celestial body caught in the gravity of a blazing sun.

Blane feinted right and I fell for it, not moving quickly enough when he snagged me around the waist and brought me up hard against his body, imprisoning me in his arms. My breath caught and I tipped my head back. The look in his eyes was a mix of hunger and anger, his hold on me branding his possession. His cologne had faded, leaving just his own scent on his skin.

"You're damn right I'm jealous," he growled.

His mouth came down on mine with bruising force. I gasped, and his tongue surged inside. Fire blazed in my veins and I forgot what we were arguing about. He licked and bit his way down my neck, the scrape of his teeth against my skin more intoxicating than I would have believed.

I held tightly to his shoulders, my fingernails digging into his skin, as he shoved my shorts and underwear down my hips to drop to the floor. His hand was between my legs, stroking and then plunging inside of me.

I gasped, the suddenness of his assault both thrilling and frightening me.

"I need you." His voice was a husky whisper against my skin.

"Yes," I breathed.

Lifting me off my feet, he had me at the couch in two strides. Blane sat me on the arm, caught the bottom of my T-shirt, and yanked it upward until it tangled around my wrists. But instead of jerking the fabric free, he pushed me down so I lay with my back against the seat cushions, hands imprisoned behind me, and hips positioned on the raised arm. My feet couldn't reach the floor, and I watched with breathless anticipation as Blane tossed his shirt aside and freed himself from his pants.

Without any leverage to move, all I could do was watch as he grasped my hips, nudging my thighs farther apart to accommodate him. Just when I thought he would thrust into me hard and fast, he surprised me. Pushing forward, he allowed just the head of his cock to penetrate my body. I moaned, my eyes slipping shut as heat flooded me.

"Open your eyes."

The command in his voice couldn't be denied. I forced my eyes open. He was looking at me with an intensity that made my pulse pound. His face was stark with need and ferocity.

"Watch me."

The order was unnecessary, I already couldn't take my eyes off him. The muscles in his arms and chest flexed as he held me, his abdomen rippling with the movement of his hips as he pushed farther into me. He teased me, only partly filling me before withdrawing. My gaze was riveted to his cock—thick, hard, and glistening from being inside me. My mouth ran dry at the sight.

"Do you want me inside you, Kat?" he asked, his voice rough.

I jerked my head in a nod.

"Say it. Tell me what you want."

I swallowed, my cheeks burning. "I want you," I pushed past dry lips.

"Want me to what?"

The head of his cock teased my entrance, and I tried to push my hips forward, but his grip tightened, holding me in place.

My restraint broke. "Please, Blane," I begged. "I want you inside me."

A strangled cry fell from my lips when he thrust inside of me hard, not at all gentle. The position of my hips allowed him to press deep inside me, and before long the sound of my moans and gasps filled the room. The helplessness of my position only accentuated my arousal, the feeling of being completely in Blane's power overwhelming me.

"You're mine. I want to hear you say it," he ground out. One of his hands moved between my legs, stroking the taut bundle of nerves at the apex of my thighs.

"Oh God, oh God. Blane!"

"Say it. You're mine." His hand and cock moved in sync, harder and faster.

"God, yes! I'm yours! Oh God!" My orgasm crashed into me, and I cried out from the force of it. Blane's release was a mere moment later, his cock swelling as he gave a wordless shout, his body jerking into mine.

My body felt boneless as I lay there. I lazily lifted my eyes to meet Blane's. He looked as overcome as I felt. Where he found the strength to pick me up and carry me to the bedroom, I don't know, but soon we were nestled spoon-fashion in my bed. He pressed gentle kisses to my hand, my shoulder, my neck, my cheek, my brow.

"God, I love you," he whispered huskily in my ear.

"I love you too," I whispered back.

"Thank you," he said, "for that." The gratitude in his voice was real.

I realized that whatever was going on with Blane, I'd given him the opportunity to be in control. Being in control was as necessary to Blane as breathing. I wondered how far his need to control me went, and if that made me feel smothered or cherished. At the moment, it was the latter. That was my last thought as I drifted to sleep.

~

When I woke, it was after seven and the sun was up. Blane was no longer in bed with me. Pulling on my robe and fuzzy pink slippers, I went in search of him and coffee, not necessarily in that order. The long night had given me a pounding headache, though the rest of me felt very nice indeed. The welcome soreness between my legs was a testament to a roughness that Blane usually kept under careful restraint. Not that I minded, but it was very obvious something was bothering him. I assumed it was the case he was working on, though if it was something else, I didn't know if he would tell me.

The bathroom was empty, as was the rest of the apartment. For a stricken moment, I thought he'd left. Then I heard the low rumble of his voice outside.

Moving toward the door, I hesitated. Maybe he hadn't wanted to wake me, or maybe he didn't want me to hear. Knowing I might regret it and already feeling guilty, I crouched down on the floor under the window. I silently eased it open and put my ear to the crack. I could hear Blane plainly now.

"If you don't find out, the guy is gonna walk and there's not a damn thing I can do about it."

Silence.

"Killing him is immensely appealing. Don't tempt me." His tone was dry as dust.

"Nothing yet. He's keeping his word. But I don't expect that to last."

I could smell cigarette smoke, and I realized that Blane was smoking while he was outside on his phone. I had never, ever seen him smoke before.

"Yeah, I'm with her . . . No, she doesn't and that's not going to change, so don't even go there. May I remind you that you're an integral part of this mess?"

A deep sigh.

"I know, I would've done the same. I just didn't know it'd come back to bite us in the ass."

Another silence. I could hear Blane take a long drag of his cigarette.

"Got it. I'll be in touch."

That sounded like the end of the call to me, and though I waited a few more seconds, he said nothing more.

Quietly, I closed the window before going to join him outside.

The morning was cloudy and chilly, as though winter was hanging on with a persistent tenacity. Blane was leaning on the railing, both arms braced on the rusting wrought iron, when he saw me. A quick flick of his fingers, and the cigarette went plummeting to its demise on the concrete below. He stood, opening his arms to me as I nestled against his side. Even in the cold, his skin was warm.

"I didn't know you smoked," I said by way of greeting.

"It's a bad habit left over from my Navy days," he replied. "I don't often indulge. Sorry if it bothers you."

I shrugged. "My dad smoked. It doesn't bother me."

I paused. "So why are you 'indulging' this morning?" I hoped he would open up to me, tell me who he'd been talking to and what they'd been talking about, and why he'd been so upset earlier.

A man was out early walking his dog, a Pekingese, oddly enough. For some reason, I always thought men should have manly dogs, like German shepherds or Dobermans. A yippy, high-maintenance dog seemed incongruous with a man, though I guess that was sexist of me. I watched them go by on the sidewalk next to the street while I waited for Blane's reply.

He didn't answer for a minute, his hand restlessly rubbing my shoulder. "I tend to when things are more stressful than usual."

"What's stressing you? This case?"

"That. Among other things. Nothing you need to worry about." His lips brushed the top of my head. "Let's go inside. You're cold."

Back in my apartment, I rounded on him. I hadn't been appeased by his answer or his kiss. If anything, I was more frustrated. "Who were you talking to?" I asked bluntly.

"Listening at the window, Kat?"

His words were light, but I detected an undercurrent of warning.

"How else am I supposed to know anything?" I retorted, crossing my arms over my chest. "You refuse to talk to me. You don't treat me like a friend and lover who wants to share your life, your burdens. Instead, you treat me like a child, to be coddled and protected."

His jaw tightened. "That's not true. Though at the moment, you're acting like one."

For a moment, I literally saw red. "Are you kidding me?" I gritted out from between clenched teeth.

"Midnight visitors you refuse to name. Playing at being an investigator, of all things. Eavesdropping on me. What would you call that?"

I tried desperately to keep my temper in check. "For your information, I have a very good reason for not telling you who was here. It might even be as good a reason as you have for not telling me why you're defending Matt Summers. And like I've already said, eavesdropping is the only way to know what's going on in your life." The tears were coming now, and I angrily blinked them away. "And lastly, my 'playing' at investigator is the first time anyone's given me a chance to prove myself at anything!"

"Giving you a chance to prove yourself and putting you in immediate danger of being hurt or killed are two very different things," he said tightly. "And who are you trying to prove yourself to?"

"To you!" I exclaimed in exasperation.

Blane looked stunned, and his whole body went still. "To me? Why?"

"Isn't it obvious?" I asked incredulously. "Look at us, Blane. We come from totally different worlds. You have a successful career, ambitions. You come from a well-known political family. Me? I'm a cop's daughter from a little bit of nowhere, Indiana. I'm a bartender who's 'playing' at investigator."

The anger drained out of me and I pushed a hand through my sleep-tousled hair. None of these things were revelations to me, but they were depressing all the same. "Maybe that's why you won't open up to me." I sighed in defeat.

Blane was next to me in an instant, his hand under my chin, forcing me to look at him.

"You don't have to prove a damn thing to me, Kat," he said earnestly. "I love you for who you are, not for where you're from or who your parents were."

I wanted to believe him, I really did.

"Then why do you hold me at arm's length?" I asked.

His expression shuttered, even as his fingers trailed a featherlight path down my cheek. "Maybe you're right," he said quietly. "Maybe I do hold back. I don't mean to. I don't want to." He paused. "But I don't know if I can change. If I can give you what you want."

Disappointment deflated me, but I forced my expression to remain stoic. I gave a short nod.

"I've spent my whole life being the one in charge, the protector, defender, the one everyone goes to for help, the one who knows what to do," he said. "It goes against my nature to burden anyone with my responsibilities, especially when it comes to defending my own."

I searched his eyes, seeing in them the warrior that he was at heart. Whether he was fighting on a battlefield or in the courtroom, he saw it in black and white, us versus them. How could I find fault with him for that? He'd protected me, defended me, avenged me.

"I don't want to lose you," he said. "But all I can promise is that I'll try." His hand captured a lock of my hair, winding it around his finger and giving it a gentle tug.

I rose on my toes, answering his silent request. His lips met mine in what felt like a pledge, from him to me.

"I have to go," he said, once we'd parted. "I'll see you at the office, all right?"

"Yeah." I nodded. "Okay."

The meaning of something he'd said occurred to me only after he'd gone, and I was left wondering, who was he "defending" me from?

When I got to the office, it had started to rain. Cursing the fact that I'd left my umbrella in my cube, I dashed to the building. A man held the door for me as I hurried past. I turned around to thank him, and stopped—the words I'd been about to say dying on my tongue.

It was Matt Summers.

"Got a little wet this morning?" he asked with a genial smile.

Matt wasn't bad-looking, he was actually rather attractive. He was maybe five ten with a wiry build, like a runner rather than weight lifter. He had sandy-brown hair and blue eyes, and skin that was rather fair, like mine. High cheekbones and a pointed chin might have seemed feminine, if not for the look in his eye.

I forced my lips to curve politely. "Yeah." I turned away.

As I watched him from the corner of my eye, he sauntered toward a woman waiting for the elevator. I couldn't remember her name, but I thought she was a new paralegal, and he struck up a conversation with her. I eased closer as nonchalantly as I could, trying to overhear what they were saying.

Blane entered the building from the other set of doors, across the foyer. He shook his head and ran a hand through his hair to dislodge the raindrops. Carrying his briefcase and dressed in a neatly pressed charcoal-gray suit and a black trench coat, he looked a far cry from the man who had been at my apartment just a short time ago.

A flash of memory hit me—Blane standing over me, palms grasping my hips as he thrust into me—and I shivered.

Blane caught sight of me, standing a few feet behind Matt as though I were also waiting for the elevator. His body stiffened and his long strides ate up the floor as he walked toward us.

"Matt," Blane said with a curt nod, once he was within a few feet. "It appears I'm running a few minutes late this morning. Shall we head to my office?"

He completely ignored me.

"Of course," Matt replied amiably. He turned to the girl. "Lovely to meet you, Amy."

Amy smiled, a flicker of interest in her eyes.

Then Matt caught sight of me waiting for the elevator as well. "I'm sorry, sweetheart, I didn't get your name."

I opened my mouth, but Blane abruptly cut me off. "I thought your uncle would be coming today as well?" he asked, directing his words to Matt. Blane had yet to even acknowledge my presence.

Matt glanced back to Blane, his eyes narrowing. "I'm perfectly capable of handling this, Kirk." His words held an edge that made my breath catch, but they didn't seem to have an effect on Blane.

"Excellent," Blane said flatly.

The elevator opened then and Blane gestured for Matt and Amy to precede him inside. When their backs were turned, he grabbed my arm and jerked me out of sight to the side.

"Stay away from Matt," he hissed.

With that admonition, he disappeared into the elevator as well, the doors sliding shut behind him.

It was several moments before I moved, my mind busy puzzling through Blane's behavior. At my cube, I sat staring into space, replaying it in my mind. Did Blane think Matt was so dangerous that he didn't want to even let on that he knew me?

"Got a minute?"

I jerked my head up to see Derrick Trent, the other partner in the firm, standing by my cube.

I jumped to my feet. "Absolutely. What can I do for you?"

Derrick sat in the only other chair in my cube and handed me a manila file folder. I took it and sat as well.

"I'm working a case where a girl has disappeared and her boyfriend's being charged with her murder," he began. "There's no body, all the evidence is circumstantial. It shouldn't have even gone to trial, but it has. I need you to see if you can dig up anything more on the girl. The boy says he didn't kill her, and I believe him. Maybe she had another boyfriend, maybe she just got sick of Indiana. But whatever it was, I need to know what happened to her."

Skimming through the file, something caught my eye. "She worked at the same place Julie Vale worked," I said. "That's quite a coincidence."

Derrick frowned. "Check it out. There might be a connection." He shrugged. "Or it could be just random fate."

He left and I got online to check out the place. It was a bar and strip club in a seedy part of the city. Definitely an unusual place for both girls to work, given the fact that they'd come from reasonably middle-class families. The club, called Xtreme, opened at four.

I grabbed a sandwich for lunch and spent the afternoon doing research on the missing girl and Julie, reading through their files again, Googling them, and checking out their Facebook and Twitter accounts. Both girls were pretty and young, barely in their twenties. I made note of the high school that Derrick's girl, an Amanda Webber, had attended. The town wasn't far from Rushville, where I'd grown up.

I'd hoped Blane would visit or call me at some point, but I didn't hear from him. So at four, I headed to the club. Before going in, I pulled my hair up into a ponytail and popped a piece of gum in my mouth.

The inside of the club was nicer than I had expected. Leather booths and dark wood chairs surrounded a raised stage, and the bar top was black granite. A smattering of patrons were seated, watching a young woman onstage. Her movements were sensuous and graceful, as she worked the pole center stage with admirable skill while dancing to the strains of Sade. Barely covered in a G-string and pasties, her body was enviably toned.

Hopping up onto a barstool, I signaled the bartender, a wiry guy with full tattoo sleeves on display. His black T-shirt bore an intricate woven design, but I couldn't make it out clearly.

"What can I get you, blondie?" he asked.

I smiled and smacked my gum. "Nice tats," I complimented him. "I'm looking for a friend of mine. We went to the same high school. She told me she worked here, made good money. I just moved into town, thought I could hook up with her."

"Sure," he said. "What's her name?"

"Amanda Webber. Know her?"

He shook his head. "Nah, man. She ran off with some guy. Four, maybe five months ago."

I pretended dismay. "You're kidding me! I can't believe she didn't tell me!"

The bartender shrugged. "Sorry. She didn't keep in touch or anything."

"Now what am I going to do?" I asked rhetorically. "I need a job."

He nodded toward the stage. "Can you dance?"

"No," I said. "But I can tend bar."

"How long have you done that?"

"A few years."

He studied me, then stuck out his hand. "Name's Jack."

"Kathleen."

"When can you start, Kathleen?"

I grinned. "I'm at your disposal."

"Perfect. Start tomorrow. Be here by three for training."

"Great! Thanks!"

I didn't breathe properly until I was back in my car. My heart was racing and my palms sweating, aftershocks from my performance. Apparently, I was getting better at acting, no matter what Kade had said about me being a shitty liar.

Kade. I wondered as I drove to my apartment if he was okay, or if whoever was after him had caught up to him. When I thought about it, which I tried not to do, it made me sick with worry. I hated not knowing where he was or what he was doing.

I pulled into my parking lot, shut the car off, and grabbed my cell phone. I stared at Kade's number for several long moments, trying to decide whether or not to call.

He was a big boy, he could take care of himself. No doubt he would not appreciate my checking up on him like a nagging mother.

Even with all these recriminations and warnings going through my mind, I saw my finger move to dial the number.

I waited, barely breathing, as it rang—once, twice, three times—before voice mail picked up.

"Leave a message."

"Kade . . . hey . . . it's me . . . Kathleen." My tongue stumbled over the words. I had no idea what I was going to say on this impulse call. "I just . . . just wanted to call. See how you were doing. If everything's okay." My voice faltered as I wondered if things might not be okay at all. "Um . . . anyway. I'll . . . uh . . . talk to you later, I guess. Bye."

I ended the call, leaned forward, and knocked my forehead against the steering wheel. "Stupid, stupid, stupid," I muttered to myself, wishing I'd just hung up when the voice mail had kicked in.

My phone rang and I jumped. Had Kade called back?

Looking at the screen, I saw that it was Blane, not Kade. "Hello?"

"Kat, where are you?"

"In my parking lot."

"Have you had dinner yet?"

"No."

"Okay. I'll pick something up and be by shortly."

"Sounds good. See you soon."

I could smell the smoke from the club on me, so I decided to shower and change before Blane got there. When he knocked on my door, bearing a large pizza box, my hair was wet and I had on my flannel pants and T-shirt.

"Isn't it a little early to be going to bed?" Blane asked, setting the pizza on my kitchen table before taking off his jacket and tie. "Though I guess you didn't get much sleep last night."

I stiffened. Blane hadn't brought Chance up again since we'd argued, and I didn't want to reopen the discussion.

"I could say the same for you," I replied evenly, grabbing two plates and putting pizza slices on them. "Matt seems like a real charmer. What were you doing last night?"

"He had a couple of hookers at his place. One of them realized who he was, what he's on trial for. She panicked, and called the cops."

"Did he do anything to her?" I asked as Blane uncorked a bottle and poured two glasses of red wine.

"He said he didn't," Blane answered noncommittally.

As we sat down at the table, Blane's presence made me acutely aware of how small my apartment was. He didn't seem to fit, though he'd never said a word about where I lived. His house suited him. Grand and reeking of old money, he fit in there.

"What did you do today?" he asked.

I took a sip of wine before answering. Blane was something of a wine snob, which I could appreciate, and it was a good bottle. "Derrick asked me to look into this case he's working on."

"The Webber case?"

I nodded. "Turns out both she and Julie worked at the same strip club. Did you know that?"

Blane stopped chewing for a moment, then took an abrupt drink of wine before answering. "Yes, I did. I'm looking into it."

I frowned. "Maybe you should tell Derrick you're looking into it, since he didn't seem to know."

Blane only nodded, so I continued.

"Anyway, I went by there and got a job bartending. I figured that might get me more information about Julie and Amanda."

Blane choked on his wine.

Alarmed, I watched as he recovered. "You okay?"

"Are you out of your fucking mind?"

His anger scared me and his words ticked me off. "Thanks a lot, Blane," I replied coolly. "Way to show some confidence in me."

"You met Matt today," he retorted. "You saw what he did to Julie. I'm doing everything in my power to protect you, and you waltz right in to the lion's den and ask for a job. How did you think I was going to react?"

I stiffened. "To protect me? From what? From Matt?"

Blane didn't answer.

"Since when did I become a part of this? I can be careful. I know how to protect myself, and I know what to look for."

We sat in silence, regarding one another. Blane leaned back in his chair, studying me. I waited uneasily, wondering what he was going to say, how he'd react.

Between our argument last night and the one we were currently embroiled in, now more than ever I was expecting that proverbial shoe to drop. Surely at any moment Blane would tell me it wasn't going to work, that it was over.

Instead, he shocked me.

"Why don't you come live with me?"

I stared at him, speechless. When I finally found my voice, I could only say, "What?"

"Come live with me," he repeated.

My mind was trying to process this. What did it mean? Other than the short time I'd spent recuperating at Blane's, I had never lived with a man before, had never been asked. I wasn't sure what to do or say.

On one hand, the fact that he wanted to make our relationship more permanent made me ecstatic. But on the other hand, I'd never had childhood dreams of a man saying, "I love you madly. Come live with me." The dreams had usually involved a white dress and reciprocal "I do's."

That helped focus my thoughts.

"Blane . . . that's really great, really sweet of you."

His eyes narrowed. "But?"

"But that's just not for me." Reaching across the table, I took his hand in both of mine. The calluses on his palm were rough beneath the pads of my fingers. "Please understand. I really appreciate the offer, though."

"Why is living with me not for you?" he asked.

My face heated with embarrassment. My opinions were probably not the norm, but I wasn't going to lie. "I just don't think it's a good idea," I said. "If we were married, that's one thing, but we're not."

"That can be arranged."

I stared at him. Had he just said what I thought he'd said?

"What did you say?"

"I said, 'That can be arranged,'" he repeated calmly, taking another swallow of wine. "If being married is what you require to come live with me, that can be rectified with a trip downtown and calling in a few favors."

I could barely breathe. Blane was suggesting we get married as though he were discussing what movie we should go see. It was an awful parody of what I wanted, and I didn't know if I could remain as detached from the situation as Blane appeared to be. His body seemed relaxed as he sat in his chair, one ankle resting on his knee, while his fingers toyed with the stem of his wineglass.

I didn't know what to say. Was he serious that we should get married? Was that what I wanted? Should I care about the completely lackadaisical way in which he'd asked or just go with it? Thoughts of being with Blane—having his face be the first I saw in the morning and the last I saw at night—tempted me. Wispy visions of children and laughter ran through my mind. My dream was within reach. I just had to say the word.

Then another thought occurred to me, one that made the blood drain from my face. My eyes lifted to Blane's, who was watching me carefully.

"Are you saying all this because you're trying to protect me?"

I could tell immediately that I'd hit the nail on the head. Blane's face was a blank slate, and he took too long to speak.

"Kat, that's not—"

"Oh my God," I breathed. "You'd actually marry me out of a sense of duty to protect me?" The thought was as demoralizing as it was mortifying.

"I love you—" he began.

"But that's not what this is about," I interrupted. "You're not asking me to marry you because you love me and want to spend the rest of your life with me. You didn't even ask, now that I think about it. You just suggested. God, Blane, I don't know what's more humiliating. Your obvious belief that I can do nothing for myself, or a pity marriage proposal."

Anger was coming in waves now, temporarily burning away the hurt. I leapt to my feet, needing to put some space between us.

"You're taking this all wrong, Kat." Blane jumped up and came after me. His hand landed on my arm. I jerked out of his grasp, rounding on him.

"I'm taking this wrong? *I* am?" My voice was laced with incredulity. He'd just made a mockery of not only me, but of all my hopes and dreams that revolved around him, and I was the one taking it wrong?

Blane pushed his hand through his hair in frustration. "I didn't mean that. Damn it, I'm not doing this right."

"You've got that right. Get out." I was surprised at how cold I sounded.

Blane looked at me, his expression pained.

"I mean it. Leave." I crossed my arms over my chest, trying to hold myself together. I felt like I was breaking apart from the inside out.

His jaw set in bands of steel, Blane finally grabbed his coat and let himself out. When the door closed behind him, my knees gave way and I slid down the wall to the kitchen floor, too stunned at what had just happened to cry.

CHAPTER SEVEN

I couldn't sleep once Blane left, and I laid on my couch, staring mindlessly at the television. An old rerun of *Seinfeld* was on, though the humor was lost on me as I replayed the scene with Blane in my head.

I didn't regret throwing him out. My humiliation and anger still burned inside me. There was a limit to how much Blane could control and protect me, and hearing him using my own dreams of marriage and family against me had been the last straw.

I'd tried talking to him, tried understanding who he was. Yet it seemed he was determined to keep me in a glass box. I didn't want that, couldn't live like that.

I drifted off to sleep, not wanting to go to my bed, where Blane had lain with me just this morning. Despair loomed underneath my anger, and the smell of him on my sheets would undo me.

A pounding at my door startled me awake. Rubbing my eyes, I glanced at the clock and groaned. It was barely after three. These nocturnal visits were killing me.

Hoping it was Chance, I opened the door, only to be surprised once again.

"You called, princess?"

My jaw was agape, staring at Kade, and it took a moment for me to regain my bearings.

"Um, yeah, I did."

"You going to let me in—?"

His voice faltered, a grimace crossing his face. I noticed that his left hand was under his jacket, holding his side.

"Kade? Are you all right?" I asked anxiously, grasping his arm.

To my horror, his knees began to buckle. I grabbed him around the waist, struggling to keep us upright.

"Kade! What's wrong?"

He didn't answer, but he wasn't unconscious. Yet. I hobbled inside, Kade half-walking, half-leaning against me. He was heavy and I thought I was going to topple over any moment, but somehow I managed to get him to the couch and sat him down.

Breathing hard from exertion and panic, I hurried to turn on the lamp. When I got a good look at Kade, I was struck by the paleness of his skin. Beads of sweat stood out on his forehead even though it was cold outside. Falling to my knees, I pushed back his jacket, sucking in a breath when I saw blood on his hand and a dark stain on his shirt.

"Oh my God. What happened? Why are you bleeding?"

He let me pull his hand away from his shirt. I pushed it up to reveal a raw wound, oozing blood.

"Kade"—my voice was shaking—"have you been shot?"

"Bingo, princess," he breathed. His eyes slid shut.

Reaching behind me, I grabbed my cell phone, but found my wrist in a viselike grip.

"No police," Kade said, his eyes open again and clear.

"I need to call 911," I argued. "You need to go to a hospital."

"Can't," he rasped. "No hospital. They'll kill me."

Oh God. They were still after him, whoever "they" were.

"Who did this to you, Kade?"

He didn't answer.

I was starting to panic. If he wouldn't let me call an ambulance, I didn't know what to do, how to help him.

Kade seemed to be losing consciousness now, his grip slackening on my wrist. Jumping to my feet, I hurried into the kitchen, rummaging through my junk drawer until I found what I needed. The blood on my hands smeared the pristine white of the business card, but I dialed the number, holding my breath and praying.

When I heard the voice on the other end of the line, my knees nearly buckled in relief.

"Dr. Sanchez?" I asked. "It's Kathleen Turner. Blane's . . . employee. Do you remember me?" Dr. Sanchez had been the doctor Blane had called to my apartment in the middle of the night when I'd been ill. He'd left his card on the table. I hoped he'd be as nice tonight as he'd been then. "I have a friend who's been shot and can't go to the hospital. Will you help me?"

Although he sounded surprised to hear from me, Dr. Sanchez readily agreed to come and assured me he'd be there soon.

I went back to Kade and dialed Blane's number. It didn't matter that we'd had a fight, Kade was his brother.

Blane picked up on the first ring. "Kirk."

"Blane, it's me. Kade just showed up at my door. He's been shot. He won't go to the hospital, so I called Dr. Sanchez."

There was a moment of silence before "I'm on my way."

The minutes dragged by. Finally, there was a loud knock on the door.

Kade's eyes flew open and he grabbed my arm as I stood.

"It's okay," I assured him. "It's a doctor. A friend of mine. He'll help you."

I opened the door to the familiar figure of Dr. Eric Sanchez. He was taller than me, but not by much; his dark hair blended into the shadows of the night.

"Please come in," I said, stepping back to allow him inside. "Thank you for coming."

The dark eyes behind the wire frames of his glasses gazed shrewdly at me. "I got here as fast as I could," he said.

He moved quickly to the couch, assessing Kade's injury. "Help me get him to the bed," he ordered.

Kade was only semiconscious at this point, but the two of us managed to move him. Dr. Sanchez swiftly and efficiently cut through Kade's shirt.

"We need clean towels," the doctor barked. "Lots of them."

I scurried to do his bidding, returning with a tall stack. In my absence, he had jerked all the sheets and blankets off the bed, save for the bottom sheet. He'd also removed an array of tools and needles from his bag, all encased in sterile plastic wrapping. When he pulled out a needle to inject something into Kade's gaping wound, I had to turn away, bile rising in the back of my throat.

Standing uncertainly nearby, I fidgeted, not knowing what to do. Dr. Sanchez didn't speak while he worked, and the few times I glanced over, I had to quickly look away. The gloves he wore on his hands were now red and I could hear the ripping of plastic as he opened more instruments. Kade, thankfully, seemed to have lost consciousness.

I heard a knock on my door and rushed to answer, knowing it had to be Blane. Sure enough, he was waiting impatiently outside.

"He's in the bedroom," I said by way of greeting.

Blane gave a curt nod before hurrying past me.

When I returned to the bedroom, Blane was standing next to Kade, opposite the doctor. A combination of anguish, pain, and guilt was written on his face.

"There," the doctor finally said. He discarded a small brass-colored object covered in blood.

He carefully stitched together the wound, then called me over. "I need to show you how to dress this, because it'll need cleaning and redressing three times a day for the next couple of days," he said, removing his bloody gloves.

"I can take him to my house," Blane interjected, his voice rough.

Dr. Sanchez shook his head. "I'd rather he not be moved for now. For a bullet wound, he's lucky, but he needs to rest and mend. It's best if he stays here, Blane, at least for tonight."

Blane looked at me. "Is that okay with you?"

I nodded, then watched as the doctor showed me how to clean and bandage the wound. After that, he handed me two pill bottles.

"This one is for infection," he said. "He's not allergic to penicillin, is he?"

"No," Blane said. "He's not."

"Good. This is for pain. Both twice a day, with food."

"Got it."

Gathering his things, he asked for a trash bag and discarded the bloody gloves and towels, now stained beyond recovery. "I'll take this with me," he said, "to dispose of properly."

Blane stepped forward to shake his hand. "Thanks, Eric," he said. "I owe you one."

"That's actually two that you owe me," Eric replied with a good-natured grin. "But who's keeping track?"

Blane smiled tightly. I showed Dr. Sanchez out, giving him my own words of thanks for coming so quickly. When I returned, Blane still stood next to Kade's unconscious form.

"Did he say anything when he showed up?" Blane asked, his eyes on Kade.

"No, nothing," I replied.

"But he came to you," Blane said flatly.

I flushed but didn't know what to say, so I remained silent.

"When I find out who did this to him," Blane quietly gritted out, his fists clenching, "I swear to God I'm going to kill them."

Grabbing a tissue from a nearby box, Blane picked up the bullet Dr. Sanchez had left. He wrapped it and pushed it into his pants pocket. With one last look at Kade, he turned and left the room.

I followed him, closing my bedroom door quietly behind me. Blane stood in my living room, arms crossed over his chest as he stared out the window. I stopped a few feet away, unsure what to say, if anything. After a moment, Blane seemed to pull himself together and turned to face me.

"I'm sorry, Kathleen . . . for earlier."

I shook my head, dropping my gaze to the floor. "I don't want to talk about it."

And I didn't. I was tired, physically and emotionally, and couldn't handle another heart-to-heart conversation—or argument.

Blane moved toward me, not stopping until we were mere inches apart. He studied the locket resting against my skin before looking me in the eyes.

"Take care of Kade."

His lips pressed against my forehead and I squeezed my eyes shut.

Then he was gone.

I couldn't think about all that had been left unsaid between us, didn't want to dwell on it. I didn't know what I should think or feel, but it didn't matter right now anyway. I had a patient to nurse back to health. Kade needed me.

That thought spurred me to action, and I went to the kitchen, filling a glass with ice water and carrying it into the bedroom. Kade was still asleep. I set the glass on the bedside table, then curled up cross-legged on the bed, watching him.

His jaw was roughened and I could tell he hadn't shaved in a few days. While the doctor had removed his shirt, he still wore his jeans. That seemed uncomfortable to me, but I wasn't about to try and pull them off.

Kade moved restlessly, and the blanket covering him fell away. His chest lightly rose and fell with his breathing, which comforted me. He was going to be okay.

It was chilly in the room, and Kade's bare skin bothered me. I reached over to drag the blanket back up.

A hand shot out to grasp my wrist, and I found myself flipped onto my back, with Kade's arm pressed against my throat.

"Jesus, Kathleen," Kade snarled, his face contorted in pain.

He released me, collapsing back against the mattress. "You've got to learn not to sneak up on people when they're sleeping."

"I wasn't sneaking," I groused, sitting back up. "I was trying to help."

"What happened?" He touched the bandage on his side. "Did you do this?"

"No, and don't touch it," I admonished. "A friend of Blane's is a doctor. He dug out the bullet and stitched you up."

I grabbed the pill bottles off the table, dumping one of each into my palm. "Here," I said, holding them out to him with one hand, the glass of water in the other. "You're supposed to take these."

"What are they?" He made no move to take them from me.

"One's for pain, one's for infection."

"Just give me the one for infection," he said.

"Don't be an idiot," I snapped. "Take the damn pain pill. I've had a shitty couple of days and I'm not going to deal with your macho crap."

Kade's eyes met mine and I held his stare for a long moment. Finally, he reached out and took the pills and water. I watched as he swallowed both of them.

"If you're going to check that I swallowed them, I've got a great idea for that."

I couldn't muster the energy to smile at his wisecrack. Instead I turned and lay down on the bed, fixing my attention on the ceiling. Kade settled back as well and we rested silently for a while, watching the room slowly brighten with the morning sun.

Kade broke the silence. "So why have you had a shitty couple of days?"

I thought about not telling him, since talking to either Blane or Kade about the other seemed vaguely tacky to me, but gave a mental shrug. "Blane and I had a couple of fights," I explained.

"About what?" He adjusted his position on the bed, carefully turning onto his uninjured side to look at me.

"About this case he's working. How he wouldn't tell me why he's defending that asshole. Then he gets this bright idea that the best way to protect me is to—"

I stopped, realizing I may have said too much.

"To what?" Kade prompted.

"To marry me," I muttered.

Kade said nothing. He merely reached down to grasp my left hand. Holding it up, he said, "I don't see a ring here. I'm guessing your answer wasn't what he had expected?"

"There was no question to answer," I said. "He didn't even ask, just suggested we go down to the courthouse."

"Ouch." Kade lowered my hand back to the mattress but didn't let go. "For a suave kind of guy, I'd have expected better."

I gave a small huff of laughter despite myself. "Yeah. Me, too."

There was a pause.

"So if he had asked, would you have said yes?"

The feel of his hand enveloping mine pressed against my senses. While it should have seemed weird to have Kade, of all people, lying next to me in my bed, it didn't.

"I don't know."

The words fell out without my consciously having decided to speak them, and I realized it was true. I loved Blane, but the last few days had shown me that rather than growing more trusting of me as we'd been dating, Blane had instead gotten even more protective, more determined to not let anything harm me, no matter the cost.

Kade pressed my hand open until our fingers were threaded together, palms touching. I turned my head to look at him, but his eyes were shut. I pulled the blanket up and over us, and with a deep sigh, I closed my eyes as well.

∼

A clap of thunder woke me. My eyes fluttered open and I saw that the bedroom was now dark. The sound of rain on the window confirmed that a storm had moved in.

Kade was still sleeping. He hadn't moved from his position and I hoped the pain medicine would help him stay asleep.

The pain medicine.

I grimaced. Some nurse I was. The doctor had told me to give it to him with food. Crap.

Untangling my hand from Kade's, I eased out of the bed. Closing the bedroom door behind me, I rummaged in my kitchen cabinets for something I could make him to eat.

"This'll have to do," I muttered to myself, holding a box of blueberry muffin mix.

Grabbing the ingredients, a bowl, and muffin pan, I mixed everything together and put them in the oven. I had about fifteen minutes while they cooked, so I got in the shower. It wasn't until I was pouring the thick conditioner into the palm of my hand that I realized I'd forgotten to put oil in the mix.

"Shit, shit, shit!"

I hurriedly turned off the water and reached for a towel. Only there wasn't one. I'd given them all to Dr. Sanchez.

If I didn't hurry to add the oil, the damn muffins would turn out hard as rocks.

Cursing under my breath, I scurried into the kitchen, naked and dripping. I took the muffins out of the oven and, thankfully, they were still sort of liquidy in the middle. The recipe called for a quarter cup of oil. Okay, dividing that evenly among twelve muffins was . . .

Math wasn't my strong suit, so I eyeballed it, dumping a little oil in each one and giving a stir with a toothpick. When I was done, I looked them over critically. I had no clue how they were going to turn out, but it was worth a try.

Grabbing the pan with a pot holder, I slid it back onto the oven rack, heaving a sigh. Gourmet cook, I was not.

"I've heard of barefoot and pregnant in the kitchen, but I think I like this better."

Startled, I jumped, bumping my fingers against the side of the four-hundred-degree oven. I cried out, jerking back my hand. Spinning around, I saw Kade striding toward me.

For a moment, the absolute embarrassment of the situation rendered me immobile. Then Kade was next to me, grabbing the hand I had cradled against my body.

"What happened?" he asked, examining the livid skin. "Don't you know the purpose of an oven mitt?" Reaching over, he turned on the cold water, putting my hand in the steady stream. I hissed.

"If you hadn't scared me, I wouldn't have burned myself," I gritted out. Groping behind myself with my other hand, I found the roll of paper towels. Jerking a handful free, I tried to cover myself.

"Seriously?" Kade deadpanned with a quirk of an eyebrow.

My cheeks heated. I was too cheap to buy the nice, thick paper towels, and the no-name brand was soaking up the water on my skin and becoming instantly transparent goo. I cursed my own frugality and stubbornly clutched the soggy mess to my body anyway, trying to use my arm to cover my breasts.

"How does your hand feel?" Kade asked.

The water coursing over my skin had eased the pain and I gave a curt nod. Kade shut the water off.

His body blocked mine where I stood. Tipping my head back, I looked up at him. His eyes burned a path down my body.

"Fuck bullets," he rasped. "You're going to be the death of me."

I swallowed. "You're supposed to be sleeping," I said as calmly as my racing pulse would allow. I was all too aware of how close he was, and how very naked I was. "What are you doing up?"

"You're demanding I get back in your bed?" he asked, all innocence.

"You know what I mean."

"I woke up, saw you weren't there, and came looking for you." His lips twisted. Leaning forward, he whispered in my ear, "Has anyone told you how magnificent you look in wet paper towels? I bet those peacock-blue stilettos would go great with that outfit."

I abruptly remembered what he'd said about those shoes once before: *And the next time I see you wearing those shoes, they'll be the only thing you're wearing.*

I felt my breath catch. "I need to get dressed."

"By all means," he readily agreed. Kade took a big step back, and I abruptly realized he could see more of me now, with space between us, than he had been able to before.

"Cover your eyes," I insisted as I fought a losing battle with my bargain-basement quicker-picker-uppers.

"Not a chance in hell."

Cheeks burning, but with as much dignity as I could muster, I turned literal tail and hurried into the bedroom, shutting the door behind me. I felt his eyes on me the whole way.

I put on clothes that covered me from neck to ankle—a turtleneck and jeans. Running a brush through my hair, I decided to let it dry on its own. I hadn't forgotten that Kade still needed food with his medication, so in a matter of moments, I was back in the kitchen.

Kade had taken up residence at my kitchen table, making the room seem smaller with him in it. The smirk he gave when he saw what I was wearing told me I hadn't fooled him, he knew I was donning armor.

The timer beeped and I took the muffins out of the oven. I could tell at once that my attempt to save them had been in vain. The outsides were hard as a rock, while the middles were still too squishy and undercooked to eat. Dismayed, I just stood looking at them. Tears pricked my eyes.

Damn it, I couldn't even cook a box of muffins.

When I sniffed, Kade moved to stand next to me. "Hey, what's the matter?" he asked gently.

His question just made the waterworks start. "These stupid things," I blubbered. "They only had like three ingredients, and I still screwed it up."

He laughed lightly, pulling me into his arms and hugging me. "So you can't cook. I can live with that."

Kade's sweetness only made me bawl harder.

"Come on now," he said nervously, reaching behind me for more of the paper towels I now despised. "It's really okay. Please stop crying, all right? We'll just order in. No big deal."

I swiped the rough cloth across my eyes and nodded. The only thing I could cook was potato soup, which I'd made for Blane, but it wasn't like we could eat it every night. He'd quickly realized my lack of culinary skills and we'd gotten in the habit of either going out to dinner, ordering takeout, or having his housekeeper, Mona, drop things by.

The thought of Blane made my stomach hurt. Tears welled up again, but I assiduously blinked them back. Now wasn't the time to start mooning over Blane.

Flipping through my stack of take-out menus, we decided on Chinese, then sat on the couch to watch TV while we waited. Kade wanted to take a shower, and after I scrounged up a beach towel (I certainly didn't need him waltzing out naked) and admonished him to not get his bandage wet, he disappeared into the bathroom.

"So who shot you?" I asked when he was out of the shower and we were finishing off our plates of kung pao.

"A bad guy."

I rolled my eyes. "Really? Come on. Tell me. Did you find out who's after you?"

Kade ignored me for a moment, setting his empty plate on the coffee table before settling back against the couch. I'd managed to rummage up a T-shirt that would fit him, and thank God he'd put it on. Bending his leg, he pulled his bare foot up onto the couch, resting his arm across his denim-clad knee as he looked at me. The casualness of his posture only seemed to accentuate his maleness. Kade oozed raw sexuality.

I took a nervous sip of Pepsi and tried to unobtrusively edge farther onto my side of the couch.

"These people like to make sure there are no loose ends," he finally said.

"How are you a loose end?"

"Because I got close enough to know that Ryan Sheffield had orders from some very powerful people."

I frowned. "Who?"

"David Summers."

My eyes widened in surprise. "Matt Summers's uncle? The guy in charge of that group, that political group?" The name escaped me, even though I'd heard it on the news a few nights ago.

"IAN," Kade said. "Improving America Now."

"Yeah, that one. But why would he have anything to do with Ryan Sheffield?"

"David Summers has a lot of money, and a lot of power," Kade explained. "Politicians fall all over themselves to get in his good graces. He's very antimilitary and, ironically enough, anticapitalism, though that's how he made his fortune."

"If you know he was behind Sheffield, why can't he be arrested?" I asked. "Sheffield nearly killed me."

"It would do nothing," Kade replied. "He'd be out in the blink of an eye. The best thing to do—what Blane and I are doing—is find out what his endgame is, if there's anyone else besides him pulling the strings."

"Blane and you?"

"Yeah, that's the part he probably didn't tell you."

I just looked at him.

Kade shrugged. "Summers is a ruthless guy. If he's responsible for even half of what we suspect, he'll stop at nothing to get what he wants."

"And what's that?"

Kade smirked. "When I know, I'll tell you." He eyed my frown for a moment. "Don't get all bent out of shape. I don't want you drawing attention from Summers either."

"I met Matt Summers the other day," I told him, "in the lobby at the firm. Blane got a little freaked out."

"No shit," Kade retorted. "Matt is bad news. His uncle's money has shielded him for years."

"And he's using that as leverage to make Blane be that shield now," I said.

Kade looked straight into my eyes. "Sure."

His answer made me frown, but as I was thinking about pursuing it, I glanced at the clock.

"Hey, I need to change your bandage before I go." Jumping up, I hurried into my bedroom to get the supplies Dr. Sanchez had left.

"Going where?" Kade asked when I returned.

"I'm looking into this place where Matt's victim worked. Derrick's also working a case where a girl disappeared, and she worked there, too."

Settling next to him on the couch, I ripped open a new bandage. "By the way," I said, "Blane took the bullet the doctor got out of you. He was pretty upset that you'd been shot."

I reached to pull up his shirt, but his hand grabbed my wrist, stopping me.

"Tell me you didn't call Blane."

"Of course I did. He's your brother." The "duh" was in my tone, but I was smart enough to not say it aloud.

Kade cursed and he scrubbed a hand across his face.

"What's wrong?" I asked. "Why shouldn't I have told him?"

He looked me straight in the eyes. "You of all people should know," he said. "If you look up 'overprotective' in the dictionary, there's a picture of Blane's face."

Okay, he had a point there.

"Well, it doesn't matter now, because it's done. Now let me go, I need to do your bandage."

Kade released my hand and I gave him a gentle shove so he was reclined enough for me to get to the wound. Unfortunately, that meant I was also now positioned squarely between his legs.

I cleared my throat, reconsidering. "You know, it might be easier if you did it." It wasn't like the wound was on his back.

"You ruined the muffins," he reminded me. "The least you can do is put a bandage on me." His aggrieved tone was a stark contrast to the mischief dancing in his eyes.

"Fine," I huffed. "Be good." I poked him in the chest with my fingernail, emphasizing my words.

"Cross my heart."

I frowned at his flippancy, not trusting him, but the clock was ticking and I had no time to argue. Leaning over him, I tried to ignore the closeness of our bodies as I took off the bloody bandage, cleaned the wound, and pressed a new bandage in place. I'd been balanced precariously so I wouldn't touch him any more than necessary, and I gave a sigh of relief once I was finished.

"There," I said with satisfaction. "That should—"

My words were abruptly cut off when Kade shifted, upsetting my balance. I landed on top of him, and his leg wrapped over mine, trapping me. Our faces were inches apart as I stared, wide-eyed, into the sapphire depths of his eyes.

"You said you'd be good," I reminded him, my words more breathless than I liked.

"I lie."

The silence was thick between us, and I barely breathed. Kade reached out, his fingers running slowly through my loose hair. Dry now, it was wavy and soft, and he brought a long lock to his nose and inhaled deeply. His gaze was still fixed on mine, and I couldn't look away.

"You make me want things," he said, his voice barely above a whisper. "Impossible things."

His gaze dropped to my mouth, which was suddenly dry as dust. My tongue darted out nervously to wet my lips, and I felt the surge of his response against my abdomen. Time seemed to stand still, my senses cataloguing the smell of his skin, the rise and fall of his chest underneath my palms, the patter of the rain still falling outside.

The thought I'd been avoiding since Kade had shown up last night was suddenly front and center in my mind. He could've died. I didn't know who had shot him, or if Kade had killed that person. What if the bullet had been farther to the left? What if the next time it was? Kade could be taken from me in an instant, and I might not even know.

Just like Blane, if he returned to the battlefield.

I rested my head against Kade's chest. I could hear the strong sound of his heart beating. Squeezing my eyes shut, I sent up a prayer of thanks, as well as a plea for strength. Kade was temptation. Blane would never forgive me, or Kade, if anything happened between us.

Kade would find his happily ever after. He had to. It just couldn't be with me.

"I have to go," I said, my voice strained.

Squirming to get out of his grip caused a muffled groan from Kade, his hips pressing up against me. I wasn't proud of the thoughts that flashed through my head at the feel of his arousal—wanton images of what I could do to him if I slid just a little lower . . .

I scrambled frantically now and Kade released me. Stumbling to my feet, I couldn't meet his eyes, couldn't look at him sprawled on my couch with desire in his eyes and a raging hard-on.

"I'll be back later," I babbled, grabbing my purse and shoving my feet into the first pair of shoes I found. "The place is called Xtreme and I start tonight. Don't forget to take your medicine, and would you mind feeding Tigger?"

I didn't wait for an answer, but hurried out the door and into my SUV, not breathing properly until I was driving down the road.

I cursed myself six ways from Sunday for the things I'd contemplated—all involving myself and Kade in various states of undress—no matter how briefly I'd thought them. I couldn't be that girl, wouldn't be that girl who falls in love with two brothers. I loved Blane and cared about Kade. A lot. That was all. He was like . . . like a brother to me, too. Yes, that was it. That's why my feelings were so strong for him.

The little voice in the back of my head reminded me that fraternal feelings usually didn't include a mad desire to unzip his pants and . . .

I groaned in dismay, smacking myself in the head with my palm to dislodge the image. While I wanted to help Kade recover from his wound, a part of me fervently hoped he wouldn't be there when I got home tonight.

I arrived at Xtreme at the appointed time and hurried inside, pulling my hair back into a ponytail as I walked. No one likes a hair in their drink, even if their attention is focused on the naked women onstage.

Inside was darker than outside, despite the gloom and rain, and it took a minute for my eyes to adjust. When they did, I saw Jack behind the bar. He waved me over.

"Fill out this form," he said, handing me a clipboard with a single sheet of paper attached. "You'll be paid minimum wage, but the tips you get are yours to keep." He eyed my clothes with raised eyebrows. "You might consider dressing more for the clientele. There are some items in back you can borrow, if you want."

"Okay, thanks," I said.

In short order, he'd shown me where things were kept, the stockroom, and his method for running the bar. None of it was anything unfamiliar, and I relaxed slightly. Bartending was something I could do very well.

"The girls like a drink before we open," Jack said. "Penny likes a sloe gin fizz, Holly drinks bourbon on the rocks, Crystal always has a cosmo, and Lucy prefers white wine." He made the drinks as he talked, setting them on a tray, which he handed to me. "They're back in the dressing room."

I headed that way, wondering what the women would be like. I'd never met a stripper before. High-priced escorts, yes, but not an actual stripper. I was both nervous and curious.

I knocked on the dressing-room door, decorated with peeling white paint and a faded blue star, but no one responded. I could hear music and chattering, so I eased open the door.

Four women, all in various states of undress, lounged in the small room. It was crowded to overflowing with clothes racks full of costumes in assorted colors, and several vanities with brightly lit mirrors and small padded stools. Piles of shoes were under furniture or randomly scattered around. Every kind of makeup—some I didn't recognize—covered the tops of the vanities, along with hairbrushes, curling irons, and various bottles of sprays.

Their chatter abruptly stopped when I stepped inside. A brassy blonde with legs a mile long and lips a brightly painted red asked, "Who are you?"

I forced a nervous smile. "I'm Kathleen. The new bartender. Jack sent me with your drinks."

"Well, hello, Kathleen-the-new-bartender," a redhead piped up. Shorter than the blonde, she was round in all the right places. "I'm Holly," she said with a friendly smile.

I smiled back, trying to keep from staring. She wore only a thong, pasties, and fishnet thigh-highs.

"When'd Mike hire you?" asked the blonde, with the same belligerence she'd displayed with her first question.

"Mike? I don't know Mike," I said. "Jack hired me."

"Well, Jack's got shit for brains if he thinks a chick servin' booze lookin' like a nun's gonna help us out any," the blonde retorted. Reaching for the tray I'd set down, she picked up the cosmo.

Ah. That must be Crystal.

"Give her a chance," said a woman with hazel eyes and dyed-black hair. She seemed to have more steel in her spine than her appearance let on. "You're always so negative." She turned to me. "You seem real nice, honey," she said kindly, taking the gin fizz.

Penny.

Which left Lucy. She was young, perhaps my age or a shade younger, with ash-blonde hair and a guarded expression.

"You must be Lucy," I said, handing her the glass of wine. "It's nice to meet you."

"Nice to meet you, too," she said with a tight smile before looking away.

Thinking this would be a good time to see if any of them might know anything about Amanda Webber, I said, "I went to school with Amanda Webber, but I lost touch the last few months. I don't suppose any of you know where she went?"

The room grew silent when I spoke Amanda's name, and I glanced curiously around. Everyone looked a little frightened—except Crystal, who studied me with suspicion, and Lucy, who looked downright terrified.

"Fifteen minutes!"

I turned my head toward the door, where the shout had come from.

"That's just Mike," explained Holly with a wave of her hand. "As if we don't know by now what time the show starts."

Her comment seemed to have unfrozen everyone, who continued on as though I hadn't said a word about Amanda.

The door opened behind me, and a man shoved his bald head inside. I thought it was odd, but the women didn't seem to think anything amiss. When his dark eyes landed on me, he opened the door fully and stepped inside.

"You the new bartender?" he barked at me.

I jumped. The man was at least a foot taller than me and outweighed me twice over. The only hair on his head was a thick handlebar mustache. He wore jeans and a black T-shirt, and a heavy gold chain around his tattooed neck.

"Well? Are ya?" he said, even more loudly.

I jerked my head in a nod.

"Mike, stop it, you're scaring the poor girl," Penny admonished.

"What's your name?" he asked, ignoring her.

"K-Kathleen," I stammered, taking a small step back.

"Well, K-Kathleen," he mocked, "change your clothes. I'm running a strip joint, and unless you're going to show some fuckin' skin, get out."

"Mike, go on, I'll take care of her," Penny said, shooing him away. He grumbled but did as she said, slamming the door behind him.

"Don't worry about Mike," she said. "He's a little rough around the edges, but he's a businessman at heart."

I certainly hoped I'd have no opportunity to be the center of Mike's attention again. He could crush me into a fine powder, and probably enjoy doing it.

Penny eyed me critically, then dug into one of the clothes racks behind her. After some rummaging, she pulled out a scrap of red fabric.

"Here," she said, pushing it into my arms. "Wear this top instead."

"This is a top?" I asked, bemused. I couldn't even figure out what it covered, let alone how, there was so little to it.

"Let me help you," she said. "Take off your shirt."

Dubious, I just looked at her. She rolled her eyes, cocked an eyebrow, and waited. No one was paying the slightest attention to us, so I quickly shed my turtleneck. In a moment, she had the top on me, and I could see how it was supposed to fit.

An extremely low-cut—like nearly to my waist—halter top, it wrapped around me, leaving my arms and back bare. With a quick flick of her fingers, Penny had undone my bra and slipped it off.

"Now, with a few well-placed pieces of double-sided tape"—she strategically fastened the fabric to my skin with said adhesive—"you'll be set." Putting her hands on my shoulders, she turned me to face the mirror.

I usually avoided red, but the deep crimson of the shirt brought out the red in my hair and set off my fair skin.

Seeing the curves of my breasts on display brought a blush to my cheeks, but I knew it could be worse. At least I got to keep on my own jeans.

"Add some lipstick," Penny said, doing just that with a red that matched my shirt, "and give your hair the just-fucked look . . ." She pulled out my ponytail, sprayed some hair spray, then tousled my hair with her fingers. "And ta-da! You're a knockout."

I examined myself in the mirror, and I had to admit she had an eye for this sort of thing. "Thanks, Penny," I said sincerely. "Hope this helps my tips tonight."

"I'm sure it will, honey." Her smile was warm and I found that I liked her. "You'd better go," she said, waving me out the door. "Mike doesn't like it if his workers don't seem ready when the doors open."

"Okay, thanks again," I said, retreating out the door. "Nice to meet all of you," I called over my shoulder.

I thought I heard a couple of them reply, and I'd definitely seen Crystal's eyes narrow as I left. She had to know something about Amanda. Her reaction was too telling. As was Lucy's. I'd have to get each of them alone and try to get them to tell me what they knew.

Jack did a double take when I reappeared, his eyes lingering longer than they should have on my breasts. "Looks like the ladies fixed you up," he observed.

"Yeah. Penny is nice."

The doors opened then and people began to trickle in, mostly men, but occasionally couples as well. I got my share of leers and suggestive remarks, but it wasn't anything I hadn't dealt with before.

The women took the stage one by one to raucous cheers and catcalls that became louder as the evening wore on. The place definitely had a different feel to it than The Drop. The air was thick with carnality, and the way some of the men eyed me as I served their drinks made my skin crawl. The tips were good, but I felt I earned every nickel. I knew I'd be asking Jack to walk me to my car after my shift.

During Holly's dance, a couple of the guys who'd had too much to drink got carried away, and one of them climbed up on stage with her. Before I could even make out what was happening, a bouncer had grabbed the guy by the collar and was hauling him to the door nearest to me.

Hurrying out from behind the bar, I opened the door for the bouncer. He tossed the guy out like he was nothing but a sack of potatoes, which was impressive because the heckler hadn't been a small guy.

"Nice job," I said to the bouncer. I had to tip my head back since he was quite a bit taller than me.

The dim light fell across his face, and I froze.

"Strawbs?"

CHAPTER EIGHT

W Jhat the hell are you doing here?" Chance asked.
"I work here," I replied. "For now."
"You . . ." he sputtered.

With a quick glance around, he grabbed my arm none too gently and yanked me through the doorway. Once we were outside, he dragged me away from the door and into the shadows at the side of the building. "You've got to be fucking kidding me," Chance gritted out. "I thought you worked at a law firm."

"I do," I snapped, rubbing my abused arm. "I'm here on assignment. What's your excuse?" It was a cold night and I shivered, wrapping my arms around myself to try and cover as much of my exposed skin as I could.

Chance scrubbed a hand over his face. "Jesus," he breathed. He glared at me for a moment. "Well, your assignment is over, as of now. I want you to get in your car, go home, and don't come back."

I stared at him in surprise, my mouth gaping, before surprise gave way to anger. "I will not," I retorted. "I'm here to find out what happened to two women, and I'm not going to drop that just because you say so."

"Oh yes, you are," he said, his voice hard.

I didn't reply, my eyes narrowing as I lifted my chin and glared at him. The darkness of the lot was broken every few moments by the headlights of a passing car, the glare illuminating Chance's implacable face.

The next thing I knew, Chance had wrapped an arm around my waist, picking me up bodily like I weighed nothing. "Where'd you park?" he asked.

I struggled in his grip, my face heating in humiliation. "Let me go!" I yelled, ineffectually squirming and beating my fists against any part of him I could reach. He didn't even break his stride. "I said, let me go!"

"Hey buddy, why don't you pick on somebody your own size."

The words were a sibilant hiss in the dark, and in the moment it took me to recognize the voice that had spoken them, Chance grunted and dropped me to the concrete.

I ignored the pain in my hands and knees, which had caught the brunt of my fall, and launched myself to my feet, panic twisting in my stomach.

Chance was on the receiving end of an ass-kicking, though he valiantly landed a few hits to the black shape moving in the darkness. I knew that shape, had seen the lethal grace bring more than one man to his knees . . . and his grave.

Chance dropped to his knees, and terror shot through me.

"No!" I cried, running toward him. "Kade, stop!" I'd seen Kade kill with an ease that now made my blood ice in fear as I watched him move in close to Chance.

"No!"

I threw myself between them, shielding Chance with my body, the hard pavement and gravel scraping my already sore knees through the denim. My arms wrapped around Chance's heaving torso, my body braced for Kade's assault. When nothing happened, I turned my head.

Kade stood inches away, looking at me wrapped around Chance, wearing an inscrutable expression, his own breath coming in quick pants that clouded in the frigid air. Lines of pain creased his face, and I wondered what it had cost him to fight as he had while wounded.

A groan escaped from Chance, and I quickly turned my attention back to him. Blood was dripping from his nose and there was a gash by his eye. Sweat was slick and shining on his forehead. Fury filled me and I rounded on Kade.

"How could you do that?" I yelled at him. "What were you going to do, Kade? Kill him?"

"The thought crossed my mind," Kade replied dryly, which only infuriated me more.

"You have so much blood on your hands, I don't know how you sleep at night," I hissed. "I didn't need your help, if you even want to call it that, and I don't want it."

My hands shook with the force of my anger and fear, fear that I could've lost Chance in the blink of an eye and a twist of Kade's hands. "Go away, Kade, and leave me alone."

Kade's face was unfathomable in the dark.

Our eyes remained locked until Chance let out a hiss of pain as he tried to get to his feet. I helped him up the best I could, guilt knifing through me at what Kade had done. When I glanced back around to where Kade had stood, he had disappeared without a sound. A sliver of regret for my harsh words whispered through my mind, but I looked at Chance and shoved it away.

"Are you all right?" I asked tentatively.

Chance painfully made his way to the building and leaned back against it. Fishing a pack of cigarettes out of his pocket, he didn't answer until he'd lit one and taken a long drag.

"Tell me that wasn't Kade Dennon," he said flatly.

I looked at him with surprise. "You know him?"

Chance snorted and took another drag at his cigarette, blowing it out before answering me. "I know of him. What I want to know, is how the fuck do you know him?"

"I . . . met him a few months ago," I stammered, taken aback that Chance knew who Kade was.

"And it was just a happy coincidence he was here to-night?" he asked.

I shook my head. "No. He must have followed me."

Chance froze, the cigarette halfway to his mouth. "Next you're going to tell me he's your boyfriend."

My face heated. "Of course not," I denied. "We're just . . . friends . . . sort of. And he's my boss." I frowned.

Minor technicality, that. Maybe I shouldn't have yelled at him. I chewed my lip in consternation.

"Your boss?" Chance's eyebrows rose. "At the law firm?"

"He . . . knows the owner," I said evasively, not wanting to divulge the relationship between Blane and Kade. "Blane Kirk."

Chance let out a huff of laughter that was devoid of humor. "That's fucking fantastic." He dropped his cigarette and ground it out under the toe of his boot. "You're friends with an assassin and you work for the most powerful, twisted lawyer in town. That's just un-fucking-believable."

My eyes narrowed. "I don't know what you've heard," I said stiffly, "but Blane Kirk is a good man and an amazing attorney. He fought for this country, and I don't appreciate you bad-mouthing him."

"I know more about Blane Kirk than you do, Strawbs," he said coldly. "Stuff that would make you think twice about spouting off how wonderful he is."

Voices from the lot jerked our attention away, and before I could react, Chance pulled me behind him, farther into the shadows.

Two men had driven up in an unmarked white van. They were talking to each other as they got out, but in Spanish, so I couldn't understand them. Another man, who must have been waiting, joined them. Walking around to the back of the van, the two men opened it, standing aside so the third man could see. From where we were, I couldn't tell what was inside, but the third man nodded, firing off rapid Spanish as they closed the van doors again. In a few moments, the van had driven away and the third man had disappeared back inside the club.

"Go home," Chance ordered before turning away from me.

"Where are you going?" I asked as he jumped on his motorcycle.

"Don't worry about it," he replied. "Now do as I say, go home, and don't come back."

I didn't get a chance to say anything more as he started the bike with a roar and shot off down the street in the same direction the van had gone.

I stood uncertainly in the lot, not knowing what to do. I didn't know why Chance was working there and yet warning me off so starkly, nor did I know where he'd gone so suddenly or why.

The decision was made for me when Mike stuck his head out the door, scanning the lot. Spying me, he barked, "Smoke break's over. Get back to work."

I scurried inside, glad for the warmth of the club. Back behind the bar, I grabbed a ticket and started mixing the drinks listed.

"Cold outside?" Jack asked, leering at my chest as he filled a frosted beer mug from the tap.

I smiled tightly, wishing I'd kept my bra and turtleneck on. "A bit," I answered curtly.

The rest of the evening was uneventful, and though I watched the door assiduously, I didn't see Chance return. Though I hated the skimpy shirt I wore, it did help with tips and I went home with a heavy pocket—a not unwelcome occurrence as I wondered if I'd be keeping my job at the law firm much longer after what I'd said to Kade.

Kade was no longer in my apartment. I told myself I was glad he was gone. Kade was dangerous, impulsive, impossible to predict. He was cold, calculating, more deadly and remorseless than anyone I had ever known.

The image of him smelling my hair, the look in his eyes as he'd said I made him want "impossible things" flashed through my mind. I shook my head to dislodge the memory.

I pulled out the bottle of vodka I kept in my freezer. I paused when I saw a pint of Häagen-Dazs rocky road in the back, remembering that Blane had bought it. He'd teased me, saying he didn't want to see me without my rocky-road fix. I'd retaliated by licking several ice-cold spoonfuls off his bare chest.

My stomach twisted and I hurriedly shut the freezer door. Grabbing a glass, I downed a shot of vodka. I wanted to sleep, needed to sleep, I just didn't know if I could. Now that I was alone, with nothing to distract me, my thoughts turned to the mess that was my life at the moment.

Everywhere I looked in my apartment, I saw them. Blane in my bed, his body spooned around mine. Kade in my bed, hurt and bleeding. Blane making love to me on the couch. Kade standing in my kitchen, his eyes burning as he drank in my naked body.

I tossed back another shot and grabbed my keys and purse, shrugging my black jacket on over the halter I hadn't bothered discarding.

It was late, but I knew a few bars that stayed open until three. I parked near one downtown. From the outside it looked like a hole-in-the-wall, so there were probably few tourists and mainly locals frequenting the place.

Long and narrow, the bar had a row of backless stools while two-seater tables lined the wall. I only saw a couple of other women, the rest were all men. I ignored any looks I got as I made my way to the end of the bar, where a few empty stools stood.

"Vodka, neat," I ordered as I sat.

Mindful of the top I wore, I kept my jacket on. I really didn't want anyone hitting on me tonight. I downed the shot as soon as the bartender placed it in front of me, tapping it for a refill. With a shrug, he complied.

"A beer, too," I said. I hated beer, but I didn't want to end up puking, either. I'd drink beer more slowly than I would vodka.

I tossed back the vodka as he slid a frosty beer bottle in front of me.

"Want a mug for that?" he asked. I shook my head.

I sipped at the beer, staring at nothing, and replaying last night with Blane. Even now, I couldn't believe he'd suggested getting married. Like the ruthless attorney I knew he was, he'd used my own weakness against me, tried to manipulate me to get what he wanted. Unfortunately, we'd wanted the same thing for very different reasons.

It hurt more than I wanted to admit, what he'd done. Naively, I still held the girlish fantasy of the man I loved getting down on one knee, ring box in hand, and declaring his love before popping The Question.

The thought of Blane doing that had me snorting in derision. How foolish I was. Why had I thought that when we said "I love you" it was a new beginning for us? The idea of Blane making a lifelong commitment to me was the stuff fantasies were made of, not reality. Holding a man like him would be like trying to hold smoke.

The words Kade had said to me in Denver came back to haunt me: *Neither Blane nor I are your happily-ever-after, princess. Blane will break your heart, and I'm the guy your mom warned you about. Don't kid yourself about that.*

I hadn't wanted to admit at the time how afraid I'd been that he was right, but I couldn't hide from the truth of his words any longer.

I didn't realize I was crying until a man sat down on the empty stool next to me and handed me a napkin.

"You wanna talk about it?" he asked quietly.

He appeared to be in his mid- to late fifties, with brown hair, thinning on top. At first I thought he might have ulterior motives, but his blue eyes were kind and the small smile he gave me was friendly in a nonpervert kind of way.

I used the napkin to wipe my face, still sniffling even though the tears had stopped. "Thanks," I muttered. The booze had really taken hold now, but instead of helping me to not care, it had only increased the width and depth of my depression and loneliness.

"Boyfriend trouble?" the man asked.

I nodded, heaving a tremulous sigh. "Ex-boyfriend now, I guess."

"I'm sorry to hear that. I'm Rick, by the way." He held out his hand.

"Kathleen." I gave his hand a squeeze.

"So what kind of moronic idiot would let a girl like you get away?" he asked so bluntly that I gave a huff of laughter in spite of myself.

"Yeah, I gotta know the answer to that one, too." Turning, I saw that a second man had sat down on my other side. He held a bottle of beer, taking a swig as he waited for my answer. About the same age as Rick, he wore a sweatshirt and a Colts ball cap.

"Kathleen, this is Jay." Jay gave a nod to me. "And this is Hal." He jerked his thumb to the man who'd slid onto the stool next to him. "We're buddies, so no worries."

"That's right, little lady," Hal confirmed. "Just having a friendly drink and wondering why a pretty little thing like you is all alone in a bar this time of night." He shook his head sadly. "It's not anyplace I'd want my daughter to be, that's for sure."

"Damn straight," Rick said, a southern accent coloring his words.

"So tell us your problems, Kathleen," Jay said. "Maybe we can help."

I sincerely doubted that, but the vodka had loosened my tongue, and it would feel so good to lay it out there, so I did. I told them about how Blane and I had been dating, how he'd told me he loved me. How happy I'd been after seeing him go through woman after woman, that he had picked me to love. Then I told them how overprotective he was, how he wouldn't open up to me. And lastly, I told him about Blane's latest solution—a quickie ceremony in front of a judge that would guarantee I'd be kept safe . . . and a prisoner in his house.

They made sympathetic noises all through my story, even when I was talking about feelings, and they listened, encouraging me to continue. When I had finished, they were all riled up.

"What a fuckin' asshole!" Jay exclaimed, taking a swig of the fresh beer the bartender had sat in front of him.

"He obviously has no idea what the hell he's doing," Rick chimed in with a disgusted shake of his head.

"If a man can't propose the right way, then he definitely can't fuck the right way," Hal added sagely.

"For God's sake, Hal!" Rick shot him a glare. "Kathleen's a lady. Will you watch your fuckin' mouth?"

I stifled a snort of laughter, and refrained from letting them know that Blane had no problems in the "fucking" department.

"Yeah, Hal," Jay joined in, his words slurring slightly. "Watch yer mouth."

"So you dumped his ass," Rick said, and I nodded. "Probably a good decision," he added.

My eyes filled with tears again and I couldn't speak, so I just gave a ragged nod.

"It still pisses me off, though," Rick said to Hal. "Lettin' a woman come to a bar in the middle of the night to cry her eyes out. He's the one should be beggin' her forgiveness, right?"

Hal nodded in agreement, his face comically serious.

The bartender set another shot of vodka in front of me. I'd lost count now of how many I'd had, and I drank it down. When I was done, I saw that Rick had gotten my phone out of my purse.

"What are you doing?" I asked, my brain sluggish.

He didn't answer, holding the phone to his ear. I was suddenly tired. And hot. It was hot in here.

I shrugged off my jacket, letting it fall behind me, and breathed a sigh at the cool air on my overheated skin. All three men fell silent, staring at me.

"What?" I asked.

Hal jumped off his stool, retrieving the jacket and placing it back over my shoulders.

"You keep that jacket on, missy," Jay said. "I wouldn't let my daughter out of the house in a getup like that."

Their protectiveness was sweet, reminding me of my father and what he'd say if he saw me wearing a shirt like this out in public.

"Hello, is this Blane?" Rick said into my phone.

My head jerked around and I groaned, instantly regretting the action as the room tilted and spun.

"Blane, you're an asshole," Rick blustered into the phone. "If you want to stop being an asshole, you can come get your girl here. Poor thing's all upset and you just let her go cry her eyes out in some bar with a bunch of strangers. Shame on you."

I listened in horror as Rick chewed Blane's ass. The ludicrousness of Blane getting a lecture from a five-foot-six Texan nearly twice his age struck my inebriated funny bone until I had to clap a hand over my mouth to stifle my giggles. I didn't hear much of the rest of the conversation. Jay had put money into the jukebox and the strains of Bryan Adams filled the bar.

I loudly sang along with Jay, who was dancing the two-step with me in the small space by the bar. My jacket had slipped off again, but by that point we were all too drunk to care. Hal and Rick watched us, grinning as they drank their beers.

I was belting out the lyrics to the latest in the string of '80s hits when Jay suddenly froze, his eyes glued on something over my shoulder. Blane had entered the bar and now stood mere feet away. He was clad in a black shirt and jeans, and the look in his eyes and the stiffness in his body all screamed danger. My breath caught at the sight of him.

"Holy shit," Jay breathed, his face paling.

"Is that him?" Rick asked incredulously.

Hal choked on his beer.

"Yeah, that's him," I confirmed as Blane stalked toward us.

Jay hurriedly dropped my hand and took a step back. I held my ground. Blane stopped right in front of me and I had to tip my head back to look at him. Vaguely, I could hear Jay and Rick talking, but I couldn't concentrate enough to make out their words. Blane's eyes burned with an unholy fire as his gaze traveled down and back up my body. I couldn't tell if I saw fury or lust in his eyes, maybe both. My breath came more quickly, my breasts heavy and aroused just from Blane's mere proximity.

Blane's gaze lowered and my nipples tightened, pushing brazenly against the scraps of cloth covering them. His face darkened, his jaw locking as he shrugged out of his leather jacket and swung it over my shoulders. It swallowed me up and I breathed deeply, inhaling the scent of Blane.

Blane's gaze suddenly narrowed, swinging around to pin Jay, Hal, and Rick.

"Did you just call me a dick?" he asked, his voice like steel.

"I called you a dick three times," Jay shot back with drunken glee. "Ya just didn't hear me the first two, motherfucker."

I snorted with laughter. "Blane," I said, once I had my amusement under control, "meet my three fairy godfathers. Jay, Hal, and Rick."

The men all gave each other a grudging nod.

"Come on, Kat," Blane said. "Let's go home."

"Just a second," I said. Turning to the men, I gave them each a kiss on the cheek. "Thanks for listening."

"Anytime," Rick said with a grin, then turned a more serious expression on Blane. "Now you take care of our little girl here, you understand? I don't wanna see her in some bar by herself again 'cause you're treatin' her bad."

"Yes, sir," Blane replied evenly. That seemed to placate Rick.

"This should take care of her tab," Blane said, pulling a few bills out of his wallet and tossing them onto the bar.

Another song came on the jukebox, and I started singing along, weaving my way to the door. Blane was next to me in an instant, supporting my back while tucking my jacket and purse under his arm.

The cold air had a sobering effect, clearing some of the cobwebs from my mind. Blane steered me toward his car, but I twisted away.

"Where's my keys?" I asked. "I can drive."

"You are in absolutely no condition to drive," he retorted, opening the passenger door and tossing my purse and jacket in the back. "Get in."

"You can't order me around, Blane," I shot back, then stumbled and nearly fell flat on my face, which robbed any seriousness from my words.

Blane snorted with derision, hooking an arm around my waist and pulling me back to the car with ease.

I slapped ineffectually at his hands. "Let me go," I huffed. "I don't want your help. Or Kade's. Or anyone's." I shrugged off his coat and shoved it at him.

"Well, that's too bad," Blane gritted out, tossing the coat into the car, "because you did something stupid tonight, and I'm here to bail you out of it."

"That seems to be a recurring theme, don't you think?" I sneered. "Kathleen's in trouble again. Time to swoop in and save the day! And nearly get killed doing it. I bet you thought you were done with that shit after you left the Navy."

Blane just looked at me. "Is that what this is about? You think I'd lay my life on the line for just anyone?"

I swallowed. "Isn't that what you do?"

His hands closed over my upper arms and he jerked me into him. "I don't lay my life down for anyone but my brother," he hissed. "The Navy was different. The men I fought with, they were my brothers, too. I'd die for them. But I'm not some comic-book hero, Kat. I watch over those I love, and that's all."

I heard him, but the feel of his hands on me, the press of his body against mine made my head swim, and I forgot anything I was going to say. My eyes dropped to his mouth, and I couldn't look away.

Blane swore, spinning me around, pushing me unceremoniously into the car, and slamming the door shut before I had even realized what was happening.

Moments later, we were speeding down the road. The heated leather of his seats made me sigh in comfort.

I loved his car. I loved being with him in his car. It was sleek and powerful, just like him.

"Is that so?" he asked, amusement lacing his voice, and I realized I must have spoken the words aloud.

"Absolutely," I purred. It also did fantastic things to my libido, which I made sure I didn't say. The alcohol had had the usual effect on my inhibitions, and I found myself contemplating some wicked scenarios.

"It's hot in here," I complained. Blane obligingly turned down the heat. "Still hot," I murmured, unfastening my jeans. Blane's hands tightened their grip on the steering wheel as I slid my zipper down. The sound was loud in the quiet car.

"What are you doing?" he asked, his voice menacing. If I'd been in the proper frame of mind, it would have frightened me. As it was, it only served to make the blood flow faster in my veins.

"Cooling off," I said simply. A lift of my hips and a quick shove down my legs, and the jeans were off, taking my shoes with them. I sighed in pleasure, reaching down to move the seat farther back so I could put my feet up on the dash, one ankle crossed primly over the other.

"You get like this when you're drunk," Blane said flatly, his eyes darting to my legs and quickly glancing away.

"Like what?" I asked, all innocence.

He just looked at me. The look I gave him in return had him muttering a string of curses under his breath when he looked back at the road.

Reaching across the small confines of the sports car, I pried one of Blane's hands from the steering wheel. He reluctantly let me, and I caressed the rough callousness of his fingers and his palm. When his hand finally relaxed, I placed it on my thigh. His whole body stiffened, but I ignored his reaction, moving his hand so it stroked my skin. I hummed with approval at the sensation. After a moment, I saw with satisfaction that I was no longer forcing his hand to move, it did so of its own accord.

Soon, it wasn't enough. Taking control of his hand again, I brought it between my thighs. I uncrossed my ankles, letting my knees fall open. His hand pressed against the silk of my panties and I moaned, feeling the heat of my arousal through the thin layer of fabric.

"Take them off," he rasped, and I wasted no time in obeying him, mewling in pleasure when his hand returned between my legs. "Christ, you're wet," he growled.

I watched, unable to take my eyes off his hand, as his middle finger slipped inside me. Another moan fell from my lips at the sensation.

"Touch your breasts," Blane ordered.

My cheeks burned, but I did it, pulling the fabric from the tape attached to my skin and allowing my breasts to spill into my hands. I squeezed, my thumbs flicking over my aching nipples. This wasn't something I normally did, and it didn't do much for me, but judging by Blane's reaction, it certainly did a lot for him.

His hand moved faster, pumping in and out of me, my hips lifting in time to his thrusts. Glancing over, I saw the strain of his erection pressing against the denim of his jeans. Abruptly deciding on a new course of action, I yanked his hand from between my legs and pulled my knees up underneath me.

"What are you—"

His voice abruptly cut off when I leaned across the seat and started undoing his pants. Thankfully, I was short enough to accomplish this position in his car, though it did leave my bare ass in the air and my breasts hanging out. Judging by the beads of sweat on Blane's forehead, he wasn't going to complain.

I freed his cock from his jeans a moment later and wasted no time taking him into my mouth. I moaned as a strangled sound escaped Blane's throat. I took as much of him as I could, loving the feel of satin-encased steel. I was startled when I felt Blane's fingers thrust inside me again, then I quickly took up the same rhythm as his fingers, wrapping my hand around the base of his erection since I couldn't fit all of it in my mouth.

I had no idea how Blane was able to drive, and I didn't want to know how fast we were going. I was much more consumed with the feel and taste of him against my tongue, and the roughness of his fingers as they fucked me.

"Stop, Kat," I heard Blane grit out.

I wanted no part of him trying to make me stop. He always made me stop. Just this once, I refused to let him.

Since one hand was on the steering wheel and the other was buried inside me, he couldn't force me to release him.

His fingers moved a certain way, curving and pressing, and I shattered, my scream muffled by his cock deep in my mouth. Then Blane was cursing, his hips jerking upward and his erection thickening, pushing down my throat as his orgasm overtook him. I gagged and my eyes watered, but I stayed with him, swallowing until the spasms eased and stopped.

Sitting up, I gasped for breath. Blane reached into the backseat, rummaging in the gym bag he always kept there until he unearthed a towel, which he handed me.

"Thanks," I muttered, wiping my mouth.

Glancing around, I saw that we were stopped, parked in Blane's driveway. Huh. I didn't say anything, just reached down and pulled my jeans back on, forgoing the underwear in favor of speed. I wouldn't say I was sober by any means, but I wasn't drunk enough to saunter into the house with my ass hanging out.

"Is that what you wore tonight?" Blane asked, watching me as I tried to readjust the halter enough to cover Thing 1 and Thing 2.

I didn't see how answering that question was going to lead anywhere good, so I ignored him.

"Why did you bring me here?" I asked instead. "We broke up. You're not obligated for a sleepover." I couldn't keep the sarcasm out of my voice.

"I don't give a shit if you say we broke up or not," he shot back. "God knows how much you've had to drink tonight, and I'm not leaving you alone to choke on your own vomit."

"What a guy," I retorted. "Be still my heart."

The look on Blane's face said he didn't appreciate my attitude, so I smiled.

His face turned to granite, but I kept my smile in place. I'd be damned if he was going to intimidate me. After all, I could still taste him on my tongue.

Blane was out of the car and around to my side before I could savor my victory. Although I was a bit wobbly on my feet, I managed to extricate myself from the Jaguar without falling over.

Pressing my body against Blane's, I tucked my panties into the pocket of his shirt. Blane sucked in a breath, his eyes burning.

Giving him another sweet-as-sugar smile, I turned and sashayed my way up to the front door. I didn't hear Blane following, but I wasn't surprised when his hand shot out to open the door for me.

I didn't bother thanking him, instead just strolled inside. I pushed my hands into the back pockets of my jeans, which thrust my breasts forward. Blane's eyes were glued to my chest as I made a slow circle around the foyer before coming to a stop.

"It's rude to stare," I said.

His eyes jerked up to mine and I saw a muscle twitch in his jaw.

I raised an eyebrow. Spying the tray Mona always left for Blane on the sideboard, I walked over to it. As I'd expected, the ice bucket had been filled. Picking up a piece of ice, I turned around, leaning against the wall.

"Thirsty?" I asked. I licked the ice, wrapping my lips around it and sucking lightly. Blane watched avidly, his hands fisting at his sides. Keeping my eyes on his, I dragged the piece of ice over my lips and down my chin. Tilting my head to the side, I traced the ice slowly down the skin of my neck, between my breasts, and down my stomach.

A pained expression came across Blane's face. Popping the remaining ice in my mouth, I bit down, my lips turned up in a satisfied smile.

The next moment, I was gulping the ice down as Blane pinned me to the wall.

"You're playing with fire, little girl," he hissed. "Isn't that what they called you? 'Little girl'?"

I instinctively cringed, then straightened my spine. I'd make him see me as a woman, and his equal, if it was the last thing I did. No more biting my tongue against words that might upset the balance between us or make him angry. No more assuming he was going to leave me if I did this or didn't do that. If he left me, so be it, but it would be on my terms.

I lifted an eyebrow. "I thought I was just using you for sex." My hand traced the outline of his erection through his jeans.

Blane's head lowered, but I twisted, ducking under his arm and quickly sidestepping his reach.

"Good night, Blane."

I felt his eyes burning a hole in my back as I climbed the stairs to my old bedroom.

I fell asleep almost immediately, waking at some point during the night because I was cold. Everything was fuzzy, and for a moment, I didn't know where I was. Groping for a blanket, I suddenly found one being dragged up to my shoulders.

The shadowy outline of Blane stood over me. He said nothing, and I closed my eyes with a sigh, too tired and drunk to even think. Prying my eyes open a few moments later, I saw him sitting in the chair by the window. The light filtered in through the blinds, slashing moonlight in silver streaks across his face. His gaze was captivating. I knew he was there to watch over me, silent and steady in his vigil. It made my chest ache.

I squeezed my eyes shut and knew no more.

~

The next morning, I awoke with a headache that reminded me of how stupid I'd been the night before. Glancing blearily at the clock, I saw that it was barely after seven. I was alone.

Everything I'd said and done came back with a rush and I groaned, mortification making me want to crawl under the bed. I'd come out, but not until they invented those light thingies to make people forget, like Will Smith used in *Men in Black*. Then I'd point it at Blane.

"Never ever, ever, ever going to drink again," I muttered to myself as I made my way to the bathroom. I chose not to think about how many times I'd said that same phrase in the past.

I had absolutely no wish to run into Blane this morning, so I ignored my headache, brushed my teeth, and splashed some water on my face. I shoved my feet in my shoes, scoured the closet for an old shirt of Blane's to throw on over my halter, and hightailed it downstairs. I vaguely re-membered that Blane had tossed my purse into the backseat of his car. Since my car was still at the bar and I knew Blane had the SUV, I felt no compunction against grabbing the keys to his Jag off the sideboard. Okay, maybe a little, but not enough to stop.

Throwing open the front door, I stopped in my tracks.

Charlotte was standing there, her hand poised to knock.

We stood in stark silence. I took in her perfect hair and makeup, skirt, heels, and overcoat, while she took in my jeans, Blane's shirt, bedhead, and last night's mascara smeared under my eyes.

The very last thing I'd expected this morning was to have to do the walk of shame in front of the newest lawyer at the firm of Kirk and Trent.

I cleared my throat and pasted on the best smile I could manage. "Hi, Charlotte," I said. "How are you?"

It took her a moment to recover from her surprise, then she said, "I'm wonderful, thank you for asking."

I stood awkwardly before saying, "Um, would you like to come in?"

"Yes, thank you."

She entered the foyer, looking around interestedly.

"Um, why are you here?" I asked bluntly.

"Blane texted me," she said. "He has some documents I need. I offered to drop by and retrieve them since he said he was going to be late this morning." She gave me another once-over from head to foot, and I tried not to squirm in embarrassment. "I didn't realize you and Blane were . . . together."

"We're not," I blurted, then flushed as her eyebrows rose.

Great. So I'd just told her that Blane and I weren't in a relationship, we were just sleeping together. Or worse, I was a one-night stand.

To my horror, Mona appeared from the kitchen. "Kathleen!" she exclaimed in delight. "How wonderful to see you!"

If possible, Charlotte's eyebrows climbed even higher.

"Hi, Mona," I said with a tight smile. "I've got to go. Have to get home, and get . . . to work." I stammered, my heart hammering in my chest as Blane appeared at the top of the stairs, decked out for work in a suit and tie. His eyes met mine, but I couldn't read his expression.

"I'll see you later," I said in a rush before hurrying out the door.

"Kathleen, wait!"

I heard Blane call out, but I was already climbing into the car. It roared to life immediately, and I took off. In the rearview mirror, I saw Blane standing in the drive, staring after me.

CHAPTER NINE

My head pounded as I drove, but it didn't begin to compare to the embarrassment crawling over my skin as memories of last night played through my mind. I remembered everything; the only part that got fuzzy was after I'd fallen asleep at Blane's.

Had I really told Blane that I was "just using" him for sex? I groaned aloud. I remembered the hurt and anger I'd felt last night—I'd wanted to retaliate after Blane's inadequate proposal, to hurt him back. I liked to think I wasn't that sort of person, but I also didn't want to lie to myself. I'd not only treated Blane badly, but I'd also been cruel to Kade. He'd just been trying to help me outside the bar.

I hated feeling this way, hated the regret and guilt that washed over me like a thick, oily pool. I sighed. Well, there was nothing for it. I was just going to have to put on my big-girl panties, suck it up, and apologize. After all the times I'd insinuated or accused Blane of just toying with me until something better came along, I'd been no better last night, using sex as a means to an end rather than as a natural offspring of our relationship and how we felt for one another.

Never once had Blane made me feel like a tramp or a slut—no, I'd done that all on my own.

To top it off, I was sure Blane was just thrilled that Charlotte had been there this morning to witness the sordid morning after. I snorted. So much for trying to keep a professional appearance at work.

And then there was what had to be the last straw—I'd taken Blane's Jag.

Okay, I had to be honest. I knew I shouldn't have taken it—more guilt to add to my already heaping pile—but wow, was it incredible to drive. The miles to my apartment flew by easily and before I knew it, I was pulling into my parking lot while still self-flagellating over everything I'd done and said the night before.

Tigger was glad to see me, and I felt another stab of guilt that he'd been alone for so long yesterday. I fed him and gave him a scratch behind his marmalade ears before I jumped in the shower. He complained long and loud about my lack of attention while I got ready for work.

Striving for a professional look today, though I doubted anything would erase the picture Charlotte had of me from this morning, I dressed up in nylons, heels, a formfitting black pencil skirt, and an ivory silk blouse. I pulled my hair back in a French twist and applied minimal makeup. Gulping down a cup of coffee, I grabbed a granola bar, my coat, and my purse, and headed out the door.

It was impossible to drive the Jag properly in heels. Slipping them off, I drove barefoot, wondering how I was going to get my car back. Maybe Clarice would take me, if she had time.

I was able to get some things done at work, the stack of files on my desk higher than normal since I'd been out a lot the past few days. At some point, I knew I'd have to go upstairs and return Blane's keys, but I put it off, cringing in embarrassment when I thought of looking him in the eye after last night.

Finally after lunch, I knew I couldn't put it off any longer. I had to leave soon to make it to Xtreme for my shift. Scooping up his keys, I headed for the elevator.

It felt like I was headed to my execution rather than just going to see Blane, and I swore to myself that I was never, ever, ever going to drink again.

Ever.

Really.

The elevator doors swooped open, and I was disappointed to see that Clarice was not at her desk. Damn. Blane's door was closed, which made me hesitate. I definitely did not want to make things worse by interrupting an important meeting.

Just as I was debating leaving the keys on Clarice's desk and forgoing seeing Blane altogether, his door swung open.

My breath caught in surprise to see Blane ushering out Senator Robert Keaston from the state of Massachusetts. The senator had been in Congress long enough that his name was spoken with reverence and awe. A powerful and intimidating man, he reminded me of Blane, which was fitting since he was Blane's great-uncle. I'd met both the senator and his wife, Vivian, a few months ago.

It seemed the eyes of both men fell on me at the same time. The senator seemed momentarily surprised, and Blane's gaze shuttered immediately, leaving his expression an unreadable mask.

Oh God—he was mad, disappointed, disgusted. Any one of a hundred possibilities, each more discouraging than the last, ran through my mind. Tearing my eyes from his, I forced a smile.

"It's nice to see you again, Senator," I said.

Senator Keaston seemed to have recovered himself, the politician's smile I'd seen too many times on Blane's face now gracing the senator's face. "Likewise, my dear," he replied.

My smile faltered slightly at the tone of his words. Though polite on the surface, they held an undercurrent of disapproval. Before I could say anything more, he'd turned back to Blane, effectively dismissing me.

"Remember what we talked about," he admonished.

Blane gave a curt nod. The senator passed by me on his way to the elevator, not saying anything further, and I watched until the doors closed behind him before reluctantly turning to face Blane again.

He hadn't moved from his spot in the doorway. He emanated danger, no less lethal for being encased in a dark suit and tie. I fancied I could feel the magnetic pull of his presence, even though he was several feet from me. I fidgeted for a moment, meeting his steady gaze before glancing away.

"I . . . um . . . brought back your keys," I finally stammered when the silence became too much for me to take.

He didn't reply, so I blundered on. "Listen, I . . . um . . . I'm really sorry." Gathering my flagging courage, I raised my chin to look him in the eye.

"You can borrow the car anytime you want," he said with a shrug.

My face heated at his misunderstanding. Now I was going to have to be more specific. I forced the words out. "I meant, I'm sorry for . . . for doing that. In the car. And for what I said at your house. I . . . wanted to get back at you, which is wrong . . . and I'm sorry."

Guilt and shame washed over me, making me want to cringe, but I refused to give in to the impulse. I harshly reminded myself that this wasn't about me feeling bad for what I'd done; I should feel bad. It was about apologizing to someone I'd hurt.

Blane pulled me into his office and closed the door. Cradling my face in his hands, he said, "Are you kidding me? You're apologizing for the best car ride I've ever had?"

My mind reeled in confusion. "What?"

Blane laughed lightly. "Kat, anytime you want to get drunk and horny, I've got no problem with that. Just so long as it's always me you call."

"You're not mad?"

His fingers brushed my cheek. "I'm mad at myself, for hurting you. I'm mad that I've done things, said things, that have pushed you away, made you feel you couldn't talk to me. But am I mad at you? No."

I shook my head. "Even if you're not, I was wrong. My intentions were wrong."

"You mean you didn't want me to touch you last night?" he asked. His voice was lower now, and it sent a shiver through me. His eyes flared green in their depths and I couldn't look away. Somehow he'd drawn even closer, our bodies nearly touching. "Didn't want me to stroke you, make you come? Didn't want me in your mouth, on your tongue? Because I've got to be honest." His lips were by my ear now, and my eyes slipped shut at the brush of his warm breath. "That's a memory I'll take to my grave."

My heart was hammering in my chest now, my embarrassment and guilt forgotten in light of his words. Our eyes locked again and his gaze dropped to my mouth. I nervously wet my lips, feeling as anxious as though he were about to kiss me for the first time.

The crackle of the intercom made me jump, and Clarice's voice had me scurrying a step or two away from Blane.

"Sir, your two o'clock is here."

Blane rounded the desk and pressed a button on the phone. "Give me a few minutes, please, Clarice."

"Yes, sir."

Our eyes met and I swallowed. Sexual tension notwithstanding, we needed to talk. I was suddenly grateful for the polished walnut desk separating us.

"I'm still upset about the other night," I confessed, "and I know you apologized, and I accept that. It's just . . . going to take me some time to get over it."

He studied me. "Understood."

I took a deep breath, then said what had to be said. "I haven't changed my mind about the Summers case. I want you to drop it."

"I can't do that." Blane's gaze was steady, his tone flat.

I'd expected that response, but had hoped for another. "Blane, I don't care how much he's paying you or what he's offering you for your career. It's not right. And what if he does it again?"

Blane's face darkened, but he didn't raise his voice. "I understand how you feel," he said flatly, "but I won't be dropping the case."

I tried a different angle. "Kade said you and he were working on this together. To take down his uncle, that he's the one you're after. Maybe I can help."

"If you want to help," Blane countered, "you'll tell me who the guy was in your apartment. The same guy that tried to drag you across the parking lot of that club last night. The man who knows you well enough to call you 'Strawbs.'"

"How'd you—" I started, then stopped. Of course. "Kade told you."

"Who is he, Kat?" Blane persisted. "And why are you protecting him?"

The urge to tell Blane the truth was strong, but I didn't dare. Chance thought Blane was twisted, hated the fact I was involved with him. God knew what he'd do if he found out I'd told Blane who he was. Not that I even knew why I couldn't tell him, only that Chance had told me not to.

When I didn't answer, Blane sighed, the look he gave me one of resignation. "After everything, you still don't trust me?"

"It's not that," I denied. "And isn't that the pot calling the kettle black. You won't even tell me what you and Kade are planning."

"The less you know, the better in this case," he retorted.

"Isn't that always the case with you?" I shot back. "At least Kade doesn't treat me like I'm twelve years old."

I knew the instant the words were out of my mouth that I shouldn't have said them. Blane went utterly still, pinning me with his steely gaze.

"Is that so," he said softly. "How does he treat you? Do enlighten me."

The anger underlying his words made my skin go cold. I'd done what I'd said I wouldn't. Had said something to compare one brother to the other, pit them against each other.

"Nothing." I backtracked. "Forget it. I didn't mean anything by it. I should go."

I tried to head to the door, but my way was blocked by Blane, who'd risen and rounded his desk.

"What happened, Kat? Has he stepped out of line? Touched you? Hit on you?" The questions came in a barrage and I instinctively recoiled.

"N-no, of course not." There was no way I was going to say a word to Blane about all Kade had said and done.

Blane studied me. "You're lying to me," he declared. "Why? What did he do?"

I pressed my lips together, dismayed that he could read me so easily. My pulse was racing until I felt light-headed. I was near to panicking at the thought of Blane and Kade at each other's throats.

"Please don't fight with Kade," I whispered through lips gone numb.

"Don't give me a reason to."

After a moment, Blane turned away. I blew out my breath, my eyes slipping shut in relief that he'd let it drop. I watched as he stared out the window, one arm leaning against the window frame. The view outside was bleak. The dismal gray sky was unrelenting, the clouds dark and heavy with impending snow.

"I'd better go," I said hesitantly. "You have someone here to see you."

I waited for an acknowledgment, and when none came, I opened the door, glancing back one more time to see Blane with his back still turned to me, stiff and forbidding.

Clarice said she'd give me a ride to my car, which was a relief. After agreeing to meet in the lobby, I hurried downstairs to get my things from my cube. The floor was quiet—all the paralegals were in their weekly staff meeting. However, my cube wasn't empty.

"Hello again, Kathleen," Senator Keaston said. He was sitting in a chair next to my desk, obviously awaiting my return.

I was immediately on guard. I'd gotten the definite feeling that he didn't like me very much, despite the kindness of his wife.

"Hello," I replied. "What can I do for you, Senator?"

"I'm glad you asked that, Kathleen. Please, sit." He motioned to my chair.

Uneasily, I perched on the edge of my seat. The senator waited until I was settled before continuing.

"Kathleen, I'm sure you're not ignorant of the very different backgrounds from which you and Blane come," he began. "Blane was born into a highly political, very powerful, very wealthy family."

He paused and I forced a small nod.

"Now I know your father was a good man, killed in the line of duty"—I stiffened—"but, needless to say, you and Blane are on opposite sides of the proverbial tracks. Blane has a wonderful future ahead of him, ambitions that could take him far, very far." His gaze was shrewd as he studied me. "I'm sure, if you love Blane as much as I think you do, that you want that for him. It's all he's ever dreamed about, worked toward."

He paused again, and I thought he expected me to say something.

"Of course," I murmured.

"Then I'm sure you also realize what a . . . liability someone like you could be for him. Blane needs someone with breeding, education. Someone with skills to complement his. Someone, in fact, wholly unlike you."

My stomach twisted. It was one thing to think something like that in the back of my mind, and quite another to have it spelled out so plainly by someone Blane loved and respected very much.

Senator Keaston reached out and gave the hand resting on my knee a little pat. "I'm sure you'd have come to that conclusion at some point, I'd just prefer it be sooner rather than later. Blane has made some choices lately that I can't say meet my approval, and I think it's best if you and I came to an understanding."

I frowned. "What do you mean, 'an understanding'?"

His look turned calculating, and I was forcibly reminded that I was dealing with one of the most powerful men in the United States Senate. He hadn't gotten that position by being anything less than ruthless.

"I know that you're in a lot of debt, due to your mother's illness," he said reasonably. "Debt is hard on people. It changes their lives, puts a halt to their dreams, especially someone as young as yourself."

"What's your point?" I asked stiffly, unsurprised that he knew such details about my life.

"My point is that I can help with that."

I just looked at him, waiting for the other shoe to drop. I didn't have to wait long.

"I can get rid of your debts, and get you accepted at the school of your choice. I believe you once harbored ambitions for a career in law, if I'm not mistaken. Acceptance to any one of a number of prestigious law schools can be provided, as well as anything you might need while you're being educated. The only thing I require in return is that you break it off with Blane, and choose another state in which to pursue that education."

My stomach felt like lead. A part of my brain seemed detached from the whole conversation, observing what was happening in stunned amazement.

"You're offering to buy me off?" I finally forced out.

The senator smiled a thin-lipped smile. "I prefer to look at it as helping you fulfill your dreams. Dreams I'm sure your mother and father would have wanted you to have a chance of realizing."

"What if those dreams include Blane?"

His smile faded and his eyes turned cold. "I'm afraid that's not going to be possible."

"Does he know you're telling me this?"

"He does not, and it would be in your best interest if it remained that way."

The unspoken threat lay there between us.

"I see." My mouth was dry and my hands shook. I clenched them into fists at my side. I was angry and scared at the same time.

"I knew you would, my dear." The senator stood. "Think it over. I'll be in touch."

He left my cube, but I didn't move. I was appalled at his interference in Blane's life, in my life. I didn't know what he'd meant by it being in my "best interest" not to tell Blane what had happened, and I didn't want to find out. Would he hurt me? Pay someone to do me bodily harm? I wasn't stupid enough to not know he had the means to make me disappear, if he chose to.

Although Blane and I were having problems, the idea of being told to break it off permanently and move to another state infuriated me. But I honestly didn't know what I could do. I had no means to protect myself from whatever Senator Keaston would do to retaliate if I refused. Likewise, telling Blane was out of the question. He idolized his uncle.

"Hey, are you coming or what?"

Looking up, I saw Clarice standing in my cube. "Yeah, sorry." I jumped up, grabbing my coat and purse.

"Was that Senator Keaston I just saw?"

"Yeah."

"What did he want?"

I shook my head, brushing by her into the hallway. "I don't want to talk about it."

It was cold outside and we didn't speak again until we were in her car and the heater was going full blast.

"I've never liked him," Clarice said.

"Who?"

"Senator Keaston," she said as though it were obvious. "He's always given me the willies."

I didn't reply, just turned to stare out the window. On that point, we completely agreed.

"Blane thinks he walks on water, though," she continued. "I guess some people are just blind to their family's faults."

My heart sank. Blane might not even believe me if I did tell him what the senator had said. And who was I to disillusion Blane about who his uncle really was?

I thanked Clarice for the ride and drove home quickly to change for Xtreme. I had no desire to borrow clothes from the strippers again, so I put on the tightest T-shirt I owned and paired it with jeans. Hopefully, Mike wouldn't complain about that.

Jack greeted me as I stowed my purse under the bar. The ice needed filling, so I offered to get it from the back.

As I walked to the ice machine, I took a quick detour by the dressing room, hoping it was early enough that one of the women might be alone. Giving the door a quick knock, I pushed it open.

I was in luck. Crystal was the only one there. She sat at one of the vanities, carefully applying mascara to her false eyelashes.

"Hey," I said with a friendly smile. "How's it going?"

Crystal paused in her work for a moment, glancing at my reflection in the mirror as I stood off to the side behind her. She didn't deign to answer me but resumed her makeup application, finishing her lashes and reaching for lipstick.

"Can I talk to you for a minute?" I asked, determined to get her to speak to me.

"It seems you already are, whether I want you to or not," she replied, her tone blasé.

So she didn't like me. I didn't give a shit. I just wanted to know what she knew about Amanda and Julie.

"I really need to find my friend Amanda," I said. "Anything you might know or remember about who she hung out with, any boyfriends she had, would be really helpful."

For just a split second, fear flashed across Crystal's face before she masked it. "Amanda only danced here for a short while, then she left. I didn't waste my time on her. Much too young and stupid to bother with." The look she gave me in the mirror said she lumped me in the same category.

"She danced?" I asked. "She told me she was a waitress, not a dancer."

Crystal's laugh was brittle. "None of those college girls that come through here tell people they dance. They're always the 'waitress' or 'bartender.'" Her sneer was full of loathing. "They're too embarrassed by the truth."

"And what's that?" I pushed.

"That they make damn good money dancing, taking their clothes off. Much more than pouring drinks or working their asses off waitressing. They may start by doing that, but before long they're up on stage with the rest of us."

"Was that what Julie Vale did, too?"

Crystal froze for a moment, then seemed to recover herself. She carefully capped the lipstick before turning to face me. "If I were you, and thank God I'm not, I wouldn't bring up that name again in this place."

"Why not?"

She eyed me, her lips curving in a sad yet patronizing smile. "Young and stupid," she said quietly. "You're all the same."

Before I could question her further, the door opened and Holly stepped inside. The petite redhead flashed a grin at me.

"Hey there, Kathleen! How are you?"

"Great," I replied, forcing a smile. "I'm great, thanks."

I exchanged a bit more chitchat with Holly, watching Crystal ignore us out of the corner of my eye, before making my excuses and leaving. I mulled over what Crystal had told me, and what she hadn't told me, as I filled a bucket with ice and carried it to the bar.

"Took you long enough," Jack groused.

"Sorry."

I didn't like Jack much. While he seemed nice enough on the surface, he looked out for himself first and foremost. If I got behind or needed a hand, he didn't offer to help. When I'd bartended at The Drop, Scott and I had always helped each other out if things got real busy. As I filled a beer mug, it struck me that I missed him, missed working at The Drop, missed my friends there.

The place grew packed and I yanked my hair up into a ponytail when it started getting in my way and clinging in wet tendrils to my damp neck. I managed to keep up, but only just, not finding time to even take a bathroom break until nearly midnight.

"Cover for me?" I asked Jack.

He shrugged and I took that to mean that yes, he would.

"Asshole," I muttered under my breath as I hurried to the back. I emerged a few minutes later, feeling much better.

It was dark and quiet back here, the raucousness of the main floor muted, the music a dull thumping of the bass. I took a moment to just take a breath, leaning against the wall and appreciating the cold that seeped through the thin T-shirt onto my skin.

"Come on, baby, don't be like that."

The voice startled me, then I realized it wasn't directed at me, but at a woman who'd just stepped around the corner. She paused, turning around, and I saw a man behind her.

They hadn't seen me, so I silently slipped farther back into the shadows.

"I have to go on in fifteen minutes," the woman said.

I squinted at her, wishing she'd step into the light. As if she'd heard me, she moved. Light streamed across her face. It was Lucy.

"This shouldn't take longer than five," the man said, a leer in his voice.

"I said, not now," the woman snapped.

"Don't take that tone with me," the man growled, grabbing her arm and jerking her toward him. Lucy gasped in pain. "You think you're all high-and-mighty. You're just a fucking whore, and don't you forget it."

He shoved her against the wall and I heard the rip of fabric. I looked around frantically. He was going to rape her if I didn't do something.

Spotting a metal bar from a clothes rack in the corner, I crept to it. The woman whimpered as I closed my hand around the cold metal. Adrenaline was flowing through my veins, and I felt pure rage at the sound of the man's grunts. He'd pressed her against the wall, shoving between her legs.

Quietly, I crept up behind him. I was only a few feet away when Lucy spotted me.

Her eyes went wide with surprise, then to my shock, she threw up a hand as if to ward me off.

I stopped, staring at her in confusion. She didn't want me to help her?

When I didn't move away, she shook her head fractionally. The man's face was buried against her neck.

The man's grunts were coming more frequently now, his hips moving faster. I was struck by the sordid horror of the scene, desperately wanting to get him to stop.

My hands tightened on the metal and I moved closer. He needed to be stopped.

The woman looked at me, her eyes pleading. She raised a hand and silently placed a finger against her lips in the universal sign to be quiet.

I had no choice. I had to back off. I couldn't do what she obviously didn't want me to do, though I couldn't understand why. Backing up, my shoe scuffed against the concrete floor.

The man's head lifted and I froze. But Lucy grabbed his face, smashing her lips against his, and he seemed to forget what he'd heard. The woman's eyes opened and she watched me retreat back into the shadows.

I waited another moment, cringing as the man jerked into her. Finally, he was done. He let her go and she slid down the wall, a grimace of pain crossing her face. I heard the sound of a zipper as he rearranged his clothing.

"Don't ever turn me down again, Lucy," he said, still breathing heavily. His arm struck out and he backhanded her across the face.

Lucy cried out, falling to her knees and cradling her cheek.

The man turned away with a snort of disgust and I saw his face clearly.

Matt Summers.

He left the way they'd come, and when I was sure he was out of sight, I hurried over to Lucy.

"Are you all right?" I asked, crouching down beside her.

"I'm fine," she said tonelessly.

I helped her to her feet. "Why didn't you let me help? I know I could have stopped him!"

I was furious with Matt for what he'd done, and angry with Lucy for not letting me crack him upside the skull.

Lucy pinned me with her eyes, which seemed filled with far too much knowledge and despair for someone her age. "You know nothing," she said flatly. "Don't interfere again."

She swiped some blood from her lip before turning and walking away. Stunned, I could only stare after her, trying to figure out what had just happened.

Back at the bar, Jack shot me a dirty look, which I ignored, still shaken by what I'd seen. My heart broke for Lucy. Why did she let Matt do that to her? Now more than ever, I knew Lucy held the answers to what had happened to Amanda and Julie. Was she afraid she'd end up like them? That she'd be beaten like Julie, or that she'd disappear like Amanda?

Though I kept a lookout, I didn't see Chance. I worried about him, wondering where he'd gone last night when he'd left the parking lot, if he'd been following that van and why.

"Hey."

I looked up to see Mike standing at the bar.

I cleared my throat. "Yeah?"

"Tomorrow's Valentine's Day," he said. "We have a few private parties coming in and I'm short a couple dancers. Come early and Penny'll dress you for the part."

I just stared at him. No one messed with Mike, no one with any sense, anyway. "But . . . I don't do that," I finally stammered in protest.

"You will tomorrow," he shot back. "Or you can call tonight your last night here."

Shit. I couldn't leave yet. I still hadn't figured out what was going on with Lucy or if she knew what had happened to those girls. Gritting my teeth, I said, "Fine."

I'd figure some way out of it tomorrow, but I couldn't let him fire me tonight.

"Don't get all bitchy," Mike grunted. "It's just for one night. Some fancy politicians or something. Do a couple lap dances, give 'em a show, you'll have a thousand bucks to take home by the end of the night."

I blanched. A thousand dollars? For one night? Crystal had been right. That kind of money would certainly come in handy for struggling college students.

After I'd cleaned and restocked, I grabbed my purse to leave. Not bothering to say good-bye to Jack, I headed out the door.

It was late, but I knew where I had to go, and I pointed my car in the direction of downtown.

A short while later, I was knocking on Kade's door. Nerves tangled in my stomach as I waited for him to answer, rehearsing in my head the apology I wanted to make.

The door opened and I stood there, mouth agape.

A woman had answered. About my height, she was reddish-blonde like me, and well-endowed, with blue bedroom eyes. She studied me for a moment before glancing back over her shoulder.

"Is this the next one, or did you want to make a party of it?" Her voice had a sensual, throaty quality that I immediately envied.

I heard Kade before I saw him as he stepped around the corner into view. "What are you—"

He abruptly stopped speaking when he saw me.

Kade's black hair was wet, as though he'd just taken a shower. He was barefoot and shirtless, his jeans zipped but not fastened. I knew immediately what the woman was here for and what they'd been doing.

My face grew hot and I backed away. "Sorry to . . . interrupt," I stammered. "I didn't know you had . . . company."

"She was just leaving. Weren't you, sweetheart?"

I unwillingly glanced over to see the blonde standing behind him, her purse and coat slung over her arm. She gave me a smile, which I didn't return.

"Come inside," Kade ordered.

Reluctantly, I walked into his apartment, the blonde passing me by on her way out the door.

I didn't know what to do or say, my thoughts and feelings a jumbled mess at seeing the unknown woman and knowing she'd just had sex with Kade. I stood awkwardly in the middle of the living room.

Kade came up behind me but didn't speak, just walked into the kitchen and grabbed a bottle of wine from the wine rack. I watched as he uncorked it and poured the red liquid into a glass.

Settling himself onto the couch, he took a drink, his eyes on me. "So to what do I owe the pleasure?" he asked, his tone suggesting that this visit was anything but pleasurable for him.

"Who was she?" I countered, the question popping out of my mouth. I inwardly cringed at the peevish tone of my voice.

Kade raised an eyebrow. "What the fuck do you care?"

"I don't," I sputtered, backtracking. "I was just . . . curious, that's all."

"Well," he sneered, "I couldn't sleep, so . . . you know . . . thought she'd be a good diversion." He took another drink, watching me.

I winced at the reminder of what I'd said to him last night. I swallowed, trying not to stare at his chest, or the way his jeans gaped at the top as I summoned the courage to say what I needed to say.

"Why are you here?" he asked, interrupting my thoughts. "I'm a remorseless killer with blood on my hands, remember?"

I flinched. "Um, yeah, about that." I took a deep breath. "I want to apologize for what I said, Kade. You were just trying to help and I . . . I shouldn't have said those things . . . reacted like I did."

Kade gave a careless shrug. "Like I give a fuck what you think about me."

His gaze was cold and hard, very much like it had been at first between us. I could practically see the wall he'd put back up, shutting me out. Not that I blamed him.

My heart sank. Deep down, I'd been afraid of this. "I'm sorry, Kade." I just looked at him, hoping he could see how I felt, hoping I hadn't permanently broken the tenuous peace between us.

Tipping the glass back, Kade finished his wine. He rose from the couch and stood directly in front of me. I flinched but didn't back away. Tipping my head back, I could see his icy blue eyes as he gazed down at me.

"I don't want you, and I don't want your apology," he said in a low voice rife with contempt. "Now get the fuck out."

Stunned, I watched as he turned his back, dismissing me, and walked away. A moment later, the door to the bedroom closed.

I couldn't move. The pain gnawing my gut threatened to engulf me. I hadn't known, hadn't expected, that he wouldn't forgive me. That the things I'd said would kill whatever friendship we'd had. I wrapped my arms tightly around my waist, as if I wouldn't fall apart if I just squeezed hard enough.

Blane was forbidden to me, and now I'd lost Kade as well?

A persistent buzzing wouldn't go away, and I finally looked up to see what it was. Kade had left his phone on the kitchen counter. I walked numbly toward it and stood staring at the metal rectangle.

The caller ID said only "Terrance." I knew Terrance. He'd been the terrifyingly large black man who'd helped Kade and me infiltrate TecSol. It felt like ages ago.

Without thinking, I reached for the phone.

"Hello?"

"Yo, who's this? Where's Kade?"

"Terrance," I said. "I...it's Kathleen. I'll get Kade. Hold on."

Numbly, I walked to Kade's forbidding bedroom door and knocked. The thought occurred to me that the unknown blonde had been in there with him just a short while ago. I roughly pushed the image aside as Kade jerked the door open.

"I thought I told you—" he began.

"It's Terrance," I interrupted. "For you." I held the phone out to him.

The look he gave me sent a shiver down my spine, and I took an instinctive step back.

"Yeah," he barked into the phone.

I watched him as he listened, and he never took his eyes off me. After a few moments, I had to look away from his piercing gaze.

"Got it. Thanks."

He slid the phone into the pocket of his jeans.

"Don't ever, ever answer my phone again," Kade threatened.

I flushed hotly but nodded. "I'm sorry," I managed, my voice strained and weak to my ears. "I saw it was Terrance and thought it might be important."

I still couldn't look him in the eye. I felt horrible, and every moment that passed in Kade's presence was only making it worse. Regret smothered me, threatened to choke me.

"I was right about you all along," Kade sneered.

I jerked my head up, confused. "What?"

"Does Blane know you're screwing some guy behind his back?"

I just stared at him, nonplussed. "What are you talking about?"

"The bouncer you were all over last night. I assumed you didn't want to be carried out of the fucking parking lot, but I guess you like to play rough." Kade's insolent shrug belied the fury in his eyes.

"That's not . . . I'm not involved with him," I denied.

"Blane said he was at your apartment in the middle of the night," Kade accused. "Calls you 'Strawbs.'" He leaned forward to hiss in my ear. "What does he call you when he's fucking you?"

I didn't think, just reacted. My hand lashed out toward his face. Kade caught my wrist in midair before it could strike. The look in his eyes made me starkly afraid of him for the first time in a long time, but it didn't quell my anger.

"I'm not sleeping with him, you jackass," I spat. "He's a friend. That's all." I jerked my wrist out of his grip. "And what's with the anger? Haven't you been trying to sleep with me for weeks now? Where was all this righteous indignation for your brother when we were in Denver?"

"That's different—"

"How in the hell is that any different?" I yelled. "You love Blane, you'd do anything for him, yet you've been trying to steal his girlfriend from under his nose. What kind of brother does that make you?"

Kade gripped my upper arms, yanking me toward him. I winced as his fingers dug into my skin. "Me wanting a shot with my brother's plaything is completely different than you making an ass out of him by sleeping with some loser," he gritted out.

"Fuck you, Kade," I hissed, struggling to get out of his grip. "I'm not Blane's play anything. He loves me."

"Bullshit," Kade scoffed, easily holding me prisoner. "You're delusional if you believe that."

"You calling Blane a liar?" I shot back.

"I'm saying he can't possibly be in love with you."

My heart twisted at those words and tears stung my eyes.

"Why the hell not, Kade?" I retorted. "I'm not good enough for him or something? You think he deserves better—"

Then the world exploded.

CHAPTER TEN

When I opened my eyes, I couldn't make sense out of what had happened.

I was lying on my back and my head was aching. Moving slowly, I verified that all my limbs were still attached and functioning. Groaning with pain, I carefully sat up.

Kade.

I gasped, memory hitting me now. I was in Kade's apartment—what was left of Kade's apartment—but Kade was nowhere in sight.

Debris was everywhere, clouds of dust obscuring my vision. I coughed, the effect on my headache making me want to disconnect my head from my neck. With shaking hands, I started picking through piles of wood and plaster, crawling because I couldn't trust my legs to hold me if I stood.

"Kade?" I called, my voice weaker than I would have liked, or maybe it was just that the blast had left a persistent ringing in my ears. I tried again. "Kade!"

Nothing. I started to panic. Where was he? How far had the blast thrown him? What if . . .

I couldn't finish the thought, just started moving faster, crawling through the mess, wondering if each piece of debris I moved would reveal Kade's body.

"Kade!" I croaked.

A hand landed on my shoulder and I spun around to see Kade crouched next to me, alive and whole.

Without thinking, I threw myself into his arms, wrapping my arms tightly around his waist. His skin was warm and alive, albeit coated in dust. I could feel his breath and the strong beat of his heart.

"Hey, easy now. It's all right," he said, cradling me close.

"It's not all right," I choked out. "I thought you were . . . were dead."

His hand cupped the back of my head as he held me. "I keep trying to tell you, I'm hard to kill." At his words, I pressed closer to him, inhaling the scent of sweat on his skin.

"It's not funny," I muttered.

"You're right, it's not," he said, pulling away. I let him disentangle my arms. "Are you hurt?"

I shook my head, but he frowned at something on his hand. Pushing my face down, he probed the back of my head.

"Ow," I complained, jerking away.

"You have a nasty cut on the back of your head," he said, his face grim. Blood was smeared against his palm.

"That's why I have such a headache then," I mused. "But other than that, I'm fine. You?"

"Fine," he said curtly.

I started to speak, but he cut me off. "Wait here a sec."

He was gone and I heard things falling as he dug through the debris, returning in a few moments with shoes on his feet and a couple of guns.

"We have to get out of here." His tone was calm but firm, and I realized that whoever had set off the explosion might want to make sure no one made it out alive.

"You well enough to shoot?" he asked.

"Yeah." Though I quaked inside to think of having to do so.

Wordlessly, Kade handed me an automatic pistol while he kept the other, much larger, gun. He pulled his black leather jacket out from under a pile of rubble and put it on.

Standing, Kade went to a door off his living room, which I'd always assumed was a closet. Opening it, he crouched down and jerked up the carpet. Once that was up, he pulled up an honest-to-goodness trapdoor.

At my openmouthed stare, he said dryly, "You didn't think I'd live on the top floor without having an escape hatch, did you?"

I gave a huff of laughter despite myself.

"Come on, let's go," he ordered, reaching for my hand. "I'll lower you down."

Tucking the gun in my waistband, I sat on the edge of the hole, legs dangling, and stared nervously into the gaping darkness below me.

"Trust me."

I looked up at Kade. Without hesitation, I raised my hands so he could grasp my forearms, lowering me slowly into inky shadows.

My feet touched something solid and I found myself standing alone in the dark. A moment later, Kade dropped beside me. I couldn't see a thing, the darkness nearly complete.

I heard Kade rustling around. Then a sudden bright light made me squint and shield my eyes. Kade held a battery-operated torch, which gave out a strong, steady glow.

"Follow me," he said.

I looked at him. "What else would I do, exactly?"

His lips twitched in a near smirk before he started down the tunnel, gun in hand. The fact that he was expecting trouble had me reaching for my gun as well, the cold metal sliding against my sweaty palms.

The tunnel was barely wide enough for Kade's shoulders, and he had to bend down to avoid hitting his head.

"So what happened?" I asked. "Who blew up your apartment?"

"No idea," he replied. "They shouldn't have been able to trace me here."

"Then how did they?"

"I'm guessing they followed you."

His words were like a shock of cold water, and I stumbled. Kade grabbed my arm to steady me.

"But how . . . why—"

"Don't worry about it," Kade cut me off. "Let's just concentrate on getting out of here."

We walked for a while, the tunnel sloping steeply downwards at points, before Kade paused in front of a hatch in the wall. "Hold this." He handed me the torch and pulled the metal plate off the wall. "Get in."

Obediently, I climbed into the hole, big enough only to crawl. It didn't go far before I hit a grate barring my path.

"Now what?" I asked.

At my words, the grate abruptly swung outward. I could see someone's legs as they pulled it open. I scrambled back in surprise and fear, grabbing for my gun.

"It's all right." Kade's voice was by my ear, his hand closing like a vise on my arm. "Don't shoot."

To my shock, I saw Blane, crouching down to peer inside the opening.

"Kat?" he asked, disbelief in his voice. "What the hell—"

"Go," Kade prodded me, cutting Blane off.

I swallowed, then scooted forward. There was no graceful way to climb out face-first, but before I could contemplate the particulars, Blane grasped me under the arms and easily pulled me out, setting me on my feet.

I drank him in. He wore jeans and a long-sleeved black T-shirt that fit him closely. With no coat or jacket, I could plainly see the dual-holster he wore, a gun on each side. I had no idea how he'd known to come or why he was even there. I just knew that seeing him meant I didn't have to be strong anymore.

"Are you all right?" he asked anxiously.

"Fine," I choked out, tears clogging my throat. His eyes met mine, and I knew he understood all I was hiding, that I was moments away from losing it entirely.

His hand closed around mine, warm, solid, and reassuring.

"Let's get out of here," Kade said, having climbed out himself. "See anyone on your way in?"

Blane's gaze swiveled to Kade. "I counted two that I could see, probably more that I couldn't." His hand tightened on mine. "I didn't realize you wouldn't be alone." There was a warning in his voice.

"Let's argue about it later," Kade said curtly, avoiding my eyes as he moved past us down the hallway.

Blane kept me tucked close to his side as we followed. He'd taken the gun from my shaking hand, shoving it into the back of his jeans and drawing his own weapon. Both Kade and Blane moved silently and I tried to emulate them, but blood loss and shock were starting to get to me and I stumbled several times, only to be caught by Blane.

"Sorry," I murmured quietly the third time it happened, blinking hard to clear my vision.

"Don't fucking apologize," Blane bit out, his jaw like granite.

Okay then.

Kade stopped at the exit door, which had no window. After a moment of silent communication with Blane, who nodded, Kade slowly pushed the door open. No gunshots sounded and I let out the breath I'd been holding.

We crept through the doorway, sliding stealthily along the rough brick wall of the building. Well, Blane and Kade were stealthy, moving like shadows. I couldn't say the same for myself. Fear made my heart pound, and a cold sweat chilled my skin.

It was almost preternaturally quiet, and I was reminded that it was the middle of the night. Not even the bars that stayed open extra late or the hookers who hawked their wares could be seen at this hour. It felt like Kade, Blane, and I were the only people alive.

Right up until a gunshot shattered the bricks above my head.

I yelped. My first instinct was to cower in fear, not shoot back. Blane grabbed me by the arm, dragging me along with him as he ran for cover. A hail of gunfire followed us. Blane shoved me to the ground, turning to shoot back.

Kade made a motion with his hand and Blane nodded. I watched in horror as Kade took off. Blane's gun spit bullets as he provided cover for Kade's retreating back.

Blane kept firing, reloading twice as the minutes passed with agonizing slowness. Finally, his SUV squealed to a stop in front of us, with Kade at the wheel. Blane pulled me to my feet.

"Get in!" Kade shouted.

Blane wasted no time in complying. Swinging me up onto his shoulder in a fireman's carry, he jerked open the back door.

I saw movement. A man stood fifty yards away, a lethal-looking gun in his hand aimed straight at Blane's back.

Pulling my gun from Blane's belt, I fired. To my surprise and relief, the man fell.

Blane shoved me in the car and then pivoted, his gun swinging up to face the neutralized threat. When there was nothing more, he followed me into the car.

"Go!"

Kade stomped on the gas and we shot down the street. He drove fast and I barely had time to process all that had happened tonight before we pulled to a stop in front of Blane's house.

"Kathleen needs to go to the hospital," Blane said roughly. "She could barely walk back there."

"Not going to the hospital," I declared, climbing out of the car. "I'll be fine. I just need a few minutes of not being shot at, that's all."

And I thought it was true, mostly. My head really hurt, but there was no way I was going to get stitches. They'd have to shave that part of my head. That was so not happening. Not to mention that I'd rather pay a visit to the taxidermist than the hospital.

Neither man replied and I walked inside unaided. I felt the need for a stiff drink, regardless of my recent vows of sobriety, so I headed in the direction of the library. The crystal decanter seemed unusually heavy and I had difficulty with the stopper. Then it was lifted out of my hands.

"I'll do that," Blane said quietly. "Go sit down."

I obeyed, heaving a tired sigh as I sank down onto the leather couch. I shrugged off my tattered coat, dismayed at the level of damage done to it. It was the coat Blane had given me months ago. Absurdly, tears stung my eyes. It was just a coat, yet I couldn't help the sobs that started.

"Kathleen! Hey, it's okay." Kade tried to soothe me, his hand gently rubbing my back.

"My c-c-coat," I babbled through my tears. "It's r-ruined!" I sobbed harder.

His hand paused, then he gave a snort of laughter. "You're crying because of your coat?"

"I l-l-love that c-coat!" I felt inconsolable, which was ridiculous. It was just piece of clothing, but I couldn't help it.

I felt the eyes of both men on me and knew they were probably stymied at what to do with a hysterical woman sobbing over a coat. Valiantly, I tried to stem the tears until finally I was left with only hiccups and sniffles.

Blane pressed a glass into my hand, a healthy dose of amber fluid in its depths. I drank it down at once, welcoming the heat that burned a path down my throat to my belly.

There was a fire in the fireplace and I watched the flames dance, transfixed. Several minutes of blessed silence passed.

"Well," Kade finally sighed, "it's been a hell of a night. But we make a good team, brother." He lifted his glass in toast to Blane, who merely stood watching him.

"You want to tell me what the hell happened?" Blane's voice was like ice. "And why you nearly got Kathleen killed. Again. Not to mention why she was even there in the first place."

Kade stiffened. "Kathleen is fine," he shot back.

I jumped a foot when Blane's glass shattered in the fireplace.

"She is not fucking fine!" Blane snarled, grabbing the lapels of Kade's jacket with both hands and hauling him to his feet. "She's hurt and in shock. Or are you too much of a selfish bastard to see that?"

"Fuck you," Kade gritted out. "You think I wanted this to happen? You think I wanted her to get hurt?" He shoved Blane's arms away, jerking out of his grip.

I watched with growing dismay, my clouded brain struggling to keep up with the scene playing out in front of me.

"I just wish for once you'd think of someone besides yourself," Blane shot back.

"What's the fun in that?" Kade sneered.

"She could've died!"

I couldn't take it anymore. "Stop it! Both of you! Stop!" I jumped to my feet. The room tilted, but I stoically remained standing. "It's not his fault, Blane! They followed me."

Blane's eyes snapped to mine, then turned to Kade. "What's she talking about, Kade?"

Kade shrugged insolently. "What the fuck do you care?"

"Don't give me that martyr shit," Blane snapped.

Kade's eyes narrowed. "The same people that tried to kill me in Denver traced me here. I'm guessing they followed her to my apartment. And for the record, I didn't ask for her to show up tonight, she just did."

Blane's hands fisted at his side as he processed this information. "We'll fix this, with you, but you have to stay away from her. Especially if they know she's tied to you."

I would have protested the fact that they were talking about me as though I weren't right there in the room, but I was too tired and dizzy to form the words. I brushed a shaky hand across my eyes, watching my fingers as though they were disconnected from my body. How odd.

"That's not going to happen." Kade said flatly.

Blane was suddenly in Kade's face. "You want her to die right along with you?"

The menace in his tone made me shiver, and Kade's was no less threatening when he replied.

"I'm saying I won't stay away."

"This isn't a fucking game, Kade!" The anguish in Blane's voice made my chest hurt.

"You think I don't know that?" Kade said.

"Everything I'm doing is for her!"

The tension in the room was so thick I felt as though it was smothering me, pressing against my chest like a leaden weight. The room tilted again and my knees buckled. I heard someone curse, and it seemed like a really good time to close my eyes and let the encroaching darkness consume me.

≈

I woke to a sharp stinging on the back of my head.

"Ow, stop," I muttered, waving my arm blearily in an effort to halt the pain.

"Shh. If you refuse to go to the hospital, the cut has to be cleaned."

My arm was caught in a gentle but firm grip and the stinging recommenced.

I gritted my teeth, fully awake now, and stared ahead at my surroundings. Blane had brought me to his bedroom, where I lay on my side while he medicated the wound. I hoped I wasn't getting the duvet on his bed dirty. I felt gross. My jeans were covered in dust, as was my hair, which had the added attractiveness of being matted with dried blood. Not one of my best looks. Blane had removed my shoes, which was a good thing since they'd been covered in dust, too.

My head was clearer now, and I remembered the argument in the library. What had happened after I passed out? Blane was angry with Kade, but it hadn't been Kade's fault I'd been there when someone had tried to kill him. It was my fault they'd even found him in the first place.

"There, that should take care of it," Blane said quietly. "Feel any better?"

I carefully turned toward him. He brushed the backs of his knuckles against my cheek. I nodded, unsure what to say from here. Tonight had been a strange night.

"Good." His hand moved down my arm to lightly grasp my palm, slotting his fingers with mine.

"Are you and Kade okay?" I didn't mean physically.

Blane didn't answer for a moment, his gaze still on our entwined hands. Finally, he said, "That's not important right now." He lifted his eyes to mine. "What's important is that you and I are okay." A pause. "Are we?"

I slowly shook my head. "Not if you and Kade aren't."

Blane studied me. "Why are you so insistent on this?"

"Because," I sputtered. "You're family. Brothers. I won't come between you."

Blane sighed. "We've disagreed before, Kat, and I'm sure we will again. That doesn't stop making us brothers."

His words reassured me, but I still felt compelled to add, "I don't feel about Kade the way he feels about me. I just want you to know that."

Blane looked at me, really looked at me, until I wanted to squirm.

"What?" I asked in frustration. "You don't believe me?"

"I believe you," he said. "But your point of view and Kade's may be . . . drastically different."

I held his gaze. "I'm not going to lie to you," I said firmly. "I care about him. He's a good man, underneath everything. I don't want anything to happen to him, not least because of what that would do to you."

"You wouldn't be the kind of person I know you to be if you didn't care what happened to Kade," he said.

That brought a tiny smile to my face and I breathed a sigh of relief. My resolve to kick Kade's ass the next time he made some suggestive remark or innuendo was strengthened. I wasn't going to let him goad me into doing something that would hurt all three of us.

At my insistence, Blane helped me into the shower. There was no way I was going to sleep like this, and he was waiting for me when I got out. He didn't suggest I go to a different room, and I didn't say anything either. I climbed into bed beside him and crawled into his waiting arms. I sighed in contentment. The warm skin of his chest pressed against my cheek. His arms and body surrounding me made me feel safe and protected. His lips brushed my forehead.

I wondered where Kade was but didn't dare ask. I hoped he was okay, that he was getting some rest.

The last thing that stole unbidden through my mind before I drifted to sleep was the image of the senator lying in wait for me.

~

I was choking on dust, the gritty feel of it clogging my throat, my nose. The explosion had ripped everything apart and I recognized nothing that had been.

They were coming. I could hear them, their voices, coming closer.

I had to find him, had to get to him before they found me.

I tore through the debris, each piece seeming heavier than the last. The sense of urgency overwhelmed me as I heard the sound of approaching footsteps.

Gunshots. I cried out. Standing, I tried to run, but there was nowhere to go. More gunshots. I fell, tripping over something. It was a man's body. Dreading the truth, but unable to halt the compulsion to see, I crept closer. My hand shook as I pushed away the cloth covering his face.

Blood trailed from his mouth in a sluggish stream while sightless green eyes stared up at me.

I screamed and screamed and screamed.

"Kathleen!"

I came abruptly awake, panic and despair still clawing at my throat. The dream had felt so real, the taste of dust still in my mouth.

A cold sweat covered my skin, and my chest heaved from my frantic gasps for air. Blane brushed my tangled hair back from my face.

"It's just a nightmare," he said quietly. "You're all right."

I turned to him, the pale moonlight streaming through the window behind him casting shadows and pools of light across his shoulders. His face remained in darkness.

I felt cold from the inside out and brittle as glass, my emotions balanced on the edge of a knife. I'd never felt this way before, this out of control, as though my life were in a tailspin.

But Blane was real. He could anchor me, ground me.

Without a word, I got to my knees, my arms crossing over my chest to tug my nightgown over my head. I let the gossamer fabric fall from my fingers as my arms rested against my sides. The moonlight caressed my naked breasts like a lover's touch. The length of my hair brushed the middle of my back.

I could feel Blane's eyes on me. The width and breadth of his shoulders was clearly outlined in the moonlit glow. He was still, so I remained still as well. My gaze was locked on his unfathomable eyes, denied to me in the shadows.

Finally, he spoke. "You're perfect, Kat. We're perfect together." His voice was a gravelly rasp. At some other time, perhaps I would consider his words and preen with feminine pride at the awe in his voice. But not tonight.

"Show me." My request was breathless, but perhaps only I could hear the tinge of desperation.

"With pleasure."

He took his time, mapping and relearning every curve, dip, and hollow of my body. His hands touched, caressed, stroked. And where his hands went, his mouth followed, until I was begging for him, needing to feel him inside me. He covered my body with his much larger one, and I felt the fragility of being the weaker sex, but I didn't mind. He was hard and strong everywhere, under my palms, against my belly, between my thighs. When I cried out his name, his lips took the syllables from my mouth. And afterward, when I lay boneless and sated in his arms, my thoughts were finally, thankfully, quiet.

∽

The sun was streaming through the window when I woke, and when I moved, my whole body protested.

I blinked, clearing the sleep from my eyes, automatically reaching for Blane. My hand encountered nothing but sheets and empty space. Sitting up, I glanced toward his pillow and saw a single red rose and a folded piece of paper. There were only two words written inside, and I recognized Blane's handwriting.

Be mine.

I smiled. Today was Valentine's Day.

That lifted my spirits. I loved holidays, any holiday, and Valentine's had always been a favorite, though I'd seldom had a boyfriend for the occasion. Rather, I'd enjoyed using the holiday to surprise friends with little tokens of affection, a box of candy, or a funny card. People always appreciated the unexpected. As for me, I never expected anything, which was good, considering I rarely received anything.

I showered and dressed, changing into a pair of jeans and thick sweater I found in the other bedroom, and I wondered where Blane had gone. It was nearing noon—I'd slept the morning away. I headed downstairs, in search of him and coffee.

Voices were coming from Blane's study, but when I recognized one of them as Kade's, I hesitated.

I didn't know how to act after last night, how to behave. While it may have been fine to handle the situation alone with Blane, I felt very anxious about being in the same room with both him and Kade. If they were talking, that meant they were getting along and working together. My being there would only cause awkwardness and tension, which I was loath to do.

Steeling my resolve, and my courage, I tentatively knocked on the half-closed door and peered inside.

Both Blane and Kade turned to look at me. My eyes brushed Kade's before I fixed my attention on Blane, though I could feel Kade's penetrating gaze on me.

"I need to head home," I told him. "I have to work this afternoon."

Blane's body stiffened, his face a mask. "I want you to stop working at Xtreme," he said.

I walked a few steps into the room, my temper igniting at his order. "Well, that's not going to happen," I said tartly, throwing his own words back at him. "A woman who works there knows what happened to Amanda, and I'm going to find her. And last night I saw Matt Summers there, too. You know, the guy you're defending? I watched him rape another woman last night. Lucky she's not pressing charges, eh?"

Blane's steely gaze met my angry one. I was still having a really hard time reconciling the man I thought I knew with the persona of an ambitious lawyer who would trade an acquittal for campaign cash.

"Maybe you'd better listen to Mr. Overprotective this time around, princess," Kade threw in. I glared at him.

Blane tossed a folder down onto the desk he stood behind. "Take a look at this, and maybe you'll change your mind." Curious, I stepped closer to see, then gasped.

Pictures of Chance stared up at me.

I snatched up the photos, thumbing through them. I could tell they'd been taken from a distance and at night, but Chance was unmistakable, though I didn't recognize the man he was with.

"Where did you get these?" I asked.

"Whoever your friend is," Blane bit out, "he's involved in some serious shit. You know who that man is with him?" He didn't wait for me to answer. "His name is Fernando Alvarez. You know what he specializes in? How he makes his money?"

Blane's anger robbed me of speech, and I only shook my head.

"He likes to sell things. Preferably women. Usually, they're from some god-awful third-world country where they think anything would be endurable, just to get to America. He gets them here, then sells them into slavery."

My eyes widened in horror. I looked back at the pictures. "That . . . that's impossible! Chance would never—"

"His name is Chance?" Kade cut in, standing now, right next to me. "Chance who?"

I closed my mouth with a snap.

"How can we find him?" Blane asked. "If he's a friend of yours, maybe we can get him to help us. Is he in it for the money?"

I shook my head. "Chance would never get involved in something like this," I denied. "You're wrong, both of you."

"He's the right-hand guy," Kade retorted. "I don't know what he's told you, but he's been in the middle of several deals going down and transports of cargo."

I looked blankly at him.

"Women," he clarified. "Girls. Some as young as thirteen, fourteen."

I felt like I was going to be sick, my stomach rolling. I had to get out of here, away from the photos that didn't lie.

Turning on my heel, I hurried out of the room.

"Kathleen—" Kade said, then Blane interrupted him.

"Let her go. Give her a minute."

I walked quickly down the hall, ending up in the kitchen without realizing where I'd been going. I couldn't think about Chance, couldn't consider the possibility that he'd do those things. No. It had to be a lie. There had to be some sort of explanation, even if I had seen him accompany that white van the other night. My stomach clenched. Had the van been full of . . . women?

"Good morning!" Mona greeted me cheerfully. "Coffee?"

"Yes, please." I smiled reflexively at her warm welcome.

"Gerard got your car for you this morning," she said as poured some coffee into a cup, added cream and sugar, and handed it to me. "If you have need of it today."

"That's great," I said, sipping the dark brew and welcoming the escape she'd just handed me. "I . . . need to get to work this afternoon anyway."

"The keys are on the counter." She motioned vaguely with her hand. "I was just getting ready to call the boys for lunch. Are you hungry?"

My eyes widened as panic set in. I wasn't ready, couldn't face seeing them with accusations in their eyes. Was I protecting someone who dealt in human trafficking?

"Actually, I need to get going," I blurted, setting down the coffee and grabbing up the keys. I'd left my purse in the car, so hopefully, it was still in there. "Please tell"—I paused, stumbling over whether to say Blane or Kade—". . . them . . . that I had to go."

"But you haven't eaten yet!" Mona protested.

"Sorry," I said, pulling open the kitchen door. "Gotta run. Happy Valentine's Day, Mona."

"You, too," she called after me.

I was such a coward. I berated myself, my procrastination, my propensity to avoid conflict, all of it, all the way home.

Mona had been right. I should have eaten. In spite of all I'd been through, my stomach was growling, so I ran through a drive-thru on the way home. It took forever and my patience was at an end when I finally pulled into my parking lot. Since it was Valentine's Day, I'd gotten a chocolate shake. Every girl should get some kind of chocolate on Valentine's Day, I figured.

Juggling my keys as I crossed the parking lot, I wasn't paying attention to anything other than the smell of the fries in the bag, which was why I was completely unprepared when I heard him.

"Where the hell have you been?"

I shrieked and spun around, dropping my shake on the ground. Chance stood behind me, arms crossed over his chest.

"Damn it!" I looked down at the oozing chocolatey mess. "Look what you made me do!"

"I've been waiting for you all night. Where were you?"

Everything that Blane and Kade had said about Chance flooded my mind. Chance had lied to me. Had turned into everything I despised. A red haze clouded my vision.

"You son of a bitch!" I yelled while flying at him, my fists hitting him anywhere I could reach. "How could you do that?"

"What the fuck, Kathleen!" Chance exclaimed, grabbing my arms. In seconds, he'd immobilized me, locking my arms together and spinning me around so my back pressed against his chest. "What the hell are you yelling about?"

"I'm yelling about your chosen career," I seethed. "The one you haven't said much about. You know, the one where you sell women and girls to be sex slaves."

Chance went utterly still, then abruptly released me. I turned around, glaring at him with hatred in my eyes.

"We need to talk," Chance said grimly. Bending down, he picked up my purse and my sack of food from the ground.

"Why don't you just do what you've done the past three years and disappear out of my life?" I sneered. "You're pretty good at that."

Chance ignored me, wrapping his hand around my arm and dragging me forward to the steps.

"Let go of me," I spat. "I don't want to talk to you."

"You always were stubborn, Strawbs." Chance sighed, pulling me up the stairs to my door.

"Don't call me that," I groused, rubbing my arm when he released me to unlock my door.

Once we were in my apartment, I ignored him, going into the kitchen to start a pot of coffee. I still hadn't gotten my quota for the day.

"Strawbs, listen to me—" he began.

"Listen to what?" I snapped at him. "Listen to you tell me why you would be involved in something so . . . so disgusting? So inhumane? You're not the man you used to be, Chance, and you're certainly not the man I thought you were."

"Will you just listen to me for a damn minute?" he said, raising his voice in frustration.

I clamped my lips shut and crossed my arms over my chest, silently waiting.

Chance sighed tiredly, swiping a hand across his eyes. He stepped closer and lightly grasped my upper arms.

"I would never, ever do anything of the sort," he said firmly. "You know me better than that."

I raised an eyebrow, but didn't say anything, waiting for more. There had to be more.

"The fact is, Strawbs, I'm working undercover. I'm a cop."

CHAPTER ELEVEN

I stared at Chance, openmouthed.

"You're what?"

"I'm a cop," he repeated, his hand dropping away from me. "Have been for a few years now."

"And you're working undercover?" It seemed like something from a television show, not real life. My mind scrambled to keep up.

Chance nodded. "We've been tracking this cell of human traffickers for over a year. I infiltrated them months ago."

"Do you know what happened to Julie Vale and Amanda Webber?"

"Julie started working at the club, and Matt Summers noticed her. He never takes no for an answer, and the more they fight, the better he likes it."

I swallowed. "What about Amanda?"

"I don't know. I think she was sold."

The thought sickened me.

"That's why you can't tell anyone about me," he said earnestly. "If they find out I'm a cop, I'm dead."

"What are you going to do?"

"I'm going to finish my assignment, and get Alvarez, that's what I'm going to do," he replied. "The only reason we haven't yet is because I'm trying to get a trace to the distributor. These women are being smuggled out of the country and sold. If we can trace Alvarez's contacts, we may be able to bring down more than just him.

"So I don't know who you were with last night," he said, "though I'm guessing it was either Dennon or Kirk, but you can't tell them I'm a cop."

"They would never—" I began.

"Dennon would do anything if the money was right, and Kirk is Summers's lawyer. I don't trust either of them, and neither should you." His voice was hard now.

"They think you're a part of it," I argued. "They have photos with you and Alvarez."

"Even more reason to not tell them the truth. Let them believe I'm a bad guy. It's not worth it otherwise. It's not worth my life. Do you get that, Strawbs?" His gaze was intense. "Your misplaced trust could kill me."

His words shook me. I took a moment to absorb the seriousness of the situation before reluctantly nodding. "Okay. I won't tell them."

Chance pulled me into a hug. "Thanks," he murmured. His hand brushed the back of my head and I cringed.

"What?" He released me. "What's wrong?"

I tentatively touched the cut. "Nothing. It's just a cut. There was an . . . explosion . . . last night." It sounded strange to say the words.

Chance's face turned hard. "You were in the explosion downtown? The gas leak in that apartment building?"

I nodded. "Yeah, but it wasn't a gas leak."

"How?" he asked. "Why were you there? It was the middle of the night."

"I was with Kade," I explained with a shrug.

Chance's jaw clenched. "He's a cold-blooded assassin, Strawbs. Dark and dangerous isn't usually your type."

I flushed. "I'm not dating him." I turned away from him and poured myself some coffee.

"Then what are you to him? Or should I ask what is he to you?"

I had no answer to the first question, couldn't even begin to try to make sense of the tangled relationship between Kade and me to know if he still viewed me as a friend or not. Before the explosion last night, it had seemed pretty obvious I was firmly in the "unfriended" category. After the explosion . . . well, we'd been running for our lives, hadn't we? Not exactly the best time for a heart-to-heart.

As to the second question, that was easy enough. "I care about him," I said. "He's not evil, Chance."

My words didn't seem to have any effect on Chance. "So he's not evil the same way Kirk isn't power-hungry?" His disdain for my opinion was obvious.

"You're wrong." Anger on Kade and Blane's behalf rose to the surface. "You're wrong about both of them."

"And you're blind," he retorted. "You need to understand that when the shit comes down, they'll pick themselves over you. Never forget that."

I glared at him until he stepped away, heading for the door.

"Where are you going?" I asked.

"Alvarez is expecting me," he said. "I'll call you later."

His hand was on the knob when he froze.

I frowned. "What's wrong?"

He looked through the peephole, pulled his gun, and jerked open the door.

"What the fuck do you want?"

I blanched when I saw Kade standing in the doorway. Other than a narrowing of his eyes, he didn't respond to Chance. He took in the gun Chance held before looking at me. I felt the disappointment in his eyes as if he'd spoken aloud.

"Apparently one near-death experience wasn't enough for you," Kade drawled, his eyes returning to Chance. Though his body looked relaxed as he rested his lean frame against the doorjamb, I knew him well enough now to realize it was a feint. His muscles were coiled and ready to spring at the slightest hint of provocation.

Chance got in his face, his finger pushing against Kade's chest. "You stay away from Kathleen," he hissed. "She's too naive and trusting to know you for the killer you are." Chance smiled a smile I'd never before seen on him. "But I'm not."

Kade moved so fast I couldn't follow what he did, but then Chance's gun was on the ground and Kade's knife was at his throat.

"I'll be sure to keep that in mind." Kade's tone was dry. "Now go away, before I change my mind about being nice."

Chance flushed angrily, but moved slowly away, stopping to pick up his gun and holster it. Neither of them took their eyes off each other.

I hardly dared to breathe again until Chance had left. "What are you doing here?" I asked as Chance's motorcycle pulled out of the lot.

Kade turned back to me, sheathing his knife. "I'm here to fire you," he said casually, brushing past me into my apartment.

I stood in stunned disbelief. He went to the kitchen and poured himself a cup of coffee. Shaking myself from my stupor, I shut the front door.

"Why?" I asked. "Why would you do that? I know I'm no Sherlock Holmes, but I just started. Give me a chance before you fire me."

I couldn't believe he thought I was so bad that he'd fire me already. He'd just been training me, had even taken me with him to Denver, so why fire me now?

Kade didn't meet my eyes. "Sorry, princess. You're just not cut out for this type of work. Maybe the secretary pool would be a better fit. I'll talk to Diane . . ."

Fury sparked in me, combining with my overwhelming disappointment, and I lashed out, slamming the coffee mug out of his grip. The hot liquid hit my hand as the ceramic crashed to the floor, but I was too angry to notice.

"Don't give me that condescending bullshit!" I yelled. "You were giving me a chance, a chance to do something important, make a difference, and now you're just going to take it away?"

Kade's eyes were blue chips of ice. "You want to make a difference? Go adopt a puppy. You'd have a better shot."

His words cut like razors, making my breath catch in my chest. My shock and hurt must have shown on my face.

Kade cursed viciously and turned away.

I sank down onto my couch, resting my elbows on my knees and my head in my hands. I felt, more than heard, Kade step in front of me. I didn't lift my head.

"Kathleen, I—"

"I don't want to hear it, Kade," I interrupted, forestalling what had sounded like the beginning of an apology. That or a weak-ass explanation. Neither of which I wanted to hear. "Just go."

He didn't move. "I have to do this for Blane," he said.

My head shot up. I hadn't been expecting that. "What does Blane have to do with it?"

Kade's face was a mask, carefully concealing his emotions. "Blane loves you. And I'm not going to keep putting you in situations where you'll be in danger. I won't be responsible for him losing the only woman he's ever loved."

I stiffened. "So now you decide Blane loves me, and that gives him and you the right to decide my career path?"

Kade didn't answer. He didn't have to.

I stood. I'd had enough. Enough of men deciding my life for me. Enough of my fate being tied to what they were or weren't willing to give up, what they decided my future should be, be it Blane or Kade or Senator Keaston.

"I have to go to work," I said stiffly. "You can leave now."

Kade's eyes narrowed. "You're fired. Don't go back to the club tonight. You're no longer investigating that case."

"Too bad I have bills to pay," I retorted. "And you just lost any say in what I do or where I go. So get out."

Kade's mouth was a thin line, our gazes colliding in mutual anger before he turned and stalked to the door. I followed him, stopping at the door once he'd stepped through.

"And Kade?" I called as he headed down the stairs.

He stopped and turned.

"Happy fucking Valentine's Day." I slammed the door.

And that was yet another reason why I never expected anything for Valentine's.

I cleaned up the mess in the kitchen and took a shower, still fuming from Kade's visit. I was fixing my makeup when I heard a knock at the door. For God's sake, what now?

I yanked open the door, a smart-ass comment on my lips, when I saw it was my neighbor Alisha.

"Hey." I relaxed, giving her a smile. We hadn't had a chance to talk in a while. "What's up? Want to come in?"

"Sure," she said. "I brought you something." She was carrying a small square pan, which she took into the kitchen.

"Ta-da!" She pulled off the foil cover to reveal fresh-baked brownies. "Happy Valentine's Day!"

"Alisha, they look fabulous! And just what the doctor ordered." I gave her a hug. "Thank you! But wait, I have something for you, too."

I hurried into my bedroom, coming back with a big red heart. "Happy Valentine's Day!"

Alisha was a little OCD, and she ate only a certain brand of chocolates, and then only a certain kind of chocolates that had hazelnuts in the middle. Luckily for me, they always made a ton of packages in all different sizes for the holiday. I'd gotten her the biggest heart I could find.

Her eyes lit up. "Aw, thanks! Let's eat."

I laughed. "Sounds good." A huge dose of chocolate sounded just the thing. I grabbed some plates and a knife to cut the brownies while she opened the chocolates.

"So what are you and Blane doing tonight?" she asked once we'd dug in. "Is he taking you to dinner?"

I shrugged, my mouth full of brownie. "I don't think so. He didn't say. We had a big fight a few days ago."

"So did you make up?" she asked. "Make-up sex is the best, you know."

I laughed, licking chocolate from my fingers. "I don't know. Sort of, I guess." I thought of the senator. I needed to tell someone, get it off my chest. "His uncle, this big-shot politician, wants to buy me off to stop seeing Blane."

Alisha's brownie-laden hand paused on its way to her mouth. "Are you for real?"

I nodded. "Yep. Offered to pay my way through school, living expenses, everything. I just have to break up with Blane and move to another state."

"Holy shit," she breathed, her eyes wide. "That's . . . that's insane."

"I know, right?" I crammed another brownie into my mouth. I watched as Alisha carefully nibbled her way around a chocolate.

"What are you doing?" I asked.

"I like to save the nut for last," she said simply.

"Huh." Why was I not surprised that she would have a special way to eat chocolates?

"I need milk."

"Got better than milk," I said, jumping up and pulling a bottle out of the fridge. "Champagne."

I'd been saving it, though for what, I didn't know. Now seemed as good a time to drink it as any, especially with my friend who'd brought me chocolate on Valentine's Day. I tore the wrapper off and popped the cork. Grabbing a couple of glasses, I filled them very full. "It's not Dom Pérignon, but it'll do."

"Cheers," Alisha said, clinking her glass against mine.

"Cheers."

"So what are you going to do?" she asked after taking a healthy swallow.

The bubbles tickled my nose as I drank. "I don't know," I answered. "He's a powerful guy, kind of made threatening noises if I said no, like he'd hurt me or something."

Alisha's eyes went wide again.

"It's all very . . . Romeo and Juliet," I said.

"And that ended so well," Alisha replied dryly.

I snorted. "Oh yeah," I added, scooping more brownie with my fingers. "And Kade just fired me this afternoon."

"Asshole."

"Yeah, pretty much." I sighed, refilling our glasses with the rest of the champagne.

"So, let me get this straight," Alisha said. "You had a big fight with Blane, but may or may not have made up, but it doesn't matter because his uncle is threatening you unless you agree to break up with Blane. And I'm assuming you haven't told Blane that part, either."

I shook my head. "He idolizes his uncle. Thinks he walks on water."

"So the uncle is threatening you or buying you off—depending on what you decide to do—then you got fired, and now you're unemployed."

"Not unemployed," I corrected her. "I've been working at this club at night. A strip club."

Alisha's eyes bulged. "You've been stripping?" she squeaked.

I laughed. "No, no. I bartend there. Though the owner was giving me crap about needing another dancer tonight."

Alisha grimaced.

"It's a thousand bucks a night." I watched her eyebrows climb.

"That's a lot of money," she said. I agreed.

We reached no conclusion about what I should do, but I felt better talking about things with someone. We both stared at the nearly empty brownie pan, the chocolate wrappers littering my kitchen table, and the drained bottle of champagne.

"I think I'm going to be sick," I said with a groan.

"Me, too."

We both laughed. "So what are you doing tonight?" I asked. "Anything?"

"Well . . ." she replied, drawing out the word. "You know I'm very tied into my tradition of watching *Out of Africa* and getting drunk on cheap wine . . ."

I nodded. Alisha was nuts about Robert Redford. *Out of Africa* was the "most romantic movie ever made," in her opinion. I didn't see what was so romantic about the hero dying in the end, but whatever.

"But this year I'm setting that glorious tradition aside because . . . I have a date."

I grinned. "Really? That's great! Who's the guy?"

"I met him in the library," she said. Alisha worked as a librarian at Purdue. "His name is Lewis and he's premed."

"Oooh, a doctor," I breathed in exaggerated awe, then giggled. "Daddy will be so proud."

Alisha blushed at my teasing. Her father was a wealthy man who indulged Alisha's desire to make it on her own, though he didn't keep it a secret that he wanted to see her marry someone who could take care of her.

"Anyway," she said, brushing off my comment with a wave of her hand, "he's picking me up at eight for dinner."

"Is this a first date?" I asked, and she nodded. "Wow. Valentine's Day for a first date? He must really like you."

Alisha grinned. "I hope so. We've been talking a lot in the library . . ."

"They frown on that, you know," I interrupted.

She shot me a mock dirty look before continuing. "And he's really sweet. We have a lot in common. He's been calling and we talk on the phone for hours. So tonight's our first official date."

"Well, I hope you have a great time," I said sincerely. "What are you wearing?"

We spent the next several minutes discussing clothing options before I looked at the clock and realized I should get ready for work.

"Thanks again for the brownies," I said as Alisha headed out the door. "And be sure to let me know how your date goes!" I watched her cross the hall back into her own apartment before I closed the door.

I felt a little better, but anger and bitterness, combined with despair, still formed a hard knot in my stomach. Kade's words about my ineffectiveness at my job burned like acid, and I didn't know if it was because I thought he believed them, or if I did.

I was ready to walk out the door when my cell rang. Checking the caller ID, I saw it was Blane. I almost didn't answer, then relented.

"Hello?"

"Kat, it's me."

"I know."

The flatness of my voice seemed to give him pause. "Kade said he stopped by—" he began.

"To fire me for you," I interrupted. "Yes, I'm aware."

Silence. "He said that guy, Chance, was at your apartment again."

My temper flared. "Leave Chance out of this."

"Kat, tell me what's going on," he cajoled. "I can help. Otherwise, Chance could get arrested, caught in the cross fire . . ."

"Are you threatening me?" I asked in disbelief.

"Of course not," he retorted. "I'm just telling you the truth."

"Chance is my friend," I bit out. "And I'd damn sure appreciate it if he didn't get 'caught in the cross fire,' as you so eloquently put it."

"What kind of friend?" Blane asked coolly. "I've seen your file. The last boyfriend you had before moving to Indy was a guy named Travis."

"I've known Chance for years," I corrected him, concealing my surprise that he knew about my brief time with Travis. "And what file are you talking about? The one Kade has on me?"

Blane ignored my questions. Big surprise. "Your friend is mixed up with some bad people." He was angry, but I didn't really care.

"I know who he works for," I retorted. "He told me."

"Kat, listen to me—"

"I'm done listening to you right now," I interrupted. "I told you how much it meant to me that Kade had given me this job, how it felt like I was moving in a direction, instead of being buffeted around by events as they happen. Now that's gone."

He was silent.

"You know," I said more quietly. "It seems every time I open up to you, you find a way to turn it against me, to try to manipulate me or get others to do so. It must run in the family." The last part just slipped out as my thoughts returned to the senator and his ultimatum.

"What are you talking about, 'it runs in the family'?" Blane was instantly alert, and I knew what I'd said hadn't slipped by him.

"Nothing. Listen, we're going to have to continue this later. I have to go."

"Where are you going?"

"We've been through this before, Blane," I said coldly. "When I get fired from a job, I still have to eat and pay rent. I'm going to work."

I ended the call. I despised when people hung up on me, so I usually never did it. In this case, though, I decided an exception could be made.

As I pulled up to the club, I remembered that Blane had taken my gun last night and hadn't returned it. It would have been nice to know the weapon was in my purse, within reach.

Mike had apparently decided to decorate, or more likely, had someone do it for him, as the place was filled with gaudy red streamers and balloons. Looking closely however, I saw that the streamers weren't regular streamers, but cutouts of a woman's body from the side view, repeated over and over in endless drapes of paper across the ceiling.

Nice. Class all the way.

"Mike said for you to get dressed backstage," Jack told me when I saw him.

"Why?"

He shrugged. "I'm just the messenger."

Irritated, I went in search of Mike, finding him in the stockroom unloading a case of bourbon.

"I'm not dancing tonight," I said by way of greeting.

He glanced over his shoulder and I stiffened my spine.

"Then you're fired." He turned away again.

Twice in one day. That had to be a record or something.

"You really want to fire your only other bartender, tonight of all nights?" Mike paused in stacking the bottles, so I continued. "Your customers aren't going to be real happy when it takes thirty minutes to get a drink. They might get so pissed they leave and head down the street to another strip joint."

"Fine," he barked. "You don't have to dance, but get your ass in the dressing room and have the girls pick something for you to wear. I don't need a fuckin' nun to be shillin' booze in my bar."

Inwardly, I grinned, but I wasn't stupid enough to push my luck, so I beat a hasty retreat.

Inside the dressing room were only Penny and Holly, who were busy doing their hair and makeup.

"Hi," I greeted them. "Mike sent me to you for another outfit tonight."

Holly chuckled when I made a face. "Sweetie, it's not all bad," she said, putting the cap back on her lipstick. "You've got assets. Use them to your advantage. Men are fools for a nice set of boobs."

She got up and rummaged through a drawer, pulling out a red half corset. "Let's try this."

I looked dubious but took it from her.

"And you don't want to wear a skirt—the men will get handsy—so try these jeans."

She handed me a pile of dark-blue denim. I went behind the screen in the corner to change. The jeans were so tight they fit like a second skin, and rode so low on my hips that if I bent over, I'd be imitating a plumber.

I needed help with the corset. It cinched my ribs and pushed my breasts up to display an impressive amount of cleavage. It showed even more than the outfit Romeo had made us wear back at The Drop at Christmas, but altogether I was wearing more fabric than I had feared.

Penny pulled my hair back in a messy ponytail and outlined my eyes in dark-blue liner. Lipstick that matched the red of the corset and sky-high red stilettos, which I had no idea how I'd be able to work in all night, completed my "makeover."

"Happy Valentine's Day to me," I mumbled, catching sight of myself in a mirror.

It seemed my life at holidays now had a theme—first Britney Spears's Naughty Catholic Schoolgirl for Halloween, then a Santa Slut, now Cleavage Cupid. What was next? A Lusty Leprechaun? Would I be wearing emerald lipstick and green clover pasties for Saint Patrick's Day?

I thanked the girls and headed back up front, passing Mike on the way. He grunted at me, which I guess meant I passed inspection.

Jack's eyes locked on my cleavage and he didn't look away until I snapped my fingers in front of his face.

"Hey," I said sharply. "Stare somewhere else."

"Bitch," he muttered, still stealing glances at my chest.

"Pervert," I hissed back. I really didn't like him.

Mike hadn't been kidding about how busy we'd be. The club soon grew packed with men, nearly shoulder-to-shoulder. My ears rang from some of the language and explicit propositions hurled my way—I'd never been called so many suggestively sexual slurs in all my life—but I stayed behind the bar and smiled, pocketing the money the same assholes laid down.

Chance had his hands full with the huge crowd, and he looked none too happy to see me. I ignored him and went about my work.

Shortly before midnight, a harried-looking Mike approached me.

"Hey, you," he said. I don't think he'd bothered learning my name. "I need two bottles of Hennessy in the Champagne Room, pronto."

"Got it," I replied.

After loading the bottles on a tray, I headed to the Champagne Room, the strip club's version of a VIP room. I'd only ever passed the door, never been inside. The door was painted black and nearly hidden behind a red velvet curtain. Deciding to forgo knocking, I walked right in.

If Kade had not taken me to that club in Denver, I would have been wholly unprepared for the scene that met my eyes.

The room was dark with shadows. Only small pools of red light emanated from obscure sources. Perhaps a dozen women in various states of undress littered the room. Men sat in several of the armchairs scattered around a small stage, where Lucy was dancing. The other women were either being fondled by the men, or engaged in various sexual acts being done by and/or to them.

I had stopped for a moment, still too shocked to move, when one of the girls caught my attention.

Appearing to be in her late teens, she was straddling a man in a chair, his mouth at her breasts, and looking at me over his head. Her eyes were strangely unfocused, her mouth slightly slack, and with a start I realized that she had the look of someone high or drugged.

Sickened, I made myself move, walking between the couples and chairs to the small bar in the far corner. My hands shook as I carefully set down the bottles of cognac.

"Pour me a glass, sugar."

I nearly knocked over one of the bottles. Turning, I saw it was Matt Summers.

Panic flared for a moment—I was afraid he would recognize me. Maybe it was the dark, or maybe it was his level of intoxication, but either way, there was no spark of recognition in his gaze, which was currently fastened to my breasts.

I silently handed a snifter of alcohol to him, but as I turned away, I was brought up short by his hand in the back waistband of my jeans. Jerking me back into him, I felt the press of his erection against the small of my back.

"Not so fast, sugar," he hissed in my ear. "Take off the bra. Let's have some fun."

Bile rose in my throat and I had to tamp down the panic that threatened.

"I'm not on the menu," I replied evenly.

"Well, you should be, with tits like that."

I would never understand men's fascination with breasts. At times it was useful to be well-endowed. Other times, like now, it was downright inconvenient. I tried to pull away, but his hand was still firmly lodged in my jeans.

"They real?" Matt asked.

When he started groping up my stomach to feel whether or not said endowments were "real," I decided I'd had enough.

I grabbed his groping hand, bent it downward, and pushed sharply back on his wrist. When he yelped, instinctively jerking his hand away, I raised my foot and brought the heel of my stiletto down sharply on his instep. As he grunted in pain and moved aside, I sent my fist into his groin.

Matt was doubled over when I spun around and grabbed his ear, pinching and yanking it hard between my fingers.

"You listen to me, you piece of shit," I hissed, bending so my mouth was inches from his ear. "You ever touch me again, I'll make sure your dick, tiny as it is, is rendered useless for the rest of your miserable life. You got that?"

I shoved him away and beat a hasty retreat to the door, not daring to breathe until I was back out in the hall. Heading to the bathroom, I took a moment to get myself back under control. My heart was beating wildly inside my chest, and my palms were damp. Slumping against the bathroom stall, I breathed.

In. Out. Repeat.

Deciding I was through with the stupid corset, I went back to the dressing room to put on a real shirt. But when I opened the door, the room wasn't empty.

A small boy sat curled on the tattered sofa in the corner. He looked up from the action figures in his hand when I stepped inside.

Nonplussed, we stared at each other for a moment. He couldn't have been more than five or six, his small frame belying the knowledge in his eyes. I had no idea who he was or how he'd even gotten in here. This was certainly no place for a child. Hell, it wasn't even a place for me.

"Hi," I said, easing onto the sofa next to him.

"Hi," he replied softly, his gaze dropping shyly back to the action figures. One was Batman, the other I couldn't identify.

"What's your name?" I asked.

"Billy."

"Nice to meet you, Billy," I said with a smile. "I'm Kathleen." I motioned to his toys. "Who's the bad guy?"

"Loki," he answered. "He goes with Thor, but I like Batman better."

"Batman's pretty cool," I agreed. "So, Billy. What are you doing in here?"

"Waiting."

"Waiting for?"

"My mom."

"Oh." I could think of nothing else to say. Which of the women was his mother?

"She's working."

He said that as though it wasn't a big deal, and my heart hurt a little at his innocence.

The door opened and we both looked up as Lucy stepped inside the room.

"Mom!" Billy declared happily, hopping down off the sofa and running to her. She caught him up in her arms, her eyes warily fixed on me.

"We were just chatting," I explained.

"Were you a good boy?" Lucy asked Billy. He nodded and she ruffled his hair. "Okay, get your toys. Time to go."

He came back to the couch and picked up his things, putting them in a small Spider-Man backpack. My eyes went back to Lucy, and realization struck.

This was why she'd told me to not interfere with her and Matt. He must know about Billy, must have a hold on her somehow. What mother wouldn't do whatever was required of her to keep her child safe?

"That's my mom," Billy said, jerking a thumb toward Lucy, "so I gotta go. Bye."

I forced a smile. "Bye, Billy."

"Luce, are you ready?"

My eyes widened in surprise to see Chance. Lucy gasped, shaking her head at him, her eyes cutting toward me. Chance glanced over, his lips thinning into a line when he saw me.

"I'll take care of it," he told Lucy in an undertone. "Just go. I'll be right behind you."

Grabbing Billy's hand, Lucy left without saying a word to me, leaving Chance and me alone.

"'Luce'?" I asked after a moment. "You know her?"

Chance rubbed a tired hand across his face. "You could say that," he muttered.

A thought occurred to me and I blurted, "You're not . . . that's not . . . Billy's not your son, is he?"

"No, nothing like that," Chance denied. "But you can't say anything to anyone. He'll kill her."

"Who?"

"Matt. I'm trying to help her, but if he gets wind of it, he won't think twice." He glanced out the door. "I've gotta go. Keep your head down and your mouth shut, okay?"

I nodded, our eyes meeting in a moment of mutual understanding, before he left, following Lucy and Billy out the door.

I heaved a sigh. My foolish innocence seemed like a weight on my shoulders. People were in horrible situations all around me, and I was clueless as to anything I might be able to do to help. I felt powerless in a way I hadn't ever felt before. Not to mention that my problems seemed pitiful in comparison to Lucy's.

I managed to avoid Mike and Matt for the rest of the evening, helping Jack clean up after closing as quickly as I could. Turning to Jack, I said, "I'm heading home."

He ignored me, which I took to mean he didn't care, so I grabbed my purse and coat and headed out the door.

I emerged from the stifling, smoky club into the crisp, clean air of the outdoors. It had been hot inside and I was sweating. Sometime during the evening, it had begun to snow, fat flakes falling from the dark sky. The ground was warm, though, and the snow was only sticking to the grass and not the pavement.

I shivered, but the cold felt good. And it was blessedly quiet. Walking around the corner of the building toward the employee parking, I paused and leaned back against the wall. Closing my eyes, I heaved a sigh. Some Valentine's Day.

Surrounded by men, none of whom I wanted. This had to be the worst Valentine's Day ever.

"How many times have I told you to clear the shadows before assuming you're alone?"

I gasped, my eyes flying open, though I knew that voice.

Kade stepped into the dim circle of light cast by the streetlamp. The icy blue of his eyes sucked me in, and I stood unmoving while he came closer. I was thrown back in time to when I'd first met him, the aura of danger surrounding him nearly palpable. He moved through the inky darkness as though he were a part of it, never taking his eyes off mine.

My senses seemed heightened by his presence. I was suddenly acutely conscious of the hushed quiet that only snow can bring, the tiny bits of sharp cold as the snowflakes fell on my skin and melted away.

Then I remembered how he'd fired me.

"What do you want?" I asked stiffly.

He didn't reply immediately, not until he was only an arm's length away. "I was in the neighborhood."

I snorted. "Right." Something occurred to me and I tossed him my car keys, which he caught reflexively. "I'm guessing you came for the car. No job, no wheels, right?" I'd temporarily forgotten I was driving a car owned by the firm.

Kade's jaw grew tight. "Like I give a shit about the damn car."

"Then why are you here?" I shot back.

"I could ask the same," another voice said.

Jerking around, my eyes widened to see Blane approaching. Dressed similarly to Kade, in jeans and a black leather jacket, he didn't stop until he was quite close, the two of them flanking me. Blane's body towered over mine, his stance protective. Though the only threat I could see was . . . Kade. Blane glanced at me, but his gray eyes gave nothing away.

"Why the midnight visit?" he asked Kade.

Kade's lips twisted. "I fired her, but as usual, she decided to play the brainless twit and come in tonight. I was just ensuring she made it home, brother."

My temper flared even as his words hurt. I opened my mouth to protest, but Blane spoke first.

"Well, I'm here now, so you can go."

Blane's body was stiff, his face unyielding as he studied Kade. Kade's eyes narrowed at the challenge in Blane's voice. I glanced anxiously between them, hoping there wouldn't be a repeat of last night's confrontation.

"A politician like yourself shouldn't be around a place like this," Kade remarked easily. "One grainy photo on the news and you can kiss your career good-bye."

I stiffened in alarm, realizing this was absolutely true. It hadn't even occurred to me. "We're closed, Blane," I said quickly, laying a hand on his arm. "I was just going home. Let's go."

Anything he might have said was interrupted by a woman's shrill scream, shattering the quiet.

CHAPTER TWELVE

What was—"

I didn't get the chance to say anything further. Blane's hand covered my mouth as he jerked me into his arms, pressing my back against his chest. Then he was moving us, lifting me off my feet and melting into the shadows. Kade followed, gun in his hand, covering Blane's blind spot.

It happened so fast. Before my heart could beat more than a half dozen times, the three of us were concealed in the darkness behind the building. I was sandwiched snugly between Blane and Kade, and Blane finally took his hand off my mouth to pull his gun from its holster. His other arm stayed firmly locked around my waist, as though I were planning to go somewhere, which I so wasn't.

My heart was beating a rapid staccato against my rib cage, adrenaline heightening my senses and sharpening my fear. I clutched the back of Kade's jacket with one hand, the other tightly gripping Blane's encircling arm.

Kade carefully peered around the building.

"Looks like they're taking some girls out of the club," he said softly to Blane. "They're loading them into a white van."

"It must be the girls that were in the Champagne Room tonight," I said, just as quietly.

Kade looked at me while Blane was silent.

"There were men having sex with them," I explained, "including Matt Summers. The girls, they were drugged or something. Their eyes . . . it's like they didn't know or didn't care what was happening." I shuddered, the vacant expression in the one girl's eyes still burning in my mind. "We have to help them."

"Not going to happen," Kade said flatly. "Not with you here."

"We can't just let them take them," I protested. I looked up at Blane. "Please," I implored. "Do something. God knows where they'll end up if we don't help them."

"Kade's right, Kat," Blane said. "They're all armed. Not only you, but the other women could get hurt."

"Then you just have to not use guns," I argued, a plan forming in my head. "I have an idea." When I quickly laid it out, both Blane and Kade looked furious.

"Don't give me those looks," I snapped. "It could work and you know it."

I wriggled to get out of Blane's grip, pushing at his arm. "Let me go," I demanded.

He reluctantly dropped his arm and I quickly shed my coat. The tension in Blane's body increased tenfold when he got an eyeful of my outfit, but I refused to look at him. Kade just snorted.

"See you in a minute, guys."

They looked dark and deadly in the shadows, the two of them, weapons ready in their hands. Before I could turn away, Blane pulled me close for a quick press of his lips against mine.

"Be careful," he said.

I nodded, my eyes darting uncomfortably to Kade, whose face was like stone.

Taking a deep breath and readjusting my assets inside my corset, I walked around the corner of the building.

"Hey, whatcha doin'?" I called out, wobbling on my heels as though I were drunk.

To my relief, they were still handing women inside the van, though I noticed that each woman was holding her hands in such a way that they must be bound.

Two of the men jerked around toward me, guns at the ready, and I tried not to panic, praying their fingers weren't snappy on the triggers. When they saw an apparently drunken woman tottering toward them, they both relaxed.

"I'm lookin' for my boyfriend," I called out, coming closer. "Y'all seen him?"

Two of the men quickly conversed, one gesturing toward me.

I faked a trip, falling down on the concrete and giggling like a mad hyena.

"Go get her," one of the men ordered, and I braced myself, sitting back on my heels.

"Give me a hand, would ya?" I asked as two men approached me.

Well, I hadn't counted on two of them coming for me, but I couldn't back out now.

They slung their guns behind their backs, the straps stretching across their chests. One on each side of me, both reached for my arms to pull me to my feet.

"I think I'm going to be sick," I moaned. They both hesitated, and I took my chance.

My fist shot out to land hard in one man's crotch. He immediately doubled over, grunting in pain. The other guy was still frozen in surprise when I reached up, grabbed the gun strap around his chest, and yanked downward with all my strength. His face met the back of the other guy's head with a crack, and blood spurted from his nose.

I heard commotion by the van and chanced a quick glance at Blane and Kade. They had rounded the building to take the remaining men by surprise.

The guy whose family jewels I'd nailed had fallen to the ground, his hands cupping his crotch, but the other guy had recovered from his head slam. He yanked his gun around and aimed it in the direction of Blane and Kade.

Panic hit and I launched myself to my feet and tackled him, gun and all. We hit the concrete with a thud.

Spitting out rapid-fire Spanish, the man threw me off. When I came back at him, he swung his rifle, the butt catching me in the temple with brutal force.

I collapsed to the ground and he shoved me out of the way with his booted foot. I was facedown against the cold, wet concrete. I couldn't move, the pain was excruciating, and I fought to stay conscious, a groan escaping me.

Gunshots rang out, and terror gripped me. Who had fired the shots? Had Blane or Kade been hit? Then I couldn't fight it anymore, and darkness overtook me.

～

"Is she all right?"

"Does she look all right to you?"

"Why the hell would you let her do something like that—"

"You obviously don't know her very well if you think there was a way to stop her."

"I know her better than you ever will, I can guaran-damn-tee you that."

"I wouldn't lay odds on that, boy scout."

"Will you two shut the fuck up?"

I groaned, the pain in my head feeling as though it had taken over my whole body. Prying my eyes open, I saw three anxious faces peering down at me. Blane. Kade. Chance.

I groaned again and shut my eyes, wishing I were still unconscious.

Blane was crouched next to me. "Kat, how do you feel?" he asked gently.

Reluctantly opening my eyes, I focused on Blane. "Like I got hit in the head," I rasped. I lifted a hand toward my head, but Blane caught my wrist.

"Don't touch it. You're bleeding."

"What happened?" I asked. "I heard gunshots . . ."

"Boy scout here shot the guy who hit you," Kade answered, nodding toward Chance. "Turns out he has a badge. But you already knew that, didn't you, princess?" His glare held accusation and I nervously looked away.

"You told them?" I asked Chance.

"Had to," Chance replied grimly. "They were going to shoot first, ask questions later. Especially him." He glared malevolently at Kade.

"I'm still considering it," Kade drawled.

"Stop fighting," I groused, easing upright. Blane's arm curved supportively behind my back. I stood, the blood rushing from my head making me weave slightly.

"Take it easy," Blane admonished, his arm tightening.

Both Chance and Kade started forward, as though to catch me if I fell.

I threw up a hand to ward them off. "I'm fine."

Sirens wailed in the distance. "You two get out of here," Chance ordered. "And take her with you. I'll deal with the police, and pray this little rescue operation hasn't blown my cover all to hell."

Blane didn't respond, his attention still focused on me. "You okay to walk?" he asked.

I nodded.

Kade tossed my keys to Chance. "Take her car back to her apartment when you're done."

In a quicker amount of time than I could believe, Blane had hustled me to his car, with Kade walking closely at my side. Once I was ensconced in the passenger seat, Blane turned to Kade.

"I've got her," he said.

"So I see," Kade replied dryly. "I'll come along for the ride." He slid into the backseat.

Blane was left with no choice but to shut my door and round the car to get in the driver's side.

The tension in the car was thick. Blane and Kade were both silent as Blane drove. I reflected grimly that this was the second time in as many days that I was locked in a confined space with the two of them. It wasn't any more appealing now than it had been last night.

I realized Blane was driving to his house. "Why aren't you taking me home?" I asked.

"You got hit in the head," he replied. "I should be taking you to a hospital . . ."

He glanced at me. I was already shaking my head. "But I know you won't go. So someone needs to keep an eye on you tonight."

"I volunteer," Kade piped in. "Especially if she's going to wear that."

I shot him a glare. The last thing I needed, or wanted, was him antagonizing Blane.

Kade feigned innocence. "What? Hey, it's better than what you wore in Denver."

In my peripheral vision, I saw Blane's hands tighten on the steering wheel. If I could have climbed over the seat and strangled Kade, I gladly would have.

"Just take me home," I told Blane. "Chance will be there soon. He'll stay with me."

Silence.

"Two men aren't enough, princess? You need a third?"

"What the fuck, Kade!" Blane exploded. "Give it a rest!"

I stared at them. "Is that what you think?"

When neither of them answered, anger flared. "Chance is my cousin," I bit out. "He didn't want me to tell either one of you because he doesn't trust you."

"Your cousin is William Turner," Blane argued. "Not Chance."

Kade groaned, laying his head back against the seat. "Now I remember. Chance. That's his middle name."

"He hates the name William," I confirmed.

"Well, now don't I feel like a douche," Kade groused.

My lips twitched into a smile in spite of myself.

Blane glanced my way, and our eyes caught. "You could've told me," he said softly.

"Chance knows you're defending Summers," I said with a small shrug.

Blane didn't reply, the stiff set of his body a reminder of the gulf between us when it came to this case.

"Matt Summers was with those women tonight," I said. "Did I mention that?"

That got Blane's attention.

"What the hell are you talking about?" Kade asked.

"Matt Summers was in the Champagne Room with some other men and those drugged women at the club," I explained. "I went inside—"

"You what?" exclaimed Blane.

"And he hit on me," I finished, ignoring Blane's interruption. "If you want to call it as nice a term as that."

We pulled into Blane's driveway and he stopped the car with a jerk and turned to me. "And you can't possibly understand why I don't want you doing this job anymore?" he bit out. "Why I no longer want to pay you to risk your life? You think I want you to watch someone get raped right in front of you? Know that some guy like Matt could just grab you, force you, anytime they want?"

"Then why the hell are you trying to get that bastard off?" I yelled back.

"I'm doing what I have to do! If I don't get Matt off, *you* go to jail!"

I went utterly still, stunned. "What are you talking about?"

"David Summers found out about what happened in Chicago, between you and Stephen Avery. His prints were in your room and yours in his. If I don't get Matt off for him, he's going to give it to the police. You'll be charged with murder.

"So don't tell me what I should or shouldn't do, what's right or wrong," he bit out. "I'll do what I have to do."

I paled in the face of his anger and this new information. My hand shook as I grappled with the door handle, practically falling out of the car in my haste. Then Kade was there, holding me upright.

"Quit fucking yelling at her," he growled at Blane, who'd gotten out and rounded the car.

"This is all your fault." Blane pushed his finger into Kade's chest.

"Oh really." Kade got up in Blane's face. "So what should I have done then, brother? She was naked. Avery was suffocating her while he whipped her with a fucking belt. And that was after I got there. God knows what he did before."

All the blood rushed from my face and I threw out a hand on the car, steadying my suddenly weak knees. "Kade, stop," I implored him, my voice feeble in my own ears. Just as quickly as I'd gone pale, heat infused my face at what he was divulging to Blane, the embarrassment and shame of what had happened with Avery shredding my dignity.

Neither of them seemed to hear me. Blane looked murderous, his face like granite and his jaw locked tight. Kade just looked disgusted.

"So don't tell me about whose fault this is," he snarled at Blane. "It's Avery's fucking fault. If I hadn't been there, she'd be dead. But if you're anxious to spread blame, I'd look in the mirror. If you didn't have the need to be the fucking hero all the time, you wouldn't have made the deal with Summers."

"You'd rather she be arrested for murder?" Blane spat back.

I felt close to hyperventilating. I was breathing too fast, trying to keep up with what Blane had said about the deal he'd made with Summers. Now it all made sense, why he had taken the case. But Blane and Kade were caught up fighting with each other, and the hostility between them was white-hot and dangerous.

I didn't know what to do, how to get them to dial it back. They shouldn't be fighting, they were on the same side. So although it left a sour taste in my mouth, I did the only thing I could think of that would tear their attention away from each other.

Pushing myself away from the car, I got close to them, one hand resting on each of their chests as I insinuated myself between them. They both looked at me, seeming almost surprised.

"Please," I implored. "I don't feel well. I really need to lie down. Help me inside?"

The ploy had the desired result. Blane immediately wrapped an arm around my waist, and Kade stepped back.

"Would you get my purse, please?" I asked Kade.

His lips twitched as he did as I requested, and I had the feeling both of them knew exactly what I was doing. Not that I cared. They'd stopped looking like they were going to rip each other apart, and that was all that mattered.

Once we were inside, I turned to Blane. "I want to change."

He said nothing, just watched me as I collected my purse and climbed the stairs. I gratefully shed the skintight jeans and corset, vowing to burn them at some point, and pulled on a T-shirt and pair of yoga pants that I kept in the closet. The cut on my head wasn't as bad as it had seemed. After washing my face and combing out my hair, I felt nearly like myself again, and ready to face the two men waiting for me downstairs.

I'd guessed correctly on their location and activity, as I found both of them in the library, each with a stiff drink in hand. Kade was in an elegant sprawl on the leather couch, while Blane stood, brooding as he stared at the fire dancing merrily in the grate.

I opted to curl up in the leather wingback chair, tucking my bare feet under me. The fire gave off a cozy warmth that relaxed my tense muscles. I breathed a tired sigh.

Blane approached to stand over me and run the back of his knuckles down my cheek. "Feel better?" he asked.

I nodded, too worn out to speak. The adrenaline rush from earlier had worn off and I found myself slumping in the chair, exhaustion hitting me hard. Blane pulled a blanket off the couch, unfolded it, and draped it over me.

"I'm sorry," I murmured. Guilt about what Blane was going through, what he'd been dealing with on my behalf, lay heavy on me. Summers was blackmailing him, and I was the cause.

"Don't be," Blane replied quietly. "I should have told you."

That seemed to be a recurring theme, but I was too tired to go into all that. My eyes were heavy and my blinks were slow.

Blane stepped away and my eyes met Kade's, who was staring intently at me from where he sat. I couldn't decipher the look in his eyes, but neither could I look away.

My eyes drifted shut and I fell into the quiet lethargy that presages slumber, where everything has a dreamlike quality and I couldn't tell if I was awake or asleep. The voices of Blane and Kade washed over me as they quietly spoke, the tones and lilts of their conversation comforting me, underscored by the crackling of the fire.

There was a buzzing and the rustle of clothes.

"A client texted me. I need to go out for a while," Blane said.

"Go. I'll watch her."

"I should take her upstairs."

"You'll wake her."

"She looks uncomfortable."

"She's fine. Go do what you gotta do."

A sigh. "All right. Hopefully, I won't be long."

Silence.

"Kade . . . I shouldn't have said that. Earlier. I never knew . . . she never told me . . . what happened with Avery. Not specifically. I was wrong to blame you."

"You would've killed him, too, if you'd been there."

More silence.

"She cares about you, you know. Cares what happens to you, that you're safe."

"Yeah."

"You don't have many friends."

"No."

"Then I'll tell you what you told me. Don't fuck it up."

There was quiet again, broken only by the rustling of cloth and the softness of footsteps on carpet, then a more complete quiet. I sank deeper into slumber.

~

When I woke, it was still dark, the fire having burned down to mere embers and casting only a dim glow around the room. Sitting up, I felt a crick in my neck that made me groan.

"What's wrong?" Kade was there, crouching down next to me.

"Nothing," I replied blearily, rubbing my neck. "Just scrunched."

"I'll help you upstairs." He got to his feet and lifted me in his arms. Instinctively I looped my arms around his neck.

"What are you doing?" I asked, chagrined. "Put me down. I can walk."

"I know you can." He headed out of the room and to the stairs.

"I don't need you to carry me," I insisted.

"I need to."

His simple reply took me aback, and I gazed up at him. He didn't look at me, his eyes focused on the path up the stairs and down the darkened hallway to my room. I had no choice but to accept his assistance, resting my head against his shoulder as he walked.

When he reached my bedroom, he placed me gently on the bed and pulled a blanket up over me. Then he lay down beside me, bending an arm behind his head and staring up at the ceiling.

I turned on my side to face him. "Thank you," I said.

"No worries."

Something was wrong, different. I stared at him, trying to puzzle out what it was.

"Are you still mad at me?" I asked.

"I was never mad at you."

He was quiet then, and I didn't know what to say either, so I remained silent.

"Are you my friend?" he asked.

The question surprised me. "Of course I'm your friend. Why wouldn't I be?"

Kade turned to look at me, his eyes glittering in the ambient light from the window. "Because of who I am. You can't separate what you do from who you are, and you were right. My hands are steeped in blood, and it's never going to go away."

My heart broke for him. "You're not a bad person."

"You wouldn't know," Kade argued. "You see only the good in people, or what you think is good. There's no good in me. Not anymore."

"That's not true," I protested. "I know it's not."

Kade turned away, his eyes sliding shut. "Sometimes I wish I could turn back the clock, make different decisions," he murmured. "But some things are unavoidable, and can't be undone."

His words troubled me. After a few moments, I asked, "Kade?"

"Hmm?"

"Why did you leave the FBI?"

His eyes opened and his head turned my way. "You really wanna know?"

I nodded.

He sighed and turned back to stare at the ceiling again. "Because of Blane."

That was definitely not the answer I'd been expecting. "Blane?"

"He got back from deployment, and it was rough on him for a while, the transition. All the pent-up aggression that's great for when you're at war doesn't translate so well to civilian life. I was on the road a lot, so I wasn't around. It took me a little while to see the problem. Blane's too proud to ask for help. I quit so I could be with him when he needed me. God knows he'd been there for me. It was the least I could do."

I stared at him. "You gave up your career in the FBI to help Blane?" A part of me was shocked. But another part of me, the part that seemed to know more about Kade than I wanted to acknowledge, that part wasn't surprised at all.

"Not a big deal," Kade said with a shrug. "But I gave Blane some song and dance about wanting to fly solo."

"Why didn't you tell him the truth?"

"Because he doesn't need to know. He carries around enough guilt for both of us. So if you feel like sharing that with him"—he turned to look me in the eye—"don't."

His tone left no room for argument. I gave a jerky nod and closed my eyes.

~

When I woke again, it was light outside and I was pressed snugly against Kade, who appeared to be sleeping soundly. Alarm shot through me at the position of our bodies, and I prayed Blane wouldn't suddenly walk through the door.

Careful to not wake him, I eased out of Kade's grasp, rolling out of bed and slipping out of the room. Once I was in the hallway, I let out my breath.

It was early, but my pressing need for the bathroom had me heading to the closest one, in Blane's room. He wasn't in there, so I assumed he was already downstairs. The bed had been made and the curtains on the windows pulled back to reveal a sunny day, the snow already melting from the few areas it had covered last night.

The bathroom smelled of his soap and cologne. I took a deep breath, a pang echoing inside my chest. I missed him. It didn't seem to matter, the arguments we'd had or my pushing away his overprotectiveness. I needed him, wanted him.

I showered, towel-drying my hair the best I could. I didn't want to wake Kade by rummaging around in my room for different clothes, so I wrapped myself in Blane's robe, which I knew he never wore. The hem came down past my knees, and I rolled up the sleeves. My hair was a damp, tangled mass of loose curls and waves, but there wasn't anything I could do about that, since my brush was in the other bathroom.

When I came out, I found Blane sitting in the chair by the window, his elbows resting on his spread knees, his hands loosely clasped. He was dressed casually, in jeans and a long-sleeved shirt. He sat up and our eyes met.

"How's your head?" he asked.

I walked over to him. "It's all right. Just a bruise and a small cut."

Taking my hand, he tugged me to stand between his thighs so he could inspect the sore spot at my temple. I winced as he lightly touched the raised bump.

"You're lucky," he observed. "He could have shot you instead."

There was nothing to say to that—it was the truth—so I changed the subject. "Why didn't you tell me about Summers blackmailing you about what happened with Avery?" It was hard to look him in the eye, knowing that he now knew the lurid details of that night.

"Why didn't you tell me what Avery did to you?" Blane responded with a question of his own.

"It was done. He was dead. What was the purpose in telling you?"

Blane just looked at me for a moment, the sadness in his eyes making me squirm uncomfortably. "To share it with me. To let me comfort you," he said. "You were hiding it, weren't you? The marks. The day we came back and we made love, it hurt when I touched you, but you wouldn't let me see."

I looked away, unable to meet his penetrating gaze.

"Why, Kat?" The hurt in his voice was my undoing.

"Because I didn't want you to think less of me."

"Why would I think less of you?"

"Because. Because I couldn't stop him. Because of how he made me feel. Because of how I was afraid you'd—"

I cut myself off.

"Afraid I'd what?" he prompted.

"Afraid you'd see me . . . differently," I finished.

Blane pulled me down onto his lap, cupping my chin and forcing me to look at him. We were nearly eye to eye. "I would never use anything that happened to you against you, or as a reason for not being with you. It wasn't your fault. You're not weak."

His thumb brushed my cheek, and his lips settled gently over mine in a kiss that was pure and sweet in its tenderness.

When he finally pulled away, a piece of my heart seemed to finally accept that what he felt for me was real. Maybe I could trust this intangible thing between us, binding us together.

"I never thought," he said softly, "that I'd feel this way, that I'd want to feel this way, about someone. I've spent so many years turning off my emotions, believing they made me weak. I was better, stronger, without them. Being a SEAL taught me that."

I barely breathed, listening to him, afraid that if I moved too much, breathed too hard, he'd stop talking.

The corner of his mouth lifted. "Then you came along, squeezed between the fissures, and cracked me wide open."

Any words I might have said seemed desperately inadequate for the situation, so I wrapped my arms around him, hugging him tightly. I was gratified that his grip around me was just as solid.

"I love you, too," I said, my voice husky with emotion.

"I have something for you," he said, reaching into his pocket. Taking my hand, he turned it palm up before depositing what he held.

My mouth fell open in surprise. A shimmering strand of pearls rested in my palm, spilling between my fingers.

"Blane, I . . . I don't know what to say," I stammered.

"Turn around," Blane said, taking the strand from me.

I did as I was told, lifting my hair out of the way as his hands moved to fasten the necklace on me.

"They say pearls are the moon's tears," Blane said quietly. "Or that maybe they're from angels' wings, moving through a cloud. They're beautiful in their purity, striking in their innocence, humbling in their integrity."

The pearls lay warm against my throat and I dropped my hair, turning back to face Blane.

"Just like you," he said simply.

I couldn't help the stupid smile on my face. "That's the most romantic thing anyone's ever said to me."

Blane's lips twitched, as though he were thinking about smiling, and there was no mistaking the warmth in his eyes. "Does that mean you'll have dinner with me tonight?"

"Without question." My hand rested on the perfectly matched pearls. "It appears I can be bought."

Blane laughed, the rumble in his chest making my smile even wider. "I don't know if you're interested, but some buddies of mine are in town. They wanted to meet up tonight. I'd like you to meet them."

"I'd love to. Who are they?"

"Some guys I was in the Navy with, other SEALs. Eric will be there. You know him."

"Dr. Sanchez?"

Blane nodded.

"Absolutely," I said, looping my arms around his neck. "I'd love to meet your friends."

I felt like this was a big step in our relationship. While I knew people at the office, Mona, Senator Keaston and his wife, and, of course, Kade, I hadn't met people who knew a different side of Blane. The people who had gone to war with him, who'd had his back in life-and-death situations—those people I had a burning curiosity to know.

"I need to get home, Tigger's going to be mad at me if I'm gone much longer, but you can pick me up tonight."

"Sounds good. I have to go in to the office today. Charlotte and I need to prep for court tomorrow."

I buried the niggle of jealousy that comment produced.

"But I will pick you up at seven," he continued. "And in the interest of staying in your good graces, I have a favor to ask."

I raised my eyebrows in silent question.

"Do something fun today. Go get Alisha and go shopping, get a massage, have lunch. Here, take my card." Reaching inside his jacket, he pulled out his wallet, extracted a credit card, and handed it to me.

I handled the plastic gingerly, looking at him as though he'd lost his mind. "You want me," I said in disbelief, "to go shopping, and spend your money doing it."

"Hard to believe, but yes," he said, his tone dry.

I forced back the grin that threatened. "Don't be silly," I admonished him. "I'm not going to go blow your money on clothes and getting pampered. I'm a working girl. I need to go job-hunting."

"Forget the job thing," he interrupted me. "Just for a few days. Do this for me. Go, have some girl time, be unproductive for once, and don't worry about it, okay?"

Blane was very earnest about this, which seemed odd.

"I guess," I said reluctantly. "If that's what you want?"

"I do. And I'll pick you up at seven."

"All right." I straddled his lap, pressing my knees on either side of him . "But don't be late."

"I will promise not to be late," he replied, "if you promise to model the pearls for me after dinner."

"Of course I will."

"*Only* the pearls."

Several images went through my mind, making me shiver. Then he was kissing me until I couldn't think straight, his hands pulling open the sides of the robe, baring my body for his strokes and caresses.

"I can model them now if you want," I breathed, my heart racing.

Blane groaned. "Don't tempt me. I have to go or I'll be late. Charlotte's probably waiting at the office for me."

His hands seemed reluctant to leave my skin, but after a moment he'd risen from the chair, putting some space between us.

"I could get used to this," he said. At my questioning look, he continued. "You being the last person I see before I leave for the day and the first person I'll see when I come home."

I was absurdly pleased with that statement.

"Then I'll try to make it worth your while tonight," I teased.

"Have fun. Stay out of trouble," he said, running a hand through his hair to straighten the mussed locks. His lips were wet and slightly swollen, which only made him look more appealing.

I straightened the robe so I was once again covered, trying to ignore the claws of the little green monster digging in at the thought of him being with Charlotte all day.

"Blane," I began hesitantly. "What are you going to do? About Summers? You're not going to get him off, are you? Do you and Kade have a plan?"

The thought of Blane being blackmailed into defending Summers because of something that had happened to *me* made me sick to my stomach, much less the possibility of Blane succeeding in a not-guilty verdict.

His jaw tightened. "I'm working on it."

I nodded, and before I could decide whether or not to press the issue, he was gone.

Going to the window, I watched until I saw him get in his car and leave.

"There you are."

I started in surprise. Kade was standing behind me, dripping wet and wearing nothing but a white towel.

"Barney Fife's been blowing up your phone," he said, holding the offending object out to me.

I frowned in confusion before I realized he meant Chance.

"Nice," I hissed, grabbing the phone. He only smirked.

"Hello?"

"Strawbs, it's me," Chance said.

"What's going on? Did the cops take care of those women last night?"

"Yeah, they're fine, and my cover's not blown, thank God," he answered. "Hey, I could use your help today, if you've got time."

I thought Kade would leave, but he remained in the room watching me as water dripped from his body onto the carpet. The towel concealed little, especially when damp and wrapped so low around his hips. I was surprised it hadn't yet fallen off. My face heated at the thought and I quickly turned away, focusing on Chance's voice in my ear.

"Sure. What do you need?"

"A babysitter."

CHAPTER THIRTEEN

I scooted past Kade and headed to the other bedroom. I needed clothes if I was going to babysit Lucy's son for a few hours today. Chance hadn't told me why they'd needed me and I hadn't asked. If I could help, I would.

"What did he want?" Kade asked, and I realized he'd followed me.

"I'm trying to get dressed," I said crossly. "Do you mind?"

"Not a bit," he drawled, crossing his arms over his bare chest and leaning against the wall.

I rolled my eyes and stepped inside the walk-in closet, pulling the door closed behind me.

"You were telling me what he wanted," Kade said loud enough for me to hear him through the door.

I shrugged out of the robe, dropping it to the floor, then abruptly realized there were no underthings in the closet. Well, damn it.

"He, uh, wants me to babysit today," I answered, cracking the door a smidge. "Hey, get me some . . ." I faltered. "You know. Out of the drawer. Behind you."

My cheeks turned hot at his smirk and I glared at him until he turned to rummage through the bureau.

"Whose kid are you watching?" He alternatively held up scraps of satin and lace before discarding them.

"One of the dancers—her name is Lucy—she has a little boy," I explained, impatiently waiting as he perused the choices. "Will you just pick something?"

"Got it," he said, returning to stand much too close to the door. "Open up."

"Just give them to me," I said, exasperated.

He huffed an exaggerated sigh and pushed his hand through the opening. I snatched the fabric dangling from his finger.

"Thank you," I said, then immediately reconsidered the sentiment in light of what he'd given me—a tiny lace thong in the palest of pinks with a matching bra. Nice.

Whatever. I had to get moving. I pulled on the underwear that barely deserved the name, as well as a pair of jeans and black turtleneck. I left my locket on under my shirt. The pearls I wore on the outside. When I stepped out of the closet, Kade had dressed—he was wearing a pair of jeans and a shirt, though neither was buttoned.

I was taming my hair into a French braid when I caught sight of Kade standing in the bathroom doorway, watching me.

Several minutes went by while I brushed and braided. "What?" I finally asked. He was making me nervous.

He shook his head. "It's nothing."

The expression on his face was similar to one he'd worn last night, and when I'd fastened my braid, I turned to him. "Tell me."

I almost thought he was going to answer me, then one corner of his mouth lifted in a humorless smile. "Some other time, princess."

I was still going to pursue it when he asked, "Need a ride?"

"Actually, yeah."

A few minutes later, we were heading to my apartment. I squinted in the sunlight, envying Kade his dark sunglasses.

Kade drove in silence, and I didn't break it. Things felt tenuous between Kade and me, like I was walking a tightrope. I couldn't read him, couldn't tell what the status of our friendship really was.

"Nice pearls," he said, out of the blue.

"Um, thanks." My fingers instinctively moved to touch the smooth stones at my neck. "Blane gave them to me. For Valentine's Day, I guess."

"They were his mother's."

I stared at him. Blane's mother? He'd given me her pearls? I didn't know what to say.

"So what are you going to do about a job?" he asked a few minutes later.

I looked at him. His face was unreadable and I couldn't see his eyes under the glasses. I shrugged. "I guess I'll go back to The Drop."

"And then what?"

"I don't know." I was getting irritated. "I had this new job, but got fired all of a sudden like." Kade sent me a look that had me rethinking getting lippy with him.

"What are you doing today?" I asked.

"I have a contract I need to fill."

My blood went cold as I stared at him. He couldn't possibly mean what I thought he meant, that he was going to kill someone today?

"What kind of contract?" I asked.

291

He spared me a glance. "What kind do you think?" The wry tone of the words gave me a sick feeling in my stomach.

"You don't have to . . . it's not right . . . just don't—"

"Relax," Kade interrupted. "It's a hack, not a hit."

I breathed a sigh of relief, the sick feeling in my gut easing. So he was hacking into something today and not killing someone. Then it occurred to me that the last time he'd told me he'd hacked something, it had been a government agency. The nausea was back.

"How are you going to do that with all your stuff gone?"

"I've got my laptop," Kade replied with a shrug. "Nothing's irreplaceable." He paused, then added, "Well, almost nothing."

We pulled into an empty space in my parking lot. Kade left the engine idling while I grabbed my things. My hand reached for the door handle, but I hesitated.

"Are we"—I searched for the right word—"still friends?"

"Is that what you want?"

I nodded. "I'm sorry for what I said the other night. I didn't mean it."

He studied me and I wished again that I could see his eyes.

"Sure you did," he said finally, the corner of his mouth twisting. "But we're good. So go. I'm sure Barney's waiting for you."

The reminder of Chance stopped me from saying anything else, knowing this wasn't the time or place to continue the conversation.

"Thanks for the ride," I said, climbing out and shutting the door behind me.

The window rolled down. "Be careful," Kade said. "Don't do anything stupid."

I bent down to look in the window. "I'm babysitting," I explained. "Not skydiving."

Kade smirked. "Only you could turn babysitting into a life-threatening endeavor."

I rolled my eyes. "Hey, when do you want me to bring the SUV back to the firm?"

I'd have to get a new car eventually, though I was hoping they'd let me have a couple of weeks to find one I could afford. No doubt it would be a huge step down from the luxurious Lexus I now drove, but it was what it was.

"Keep it," Kade replied with a wave of his hand.

I was taken aback. "I can't keep it," I protested. "The firm owns it."

"No they don't. I lied."

I stared at him, jaw agape. He'd lied about the firm buying the car?

"Why?" I asked. Why had he bought it? And why had he lied?

Kade shrugged. "It seemed like a good idea at the time. And you needed it."

I couldn't think what to say, my mind reeling. He'd spent thousands of dollars buying me a car just because he'd seen how much I'd needed it.

"Why would you spend that much money on me?"

Kade slid his glasses down, peering at me over the top. "Who else do I have to spend it on?"

I didn't speak, caught by the look in his eyes, which contrasted starkly with the matter-of-fact way in which he spoke.

"Catch you later, princess."

Then he was gone and I was left staring after the Mercedes receding in the distance.

Chance arrived not thirty seconds after I stepped into my apartment, Billy in tow.

"Lucy's in the car," he said, handing me Billy's Spider-Man backpack. "This is just for a few hours."

"Are you going to tell me what's going on?" I asked.

"Lucy's been with Summers for years," Chance said in an undertone, pulling me aside. Billy and Tigger were eyeing each other with mutual suspicion. "She's seen everything, knows everything. In return for protection, she's going to be a witness against him.

"Just keep Billy occupied for a few hours," he said. "I'll call when we're on our way back."

A few moments later, it was just Billy, me, and Tigger, who seemed to have gotten over his momentary aversion and was now curled half on, half off Billy's lap, purring loudly as Billy scratched his ears.

I surveyed Billy. He was playing with the same action figures he had the other night.

"Hey, Billy," I said, "what do you say to doing some shopping today?"

He looked at me dubiously. "What kind of shopping?"

"For toys. Would you like that?"

I didn't have to ask him twice.

We spent the next several hours shopping for the latest and greatest Batman action figures. Since I was a Superman fan, I convinced him he also needed the Man of Steel. It wasn't until we were eating at a pizza joint that my cell rang. The caller ID said it was Blane.

"Having fun?" he asked.

"I am," I replied as Billy reached for another slice of pizza. Batman and Superman stood as a sentinels on the corner of the table, their various archenemies trapped by Spidey's web inside the backpack.

"My credit card company called," he said.

Uh-oh. I started to panic, adding up how much I'd spent in my head. It wasn't terribly much.

"They were inquiring as to whether my card had been lost or stolen, because I have never in my life purchased anything from an establishment devoted to children's toys."

I laughed, relaxing.

"Is there something you want to tell me?" Blane asked.

I flushed, remembering how we'd thought perhaps I might be pregnant a few weeks ago, which had turned out to be a false alarm. "I'm babysitting," I explained. "The little guy needed some things, and I didn't, so I shopped for him instead. Is that okay?"

"It's fine," he replied. "And why am I not surprised that you'd find someone else to spend money on instead of yourself?"

I squirmed uncomfortably. It wasn't like I was Mother Teresa. I just didn't see what was fun about blowing money on things I didn't need. It seemed like a waste.

"Are we still on for tonight?" I asked, wanting to change the subject.

"Absolutely," he replied. "It will be the best part of my day."

"Me, too."

A bowling alley nearby provided the afternoon's entertainment, and if I'd cared, I would have been embarrassed at the fact that I needed the bumpers as much as Billy did to get the ball down to the pins. By the time four o'clock rolled around, I was ready to call it a day.

Billy seemed worn out, too, falling asleep in the back of my car on the drive back to my apartment. I got him upstairs, where he promptly curled up on my sofa.

A short while later, Chance showed up.

"Everything okay?" I asked as he collected Billy's things.

"Yeah. I may need you to do this again," he replied. "Is that all right?"

"Sure. Anytime."

After he left, I hurried to get dressed for my date with Blane. I was supposed to be ready by seven o'clock. I took a shower, blew my hair dry, then stood in front of my closet in bra and underwear, trying to figure out what to wear.

Blane had said we'd be meeting his friends tonight, and I couldn't imagine them meeting somewhere superfancy. Probably more like a bar and grill. So jeans then. But what about my shirt? I wanted to look nice, make a good impression. I wavered in indecision before finally settling on a silky aqua-blue blouse with transparent sleeves, the neckline a deep V that showed a respectable amount of cleavage. Not the warmest of picks, but it looked nice with my hair and eyes. I added makeup and the pearls.

After a moment's hesitation, I slipped on the peacock-blue stilettos that I'd bought with the money Kade had given me. I thought again about what he'd said the night he'd seen me wearing them. I pushed the uncomfortable memory aside.

A knock at the door heralded Blane's arrival. I was greeted with a dozen white roses.

"Thank you," I said, burying my nose in their fragrant depths. I stepped aside so Blane could come in. I was glad about what I'd chosen to wear. He was similarly clad in jeans and a deep navy-blue long-sleeved Henley, his black leather jacket topping it off.

"You look fantastic," he said with a pleased smile, giving me a quick kiss before we left.

As he drove, Blane assured me that the place we were going was one he knew well, a locals bar in Indy often frequented by military guys.

"So whose kid were you watching?" he asked.

"The son of one of the girls I work with," I said. "Lucy is her name. She's the one Matt raped that night. Her boy's name is Billy. Chance was taking Lucy with him for a few hours. I guess she's going to be a witness."

"His name is Billy?" Blane asked, a strange expression crossing his face.

I nodded. "I bought him some new toys. I hope you don't mind."

"That's fine," he said, his expression smoothing. "I just wanted you to have a good time today."

"I did," I assured him.

"Then mission accomplished." Blane smiled at me, a real smile that warmed me from the inside out. "I was thinking," he said, "wondering if you'd considered going back to school."

I was taken aback. "Um, I don't know. I'm still in debt from my mom's medical bills. Going back to school seems . . . unwise."

And completely out of my budget. The last thing I wanted to do was incur more debt. The twenty grand I'd received from the TecSol case had gone a long way to paying off what I owed, and now that freedom was within reach, I was loath to become indebted again.

The senator's offer came to mind, and I briefly contemplated telling Blane about it. But I was hesitant to bring up something that would no doubt upset him, right before we were to meet his friends, especially after what he'd said this morning. I'd have to find a time later to figure out how to tell him.

"What if you didn't have to worry about the cost?" Blane asked.

I stared at him. He stared at the road, sending only a quick glance my way.

"What does that mean?" I asked, afraid of what his response would be.

"Before you say anything," he began, "hear me out. I love you. I want the best for you. I want you to be happy. I know you're upset about the investigator thing not working out"—I glared, but he continued—"so I want you to go back to school. Get a degree for what you want to do. I'll pay the bill."

I didn't know what to say. His offer contrasted starkly with the senator's. Blane's was offered out of love, the senator's out of a desire to get me out of Blane's life. Suddenly, it seemed like the time to tell Blane, even if it was going to upset him.

"Blane, I need to tell you—"

His cell phone rang.

After glancing at his phone, Blane put the call on speaker. "Yeah?"

"Sorry to interrupt your date, brother." Kade's insolent tone came through over the speakers. "But I got a hit on that text you sent me."

"Can you document it?"

"For legal use or leverage?"

"Leverage."

"You bet."

"Thanks."

"No problem. You kiddos have fun."

Kade ended the call.

"What was that about?" I asked.

Blane's smile was tight-lipped this time. "Let's talk about it later, okay? We're here."

"Here" was a bar I would have been hard-pressed to ever choose to enter, whether I was with a man or not. A sign proclaimed it to be The Dive, and I couldn't disagree. A large contingent of motorcycles out front had alarm bells going off inside my head, but I followed Blane inside.

I would never have pegged this as a place Blane would frequent. It seemed clean enough, but it was old and showing its age. In one corner stood a well-worn pool table, its faded green surface dotted with balls as four rough-around-the-edges guys played a game. Bottles of beer sweated on the pool table's wooden sides, the men taking swigs in between shots.

Music played from a jukebox, surely an antique, and I recognized the tune as an old Guns N' Roses number. Taking my hand, Blane led me to a far corner table populated by five men. I nearly put the brakes on right there, my eyebrows flying upward, but Blane pulled me relentlessly forward.

The men were all a decent size, though only a couple of them were as tall as Blane, but they all had the look of someone you didn't want to meet in a dark alley. It wasn't their muscles, although several seemed as though they spent a lot of time at the gym. It was the aura they gave off—the way they held their bodies, and how their eyes moved constantly and missed nothing, no matter the smiles they wore or beers they held.

When they saw us coming, they stood, reaching out to slap Blane on the shoulder or back while eyeing me.

"Well, if it isn't the Captain!" one of the men exclaimed with a grin. "'Bout time you showed up." Shorter and squatter than Blane, the man carried himself with confidence, grasping Blane's hand in a firm grip.

"Todd! Good to see you." Blane's smile was full-on, his demeanor more relaxed than I usually ever saw him in company. Turning, he greeted the other four men. One was Eric Sanchez, who gave me a nod.

"This is Kathleen," Blane said, resting his arm across my shoulders. I automatically smiled, even though my insides were twisting nervously at being the center of male attention, especially from these men. "Kathleen, this is Todd, Sammy, Rico, Joe, and Eric."

I struggled to memorize their names and hoped there wouldn't be a quiz.

"Nice to meet you all," I said.

"Nice to meet you, little lady," the guy I thought Blane had called Joe said. He pulled out a nearby chair. "Don't let that bumbling idiot keep you standing all night. Have a seat."

I had never heard anyone call Blane a bumbling idiot, at least no one stupid enough to say it to his face, and I automatically turned to Blane. My surprise must have shown, because he just laughed.

"They've never shown me proper respect," he said, grabbing his own chair and sitting. I followed suit.

"Proper respect, my ass," Todd said while they all resumed their previous positions. "You're the one nearly court-martialed for insubordination." Todd looked at me. "You should make him tell you that story."

I grinned. "I'd love to hear it."

The waitress came by, dropping off some more beers. Blane ordered a round for us before replying. "Now, don't go ruining my excellent reputation with Kathleen by bringing up the indiscretions of my youth."

This was met by a round of guffaws, the mischief in Blane's grin making me smile again. I loved seeing him so at ease with his friends.

"So how did you and the Captain meet?" Rico asked.

"Why do you call him Captain?" I countered, not at all anxious to impart the story of my falling headfirst into Blane's lap.

"You wanna tell her or shall I?" Todd directed at Blane.

Blane turned to me. "We were on a training mission. I was a little too . . . enthusiastic in pursuing the objective."

"Took off ahead of his team like he was invincible," Todd added with a smirk.

Blane laughed. "I learned my lesson, though. Fell into a sand trap and had to be pulled out, then had my ass handed to me by the CO, who had a slightly different take."

"Yelled at him in front of the whole team, made him stand there covered in mud and sand. 'Who the fuck you think you are? Captain fucking Kirk?'"

Everyone laughed while Blane grinned good-naturedly.

"As you can see," he said to me, "the moniker stuck, and I don't think it's meant as a compliment."

I chuckled, the image of an embarrassed, mud-encrusted younger version of Blane taking form in my mind. It contrasted sharply with the picture I usually had of him.

After a few more rounds of beers, everyone was sharing their stories with me, their constant ribbing of each other making me laugh until my cheeks hurt. Blane ordered us a couple of burgers, then grabbed my hand.

"I love this song. Let's dance."

The music of 38 Special filled the bar as Blane pulled me onto what perhaps used to be a dance floor but now barely deserved the name. I didn't have the chance to speak, as he immediately spun me around, then pulled me in, only to spin me away again.

Taken by surprise, I started laughing, his happiness invigorating me. I had no idea he knew how to dance like this, twisting and turning me until I was breathless and he caught me in his arms and pulled me close.

"I didn't know you could do this," I managed, trying to catch my breath.

His eyes glittered, a wicked grin on his face as he said, "There's lots you don't know about me. I'm rectifying that." Then I was spun away again, only to have his hand catch mine and pull me back.

The end of the song came too soon and Blane led me back to the table where our food was waiting. I stayed quiet, content to listen to the men talk while I observed Blane.

His usual reserve was nowhere in evidence. His body was relaxed, the lines of worry on his face eased. I'd only ever seen him this relaxed around Mona and Gerard. It occurred to me that it must be difficult to always be on guard. Someone was always watching him, be it the press or the lawyer sitting across from him in the courtroom.

We'd finished eating and Blane had pulled my chair closer to his, slotting his fingers with mine and resting them on his denim-clad thigh. I listened as he and his friends reminisced about past missions, some of the stories making me grip Blane's hand tighter.

"Shit, that fucker nearly took your head off before Sammy got him," Rico said.

"If I hadn't been out of bullets, he wouldn't have gotten so close," Blane replied.

"You can't help it you're shit at hand-to-hand," Sammy smirked at Blane.

"Fuck off," Blane shot back with a grin. "Least I don't have to try and impress women with my knife skills."

"Good thing since you have none."

And so it went, a whole other side of Blane that fascinated me even more than what I already knew of him.

"Time to get to know your girl, Kirk," Todd said, pulling me up out of my chair. "Let's dance, sugar."

Out on the dance floor, Todd did the two-step and I learned it on the fly. "What's a girl like you doin' with an old man like Kirk?" he asked with a grin.

"I work . . . used to work"—I corrected myself—"for him. That's how we met."

"Must've made quite an impression," Todd observed. "Blane doesn't usually date girls with looks and brains."

"Thanks, I think."

He laughed. "Since you're the only one he's ever bothered to bring 'round, I'd take that as a compliment."

"Am I here to pass inspection?" I raised an eyebrow, only half-kidding.

"Yep." His matter-of-fact response took me aback. He noted my surprise. "We don't bullshit. Not when it comes to our brothers."

"Brothers?"

"That's how it is. Our lives were in each other's hands more often than they were in our own. I'd die for any one of those guys, and them for me. That makes us brothers."

His remark was sobering. "Blane says he might go back," I said. "That they offered him a position but that he'd be deployed first."

"Is that so?" Todd replied, his face hardening. "What do you think about that?"

I looked directly at him. "I don't want him to go," I said. "I love him. I don't want to lose him."

Todd smiled widely, his white teeth flashing in the semi-darkness of the bar. "Now that's the best damn thing I've heard all night."

Without another word, he spun me around and I found myself dancing with Rico, and before too long, Sammy, Joe, and even Eric took a turn. None of our conversations was as serious as the one with Todd, but I had the distinct feeling I was being assessed by all of them. I could only hope I passed whatever test or measure they were using to judge me.

When I finally got back to the table, Eric handed me into my seat, where I took a grateful drink of my beer. Blane's arm curled around my shoulders, dragging me close enough for a kiss that was longer than he usually preferred in public. I had the feeling he'd had enough beers to make this seem like a good idea. Judging from the catcalls and whistles at the table, his friends thought it was, too.

I pulled away, though the look in his eyes made me wish we could suddenly be transported somewhere private with a bed.

Okay, the bed was optional.

A few minutes later, I got up to go to the restroom. I was nearly back to the table when a big guy in a black T-shirt suddenly stepped in front of me, halting my progress. Tall and broad, he had tattoos up and down both arms.

"What's your hurry, honey?"

The man's eyes were red, as though he'd already had too much to drink.

"Let me buy you a drink."

"Um . . . thanks, but I'm okay," I stammered.

Another guy, obviously a buddy, sauntered up behind him. "We'll have a good time, sweet thang," he slurred.

"No, thanks," I blurted, sidestepping them both and making a beeline for the table. I was almost there when my arm was caught.

"It wasn't a suggestion," tattoo guy said, yanking me toward him.

Suddenly Blane was there, Rico and Todd standing with him. The rest of SEALs had gone quiet, watching the scene.

"She said no." Blane's voice was calm but implacable.

"Nobody asked you, motherfucker," retorted tattoo guy.

"Who you calling motherfucker, motherfucker," Rico drawled. I didn't mistake his seemingly relaxed pose as anything other than that, a pose.

"A spic like you may not speak English too well," the second guy snarled. "So let me spell it out for you. Fuck. Off."

I stiffened, expecting a full-on fight to break out at those words, but to my surprise, the SEALs showed admirable control. When more than one of their glances landed on Blane, I realized, somewhat belatedly, that Blane was the de facto leader.

"I think the lady turned you down, friend," Blane said. "Let me buy you and your buddies a round."

"I don't want a fuckin' drink from you," tattoo guy spat. "The whore's gonna suck all your dicks, I want my turn."

Well, so much for diplomacy.

Without so much as a by-your-leave, Blane swung, flattening the guy with one punch. Unfortunately, tattoo guy had friends, and soon I found myself in the middle of a fray of men gleefully trading hits with one another.

I was spun from one SEAL to another, always protected even as wood and glass flew about me. Never did I worry about getting hurt, and it was obvious the SEALs were enjoying themselves, beating the shit out of the guys determined to harass them.

Through the melee, I caught the sound of police sirens.

Oh no. That's all we needed—Blane getting arrested for a bar brawl.

"Beat it, Captain," Todd said over the noise, holding one guy by the scruff of the neck. "We got this."

"I don't know," Blane said, ducking a punch before landing a blow to the man's gut. "You might need a lawyer."

Rico guffawed. "Please. We'll be long gone by the time the cops get here."

I was relieved they were telling Blane to go. "This way," I said to him, again in his arms. I'd spotted the back exit when we'd first entered, courtesy of my training with Kade. I grabbed his hand and bolted, Blane having no choice but to follow me.

We were outside in the cold. The sirens were getting closer.

Blane spun me around, then his mouth was on mine. I tasted the tang of his blood; his lip had been split by a lucky punch. His body was hot under my hands, sweat from the fight leaching through his clothes. I couldn't see him well—the darkness of the building's exterior threw him into shadow—but I could feel his heat and smell his scent under his cologne.

His mouth was hard, his tongue twisting with mine. His hands moved purposefully at my waist to unbutton my jeans and shove them down my legs. My panties were a mere inconvenience, shredded and pulled from my body. The hard length of him pushed inside me as he lifted me, his hands gripping the backs of my thighs. I wrapped my legs around his waist, the wood siding of the building against my back as Blane pressed me against the wall.

My blood pounded in my veins, the beat of his pulse strong against my fingers as I pushed my hands up under his shirt to touch the skin of his chest. I clutched at him, the feel of his cock inside me, his body between my legs overwhelming me until I couldn't think, couldn't do anything but feel him.

My scream as I came was swallowed by his mouth. His hands pressed into the skin of my hips as he took me in a way that was primal, elemental. I could taste his sweat and blood on my tongue before his mouth moved to my neck. His body jerked into mine and I wrapped my arms around him, loving the feel of him losing all control.

My knees were weak when he set me back on my feet, his hand cradling my jaw as he kissed me. He bent to help me with my jeans until I was once again presentable.

Blane bundled me into his car and we headed home, my hand firmly situated in his. Comfortable silence enveloped us as he drove, and my eyes were heavy with post-orgasmic lethargy.

I must have fallen asleep, because the next thing I knew, Blane was opening my car door. I roused myself enough to walk with him to his front door. His arm was heavy on my shoulders and his breath warm in my ear as he whispered words that made my heart beat faster and the blood rise in my cheeks.

The house was dark and quiet when we entered. I took Blane's hand as he led me upstairs. Some sixth sense had me glancing behind me, only to see Kade standing in the doorway to the library. The look on his face as he watched us ascend the stairs made my chest constrict. My last glimpse of Kade before he disappeared from sight was to see him downing the amber fluid in the glass tumbler he held.

CHAPTER FOURTEEN

The next morning dawned early, and the headache I woke with reminded me why it wasn't a good idea to drink the nights before I had to work. Then I remembered I was currently unemployed.

I turned over in bed with a groan, reaching for Blane, but the bed was empty.

I sat up, rubbing my eyes, and Blane appeared next to me, clad in full courtroom armor.

"What time is it?" I asked, pushing my hair out of my face.

"Time for me to get going," he replied, sinking down next to me on the bed.

"When will you be home?" I felt vaguely self-conscious, Blane being dressed to the nines while I was naked under the sheets.

"About six." He leaned over to press a kiss to my lips. His hand dipped under the sheets and I sucked in my breath. "Think about what I said," he murmured. "Get online and check out some schools today. Purdue and IU."

"Okay." My voice was embarrassingly weak, but I couldn't think straight with him doing what he was doing, especially not enough to take him on in an argument.

"See you tonight," he said. "Will you be here?"

I nodded. "If you want me to be."

Blane's smile was broad, and satisfaction glimmered in his eyes. "I do."

Another kiss and he was gone. It occurred to me then that he'd managed to accomplish what I'd initially turned down. If I was sleeping and waking in his bed, kissing him good-bye in the morning and agreeing to be in his home when he finished work, wasn't I for all intents and purposes living with him?

This didn't sit well with me, but I wasn't sure what to do about it. Last night I'd seen a part of Blane I hadn't known existed, a part of himself he'd wanted to share with me. I didn't want to jeopardize the walls that were coming down between us, but neither did I want our relationship to move forward by accident and manipulation.

Speaking of manipulation, I was going to have to tell Blane about the senator tonight. I wasn't looking forward to that.

I fell back to sleep and woke awhile later, feeling better than I had before. I showered, blew my hair dry, and did the makeup thing, pulling on a pair of jeans with an ivory sweater that went nicely with my pearls. The forecast said it would be getting warmer, but today was still overcast and cold. February was always the dreariest of winter months in Indy.

I went downstairs, greeting Mona in the kitchen.

"Good morning," she said with a smile. "It's good to see you again. Will you be here for dinner tonight?"

"Um, I think so," I said, pouring myself a cup of coffee. "Blane didn't mention dinner plans."

"I'm just going to head to the store then," she said, untying the apron from around her waist. "Pick up a few things. Do you need anything?"

"No, but thank you."

Her gaze landed on the pearls around my neck and she froze, her eyes widening. "Did Blane give those to you?" she asked.

I nodded. "They're beautiful, aren't they?"

Mona's smile was wide. "Indeed. They were a favorite of his mother's. It's very nice to see them being worn again."

I wasn't sure what to say, and before I could decide, she added, "Gerard should be back soon. He had to take Blane's car in for maintenance."

I mumbled something in reply, my thoughts elsewhere as I touched the jewels at my neck.

"And Kade should be back soon as well."

I stiffened, remembering the look on his face last night.

A few minutes later, Mona was gone and I was left contemplating what to do about Blane's offer, and what it meant that he'd given me the pearl necklace. Did I want to go back to school? And more importantly, was I going to allow him to pay for it? That was quite a commitment, and a step I didn't know if I was comfortable taking, as generous as it was.

Carrying my coffee into the living room, I flipped on the television. I absently listened to the local news as I checked my phone for any missed calls.

". . . shocking twist today in the trial of Matt Summers . . ."

My head jerked up.

". . . allegations of prosecutorial misconduct. The defense is accusing the prosecution of secretly collaborating with law enforcement officials, inducing possible witnesses to testify against Summers in exchange for leniency. If true, the judge could declare a mistrial or even dismiss the case altogether."

Blane's face suddenly filled the screen.

"The fact that the prosecution in this case is working in secret to dig up more fraudulent charges against my client is not only outrageous, it's disappointing." Blane's solemnity lent credence to his words. "I can only hope that this isn't a pervasive guilty-until-proven-innocent, bury-the-defendant-at-all-costs culture at work in our law enforcement community."

The reporter came back on the screen. "The judge has recessed until tomorrow, when the defense is expected to present a motion to dismiss. We'll keep you updated."

I stared at the screen, trying to make sense out of what I'd just heard. The case would be dismissed? Summers would get off?

My cell phone rang.

"Hello?"

"What the fuck did you tell Kirk?" Chance yelled in my ear.

I shrank back from the phone, panicking as I tried to recall my conversation with Blane.

"Nothing, I swear," I protested. "He asked me who I was babysitting yesterday and I told him. That's all."

"You told him nothing else?"

I opened my mouth to reply, then stopped. I had told Blane more. "I told him Lucy was going to be a witness," I confessed, my stomach tying itself into knots.

"Damn it!" Chance exploded. "I told you not to tell him a damn thing! He's using that information to get the trial dismissed."

I was silent, aghast at what I had inadvertently done.

"Didn't I tell you that Kirk thinks of himself first?" Chance reminded me. "Billy is Matt Summers's son. I'm sure he knew exactly who you were watching and who the witness was once you said his name."

I was in shock. It couldn't possibly be true. Blane couldn't have used the information I'd given him to free Summers. Surely he wouldn't do that to me, even with the threat of murder charges hanging over my head.

"Chance . . . I don't know what to say," I stammered. "I'm so sorry. I didn't know, didn't think he would do this . . ."

Chance sighed. "It's not your fault, Strawbs. You trusted him. He betrayed that trust."

His words hit me hard, and I couldn't speak. I'd trusted Blane to do the right thing, not pervert justice for my sake.

"Listen, I've gotta go," he said. "Lucy's cover's been blown all to hell and I've got to get her and Billy out of town. If you don't hear from me by tomorrow, call this number."

He gave me a number, which I jotted down on a nearby pad of paper.

"Ask to speak to Detective Wells," Chance said. "He'll know how to reach me."

After a quick good-bye I was left staring into space, trying to come to grips with what had happened. I didn't want to believe it. There must be some mistake. Though I didn't know how there could be. It couldn't be mere coincidence that the day after I told Blane about Billy and Lucy, he was calling for the case to be dismissed.

I don't know how long I sat there, my coffee growing cold as my mind churned. I briefly considered calling Blane but discarded the idea. This conversation should take place in person.

Wondering if perhaps Blane had left files about the case on his desk that might help explain his actions, I decided to go to his study. Technically, I wouldn't be snooping. I'd been told to investigate this case.

I pushed open the door and stopped short.

A man was rifling through Blane's desk. He looked up, and both of us froze in place.

It took me a moment to process that I knew him. It was Garrett, Kade's friend from Denver. The second that clicked, I also realized that if he was here without Kade's knowledge, then he couldn't be up to anything good.

Garrett dropped what he was holding and sprinted around the desk. I turned to bolt and he grabbed for me, catching hold of the collar of my sweater. I felt a sharp tug, then heard the sound of dozens of pearls hitting the wooden floor, my broken necklace shedding its jewels.

I slammed my elbow back into his solar plexus and was rewarded with freedom. But it was only temporary. His hand grabbed a fistful of my hair and he yanked me backward. I yelped in pain, losing my balance and crashing to the floor. He lost his footing and came down with me. We struggled, his foot hitting a nearby table, sending a glass vase careening to the side. It fell, shattering into pieces on the floor.

On my stomach, I kicked out at him, striking him in the nose. I scrambled for the glass shards and flipped over to my back just as Garrett climbed up my body. I made to stab him with a good-sized shard, but he caught my wrist in a death grip, holding it aside as he lay on top of me. I heard the telltale click of a gun being cocked.

"Drop it or you're dead," he gritted out through the blood smeared under his nose and across his lips. The cold metal of his gun was pressed to the underside of my jaw.

The glass hit the floor with a light tinkling sound.

Garrett stood, yanking me to my feet. "You were supposed to be out of the house," he accused.

I didn't reply, still breathing hard from the fight.

"I've been following you," he continued. "You should be more careful who you spend time with. Hanging out with Kade Dennon can be hazardous to your health."

"What do you want?" I demanded.

Garrett's fist hit me hard in the stomach, and I doubled over in pain, retching. "Shut up until I tell you to speak."

He jerked me upright by my hair. In his eyes was the same icy coldness I'd seen before in Kade's, remorseless and devoid of emotion. It scared me.

"Tell me where he keeps his computer," Garrett ordered.

"I don't know—"

Garrett's hand closed around my wrist like a vise. He pulled me to Blane's desk, his gun pointing steadily at my chest. He flattened my palm against its surface. Putting the gun down, he drew a switchblade. A quick flick of his wrist, and the blade appeared, light glinting off the metal.

He pressed the razor-sharp edge to my pinkie, right above the second knuckle.

"Tell me or you're going to lose your fingers, piece by piece."

I trembled all over, tasting the sharp tang of fear in my throat.

"I swear," I said, trying to stay calm, "I don't know where it is."

The knife pressed just a fraction and I hissed in pain, bright red blood oozing from the shallow cut he'd made. He didn't stop there, continuing the cut down the back of my hand to my wrist, the slow but inexorable path of the knife leaving a trail of vivid crimson in its wake.

"Okay, okay," I babbled, my thoughts frantic as I watched the deadly blade. "I know where it is."

I had no clue where Kade kept his computer. The last time he'd mentioned it, he'd said it was in his car.

"It's not in here."

"That's more like it," Garrett smugly replied.

He abruptly released me, flipping the blade closed and pocketing it as he picked up his gun. Pointing the weapon at me, he said, "Lead the way."

I cradled my burning hand against my stomach as I walked shakily to the door. Garrett followed closely.

"Try anything and you're dead," he said.

I had no plan, I just moved forward, hoping something would present itself.

"Why do you want Kade's computer?" I asked, hoping to distract him.

"The son of a bitch froze my accounts," Garrett snarled.

"Why would he do that?"

"I'm guessing he found out I was the one who set him up." Garrett's sarcasm was thick.

"You betrayed Kade?" I asked in surprise, momentarily halting my progress. "I thought you were his friend."

"There are no friends in this business," Garrett retorted, then waved his gun at me. "Move."

"You won't be able to hide from Kade," I said. "He'll hunt you down and kill you." I knew this for a fact. Kade's declaration in Denver that he was going to find whoever had betrayed him rang in my ears.

"Not if I kill him first."

My blood turned to ice at those words. I had to do something. Once he found out I was leading him on a wild-goose chase through the house, he'd kill me without a second thought—and then he'd hunt Kade.

Making a decision and praying it was the right one, I led Garrett toward the kitchen. A kitchen filled with knives, glass, and heavy pots and pans. Surely somehow I could get my hands on something that would do some damage. There was also a door to outside there, a possible means of escape.

I did a quick scan of the room as we stepped through the doorway.

"What the fuck are we doing in here?" Garrett asked.

"There's a butler's pantry," I explained. "Kade likes to work in there."

As we passed by the stove, my eyes lit on the still-steaming kettle of water Mona had left. I was terrified, but I knew I had no choice. Once Garrett saw there was nothing in the pantry, he'd kill me.

In one smooth motion I spun, grabbed the handle of the kettle, and swung it at Garrett. Instinctively, he leaned back, but he wasn't quick enough. The kettle connected in a hard clank against the side of his head, with an added bonus when the lid popped off and steaming water cascaded out.

Garrett stumbled backward, roaring in pain and rage. He raised his gun and fired just as I knocked his arm out of the way, the bullet ricocheting off the wall behind me.

I grabbed a frying pan sitting in the drying rack by the sink, swinging it with both hands. The metal collided with his hand holding the gun and he yelled, the gun dropping from his grip. I made to swing again, but he tackled me, shoving me against the china cupboard. The edge of the wood pressed sharply into the small of my back.

Garrett slammed my hand against the plate glass of the cupboard, and sharp pain bloomed in my arm. The glass shattered as the cupboard shuddered under the assault. Plates and cups fell to the floor, their delicate porcelain making a cacophony of sound. I couldn't keep my grip and the pan fell to the tile. Then Garrett had me by the throat.

"Fucking bitch," he growled, hauling me toward him, his grip unrelenting.

I could breathe, but just barely.

"If you want your money back, may I suggest this isn't the way to go about getting it."

Garrett spun around at the sound of the voice, jerking me against him as a shield. Breathing hard, he pulled his knife and held it to my throat. I gripped his arm, trying to hold the knife at bay as its blade pressed against my skin.

Kade stood across the kitchen from us, a shard of dark in the brightness of the room.

"I thought you wanted your money, Garrett," he said coolly. "Why would I unfreeze your accounts if you kill the girl?"

"Why the fuck did you hack my accounts, Kade?" Garrett spat. "You know this is business. It's nothing personal."

Kade's eyes narrowed. "I trusted you. You betrayed me. That makes it personal." Kade's voice was silken steel. "Who were you working for, Garrett? I already know how much they paid you."

"Look," Garrett said, "just give me my money and I'll let her go."

Kade stared at him. "Fine." He held up a cell phone. "This will unfreeze your accounts. You just have to log in."

"Slide it across the floor," Garrett ordered.

Kade bent down and did as requested, the cell phone stopping at my feet.

Kade's eyes met mine. "This reminds me of when we first met."

Panic threatened at the edges of my mind and I struggled to understand. My nails dug into Garrett's arm, my breath in shallow pants.

"Pick up the phone," Garrett ordered me.

I slowly bent my knees, my upper body remaining upright against his as I scrabbled blindly. My fingers closed over the phone and he pulled me up again.

"You remember that, princess?" Kade said.

My eyes jerked to his, the brilliant blue striking a memory, and suddenly I knew what he meant.

"Hold the phone up so I can see it," Garrett said, then he told me a series of letters and numbers to punch into the screen. It all seemed like gibberish to me, but even I could see that the accounts were steadily declining, the numbers evaporating into thin air.

"What the fuck is this?" Garrett yelled. "You said you'd unfreeze my accounts!"

"I did," Kade replied evenly. "Or rather, you did, when you entered your password. They're currently being drained by the FBI. They might let you have some back, but you won't need it where you're going."

Garrett seemed frozen in shock, and I took my opportunity. Shoving his arm down and away from me with all my strength, I twisted underneath his arm. As soon as I was clear, a shot rang out. Garrett cried out in pain, falling to the floor and clutching his side.

Kade was instantly there next to me, and I fell into his arms. My whole body was shaking. Kade cupped the back of my head with one hand while his other rubbed soothingly up and down my back.

"Are you all right?" he asked.

I forced myself to pull away, making a concerted effort to keep from falling apart. I nodded, brushing my hair back from my face. "I'm fine."

Kade caught my injured hand in his and pushed the sleeve of my sweater up to inspect the jagged and bleeding cuts. Blood dripped sluggishly from my hand, staining my skin and clothes a garish red.

I pulled my wrist from his grasp, tucking my hand against my side.

"You're not fine," he said quietly.

He turned away and approached Garrett, who was half-sitting, half-lying on the floor, blood seeping from his wound. The look that had come over Kade's face was terrifying in its stark coldness, the icy fury in his eyes deeply unsettling.

"You hurt her," Kade accused. His voice was calm and quiet, and even more frightening for being so. I watched him warily.

"She wouldn't cooperate," Garrett hissed. Sweat had broken out on his forehead.

Light glinted off the blade in Kade's hand. I hadn't even seen him pull it, and I inhaled sharply.

"You hurt her. I hurt you."

"Kade!" I called out, desperation pushing aside my fear. "Don't. Please."

I moved slowly forward, a hand outstretched. I really didn't want to see Kade inflict pain on Garrett, no matter how much he may have deserved it.

Kade glanced at me, and I was relieved to see the cold rage ebb from his eyes. I let out a silent breath when he lowered the knife.

"You think this is over, Kade?" Garrett snarled. "The girl led me right to you. First to your apartment, then here."

Kade's face was an unreadable mask. "You're lying. No one knows about her."

Garrett laughed, a hissing wheeze. "You're blind. You follow her around like she's a bitch in heat." His laugh faded and his gaze turned hateful. "It's only a matter of time before you get her killed." He turned my way. "An assassin in love with you. Your life expectancy just dropped by half."

"Fuck you," Kade growled.

Garrett coughed, a hacking sound, as he clutched the wound in his side. When he stopped, he was panting for breath. "This isn't over," he hissed. "Even if I go to jail, they're going to know about her. Her name, address, where she works, her friends, what she eats, where she goes, who she fucks, everything. Everyone's going to know exactly how to break Kade Dennon."

I reacted an instant too late. "Kade, no!" I shouted, leaping for him. But even as the words left my mouth, I saw the glint of metal. A grunt left Garrett's mouth just as I reached Kade, grabbing for his hand, the hand wrapped around the hilt of his knife buried in Garrett's chest.

Garrett's body fell back onto the floor, his eyes open but unseeing.

We were locked in that macabre tableau for only an instant before Kade pulled me away. I couldn't tear my horrified gaze from Garrett, but Kade held me trapped in his arms, forcibly turning my head and moving us across the room.

Fear and horror choked me. My mind kept replaying Kade sliding the knife between Garrett's ribs.

"Kathleen, look at me," Kade said, tipping my chin up. "You're safe now. No one's going to hurt you."

"You just . . . killed him." My voice was a choked whisper. Part of me couldn't believe it. I'd known Kade had killed people, had seen him kill before, but never like that. "Why?"

"He knew about you," Kade replied simply. "Hurt you, because of me." His blue eyes turned intense. "It wasn't a difficult choice. No one is going to hurt you. Not while I'm around."

I didn't know what to say. His declaration sank deep into my gut. I couldn't explain how it made me feel. A man was dead, killed by Kade, because of me. Not that he'd been a good man. His intention to kill Kade had made him a threat no matter what deal they could have struck. But Kade had been planning to turn him over to the FBI, if it hadn't been for me. I felt as though Garrett's blood was on my hands.

Our eyes locked and I was unable to look away, trying to puzzle through the riddle that was Kade Dennon. A good man . . . who did bad things.

Kade looked away first, releasing me before pulling out his cell and dialing. "Donovan, it's Dennon. Did the wire transfers complete?" He paused. "Good. Garrett's here at the house, but didn't survive. Can you send someone over to collect the body?" A few moments later, he ended the call.

I was reeling, my thoughts spinning and my emotions hanging by a thin thread. "I want to go home," I said.

He didn't say anything, just gave a curt nod.

We walked outside and I shivered. Kade took off his coat and slung it over my shoulders before helping me into the car.

Once we were on the road, I cleared my throat.

I didn't want to do this, but knew I had to. "I need to talk to Blane," I said.

Kade wordlessly dialed a number on his cell and handed the phone to me. Holding it to my ear, I heard Blane answer.

"Yeah?"

"Blane, it's me," I said.

"Kat? What's wrong? And why are you calling me from Kade's phone?" The suspicion in his voice rankled my already fragile temper.

"Kade's taking me home," I said, then got straight to the point. "Why is the case getting dismissed?"

Blane was silent.

"Did you know Billy was Matt's son?" I asked. "Did you use the information I gave you about Lucy for your case?"

"Kat, let me explain . . ."

That was all the confirmation I needed. I hung up.

I felt curiously numb inside. It didn't feel like when I'd seen Blane with Kandi. Then, my heart had felt torn into shreds. Now, I felt detached. Perhaps I was still in shock, I didn't know. What I did know was that I was exhausted, my hand hurt like hell, and I didn't have a clue what to say to Kade about what he'd done.

We reached my apartment and he followed me inside. Tigger ran to greet me and I absently gave him a quick scratch behind the ears. I went to the kitchen sink and pushed up my sleeve. Kade reached around me and turned on the water.

I didn't speak as he gently washed the blood from my hands, dried now. A breath hissed through my teeth at the stinging sensation. When they were clean, Kade grabbed some paper towels, dabbing my skin dry.

"I'm sorry," he said.

I looked up at him in surprise.

"I wasn't careful enough," he continued. "After they got my apartment, I suspected it was Garrett that had leaked information on me in Denver. I didn't think he knew about you, though, and I should have foreseen that."

"How could you have?" I replied, shrugging my shoulders. "You thought he was a friend."

"I have no friends, remember?" he said with a bitter smile.

"You have me." Even after what had happened tonight, it was still true.

His smile faded and his eyes grew serious. "How long before you betray me?" he murmured.

"I won't betray you," I replied, shocked. "Why would you say that?"

"Because everyone does, eventually."

My heart broke a little at the resignation in his voice, the dead certainty in his eyes.

"I swear. I will never betray you."

I couldn't say whether he believed me or not, though I hoped he did. He leaned down, and my breath caught, but his lips grazed my forehead.

"I should go," he rasped, the backs of his knuckles brushing my cheek.

I allowed him to lead me to the door in silence, my fingers threaded through his.

It was cold outside, the frigid air drifting into my apartment as Kade stood, framed in the doorway. He pulled me toward him, his arms encircling me, and I rested my head on his chest.

"Be careful," I murmured.

"For once, maybe I have a reason to be," he replied, sounding surprised. His chin rested on the top of my head, and I could feel the beat of his heart against my fingers. We stood there like that, the silence comfortable, not oppressive.

"Am I interrupting?"

I jumped guiltily backward out of Kade's arms, my eyes going to the spot over Kade's shoulder where Blane now stood.

Kade leisurely turned, raising an eyebrow. "Do I detect a hint of jealousy, brother?"

The look on Blane's face was murderous. My heart lurched into my throat.

"Relax," Kade huffed in exasperation, loosely gripping Blane's shoulder as he made to pass him.

Blane grabbed Kade's wrist, pushing him away. "How many other times have you been with her when I'm not around?" he snarled.

Kade's eyes narrowed, his body stiffening. "A lot," he retorted. "In case you've forgotten, you're the one that made me stay with her to protect her when you couldn't."

"That was a mistake I don't intend to repeat."

"Good to hear," Kade shot back.

I watched, barely breathing, unsure if I should intervene, say something. To my relief, Blane said nothing further as Kade warily turned his back and left.

"Are you through playing alpha dog with your brother?" I snapped, angry at the way he'd treated Kade, and not sure I wanted to do this right now. I was exhausted, angry, and disappointed, but in the end, I relented.

Wordlessly, I opened the door wide, then turned and walked inside. I went into the bathroom, retrieving some salve for my injured hand and a few bandages for the deepest cuts. Sitting cross-legged on my couch, I examined the wounds.

Blane remained standing, watching me.

"What happened to your hand?" he asked.

Like I wanted to tell him. "Why are you here, Blane?"

"I came by to explain," he said.

I didn't reply, not trusting my emotions or temper to not say something I'd regret.

"I did use that information to get the case dismissed."

My hand faltered slightly as I fumbled with the salve, his confirmation killing something inside me. My optimism, maybe.

Blane took the seat next to me. I shifted away from him, his presence overpowering. I didn't want to succumb to his influence or manipulation. Not this time.

"Kat. Look at me."

I unwillingly met his gaze.

"Hear me out. The rape conviction, it'd give him twenty years. He'd be out in five. That's why I took what you gave me and went to the feds with what I knew."

"What are you talking about?" I asked.

"Kade got enough to give them so they can pursue the human trafficking," he explained. "They're going to prosecute him for that. The penalty for trafficking is twenty years per violation."

I stared at him, trying to understand.

"He's going away for good," Blane said. "I honored my part of the deal with Summers. You're in the clear. But the feds have enough now for warrants. They're watching and listening."

"Why didn't Chance tell me this?"

"Maybe they hadn't talked to Chance before this went down. It happened really fast," he answered. "The point is, he's not getting away."

I shook my head, partly amazed at his machinations in outwitting Summers, partly chagrined at yet again being the last to know.

"The point is, you don't trust me," I said. "Haven't trusted me. I don't think you'll ever trust me." My anger had dissipated, but not the hurt. "So much could be avoided if you'd just talk to me. You should have told me from the beginning that Summers was blackmailing you. Why didn't you?"

Blane stared at me. "Do you think I wanted you to know? Would want you to feel guilty for something that wasn't your fault?"

I tried to protest, but he interrupted.

"I know you," he said. "So don't tell me that wouldn't have happened. I could see the guilt on your face the second I did tell you."

I couldn't say he was wrong. I had felt guilty, still did.

"We're in this together," I said. "If you want me to be open and honest with you, then I have to trust you're doing the same."

"You're not going to change the fact that I'm going to protect you, whenever I can," Blane said, his voice flat. "That's too ingrained in me."

"Understood. So long as you know that I don't react well when I find out you've been keeping things from me."

"Understood."

We sat for a moment before he cracked a small grin. I couldn't help a tiny smile back.

"I do think it's really cool that you outsmarted that SOB," I admitted.

"You do, do you?" he asked, a twinkle coming into his eyes.

"I mean, for a lawyer and all, it's pretty clever," I said archly, teasing him.

Glancing down at my hand, Blane's smile faded. "You want to tell me what happened to your hand? Why Kade was here?"

I reached for the salve and bandages. "Just another day in the life," I dismissed. "A guy Kade knew broke into your house. I got in the way and he decided I could use a few less fingers, then thought he'd use me as leverage against Kade, yadda yadda yadda."

"Why would he think you could be used as leverage against Kade?" Blane asked.

I shrugged. "He followed me to Kade's apartment the night it got blown up, then to your house." I carefully smeared more salve on the cuts while Blane wordlessly placed the bandages.

After Blane had covered the last wound, he asked, "Why did you go to Kade's the other night?"

Something in his voice made me look up at him, and I remembered how angry he'd been that Kade had been here tonight. His expression was guarded.

"I'd said something," I answered, choosing my words carefully. The last thing I wanted was to cause any more discord between Blane and Kade. "Said something awful to him, and I wanted to apologize. He was . . . entertaining . . . a woman when I got there. I think she was working with Garrett."

Blane nodded, as though he understood my attempt at tactfulness. His expression eased and I relaxed.

"I wanted to tell you"—he took both my hands in his—"that I decided to not take that position the Navy offered me."

My breath caught. "So you're not going to be deployed again?" I asked, hardly daring to hope.

"No. That part of my life is over. I'm quite anxious to start the next part."

I threw my arms around his neck, squeezing him tightly. "I'm so glad! I would have hated to see you go, hated you being gone."

He hugged me back just as tight. After a few moments, he released me, easing me back and taking my hands again.

"About the next part," he said, "I've decided to announce my candidacy for governor."

"Blane, that's fantastic!" My smile was somewhat forced this time.

Governor. Wow. My heart sank. How could I possibly fit into the life of the governor of Indiana?

"My uncle Robert is arranging the announcement, a big party, press, the works. It's Friday night downtown at the Hyatt."

"Sounds great," I enthused, hoping I didn't sound fake.

"I want you there," Blane said, his grip tightening on my hands. "I need you there with me. But not as my girlfriend."

My forced smile faded. Not as his girlfriend?

"I want you there as my fiancée."

Stunned, I just stared at him. Memories of the last time we'd discussed marriage immediately came to mind.

He smiled. "I know what you're thinking, but this isn't like last time. I did everything all wrong. This time, I'm going to do it right."

He slid off the couch and got down on one knee in front of me. Then his image blurred as tears welled in my eyes.

My hands shook in his as he said, "Kathleen Turner, I'm in love with you. You're everything I'd hoped to find in a woman. I want you by my side, now and always. Would you do me the honor of being my bride?"

My tears were flowing freely now and I almost didn't notice the small velvet box he'd taken out of his pocket. Opening it, he displayed a beautiful diamond solitaire ring, its large square gem sparkling even in the muted light.

I looked back up into his gray eyes, surprised to see a hint of uncertainty there, as though he weren't positive of my answer. As if I would have any other answer than yes.

I managed to say through my tears, "Yes, I will."

His answering smile was wider than I'd ever seen it. He pulled me off the couch and into his arms, kissing me fervently. I twined my arms around his neck, hardly daring to believe what had just happened.

When he pulled away, it was only to place the ring on my finger. Slightly too big, it still fit well enough to wear.

"You look good with my ring on your finger," he whispered against my lips. Then he was carrying me into the bedroom. And we celebrated.

CHAPTER FIFTEEN

Dawn found me awake, Blane asleep next to me. I gazed at the ring on my finger, the early morning light making it sparkle. Contentment curled low in my belly, joy spreading to my limbs like warm sunshine, making sleep impossible. Afraid I'd accidentally wake Blane, I eased out of bed, pulled some clothes on over my nakedness, and put on a pot of coffee.

Checking my phone, I saw that there were no missed calls or texts from Chance, though there were several from Blane. I was worried about Chance, but resolved to give him a few more hours before I really started to panic.

I was sipping my second cup of coffee when my cell rang. I grabbed it.

"Hello?"

"Miss Turner," an unfamiliar voice said. "This is Senator Keaston."

I was immediately on guard. What was I going to tell him? What would he say when he found out about Blane's proposal?

"I trust you know by now that Blane has decided to declare his candidacy for governor, and that you remember our conversation?"

"Yes."

"Have you decided to take me up on my very generous offer?"

I steeled myself. "I'm not going to break up with Blane," I said. "Not for you or anyone. I love him and he loves me."

Silence, then, "I see."

"I know you think I'm not good enough for him," I said, "but he doesn't think like you do, and it's really his decision, not yours. He respects you very much, Senator. I'm sure he'd want your blessing. We both do."

"Blessing on what?" he snapped.

I took a deep breath. "On our engagement."

"You are incredibly naive, Miss Turner." The menace in his voice made the hair stand up on my arms. "More's the pity."

The line went dead.

My earlier happiness had evaporated, and my hand shook as I put down the phone. What was Blane going to say when he found out how much his uncle was against our engagement? Would it affect how he felt about me?

I sat staring into space, my coffee growing cold. Finally, I roused myself enough to go into the kitchen for a fresh cup.

"How's my beautiful bride this morning?" Blane pressed against my back, his arms around my waist as he nuzzled my neck.

"All right," I said, leaning into him. "But I'm worried about Chance."

Blane released me, reaching over my head to get another coffee mug out of the cabinet. "Why? Where is he?"

"That's the point," I said as he poured the steaming liquid. "He called yesterday and said that he had to get Lucy out of town. That if I hadn't heard from him by this morning, I was supposed to call this number he gave me and ask to speak to Detective Wells."

Blane took a sip of the coffee, his brow furrowing. "Have you called him?"

"I was about to."

Blane handed me my phone. "Call."

I did as he said, my stomach in knots as I dialed.

"May I speak with Detective Wells?" I asked the man that answered the phone.

I was put on hold, and then another voice came on the line.

"Detective Wells," he identified himself.

"Detective, my name is Kathleen Turner. I was given your number by my cousin, Chance Turner. He told me you would know how to reach him."

"Miss Turner, I'm sorry, but I don't have good news."

My heart lurched in my chest.

"Chance was supposed to check in with us six hours ago, and we haven't heard from him. When was the last time you spoke with him?"

"Yesterday morning," I replied. "Don't you have someone else with him? Another officer?"

"I'm sorry, I'm not at liberty to answer that question," the detective said.

My frustration mounted. "He said he was going to get Lucy and Billy out of town," I said. "Did anyone go by Xtreme? Maybe they're there."

"We can't search Xtreme," the detective said. "We have no warrant. And if Chance is still undercover, we'd be compromising him by doing so."

"Then I'll go," I retorted. "I'm supposed to work there tonight anyway."

A pause. "You work there?"

"Yes," I explained. "I was investigating the disappearance of Amanda Webber. I work for the law firm representing her boyfriend." Technically, that should have been in the past tense, but I wasn't going to argue semantics.

"Hold on, please."

I waited impatiently while he covered the phone with his hand. I could hear muffled voices. Blane sipped his coffee, watching me intently.

"Miss Turner," the detective said, "would you be willing to come down to the station and speak with me?"

"Come to the station?" I asked. Blane's gaze sharpened. "Um, sure. When?"

"As soon as possible."

"Okay."

"I'm going with you," Blane said the minute I hung up the phone.

"That's fine with me," I agreed.

We showered and dressed quickly before heading to the police station downtown. An hour later, I was asking for Detective Wells.

He was younger than I thought he'd be, looking to be in his late twenties. His hair was a dark auburn, his eyes tawny brown. At about six feet, he towered over me but didn't achieve Blane's height. He wore jeans and a long-sleeved dark-gray shirt, his gun tucked in to the holster at his side.

"Miss Turner?" he asked.

I nodded, shaking his proffered hand.

"I'm Detective Nathan Wells." His gaze shifted to Blane, who likewise held out his hand.

"Blane Kirk. Her attorney."

The detective's eyebrows climbed skyward. "An attorney wasn't necessary," he said stiffly.

"She's my fiancée."

Those words made me glow on the inside.

"Ah. I see," replied Detective Wells.

He led us back to a small conference room, motioning for us to take a seat. "Would you like some coffee? Water?"

"No, thank you," I said. Blane declined as well.

He closed the door and took a seat next to me. "Let me get right to the point, Miss Turner—" he began.

"Please call me Kathleen," I interrupted.

"Kathleen," he continued, "you're in a unique position to help us."

"Help you?"

"Other than Chance, we have no one on the inside at Xtreme," he confessed. "If you work there, have been working there, then you already have an advantage."

I just looked at him, waiting.

"We were hoping you'd consent to wear a wire tonight when you go in."

I was taken aback. "A wire? But I'm not a cop."

"I know, but you don't have to worry. All you need to do is work as usual, perhaps ask a question or two, that's all. Our team will be across the street. We'll hear every word."

"What's the point of me wearing a wire?" I asked. There was something they weren't telling me.

"We think David Summers is going to be there tonight."

"David Summers? Matt's uncle?"

Wells nodded. "If we can tie him to the illegals they're smuggling into the country, we can take his whole organization down. That's what Chance has been working on."

"Absolutely not," Blane cut in. "There's no way you're going to put a civilian in danger."

"She won't be in any danger," Detective Wells argued.

"You don't know that," Blane shot back. "It's not worth the risk."

I interjected before the detective could respond. "Will this help find Chance?"

"If we can get Summers, there's a good possibility he'll know where Chance is."

I studied Wells, hoping he was telling me the truth, though he didn't seem like the type to make empty promises. I didn't know if I agreed with him that I wouldn't be in danger, but if it meant finding Chance, then I didn't really have a choice.

"Okay," I agreed.

"Kat, don't—"

I held up my hand, silencing Blane. "It's my decision," I said quietly. "I can't just leave Chance, not if there's a possibility I could help find him."

Blane's face was like stone, his jaw locked tight. "Fine," he bit out, turning to Detective Wells. "But if she goes, she wears a GPS transmitter as well."

Wells quickly agreed.

My hand was in Blane's, his grip strong and solid.

A few hours later, I was being fitted for a wire inside an unmarked van around the corner from Xtreme.

"We'll be able to hear everything you're saying," the woman who was taping the wire to my chest said. The thin microphone was nestled between my breasts.

I buttoned up my shirt, covering the wire.

"This is the GPS transmitter." She handed me a small circular device. I slipped it in my pocket.

"You're sure you won't be far?" I nervously asked Wells, who was standing nearby.

"We'll be in at the first sign of trouble," he assured me. "If you start feeling uncomfortable, or that you're in danger, just come outside or say something into your wire."

"I still don't like this," Blane said. He stood nearby, arms crossed over his chest and an ill-tempered look on his face.

I faked a smile. "I'll be fine," I said, trying to reassure him despite my own nerves.

He pulled me in his arms, giving me a brief but hard kiss. "I'll be here, too," he whispered in my ear. "Just say the word and I'll come get you."

His words calmed me more than any of the assurances from Detective Wells. My gaze met Blane's. His eyes held a promise I knew I could rely on. Come hell or high water, he'd protect me. He'd shown me proof of that many, many times.

"I love you," I said.

"Me, too."

It was getting dark by the time I left the van and walked around to the front entrance to Xtreme. The place seemed to have a menacing air that it didn't have before, though I was sure it was just in my head. I was apprehensive about wearing a wire and even more scared that something had happened to Chance.

Jack was already there and the place was starting to pick up with customers. Holly was dancing onstage at the moment. I filled drinks for a while, then decided to start snooping.

"I'm going in back to get some more vodka," I said to Jack, who responded with a wave of his hand.

I searched the back of the place, not knowing what I was looking for. I peeked inside the Champagne Room, but it was empty.

There were a couple of doors I'd never looked behind, so I started there. One was to a closet. The other was locked. I stood there, pondering what to do. It was dark and quiet back here as usual, but this time, the silence seemed more eerie than peaceful.

A sound behind the locked door alerted me, and I barely had time to slide inside the closet before it opened.

I peered through the tiny crack in the door. It was Lucy and Billy, along with some man I'd never seen before. He held a gun, and Billy was crying. Lucy looked as pale as a sheet.

They didn't say anything as they went by, Lucy gripping Billy's hand. When they disappeared around the corner, I eased out of the closet. This time when I tried the other door's handle, it was unlocked.

My heart pounded in my chest, blood roaring in my ears as I carefully descended the concrete stairs behind the door. It was dark and it took a moment for my eyes to adjust. I was thankful the stairs weren't made of wood—concrete doesn't squeak.

I thought about saying something into my mic, but didn't want to risk being overheard, so I remained silent.

At the bottom of the staircase, I could see a little bit of light coming from a room beyond. I paused on the last step, taking several deep breaths before peering ever so slowly around the corner.

What I saw made my heart skip a beat, panic flaring inside my head.

"Chance!"

I ran over to him. He was bound hand and foot as he sat on the concrete floor, propped against the wall. His eyes were shut and blood ran freely from several gashes on his head and face. I didn't know if he was alive, and I feared the worst.

"Chance, please, wake up," I pleaded, reaching behind him and pulling at the knots in the ropes binding his hands.

His eyes cracked open and I wanted to cry with relief.

"Strawbs?" His voice was weak. "Is that you?"

"Yeah," I sniffed. "Yeah, it's me." The knots weren't yielding, but I kept working at them.

"Gotta . . . go," Chance managed, his eyes struggling to stay open. "Gotta save . . . Lucy . . . Gonna kill her."

The ropes finally gave and I yanked them off, moving to the ones around his ankles. "They're going to kill Lucy?" I asked.

Chance seemed to be coming around, his words more lucid this time. "I've got to save her," he said, wincing in pain as he moved.

"I'll tell the police," I said to him as I unwound the rope. "They'll get her."

Chance shook his head as he got unsteadily to his feet, leaning heavily on me. "Won't get here in time," he said through gritted teeth.

"They will," I said. "They're probably already on their way." Surely they'd heard me say Chance's name and would be busting down the door any second.

"They're taking her and Billy," Chance argued. "I've got to get her."

"Sit down," I said. "I'll go look for her. They might still be here somewhere. I'll come back for you."

"Can't," he panted. His knees gave out and I eased him down to the steps. "Lucy . . ."

"I'll go," I reiterated. "And I'll be back."

"No, Strawbs . . ."

Whatever he'd been about to say was lost as he passed out, which probably wasn't a bad thing, considering.

I hightailed it back up the stairs, talking into my chest as I went.

"Chance is in the basement. He's hurt. I saw Lucy and Billy being taken. Heading to see if I can find them."

I ran through the hallway to the place I'd last seen them. Rounding the corner, I stumbled to a halt.

The back door was open up ahead and I saw them being forced into the back of a van. I panicked. I was too late. They were going to take Lucy somewhere else to kill her, and possibly Billy, too.

Then I remembered. I had the GPS on me.

Without any sort of real plan, I ran forward and tackled one of the surprised guards. We fell to the ground. I climbed on top of him, slamming the back of his head onto the concrete. His body went slack.

Arms grabbed me from behind, yanking me to my feet. I whipped my head back, hitting someone and hearing them grunt with pain. Then I was free. I slammed my elbow back into his solar plexus as another man approached me from the front. His fist crashed into my jaw, and pain exploded through my cheek. My teeth came down hard on my tongue, and blood filled my mouth.

Before I could recover, another blow landed in my gut, knocking the wind from me. I doubled over in pain.

"What a hellcat," I heard someone observe in an amused tone.

My arms were yanked painfully behind my back as I was forcibly straightened and held tight.

"I have some unfinished business with this one," Matt Summers said. He stood in front of me, his lips twisted in a menacing smirk.

I spat a mouthful of blood and saliva at Matt, watching in satisfaction as it splattered on his face and clothes.

The satisfaction was short-lived. Matt backhanded me with a force that made me see stars. I struggled to stay conscious.

A shot rang out and one of the men standing next to Matt dropped. I jerked my head around and saw Blane, gun in hand, heading toward us, only fifty yards away.

Hope sprang up in my chest, until they started shooting back at Blane. He ducked behind the Dumpster, the bullets hitting the metal and ricocheting off.

I started struggling with everything I had, screaming and yelling, trying to get away. If I could just tackle Matt or the men shooting at Blane, do anything to distract them enough, maybe Blane could get a clear shot.

"Get her in the van," Matt bit out, wiping the blood off his face with his sleeve.

I let my knees go lax, my entire body weight now on the man holding me up by my arms, which hurt like hell. He cursed, dragging me as I twisted and bit his arm.

"Fucking bitch!" he yelled. His fist came flying and I braced myself for the blow, which bounced my head off the side of the van.

I was too dazed to fight as he shoved me into the van, the door slamming shut behind me. Nausea roiled in my stomach at the pain, and I spat more blood on the floor.

Staggering to my feet, I fell against the door, but it was locked. Peering through the window, I saw two more men drop from Blane's bullets.

Jack suddenly stepped out the back entrance of the club. I banged on the window, shouting. "Jack!" I yelled. "Help me!"

Recognition flared in his eyes.

I shouted again. "Help me!" We hadn't particularly gotten along, but surely he wouldn't let them take me. To my dismay, Jack turned away, disappearing back inside the club.

The van lurched into motion, pulling away, but not before I saw Blane collapse to the ground.

I screamed and banged my fists on the glass, profanities falling from my lips as I desperately tried the handle, the glass, anything to get out, to get to Blane. I couldn't see, everything was blurry, and my hands wouldn't work properly, wouldn't close around the handle. I sobbed, wiping away the blood, saliva, and tears dripping down my face while beating fruitlessly on the door.

Hands—gentle, soft hands—pulled me back from the door. I didn't have the energy or will to fight them. My breath was coming in quick, shallow gasps between sobs wrenched from my chest. A woman cradled me in her arms, speaking quietly to me, though I couldn't understand her, didn't want to understand her. I didn't care about anything. I'd failed Blane.

I lost track of time, my sobs quieting, my mind going numb. The van kept moving, and I realized it wasn't just me, Lucy, and Billy in the back. Six other women stared back at me as I looked around. I couldn't understand how they could be in here, not when we'd just rescued a handful of women the other night. And why hadn't the police come? They knew I was in here. None of it made any sense.

Finally, we stopped. I braced myself, but guns were pointed at us the moment the doors opened, giving no chance to escape.

It was dark and we were out in the middle of nowhere, it seemed, on a flat, empty stretch of land.

The men with guns herded us toward a plane waiting nearby. I stuck close to Lucy and Billy. If nothing else, perhaps I could help keep them safe, or at least safer.

I hesitated before getting on board the plane, knowing that if I did so, I might never set foot on American soil again. The police hadn't come, Blane had been shot, was perhaps dead . . .

My steps faltered. A man growled at me in Spanish, shoving me none too gently with his rifle. I stumbled and fell.

I grabbed a handful of dirt, fury spiking in me. I was ready to fling it in his face when a hand closed over mine.

"Don't do it," the woman whispered. She pulled on my arm to help me up, keeping her wary eyes on the guard. "You'll get us all killed." Her accent was thick, but I understood.

With difficulty, I tamped down my rage, opened my fist, and let the dirt fall harmlessly to the ground.

Clasping my arm firmly, the woman helped me onto the plane.

It was a kind of cargo plane, on the small side, with no seats. The guards made us sit on the metal floor while they watched over us. Lucy cradled Billy in her arms. His eyes were wide with fear, but he didn't make a sound.

The guards strapped themselves into the few utilitarian benches along the sides of the plane. The engines started with a dull roar that made the plane vibrate underneath my legs.

I was scared, and I could see from the stark faces of the women around me that they were scared, too. Where were they taking us?

As the plane took off, a part of me still felt like this was a nightmare, that I'd wake up any moment, Blane asleep next to me in bed.

The guards relaxed, talking among themselves during the flight. I put my hand in my pocket, feeling reassured by the GPS, even though I didn't know how long its battery would last.

After what felt like a couple of hours, one of the women got up, warily approaching a guard. She was Hispanic—most of the women were—and she asked him something in Spanish. The guard shook his head, speaking rapidly and waving his hand for her to go sit. The woman asked again, her voice imploring. This time the guard stood, backhanding her so hard she fell.

The women around me tensed, all of us watching. The guard yelled at the woman at his feet, kicking her in the side. She curled into a ball, drawing her knees to her chest.

I couldn't take any more. I crawled forward, shaking off the hands that tried to hold me back.

The guard had stopped kicking her and was now just yelling. He spat on her just as I reached out for her arm and pulled her toward me. Suddenly another woman was helping me, taking the other arm and pulling her back into our midst. The guards watched but didn't interfere.

The woman was weeping, clutching her side, and I now realized what she'd wanted. The pants she wore were soaked down the inside of her thighs and I could smell the foul tang of urine.

No one approached the guards again.

My head hurt, and my entire body ached. My legs were cramped from not being able to move around, and all the time I thought of Blane. Maybe the gunshot had only wounded him. Maybe he was okay. I held on to that, held onto the hope and prayer that he was alive. It was all I had.

The plane landed with a hard jolt before rolling to a stop. The door opened and the guards herded us out and down a short flight of stairs.

We were somewhere tropical. It was hot, the humidity so thick it was like trying to breathe through wet cotton. I immediately started to sweat, perspiration rolling down the sides of my face.

The sea couldn't be far—I could smell it, a salty tang in the air—but the airstrip on which the plane had landed was surrounded by jungle.

Two of the guards approached Lucy, and I watched in horror as they pulled her son out of her arms. She immediately started screaming, trying to reach Billy, who was now crying and holding his arms out for his mother. A guard shoved her down, but she scrabbled back onto her feet.

Knowing Lucy would only get herself killed if she fought them, I ran forward, wrapping my arms around her from behind and pulling her away.

"Let me go!" she screamed. "Billy!"

"We'll get him back," I hissed urgently in her ear. "But they're going to shoot you if you don't stop!"

I had to say it several times to get through to her. Then she hung in my arms, defeated, tears streaming down her face.

"We'll get him," I assured her, though I had no idea how I was going to deliver on that promise. "He'll be okay. You need to survive."

I didn't think Matt would murder his own son. At least, I desperately hoped he wouldn't.

They made us get into another van, the trip sweltering inside the metal oven. Thankfully, it was a short ride. Though what I saw when we got out made despair leach into my bones.

It was a shantytown, like something I'd see in a movie or in pictures of third-world countries. Tiny dwellings with tin roofs and curtains for doors, or just cardboard. No one was about, just a few goats and chickens wandering.

Lucy's fingers found mine and we clutched each other's hand tightly. Fear unlike anything I'd ever known coursed through me. I had no idea where I was, or what was going to become of me. How would anyone ever find me? And was there anyone who would be looking?

They herded us into the largest of the shanties. A man stood there, obviously someone in charge, the way the others seemed to defer to him. I realized this must be Alvarez. He spoke rapidly in Spanish to one of the guards while gesturing to the group of women. He then went from woman to woman, looking each one over in turn. Some he made turn around, others had to lift their shirts, some he told to open their mouths or smile so he could look at their teeth. It was horrible to watch, demoralizing and dehumanizing.

I dreaded my turn, which came all too quickly.

"Americano?"

I jerked my head in a nod, too scared to speak.

His lips curled in a sneer that sent a shiver of fear and revulsion through me.

"Take your hair down," he said in English.

My hands shook, but I obeyed.

"Nice," he observed. He took my chin in his hand, turning my bruised and swollen cheek so he could see it. "Hmm, too bad about this, but you'll heal."

I gathered what little courage I had left. "What are you going to do with us?" I asked.

"Make money off you, of course," he replied easily. "The rest will go to Rio, but you, you with the blue eyes and blonde hair, you could fetch a better price. The rich Arabs do like the blondes."

He laughed and I thought I was going to vomit. "It would be too much to ask, I suppose, for you to be a virgin?"

I just looked at him, my mind in numbed shock at what he'd outlined for my imminent future.

"Ah." He shook his head sadly. "Too bad. The Americans and their sex."

He looked down, then grabbed my left hand. "Married?" He pried Blane's ring off my finger. "Engaged, I think, not married."

I watched in dismay as he pocketed the diamond ring. A ring I'd had for only twenty-four hours. A ring Blane had placed on my finger after he'd asked me to marry him. Less than a day ago, I'd been safe in my apartment, where I should be right now. And this asshole, the horrifically evil bastard in front of me, was taking all that away.

Something broke inside my head and I leapt for the man. A yell of pure rage tore from my throat. My hands closed around his neck, squeezing as he tried to pry me off. The guards yelled, and there was mayhem all around. My vision was tinted red by my rage. All I could think was how I wanted to hurt him, kill him.

A lethargy crept over my limbs, but I fought it, trying to keep my fingers closed around his throat. But my body wouldn't obey and my vision began to darken. Confused, I turned my head and saw a needle buried in my arm. Then I knew nothing at all.

~

Time passed. I was moved, tossed into a room with a dirty cot and a dirt floor. Even when I was awake, I could do nothing to stop them, nothing to try and get away.

They searched me, their rough hands pushing aside my clothes and tearing away the wire taped to my skin. They found the GPS as well. I watched, unable to summon the strength to fight as a guard ground it into dust beneath his boot.

Everything was fuzzy: my thoughts, my vision, my will. I fought despair, screaming inside my head what I couldn't make come out my mouth, every time the man with the needle came and sent me back into oblivion.

～

I felt odd when I woke next. My thoughts were coherent, my body more under my control. It was a strange feeling after the dreamy, indistinct period where I hadn't had any control, no will of my own. It took me a minute to identify what was different.

Afraid the man with the needle would be coming any moment, I sat up and looked around, assessing my situation.

I was in a cell, or cage. A wall was at my back, but the other three sides had bars. It felt strange. I was moving, but not moving, and I realized after a moment that I must be on a boat.

Glancing down at myself, I saw I was still wearing my clothes, though now they were filthy and torn and several buttons on my shirt were missing. A quick check showed I was no longer wearing the wire. Vague images of hands ripping it off floated in my mind, but it was like a half-remembered dream.

My stomach growled. I was hungry, and thirsty. So thirsty. I didn't think I'd ever been so thirsty in my life. I tried to wet my dry, cracked lips, but my tongue was dry, too.

Getting off the floor proved more difficult than I had anticipated. Whatever they'd done to me had made me weak. My knees buckled and I ended up back on the floor, crying out when my knees hit the deck. The pain seemed accentuated, hurting more than I'd have thought.

I stayed on the floor, trying to catch my breath and summon the energy to try again. Turning my head, I saw a woman in the cage next to me. She was sitting with her back to the wall, her eyes shut.

"Hey," I rasped. She didn't move.

"Hey," I said more loudly.

This time she opened her eyes, tipping her head my direction as though it weighed more than what her neck could hold. To my shock, I saw that it was Lucy. She looked terrible. Her eyes were bruises in her pale face, her lips cracked and bleeding. Dirt coated her hands and bare arms.

"Where are we?" I asked.

She shrugged, her eyes sliding closed again, and I realized she must still be in the hold of the drug. A thought drifted through my mind: Was that how I looked?

A door opened to my right and light flooded into the room. I pushed myself to a sitting position, hoping I could provide some resistance if it was the man with the needle again. I didn't know whether to be relieved or more afraid when I saw who it was.

Matt Summers.

CHAPTER SIXTEEN

I stared at Matt Summers, waiting. He didn't make me wait long.

"Are you enjoying your accommodations?" he asked solicitously.

"The maid service is crappy," I rasped.

Matt laughed, clasping his hands behind his back as he sauntered closer. "Funny. You're funny. I'm glad to see you haven't lost your sense of humor."

"Where are we?" I asked, ignoring his jibe.

"On board my yacht," he explained.

"This is a yacht? You paid too much."

"The view from above is much more impressive," he said. "All you have to do is cooperate."

I eyed him warily. "Cooperate in what?"

He shrugged. "I know you're related to Detective Turner, my dear Kathleen Turner, and that he told you about Lucy here." He tipped his head toward her. Lucy didn't respond. "All you have to do is tell me what she told the police."

"Ask her yourself."

"She's been decidedly unhelpful," Matt said.

"That'll happen when you take away a woman's child."

Matt looked at me sharply. "I'm hoping you can talk some sense into her," he continued. "She should be coming off the drugs within a few hours. If she cooperates, tells me what she told the police, I'll release you."

"And if she doesn't?"

Matt just smiled. "Up until now I've spared you the fate of the rest of the women, which they are even now enduring, but that can change," he warned. "I'll let you imagine the details." He turned to go.

"Wait!" I said, my bravado melting in the face of this threat. He stopped. "Water. We really need some water."

"Then I suggest you be very convincing." The door swung shut behind him.

I collapsed back to the floor, the conversation with Matt having taken every ounce of energy I could summon or fake. As I lay there, waiting for Lucy to recover, I thought about what Matt had said.

I didn't know how both Lucy and I had made it out of the shantytown without being sold or raped, but I wasn't going to question it. Being on a yacht with Matt was preferable to being sold into sex slavery. If I could just talk with Lucy, maybe we could concoct a plan that would get us out of here.

I tried to ignore my thirst, and eventually I pushed myself up to crawl to the door of the cage. Getting to my knees, I examined the lock. With a jolt, I realized it looked very similar to the lock Kade had given me to practice picking. Renewed energy pulsed in my veins as I searched the floor, looking for anything I could use on the lock.

"Kathleen?"

It was Lucy.

"You're awake!" I said, crouching down next to the mesh separating us. "Are you okay? How do you feel?"

"Awful," she groaned, holding her head. "Where are we?"

I quickly explained where we were and what Matt had said.

"Did he say if Billy was here?" she asked anxiously when I was through.

I shook my head. "No, he didn't."

Her head bowed again, the glimmer of hope I'd seen in her eyes fading.

"Lucy, it's going to be okay," I said. "We'll get—"

I broke off, just now noticing something.

"Lucy," I said excitedly, "is that a pin in your hair?"

Confused, Lucy felt around the mass of tangles, finding the slim piece of metal I'd spied.

"Quick, give it to me!"

I took it to the door of my cage. The lock was heavier than the one Kade had given me, and my pick flimsier, but desperation worked in my favor. After several minutes, the lock clicked open. A few more minutes and Lucy's door was open, too. I helped her to her feet, but it was obvious we were both weak.

"If we can find our way to the bridge," I said, "there's probably a radio there. We can radio for help."

Lucy just looked at me, breathing hard from the mere act of standing. "How are we going to do that?"

I fought the despair inside, the same despair I saw in her eyes. "I don't know, but we have to try." The future Matt had laid out for us was more horrifying than my worst nightmares. Even if Lucy cooperated, I didn't believe he would let us go.

The door to the room was already unlocked and I opened it just a crack to peek through. Beyond was a landing and short staircase going up. No one was in sight. I guess they thought two women, drugged, dehydrated, and locked in cages, were hardly a threat.

Leading the way, I climbed the stairs on all fours, not wanting my head to pop out without knowing what or who was around. My limbs trembled, weak from disuse. I prayed I had the strength to get us out of here.

The hallway was a brilliant white. On the right were doors for what I assumed were the cabins, while to the left was a glass-walled entertainment room. A pool table and a few sofas stood at one end, and a huge flat-screen television hung on the opposite wall.

Sitting in front of the TV playing a video game was Billy.

Lucy's grip nearly crushed my hand. She'd seen him, too.

Then I saw the guard. He was standing in the back, alternately watching the video game and scanning the windows beyond, which looked out onto a lower deck and the ocean. A lethal-looking machine gun was slung over his shoulder while a handgun rested in a holster at his hip.

My nerves were stretched tight as I stared at the guard. How to get rid of him?

"Lucy," I whispered. "If I can get him over here, can you jump him from behind? We can take him down if we work together."

She gave a quick nod. "I'll do whatever I have to. Just so I get Billy back."

"Okay. Get down."

Lucy ducked back down into the stairway while I climbed out. I made no effort to hide, playing up my weakness. I slapped the palm of my hand on the window and leaned against the glass.

The guard noticed me immediately, his body straightening. He hurried to the glass door, pushing it open and coming toward me.

"How did you get up here?" he asked when he reached me.

I moaned as though I were in pain, moving toward the steps. He followed me.

"I said, how did you—"

He was in position, perfectly framed above the stairway.

Lucy leapt at him, attaching herself to his back and hooking an arm around his throat. He struggled to get her off while I grabbed the gun from his holster.

"Got it," I said to Lucy. I pointed the handgun at him and she released her hold, ripping the machine gun from his shoulders.

A slow handclap made us both spin around. Matt stood a few yards away, his applause loud in the hallway.

"Bravo," he mocked. "Well done. How resourceful you are. You subdued one guard. Now, what are you going to do about the other eleven on board? Like the one in there." He tipped his head toward the glass-enclosed room.

Billy was still playing his video game, oblivious to the everything else. A new guard was standing behind him now—with a gun pointed directly at Billy's head. The guard was watching Matt for a signal.

"One word from me and that boy's dead. I imagine a bullet at that range will splatter his brains all over the place.

I might even have to get a new couch. Some stains don't come out, you know, no matter what the manufacturer says."

Lucy sagged in defeat, not resisting when the guard pulled the gun out of her hands. I was filled with fury and bitter despair. To come so close, to have weapons in our hands, only to be recaptured was nearly too much for me to handle.

Matt walked over to me. I didn't lower the gun I held and Matt didn't stop walking until he was right in front of me, the metal barrel pressing against the white linen of his shirt.

"Now you don't want to be responsible for that, do you?" he asked quietly. His lips twisted in a sardonic sneer.

I made myself think about Billy. It was the only way I could let Matt take the gun from my hand.

He shoved it into the back of his pants "Take them to get cleaned up, then bring them to me," Matt ordered the guard. He sniffed. "They smell." Entering the room with Billy, he gave a nod to the guard who holstered his gun.

The guard at my back pushed me forward and I grabbed Lucy's hand. He made us go to the last door on the right, a small bedroom and bathroom.

"You got fifteen minutes." He closed the door behind us.

I immediately started searching the room for something I could use as a weapon, wanting to scream with frustration when I found nothing. There were no hangers in the closet, no mirror I could break for the glass. Nothing.

Lucy and I cleaned up as quickly as we could, taking long moments to quench our thirst. I was glad to be clean, feeling as though six layers of grime had been washed from my skin and hair.

When I saw the clothes laid out for us, though, a sick nausea rolled in my stomach. There were two spaghetti-strap dresses, neither of them longer than mid-thigh, made of nearly transparent material. I thought I knew what Matt had in store for us, and it made me want to vomit.

"Let's go," the guard said. He reopened the door just as I'd finished pulling the dress over my head. I'd briefly considered putting my dirty clothes back on, but I just couldn't do it. Plus, Matt might be more amenable and off his guard if we dressed as he wished.

We were escorted back to the entertainment room, Lucy and I gripping each other's hands. That seemed to give us strength. We weren't alone. We were in this together.

Matt was sitting on a couch, leisurely sipping a drink. His eyes gleamed when he saw us, and a shiver of revulsion ran through me.

"I do enjoy keeping the choicest merchandise for myself," he murmured.

Billy turned at the sound, his gaze lighting on Lucy. "Mommy!" he yelled, tossing aside his video controller and racing toward her.

Matt waved off the guard who had stepped forward to intervene and Billy launched himself into Lucy's arms. Tears ran freely down her cheeks, and my own eyes began to water. His pudgy little arms were tightly wrapped around her neck, and her hold on him was just as tight.

"Why'd you take so long to get here?" Billy asked.

Lucy loosened her grip on him, wiping her face before smoothing his hair, as though she couldn't believe he was all right. "I came as soon as I could," Lucy replied, her voice thick with tears.

"Matt said you might not come, that you didn't want me anymore." The hurt in the small boy's voice was heartbreaking. Rage filled me at Matt's malicious lies to the child, and my hands clenched into fists.

"That's not true," Lucy assured him. "That could never be true. I love you more than anything. You're my baby boy." She pulled him into her arms again, tears leaking from behind her closed eyes.

"You son of a bitch," I gritted out, glaring at Matt, who just smiled.

"Come have a seat, Kathleen," he ordered, patting the space next to him.

I complied, not having much choice with a gun leveled at me.

"So, you want to tell me what she told the police?" he asked.

"I told them the truth." Lucy spoke up before I could reply, her eyes flashing. "That you're a sniveling bastard that smuggles women illegally into the country, then sells them to the dealers in Rio."

Matt's face was turning an angry, mottled color. Afraid he was going to do something to Lucy, I asked a question of my own.

"Why bother smuggling them into the country?" I asked, making Matt look at me. "Wouldn't it be easier to just take them directly from Mexico?"

I didn't think he would reply, but he said, "The fucking cartels in Mexico won't let me. They always want their share, their cut. And you can't work with them. They'll fucking kill you as soon as look at you. Idiotic morons, the lot of them." He smiled, some of the anger fading. "But there's always women wanting to come to America. A word or two, a whispered rumor, that's all it takes to have them do almost anything to get across that border."

Matt turned back to Lucy, his gaze hardening. "But without you, they have no witness, and no case. I just have to make you disappear. An easier feat than you can possibly imagine."

"Your uncle isn't going to be happy that you've taken us," I interjected. "He went to a lot of trouble to make sure you didn't get convicted for the Vale case. What do you think Blane's going to do when he finds out you kidnapped me?"

It was a shot in the dark. The last I'd seen Blane, he'd been shot.

"Oh, I think he'll get over it," Matt sneered.

My heart leapt. Blane was alive!

"It wasn't an accident you were brought along, you know," Matt said. "Some powerful people would very much like to see you disappear, too."

My blood ran cold. I could see by the satisfied expression on his face that he was telling the truth. My mind immediately jumped to the senator's threats. Then my mind made the next logical leap.

"It was him, wasn't it?" I asked. "Your uncle, the billionaire philanthropist—and that organization of his, Improving America Now. It donates millions to politicians. I bet Senator Keaston is one of them. Keaston had him get you to do this."

I knew I was right, and it made me sick inside.

"He didn't have to work real hard." Matt shrugged. "You'll be my plaything for a while, then disappear into the wind.

"Do you prefer warm or cold weather?" The fake solicitousness in his voice was like oil on water. "Rio's nice and warm, but there are colder locales, if you don't mind the winters, though I do hear that Russian men are a bit rougher than the Hispanics."

"Blane will find me," I spat. "And he'll kill you."

"Blane Kirk has a bright future ahead of him," Matt replied, unfazed by my threat. "My uncle knows what potential he has. It's better this way anyway. If you'd been arrested for murder, Kirk would have been heroically compelled to defend you, blah blah blah."

He waved his hand. "With Keaston's endorsement and my uncle's money, Kirk will win. Serve a couple of terms as governor, then it's on to bigger and better things." His eyes gleamed. "The most powerful position in the world."

"Keaston's not going to endorse Blane," I argued, trying to conceal the panic rising in my chest. "They're of different parties. Surely even an ill-educated moron like you knows that."

He slapped me, the sound ringing out in the room. Both Billy and Lucy, who'd been talking quietly together as she rocked him on her lap, fell silent.

The force of the hit knocked me to the floor. I cradled my cheek in my hand, glaring at Matt with hatred in my eyes.

"Show me respect, or I'll teach it to you the hard way," he ordered.

"Fuck you," I snarled.

Matt raised his hand and I flinched, expecting him to hit me again, but he didn't. Instead, he signaled for the guard, who obediently came over.

"Take this one for your enjoyment, then pass her around. I don't care if she survives. Do take pictures, though. I want to make sure my uncle has leverage to keep Kirk in line in the future." Matt's smile was cold and ruthless. "Perhaps he should pick his next girlfriend with more care."

Terror streamed through my veins, then the cold rush of adrenaline. I leapt from the floor to try and get away, though where I thought I could go on a boat, I didn't know.

"No, Matt, please!"

I could hear Lucy begging on my behalf as I ran, though the guard caught me easily, grabbing my hair and yanking. I felt the stab of a needle in my arm and I cried out in pain. Then I twisted and bit his hand until I tasted blood.

The guard roared, dropping me as I dodged his grasping hand. His brutal face was livid now and he snarled curses at me as I ran. The drug he'd injected me with was starting to take hold, but I fought it, knowing that if I didn't, I was worse than dead.

The wind from the sea caught at my hair as I hit the deck running. A set of stairs heading upward caught my eye and I climbed them, twisting on the top step to send a kick toward the pursuing guard. The ball of my foot got him squarely in the nose, and blood spurted. I turned and ran again, not waiting to see if I'd slowed him down.

The upper deck was even windier, whipping my hair into a frenzy and plastering my clothes to my body. To my dismay three more guards stood post up here, all of them turning to look at me as I emerged from the stairway.

A noise behind me made me turn. The bloodied guard was coming up the stairs, his malevolent gaze unblinking as he came for me.

I backed away, my steps faltering as the drug-induced lethargy began to take hold. I blinked rapidly, trying to focus on the four encroaching men. The panic and terror were receding now, replaced by a cold nothingness that I knew was more deadly than fear.

My progress was stopped by a metal bar at my back. Turning, I saw that I was at the very front and top of the boat. The guardrail had stopped my steps, protection from the drop into the waters below.

The decision to climb over the rail was an easy one, though the execution proved more difficult. My limbs were heavy, not wanting to cooperate.

"Stupid bitch is gonna take a swan dive," one of the guards observed. They'd stopped moving forward now, just watching me.

I glanced down. The ocean was churning, the waves beckoning to me. In a corner of my mind not yet altered by the drug, I could appreciate the deadly irony of my predicament. I hadn't saved anyone, hadn't helped anyone. My sacrifice to try and help Lucy and Billy had come to nothing but my own death.

Looking back up at the guards, I took a deep breath. At least my death would be my decision, not theirs.

My hands loosened on the rails as my eyes slipped closed.

A grunt and a thud made me pry my eyes open, harder to do with each passing moment. Two guards lay sprawled on the deck, blood leaking from their heads. The remaining two had their guns in their hands, looking around wildly for the source.

Then another dropped, half his head blown away. He hadn't even hit the floor before the last guard was shot dead, too.

I was in shock, staring at the carnage around me. How had that happened? Was I dreaming?

I squeezed my eyes shut, opening them again with effort. To my amazement, I saw black-clad figures climbing over the rails of the yacht from all sides. They were silent, any sounds masked by the wind and the waves.

Gunfire rang out from below, and now I heard yelling, but it didn't seem to faze the invaders, their movements precise and deadly as they disappeared onto the deck below me.

I didn't know what to do. Glancing back over my shoulder, I saw the water. The waves seemed to hypnotize me, their randomness becoming a pattern. My grip loosened even more, it becoming nearly impossible to hold on to the rail as my muscles began refusing to obey my commands.

"Kathleen!"

My name on the wind. How strange.

I tore my gaze away from the beckoning sea. One of the invaders stood among the dead bodies, his gun slung across his back. His face was painted black, making his green eyes stand out. One arm reached for me as he slowly approached, as though fearing I'd run away.

"Kat, it's me," the man said, coming closer.

My mind sluggishly tried to process the words, unable to reconcile what he'd said with what he looked like. He had a gun over his shoulder, another at his hip, dark grease in his hair, and black body armor strapped to his chest.

"Lucy," I said, forcing the word from between lips gone numb. "Lucy and Billy. You've got to save them. He's going to kill her."

"It's all right," the man said. "They're okay. We have them."

Relief flooded me. It hadn't been for nothing after all. They were going to be okay. I hoped Chance would be, too. I thought he and Lucy would be good together. Maybe they'd have a little girl. She could be called Lana, after Lana Turner, keep the tradition going. Mom and Dad would like that. I wondered if Mom knew where I was. She worried if I came home late from work, though she knew the bar didn't close until late. Maybe Scott would fill in for me tomorrow. I didn't feel well. My stomach churned and I was so tired.

"I think I should lie down," I mumbled. I was exhausted. My eyes drifted shut.

"Kat!"

My eyes opened again. The man was still there, only much closer.

I panicked. "Stay back!" I warned him. "Don't touch me!"

He froze. "Kat, please. It's me. It's Blane. Remember me?"

The name sparked a memory, but it was too difficult to grasp. My mind was filled with cobwebs and it just took too much effort.

"I'm here to help you," the man said. "Take my hand."

I stared at the hand stretched toward me. "Okay."

I reached for him, but my foot slipped on the edge of the deck just as a gust of wind pushed at me. Then I was hurtling through the air. I stared at the man as I fell, an odd peace coming over me. I watched in detachment as he climbed on the rail and dove after me with no hesitation. Then I hit the water.

Cold water closed over my head, bringing clarity to my fogged brain. I sucked in a lungful of liquid before my head broke the surface. I was choking, gasping for air, when a wave slammed into me, submerging me yet again.

Up was down and down was up. I couldn't see a thing, and the cold seeped into my bones just as the drug had. My lungs burned with the need for air as I tried futilely to find the surface, the fear that I was swimming the wrong direction at the edges of my mind.

Something snagged me around the waist, pulling me. A moment later, my head broke through the surface and I choked, trying to get air. Hands under my armpits lifted me and I was lying flat, but I still couldn't breathe.

Pushing, painful pushing on my stomach. Water filled my mouth, streaming out through my lips and nose, again and again. Then I was coughing, retching, and was turned on my side. More water came up as I coughed, but finally I could breathe.

My body was shaking uncontrollably. Someone wrapped a blanket around me. My eyes were shut tight, but I could hear men talking.

"Rico call it in?"

"Yeah. Got the girl and kid in the other RHIB. All hostiles neutralized."

"Let's bug out."

"Roger that."

The rumble of the boat's engines was loud in my ears. A man slid his arms underneath me, picking up my limp body and cradling me on his lap, tucking the blanket securely around my shoulders and legs.

"Doc, take a look. Something's not right. She wasn't in her right mind up there. Didn't even know who I was."

My head was too heavy for my neck, and when a hand gently turned my chin, my head lolled back on the arm of the man holding me. A bright light flashed in my eyes.

"Drugged." My arms were pulled from under the blanket and examined. "Needle tracks. They've been drugging her for a while."

"Will she be all right?"

"I don't know what they gave her, so I don't want to try to counteract it. Best to let it wear off. She needs fluids, though. I'll start an IV."

Beyond the doctor, I could see a couple of others in the boat. One was driving, and another just watching. They all seemed familiar somehow, but I couldn't remember. My teeth cracked together hard as my shivering intensified. The man holding me pulled me closer, his arms wrapping tightly around my back.

"You're okay, Kat," he whispered softly in my ear. "I swear to God you're going to be okay."

I felt a stinging sensation in my arm, but I was used to it and didn't care. I focused on the green eyes staring intently into mine. They were beautiful, mesmerizing. The man's hand brushed my head, tangling in the wet mass of my hair.

"Stay with me, Kat. Stay with me, baby girl. Nothing's going to hurt you now. You're safe. I swear."

He seemed so upset, his words strangling in his throat and coming out as hoarse whispers. I wondered who he was, wished I knew of a way to comfort him. But my body wouldn't obey and neither would my tongue. So I just listened, staring into his eyes as he kept whispering to me, his promises and pleas melding into one melody of sound. I listened until I could no longer resist the warm pull of sleep and I slipped down into the depths of exhaustion.

CHAPTER SEVENTEEN

A week. I'd lost an entire week of my life, with no real memory of the events I'd witnessed or what I'd endured.

I stared at my reflection in the mirror above the sink in the hospital bathroom. The bruises on my face had finally begun to disappear, the black and blue fading to yellow. My lips were no longer swollen, cracked, or bleeding. I'd lost weight—my clavicle bones protruding sharply underneath my skin, my arms sticklike. Even the bones of my hips jutted out further than I would have wanted. Granted, I'd always wanted to be slightly less curvy, but I thought I just looked sickly now.

None of those things held my attention for long, though. It was my eyes that I couldn't look away from. The eyes that stared back at me in the mirror held a knowledge and sadness that hadn't been there before. Gone was the optimistic innocent; in its place was a woman who knew firsthand the evils there were in the world, the people who would treat other human beings as though they were cattle, to be used and slaughtered. I would have been one of them, for the rest of my life, if not for Blane.

I hadn't believed my eyes when I'd woken from my drug-induced stupor to see Blane sitting in a chair next to the hospital bed. He was leaning forward, his head resting on his folded arms, asleep. Even in sleep, his hand maintained a firm grasp on mine.

Confused, I'd looked around, realizing I was in a hospital, safe. It was late. The window showed a dark sky, and muted lights bled underneath my door.

"Blane?" I croaked.

His head shot up immediately, instantly alert.

"Where am I?"

Thankfully, he knew what I meant without me having to elaborate.

"Home," he replied. "We're in Indy."

Tears burned the back of my eyes, but I held them back. Home. I hadn't thought I'd ever see it again.

"How?" My voice was a rasp of pain, my throat burning.

"The GPS," he replied, pouring water into a paper cup nearby. Sliding an arm behind my back, he helped support me so I could take a drink. "It tracked you to an island off the coast of Cuba."

"Cuba?"

Well, that explained the tropical part.

"Yeah," he said. "Once you were in their territory, the feds couldn't do anything. Todd and Rico run a security business, they still do a few ops on the side. They put a team together to come get you."

I leaned back against the pillows, my throat feeling better now after the water.

"What happened to the cops?" I asked. "I was so sure they would come any second, and they never did."

Now Blane's face turned to cold granite. "In the middle of the operation, the feds showed up, told the police to shut it down, that they were inhibiting a federal investigation. The cops were going to come get you, but the feds wouldn't let them, told them it was more important to track where they took the women than to stop them. Their goal was to shut the whole operation down, not just this branch.

"I got out, came after you myself," he continued. "But I was outnumbered."

"They shot you."

Blane nodded. "About then the feds finally let the cops come help me. They arrested the men still standing and got Chance out."

Relief flooded me. Chance was okay.

"But that was the most they were allowed to do. They were kept from interfering when the plane took off, and I was out cold from the bullet wound." His hand brushed the hair from my forehead. "I'm so sorry, Kat. I never should have let you go. I'm sorry that I failed you."

"Stop," I said, lightly pressing my fingers to his mouth. "It's not your fault. It was my decision to try to find Chance, my decision to try and help Lucy and Billy. You did all you could. I trusted the cops. Trusted them to have my back."

He kissed my fingertips and gently held my palm against his cheek.

"I almost lost you," he rasped. "Again. Forever. When you fell from that boat . . ."

His eyes squeezed shut for a moment, then reopened, their deep gray depths tormented.

"Shh," I soothed him. "We're together now. That's all that matters."

Blane reached into his pocket, and my eyes widened when his palm opened to reveal my diamond engagement ring.

"How did you find it?" I breathed in wonder.

Blane took my hand in his, gently sliding the ring back onto my finger. "Found the bastard that took it. He regretted that action, very, very much. I . . . encouraged him to cooperate with us, tell us where Matt had taken you. That's how we found the yacht."

I didn't want to think through the details of what that "encouragement" had entailed, but I hoped it had been extremely painful.

"They were able to trace Amanda Webber's whereabouts from the intel we gathered on the island," Blane continued. "She's recuperating at home with her family now. I thought you'd want to know. The island where they took her and you is in Cuba's territory, but the Navy is keeping an eye on it. I doubt they go there again."

That was a relief. I couldn't imagine the hell the women were going through who hadn't been rescued.

"Xtreme has been shut down. Several of the employees have been arrested for their involvement in the operation."

I hoped one of them was Jack, the bastard.

"What about Matt?" I asked. "Is he in jail?"

"He's dead." Blane's voice was cold and flat. "I made sure of it."

My eyes slipped closed in relief and Blane's grip tightened on my hand.

Blane didn't leave my side again.

~

After three days in the hospital, I was more than ready to go home. Pushing away the memories that disturbed me, I pulled on the soft yoga pants and sweater Blane had brought from home. The doctor had taken his sweet time releasing me, and it was already after five and dark outside. He'd pressed a card into my hand as I left, speaking vaguely about "people to talk to" and "specialists in this sort of thing."

I wished I had something to tell a specialist, but the truth was I couldn't recall most of the ordeal. The doctor had told me the drug cocktail they'd injected me with had scopolamine as its primary ingredient, which accounted for why I couldn't remember so much of the time I was missing. Usually used to treat motion sickness, a high enough concentration of it combined with other chemicals and it acted much like a date-rape drug.

I insisted on walking out of the hospital. I'd never gotten used to their rule about wheelchairs and wasn't about to start now.

"Did you announce your candidacy while I was gone?" I asked Blane once we were in his car and headed home. He just looked at me strangely.

"You're joking, right?"

I flushed and he continued. "I put all that off. Nothing else mattered. Only finding you." His hand found mine, linking our fingers on the empty space between us.

"You're still going to run, right?" I asked. I didn't want what had happened to me to cause him to not pursue his dreams.

He hesitated. "Maybe now's not the right time," he hedged.

"Blane, you can't do that. You can't put your life on hold just because something awful happened. You want to run for governor, then run for governor."

Blane glanced at me, then back at the road.

"Are you sure?" he asked.

"It's your life," I replied.

"It's our life," he corrected. "This affects you as much as it does me."

I smiled weakly. "I don't have a degree in Politician's Wife," I said ruefully, "but I love you. I believe in you."

"That's all that's required," he said with a soft smile.

Mona greeted us when we got home, as well as Tigger, who'd fattened up since last I'd seen him.

"And you certainly could use a few home-cooked meals," Mona said, tears sparkling in her eyes as she gave me a bone-crushing hug.

"That sounds wonderful," I replied. It felt so good to have a mother figure fuss over me again. Were we ever too old to not want our mothers when life got to be too much?

I had another nightmare that night, waking screaming and drenched in sweat. Blane folded my shaking body into his arms, hushing me in gentle tones. He rocked me, pressing his lips against my temple every now and again, until I'd calmed. I'd had bad dreams in the hospital, too, refusing to take a drug that would knock me out. I was through taking any drugs I could reasonably avoid.

"I'm sorry," I whispered, wishing I didn't have to burden him with my fears, no matter how unconsciously done.

"Don't apologize," he said fiercely. "If there's anyone who can understand, it's me."

That made me feel slightly better. We sat in silence for a while, my racing heart slowing to a more normal speed.

"Is there anything you want to talk about?" Blane asked. His voice was quiet in the stillness of the night.

I tensed in his arms. "What do you mean?"

"Anything that . . . happened . . . while you were gone? Sometimes it helps. Talking about it."

Blane had been wonderful, never once asking me The Question. The question that had immediately come to mind when the drugs had worn off and I'd been able to think clearly.

"I wasn't raped," I confessed. I'd requested an exam, wanting to know everything that had happened to me during that period missing from my mind.

Blane's body went still and he was silent for a moment. "Do you remember—"

"The doctor examined me," I explained. "I don't remember anything, no." Except, apparently, in my subconscious.

"You know it wouldn't have mattered to me," Blane said carefully. "I wouldn't think differently of you if you had been."

I leaned back to look at him. "I'm not lying," I said. "I know I didn't tell you before about Avery, but I'm telling you the truth now."

He nodded wordlessly, pulling me down beside him in the bed, his body spooning mine. Surrounded by the feel and scent of him, I felt safe, and was able to drift back to sleep.

The days passed in a blur of activity. Blane announced his candidacy for governor at a press conference rather than the lavish party his uncle had planned before my disappearance. He opened a small office for his campaign staff, mostly volunteers, who wore red, white, and blue shirts proclaiming *Blane Kirk for Governor.*

I helped where I could, running errands, making copies, keeping the volunteers happy and not squabbling with one another. Blane had taken a leave of absence from the law office, transferring his cases to Charlotte, and spent his days crisscrossing the state, visiting small towns and shaking hands. Some days I went with him, others I stayed home.

Mona was helping me plan the wedding. Between all the things to be done for that, plus Blane's candidacy, I was kept plenty busy. So busy that I could sometimes sleep the whole night through. If Blane was there, I often could.

When he wasn't—well, on those nights when I woke up screaming, I wandered the house. Sometimes I'd make a cup of tea and drink it in the library, the room that most strongly reminded me of Blane. Other times I'd wrap myself in a blanket and sit on the back patio, looking up at the stars. I didn't tell Blane this, though, since he worried enough about leaving me alone. When he asked how I'd slept while he was gone, I smiled and said, "Just fine."

It was on one of these sleepless nights that I was curled up in the leather sofa in the library, staring into the dancing fire. It was late March, but the chill of winter refused to ease its grasp. I didn't know what time it was, though I thought I'd heard the grandfather clock chime three times earlier. Absently, I stroked Tigger's ears while he curled on my lap.

"Can't sleep?"

The male voice came from behind me, startling me from my reverie so badly that I screamed, for a flash of an instant plunged back into my nightmares. Tigger hissed and leapt from my lap while I scrambled, grabbing the gun I now always kept close at hand. I quickly turned, my shaking hands barely able to hold the gun steady.

"Princess? You all right?"

Kade stood staring at me, confusion written on his face.

"Oh God," I gasped, dropping my arms. I couldn't breathe, my heart racing in my chest, and tears started rolling down my cheeks.

"Holy shit, what's the matter?"

Kade gingerly took the gun and set it back on the table next to the couch. I didn't answer, my sobs shaking my whole body.

"Don't do that!" I cried out, angry that he'd inadvertently caused me to nearly have a nervous breakdown. "You . . . you scared me!"

"So I see," he said dryly.

Wrapping his arms around me, he held me close, waiting until my tears had subsided.

"You wanna tell me what that was all about?"

I sniffed, looking up at him in confusion. "Blane didn't tell you?"

His eyebrows lifted. "Tell me what?"

I looked down at the floor and haltingly told him what had happened. Since I didn't remember a huge part of it, it didn't take very long.

When I looked up again, the look on his face was terrifying.

"He let them take you?"

"It wasn't his fault," I protested. "I was stupid, and it just . . . happened." I was tired, worn out from the crying jag.

"And now you're here alone, terrified of your own shadow, and pulling a gun on anyone that sneaks up on you?"

I didn't know what to say to that. It was true. I hadn't told Blane that I always kept a gun at hand now.

Kade pulled me into his arms again, holding me close. My arms around his waist gripped him just as tight. The familiar feel and scent of him eased the knot inside my chest.

"I'm going to kill my brother for not calling me," he muttered angrily. "God, what if—"

"It's over," I interrupted, pulling back slightly. I wasn't anxious for another scene between Kade and Blane. "Just let it go. I'm fine."

"I don't think you're fine," he murmured, gently tucking a lock of hair behind my ear.

I didn't answer, instead turning to rest against his chest.

We watched the fire in silence for a few minutes. His arms curved around me as I leaned against him, the soft leather of his jacket underneath my cheek.

"Where have you been?" I asked eventually.

"Trying to find out who Garrett sold out to," he said. His fingers combed absently through my hair. "It had to be the same people who knew we were in Denver. Garrett sent us right into a trap in that club."

I didn't want to talk about Garrett, didn't want to remember that night when Kade had killed for me.

"You're going to be here for the wedding, aren't you?" I asked, changing the subject.

"Sure, princess," Kade said easily, his fingers twisting a soft curl. "Who's getting married?"

It was my turn to look at him strangely. "Me and Blane, of course, who else?"

His body went rigid, his mouth settling into a hard line. "What the fuck are you talking about?"

The harshness of his words made me jump and I moved away from him.

"Blane proposed," I explained. "Surely he told you?"

"He didn't tell me a damn thing," Kade bit out. He got to his feet, shoving a hand through his hair as he paced away from me.

"Kade, what's the matter?" His reaction hurt. "I thought you'd be happy for us." After all we'd been through, did he still feel I wasn't good enough for his brother?

His head whipped around, his blue eyes pinning mine.

"Happy for you? Are you out of your mind?" Anger mixed with incredulousness. "You think I want to see you locked in the prison of being Blane's wife? Do you even realize how much you're going to hate it?"

I was starting to get angry now. "I don't see it as a prison," I shot back. "Who are you to tell me what I'm going to love or hate? You don't know anything about my hopes or dreams."

"You're telling me you want to be saddled with a man whose career will dictate your life? Pump out a litter of kids and play June Cleaver all day?"

His derision set my teeth on edge and I jumped to my feet to confront him. "Yes," I hissed, jabbing my finger against his chest for emphasis. "That is exactly what I want, not that you would know that. Someone I love and who loves me. Someone to talk to about my day and fall asleep next to at night. I want the snotty noses and dirty diapers, midnight feedings and scraped knees. I want a family. Blane can give me all that."

Kade looked as though I'd hit him. I closed my mouth, staring at him, still breathing hard from my angry tirade.

"You think Blane's the only man that can give you that?" Kade's hands closed over my upper arms, holding me in place. "Look at what happens to you because of him. How many times have you nearly died? Look at yourself. You're not happy. You're just existing. He has you completely dependent on him, and you don't even know it."

"That's not true," I protested. "It's called love, Kade. When two people love each other, they do depend on each other, and there's nothing wrong in that."

"Then where is he if he loves you so much?" Kade sneered. "Why aren't you asleep? Where's your hero to protect you from the demons inside your head?"

"I'm not a child," I bit out. "I'm not going to make him stay at home when he has a job to do."

"So what comes first? You? Or his career?" Kade retorted. "Because there's no way in hell I'd leave you alone like this."

"You always leave! You're the first one to run away, Kade! You talk about me not seeing the truth—look in the damn mirror. I can't depend on you, Blane can't depend on you, because you are beholden to no one but yourself!"

He shook me, bringing me closer. "I leave because I'm terrified I'll cross that line in the sand," he gritted out. "The point of no return. And I don't want to stab my brother in the back and lose his trust forever."

Kade's eyes were blue pools of pain, but I didn't understand.

"Blane loves you," I said, my anger fading. "Nothing you do will ever change that."

If only Kade could trust in and accept Blane's love and affection, maybe then he wouldn't feel he had a debt to his brother. Love wasn't supposed to be like that, but my guess was that Kade had known too little of love to know what it was supposed to be.

"Ah, sweetheart," Kade sighed in defeat, his grip loosening on my arms. "If only that were true." His fingers combed through my hair. "But if Blane knew the thoughts in my head right now, he'd kill me."

"Don't say that," I implored. "That's an awful, terrible thing to say."

"It's true," Kade insisted, the timbre of his voice lowering. "I look in your eyes and see my soul written there."

I was stunned, listening to words I shouldn't hear, words he shouldn't utter. Yet I couldn't make myself push him away. The agony and adulation in his eyes held me captive.

"I want to tell you how I knew from the moment I laid eyes on you that you were destined to be my downfall."

I swallowed hard. Unable to look into his eyes any longer, I finally broke our locked gaze to stare at a point somewhere on his chest.

"Kade," I said, my voice cracking. "Don't tell me these things. I can't . . . it's just wrong. We're going to be family. I'll be your sister."

"My feelings for you are far from familial," he said bitterly.

Before I could react, his hands closed over my hips, yanking me toward him. Our bodies pressed close together, my breasts against the hard planes of his chest. His hands moved to cup my rear.

"Does that feel brotherly to you?"

I started to panic. This couldn't be happening.

"Stop," I warned. "Don't do this. Let me go."

"You were never in the plan," he whispered. "God, I wish I'd never met you." The anguish in his voice tore through me even as his words cut deep. "Just so I wouldn't have to feel this way anymore."

"I care about you. You're my friend," I insisted.

"Liar," he growled. "You feel more for me, even if you refuse to admit it."

His mouth came down hard on mine, demanding a response. I fought him, trying to twist away, but his hands cradled my face, keeping me in place as his lips moved over mine. My hands moved to his chest and gave him a hard shove.

I didn't think, just reacted, the palm of my hand cracking against his cheek in a stinging slap.

We both froze. I was horrified at what I'd done.

Kade slowly turned back to me, his eyes meeting mine. "You can lie to yourself all you want, but I'm the one you should be with, not Blane," he rasped. "You may love Blane, but it's based on all the wrong things."

"You don't know anything!" I shouted, oblivious to the tears running down my cheeks.

"I know that the only jewelry you're wearing is the necklace I gave you, not his engagement ring. You may not want to admit it, but you know I'm right."

"Get out!"

A nearby crystal clock caught my eye. I hurled it at Kade, who ducked. The clock shattered against the wall.

Kade's look was penetrating. "Don't worry. I'm not going to stay and watch you make the biggest mistake of your life." Then he disappeared though the door.

I collapsed onto the couch, a sobbing mess. The words Kade had said were ringing inside my head. It wasn't true. I loved Blane. He loved me. We were going to build a life together.

I finally fell asleep on the couch, my palm curled around the golden locket hanging from my neck.

Blane found me there the next morning.

"Hey, sleepyhead," he teased, sitting next to me on the couch. "Why are you in here? You feeling okay?"

His hands brushed my hair back from my face as I rubbed my tear-swollen eyes.

"Yeah," I muttered. "I'm fine. Just couldn't sleep last night."

"Nightmares?"

I looked up at him, hesitating, but he read the truth on my face and cursed. "I knew I shouldn't have left you alone."

"It's all right," I said. "I'm a big girl. I can handle it." I forced a smile.

His smile back was just as faint. "I brought you some coffee," he said, picking up a mug from the table and handing it to me.

I sat up, resting my back against the arm of the couch and pulling my knees to my chest. The steaming mug felt good in my cold hands and I took a sip. "Mmm, thank you."

"I'm in town today," he said, "but have to leave tonight for a fund-raiser in Fort Wayne. I was hoping you could meet me at the office and we'd have lunch today."

"Sounds good," I replied.

We settled on a time and he said, "Robert and Vivian are in town. Do you mind if they join us?"

Something niggled at the back of my mind when he spoke about the senator, something important, but I couldn't remember what it was. What I did recall was how displeased the senator had been when I'd told him of our engagement.

"Blane," I began hesitantly, ". . . you do know that the senator doesn't approve of me . . . of us."

Blane looked away, his expression unreadable. "He's always wanted me to marry some politician's daughter, that's all. He'll come around."

He looked back at me, resting his hand on my bent knee. "Vivian adores you." His smile was gentle.

"So what happened to the clock?" he asked, tipping his head to the shattered remains scattering the floor across the room.

I blanched. "Um." I scrambled for a plausible explanation. "There was a mouse."

"So you threw a clock at it?"

"It was a big mouse," I muttered, my face heating in embarrassment.

It wasn't like I could tell him the truth. I could just see how that would go over. Well, Kade came by, kissed me, then told me I was making the wrong decision and that I secretly love him. Yeah, I was sure Blane would react really well to that. I kept my mouth shut and hoped he'd drop it. I was in luck.

"I've got to get going." Blane glanced at his watch. "Just stopped in to see you before going to the office."

"Thanks," I said, a real smile curving my lips this time.

"I'll see you in a few hours, okay?"

I nodded. He pressed his lips to my forehead and was gone.

I cleaned up the mess from the clock, not wanting Mona to have to do it, before showering and getting dressed. The words Kade had said last night still bothered me, though I tried to not think about them, even as I tucked the locket under my blouse out of sight. I wore it because of the photo of my parents, not because he'd given it to me. He'd just misinterpreted it, that's all.

As I drove to the firm, I thought about how I'd reacted last night to Kade startling me. That wasn't normal. I didn't feel normal anymore, and I wondered if I ever would again. The only thing that seemed to ease the constant knot of anxiety in my stomach was when I was with Blane.

Or Kade, a little voice inside my head whispered.

But it was true. Even when Kade and I fought, the pressure inside my head hadn't been there. I hoped that time would fix what was broken between us, that we could be friends again.

It was a little before noon when I parked the car and headed inside the firm. Spring was in the air. A few of the trees were sporting buds, and vibrantly green blades of grass were pushing through the brown carpet of winter. The sun was warm on my hair and skin, easing the darkness inside, until I felt downright cheerful. It was good to be alive.

Clarice had already left for lunch, so I bypassed her desk, disappointed to not be able to see her. Maybe she'd be here when we got back.

Blane's door was closed, so I knocked before opening it. Sunlight streamed through the open blinds on the windows.

"Right on time," I said cheerily, stepping inside. Then the smile froze on my face before fading completely.

Blane sat at his desk, his head in his hands, his body bent as though in pain.

"Blane!" I cried out, rushing toward him. "What is it? What's wrong?"

He looked up at the sound of my voice, and the look on his face stopped me in my tracks. Anguish, pain, fury—all three were etched in his expression. His eyes were red-rimmed and full of agony.

"What happened?" I asked, dread consuming me. If it was something bad enough to affect Blane so deeply, it had to be very, very bad.

"How could you?" he whispered, and never had I heard so much anger and betrayal in his voice.

"What are you talking about?" My face and hands had gone ice-cold, nausea curling in my gut.

"My dear, you didn't think you could keep this a secret, did you?"

I spun around, not having realized that Senator Keaston was sitting in the office as well. He eyed me with false compassion, while satisfaction gleamed in his eyes.

"Keep what a secret?" My voice was stronger than it had been before.

"Your affair with Kade, of course."

My mouth fell open in shock. "I don't know what—"

"Stop with the innocent act," the senator interrupted with a disdainful snort. "I've known what you were all along. I just hated having to tell Blane the truth."

I turned back to Blane, panic and dread clawing at my chest. "Blane, it's not true," I protested. "Please believe me! I haven't had an affair with Kade!"

"The evidence doesn't lie," the senator intoned.

"What evidence?" I cried. "I haven't done anything!"

Blane abruptly stood, the fury on his face, which marked every inch of his body, sparking fear in me. I took a step back.

"Uncle, please give us a moment," Blane said. It wasn't a request.

The senator rose and exited the room, closing the door behind him.

"You're lying," Blane accused, once the door had shut. He grabbed a sheaf of papers from his desk. "This is my proof." He tossed the stack at me.

I threw my hands up to protect my face from the flying papers, a cry of fear strangling in my throat. The papers settled to the floor and I glanced down at them.

Pictures of Kade and me stared back. We were in Denver, inside Bar Sinister. Kade had his hands on my hips as I stood between his spread thighs. My borrowed clothes were even worse captured in color and printed on glossy 8x10. A second photo showed him leaning close, as though about to kiss me. Another was a close-up of his hands on the backs of my thighs, sliding up under my skirt.

Horrified, I looked at Blane. "Blane, it . . . it wasn't like that," I stammered. "We were on a case—"

"You shared the same fucking hotel room!"

I flinched. "Nothing happened—"

"Maybe I could have forgiven that," Blane interrupted, his voice calm now but still filled with fury. "Maybe. But now? In my own home?"

"What—"

"Tell me Kade wasn't there last night. Tell me he didn't come by when I wasn't there."

I just stared at him, horrified. He had it all wrong. Kade had come by, but I hadn't slept with him. Looking at Blane, at the rage and betrayal on his face, I knew he wouldn't be-lieve me. The photos at my feet mocked me.

My silence was telling. Some of the anger on Blane's face faded away, replaced by a cold nothingness.

"I saw you two," he said. "The morning after we rescued those women at Xtreme. I looked in to check on you, make sure you were okay."

He paused and I knew with painful certainty what was coming next.

"I saw you, wrapped in each other's arms," Blane said. "I tried to believe it was innocent, that you wouldn't do that to me. That Kade wouldn't do that to me, my own brother. But I was wrong. Wrong to trust either of you."

"No, Blane," I protested, tears coming to my eyes. "I swear. I told you I care about Kade, but it's not like that! Not like what you think!"

"I opened up to you," Blane said quietly. The pain in his voice made me wince. "Told you how hard it was for me to care about someone, love someone. Did that mean nothing to you?"

"Blane . . . I didn't . . . I swear . . . you have to believe me," I stammered. "I'd never do that to you." I didn't know what to say, how to make him believe that I hadn't slept with Kade.

His smile was cold and devoid of humor. "You know, that's how I know a client is lying. They say things like 'I'd never do that,' and 'You have to believe me.' Well, I don't have to do anything. And I'm certainly not going to marry you. Not now. Not Kade. I can't forgive you this—"

Blane's voice broke and he abruptly turned away, as though he couldn't bear the sight of me any longer. He stared out the window, arms crossed over his chest.

I stared at him in shocked horror. He was like a different person, his rage and pain a steel wall between us.

Stepping forward, I slid the engagement ring off my finger and set it on his desk. The sound of the metal hitting the wood made Blane turn, but he made no move to pick it up.

"Good-bye, Blane," I said. I swallowed hard, holding back the sob I could feel rising in my chest.

My last glimpse of Blane would stay with me for a long time. His face was like granite, unreadable and devoid of emotion. But his eyes—his eyes were filled with the pain of my supposed betrayal.

Darkness and despair filled the pit of my stomach until the pain was nearly unbearable and I thought I was going to be sick.

Turning away before I lost control, I left his office. My eyes caught again on the senator, silently watching me from where he stood by Clarice's desk.

"Congratulations," I bit out. "You won."

And I didn't cry. I couldn't. It seemed once I'd left Blane's office, my emotions had shut down and I operated on autopilot.

I drove to The Drop, smiling mechanically at my old friends as they greeted me. I was in luck. My old boss, Romeo, was there. I didn't have to grovel too much to get my job back. I guess he'd had a tough time replacing me. He gave me my schedule and a new uniform and I drove home.

Gerard was waiting for me when I arrived at my apartment. Tigger was in a pet carrier at his feet.

"Thanks for bringing him by," I said, unsure if Blane had spread the lies he believed to Mona and Gerard.

"Mona's going to miss him," he replied with a sigh, "and you. We both are."

His eyes were kind and I couldn't resist giving him a hug. "I'll miss you, too."

Gerard's eyes were watery when we parted. He cleared his throat. "Here," he said gruffly, handing me a paper bag. "Mona cooked dinner for you. Didn't want it to go to waste. Said you need to eat more, get some meat back on those bones."

Now my eyes got teary. "Tell her thank you for me," I said. "I really appreciate it."

Gerard gave a small nod and smile, blinking rapidly as he turned to go. I watched him walk down the stairs before I went inside.

Tigger meowed loudly, disgruntled at being in the pet carrier, and I hurriedly let him out before going into the kitchen to refill his food and water bowls. I put Mona's food into the refrigerator. My stomach was churning too much to consider eating at the moment.

Going into my bedroom was hard, with memories of Blane assaulting me. I steeled myself and lay down on my bed, curled into a ball on my side, and pulled the blankets up over me.

I slept.

When I woke, I used the bathroom, kicked off my shoes, climbed back into bed, and slept some more.

I lost count of the hours, the sun streaming through my window, darkness falling again. And still I slept.

I didn't know when I would have gotten out of bed if not for the incessant knocking that came the next day. I tried to just turn over and ignore it, but whoever was out there was persistent. Finally, I crawled out from under the covers and went to the door. Peeking through the peephole, I saw that it was Alisha.

She took one look at me, said, "Aw, honey," and folded me in her arms. That's when I began to cry.

Alisha sat with me, letting me cry on her shoulder, not asking any questions. When I had no more tears, I just sat there, her arms around me. She smoothed my hair, a comforting gesture, reminding me of how my mom used to hold me when I cried.

In a halting voice, I told her everything. Blane proposing, my being taken, my rescue, Kade's visit and fury over my engagement, and finally the blowup in Blane's office. She was quiet when I was finished, taking it all in.

"Considering what happened with Kandi," she finally said, "Blane has some nerve accusing you of cheating on him."

I couldn't disagree.

"I know it hurts terribly," she said, "but if he doesn't believe you now, when will he? Five years and two kids down the road?" She shook her head. "Better to have your eyes opened now than wait until kids are in the middle of every-thing and you have much more to lose."

It felt like a knife twisting in my gut to hear her say those words, but I knew deep down I agreed with her.

I sat up, grabbed a tissue, and blew my nose.

"Feel better?" Alisha asked.

I gave her a wan smile. It felt good to not be alone.

"I'm hungry," she said. "Got anything to eat?"

"Mona made something a couple of days ago," I replied. "I put it in the fridge."

"Okay, I'll scrounge us up some food while you go clean up," she ordered. "You look like you haven't seen the inside of a shower in days. Smell like it, too." She winked and I couldn't help the embarrassed huff of laughter that came out of my mouth.

I obeyed, taking a long shower and changing into clean clothes. I brushed my teeth and combed out my hair. When I came out of the bathroom, Alisha had set the table, and two plates of steaming food were waiting for us.

"Manicotti," Alisha said with a sigh. "I do love Mona."

"She's fantastic," I agreed. I was afraid I wouldn't be able to stomach more than a couple of bites, but I managed to eat half of what Alisha had piled on my plate.

"So what are your plans now?" Alisha asked, sitting back in her chair and groaning. "Sheesh, I ate too much."

"I got my job back at The Drop," I said. "I start again on Friday." I paused, thinking. "Wait, what's today?"

"Thursday."

"Good," I said with relief. "That would've been bad if I got my job back then didn't show up for work. How'd your Valentine's date with Lewis go?"

Alisha tried to hide a smile. "Really well. We've gone out a few more times since then. I really like him. But let's not talk about it."

"It's okay to talk about your love life," I said. "Don't be silly."

"I don't want to upset you," she protested.

"What kind of friend would I be if I demanded you not be happy just because I'm not?"

Alisha frowned at my rhetorical question. "I wish you were happy. How do you feel?"

I thought about it. "Sad. Depressed." I hesitated, staring over Alisha's shoulder at nothing, my concentration directed inward. "And angry. Really, really angry." Those words surprised me and I realized they were true.

"I'm angry at the cops who were supposed to protect me. I'm angry at the men who took me, who took all those other women and treated them like cattle. I'm angry at the senator for interfering and lying to Blane. I'm angry at Kade for making me doubt my feelings for Blane. And I'm really angry at Blane, for not believing in me, in us. For offering me a future with him, then snatching it away."

It occurred to me then that I'd had enough. Though I'd told Blane I was tired of being buffeted by the winds of my life, I'd succumbed once again, playing the victim to other people's machinations. I'd been nothing but collateral damage, as had my relationship with Blane. If I was ever going to be happy, it was up to me to make it happen. A family might not be in the cards right now, but someday I'd meet a man who loved me and believed in me.

"I think I'm going to go back to school," I said slowly.

"I think that's a great idea," Alisha enthused.

"I'll go to school during the day and work nights at The Drop," I said, making my decision on the spot. Yes, it would put me back in debt, but it was an investment in my future, my happiness, my life.

"What will you study?" Alisha asked.

There was really only one answer to that, and it sprang easily from my lips.

"Criminal justice."

EPILOGUE

It was late when Kade pulled into Blane's driveway. He'd wanted to leave town, meant to leave town, but he hadn't made it very far before he found himself circling back around to Indy. Now he sat in the car, engine silent, staring at the dark house.

He'd lost her last night.

Maybe he'd known all along. She was beyond him. So far above him, it felt almost a sin to look at her, touch her. Never before did he have a moment's hesitation or qualm about the life he'd chosen. Not even Blane's disapproval had dissuaded Kade from his path.

She had changed all that.

Now regret was a constant companion, the "what ifs" enough to drive him mad if he thought about them too long. What if he'd stayed, talked to her, maybe taken her to dinner those many months ago when she'd fought off her courthouse attacker? He'd felt the pull, even then, without even knowing her name. She'd looked up at him with those clear blue eyes, her cheeks pale, her long blonde hair the color of the sunrise, and it was like an electric shock had gone through him.

Now it was too late. She belonged to someone else. And not just anyone else.

His brother.

Kade had waited too long for Blane to find someone to be happy with, to really be happy with, to begrudge him it now. Blane was a good man. He'd take care of her. The words Kade had said earlier to Kathleen had been a product of his own anger and despair. Despite all Kade's futile hopes to the contrary, Blane loved her, was going to marry her.

Kade just had to find a way to live with that.

With a heavy sigh, he got out of the car. He'd apologize to Kathleen, congratulate Blane, then get the hell out of town until he had to be back.

To watch her walk down the aisle . . . into another man's arms. Piece of cake.

Right.

Kade went in through the back door into the kitchen. His steps were silent without any conscious effort. It was second nature to be a shadow inside the shadows.

Kathleen was probably asleep, but a light filtered from under the library door, so Blane must still be up. Kade turned his footsteps that direction and eased open the door.

Still in his work clothes, minus the jacket and tie, Blane was sitting on the couch in front of the cold fireplace, leaning his elbows on his knees. One hand held a crystal glass with amber liquid, the other was resting on the back of his neck as he stared at the floor. The only sound was that of the grandfather clock ticking in the corner.

Kade frowned. Attuned to his brother's moods, he knew this wasn't a pose in which Blane often appeared. A nearly empty decanter sat on the table at his side, and Kade's brows climbed. Blane drank, yes, but it had been years since Kade had seen Blane allow himself to get drunk.

Without warning, Blane suddenly flung his glass into the fireplace, the crystal shattering against the stone.

All Kade's alarms were going off inside his head now. This wasn't like Blane.

"You keep doing that, Mona's going to kick your ass. That's Mom's crystal," Kade said.

Before he'd even finished speaking, Blane was on his feet, gun in hand and pointed directly at Kade.

Kade wasn't surprised at Blane's reaction; it had been a common one when Blane had first returned from deployment. What did surprise him was the fact that the gun remained pointed at him.

"Really?" he finally said, cocking an eyebrow at Blane.

Blane stared at him, unblinking, before finally lowering the gun and tossing it onto the couch. "Get the fuck out," he said. He turned away, going to retrieve another glass from the sideboard.

Kade stood for a moment, uncertain of what was going on. "Worn out my welcome already? It usually takes at least a week to do that," he joked.

Blane ignored him, which only made Kade more concerned. Walking over to the sideboard himself, he poured a shot of bourbon into a glass.

"Bad day at work?"

Blane didn't look at him as he said, "I'm not kidding. We're through. Get out."

They were words Kade had hoped never to hear but had never been able to convince himself wouldn't come, no matter what Blane said to the contrary. He could feel it. The old fear curled in the pit of his stomach. The dead certainty that the brother he'd idolized since he first set eyes on him at the age of ten would eventually realize that Kade wasn't worth it. Wasn't worth wasting his time or his affection.

Those words were harder to take after the years of endless waiting.

Kade tossed back the liquor, embracing the burning path it left in its wake. Physical pain was always a welcome respite to the agony he felt inside.

"Right," he said tonelessly, setting the glass back on the table. Blane had yet to look at him.

Steeling himself, Kade asked, "Where's Kathleen?" He'd like to see her, to say good-bye, one last time.

Kade wasn't prepared for the onslaught that question unleashed. In seconds, Blane had him shoved against the wall, his fists gripping the front of Kade's jacket as he snarled, "Don't you even say her fucking name to me, you son of a bitch."

"What the fuck, Blane?" Kade yelled in surprise and anger.

"I opened my home to you." Blane's face was a mask of rage and betrayal. "Gave you everything I could. Tried to make up for the old man leaving you to rot. I trusted you." His face contorted in pain. "And this is how you repay me?"

Kade shoved Blane, twisting away so he was out of reach. Blane's words struck a deep chord of guilt. "I never asked you for anything! I didn't tell you to come find me! I didn't ask to come here!" He paused, his breath coming hard as he stared at his brother. "How the fuck am I supposed to repay you that?"

It was a question that kept Kade awake nights. How could he possible repay Blane for everything he'd given? It was impossible. He'd spent the last eighteen years trying.

Blane's eyes grew hard. "I certainly wouldn't have chosen to fuck my fiancée."

Kade's blood ran cold. "What are you talking about?"

"Don't bullshit me." Blane's voice was like ice. "I've seen. I know. I trusted you. I trusted her. And you both betrayed me."

"Blane, I swear, it's not what you think—"

"Don't fucking lie to me!" Blane exploded, coming after Kade. He threw a punch, catching Kade off guard.

Kade blocked the next blow, twisting Blane's arm around behind him and grabbing him in a headlock.

"Listen to me," Kade demanded, "nothing happened—"

Blane struck back at Kade, who was forced to release him. They fought, though Kade pulled his punches, not wanting to hurt his shit-for-brains brother.

"I trusted you!" Blane yelled while Kade dodged his blows. Blane was drunk and slower than he would have been normally.

The pain and rage in Blane's voice was like a steel knife sliding between Kade's ribs. Kade had no idea where Blane had gotten the idea that he'd slept with Kathleen, and wanted to make him listen to reason.

"Knock it off!" Kade shouted. "If you don't believe me, ask her! She'll tell you! I didn't sleep with her!"

"I did ask her," Blane snarled. "She lied to me. Just like you are."

Fear for Kathleen struck Kade and he quit pulling his punches and dodging. In seconds, he had Blane by the throat against the wall. "Where is she?" Kade demanded. "What did you do to her?"

Blane's gaze was unrepentant, blood and sweat dripping down his face. "What do you think I did?" he asked, his voice quiet now. "I'm not going to marry a woman who fucks my own brother behind my back."

Rage consumed Kade. In seconds, Blane was on the floor. Kade stood above him, breathing in gasps as he struggled for control. Blane groaned, turning to the side to spit a mouthful of blood.

Kade wiped away the blood seeping from his nose, staring in disgust at his brother. His hands ached, the knuckles raw and bruised.

"Kathleen was telling you the truth," Kade stated flatly. "We never slept together. Not that I didn't try, back when I thought she was just another eye-candy diversion for you. She turned me down every time. All I've heard is how much she loves you, how she belongs with you."

Blane had halfway sat up, one hand holding his side. Kade couldn't see his face.

"You got her to trust you, fall in love with you, agree to marry you, then you call her a whore and liar and break her heart?" Kade's voice held nothing but loathing. "You don't fucking deserve her. And chances are, she realizes that now, too."

Kade turned away, his emotions a mix of fury, disgust, and sorrow. He was almost out the door when he remembered.

"Oh yeah," he said. "I came here tonight to tell you congratulations"—he paused—"but it looks like you've ruined the best thing that ever happened to you."

Moments later, he was back in his car and speeding into the night.

NOTE FROM THE AUTHOR

Human trafficking is a horrendous crime that affects upward of 2.5 million people around the world. It can happen to anyone, anywhere, even in the US and other Western countries.

Under federal law, any individual who uses physical or psychological violence to force someone into labor or services, or into commercial sex acts is considered a human trafficker. Some victims experience beatings, rape, and other forms of physical violence, while other victims are controlled by traffickers through psychological means, such as threats of violence, manipulation, and lies. In many cases, traffickers use a combination of direct violence and mental abuse. The federal definition of the crime, as defined in the Trafficking Victims Protection Act of 2000 (TVPA), was created to address the wider spectrum of methods of control used by traffickers beyond "bodily harm."

The National Human Trafficking Resource Center (NHTRC), at 1-888-3737-888, is a toll-free hotline, available to answer calls from anywhere in the US, 24 hours a day, 7 days a week, every day of the year. The NHTRC is a program of Polaris Project, a nonprofit, nongovernmental organization working exclusively on the issue of human trafficking. The Polaris Project (www.polarisproject.org) is one of the leading organizations in the global fight against human trafficking and modern-day slavery. Please visit their website for more information or to find out how you can help fight human trafficking.

ABOUT THE AUTHOR

Tiffany Snow has been reading romance novels since she was too young to read romance novels. After fifteen years working in the Information Technology field, she now holds her dream job of writing full time.

Tiffany makes her home in the Midwest with her husband and two daughters. She can be reached at tiffany@tiffanyasnow.com. Visit her at her website, www.TiffanyASnow.com, to keep up with the latest in *The Kathleen Turner Series*.

Turn the page for a sneak peek at the fourth book in *The Kathleen Turner Series, Out of Turn*.

Out of Turn

CHAPTER ONE

No one had shot at me in weeks, or beat me up. I hadn't been cut, punched, or slapped. No one threatened me, stalked me, or stabbed me.

It was a nice change.

And that's what I kept telling myself as I headed to my car. It was midafternoon and the humid heat of late June in Indianapolis made perspiration slide down the middle of my back under the thin T-shirt I wore. The backpack I carried didn't help matters any.

The air inside my white Toyota Corolla was stifling, and sliding inside felt as though I were climbing into an oven. I rolled down the windows as I drove to my apartment, waiting for the AC to kick in. The air gusting through the windows was still hot, but cooled my sweat-dampened skin.

I thought longingly of the huge Lexus SUV I'd had the brief privilege of driving. It had been a gift, a wonderful gift that I'd have been happy to keep, if it hadn't cost so much to drive. Gas was too expensive for me to justify driving the luxury car, especially when I sometimes wondered how I was going to pay my rent, so I'd sold it, using the money to buy a used Toyota and what was left to help pay my tuition.

I had just enough time to feed my cat Tigger and jump in the shower before I had to leave for work at The Drop. It was Friday night and, like most downtown bars, I was sure we'd be busy.

In the summer my boss, Romeo, allowed the girls to wear black shorts and white T-shirts instead of our usual uniform. That would normally be a good thing, but Romeo believed sex always sells, so the shorts were nearly Daisy Dukes, and the T-shirts were tight with plunging necklines. Not that I could be real choosy about it. I needed my bartending job to pay the bills, especially since I was now taking classes during the day at the IU campus downtown rather than working for the law firm of Kirk and Trent.

"Hey, Kathleen! Can you give me a hand?"

That's me. Kathleen Turner, and sometimes I really wished I were *that* Kathleen Turner. I bet she never had to worry about paying her electric bill. Cursed with the family legacy, I had been the latest to be named for a famous Turner. My dad was Ted Turner, my grandma was Tina Turner, and my cousin was William Turner, though he went by his middle name, Chance. Wish I'd thought of that years ago.

"Yeah, sure," I replied to Tish as she juggled one too many plates of food. I shoved my purse under the bar and hurried to help her take the dishes to a table of five.

I was right. The bar was busy tonight and I didn't have time to even think. I was grateful for that. I didn't want to think. If I did, I'd remember.

"Another round, please."

I jerked my attention back to my job, hurrying to fill the order tossed my way. By the time closing neared, I was almost dead on my feet. Thank God. Maybe I'd get more than three or four hours sleep tonight.

"Have some cheese fries," Tish said, sliding onto a stool and placing a laden plate on the bar. "I'm exhausted," she sighed, picking up a dripping French fry and popping it in her mouth.

I grabbed us each a bottle of beer and leaned against the bar. The cold, bitter liquid felt good going down. My hair had come loose from its ponytail, so I redid it, pulling the long strawberry blonde strands up and off my neck. I hated when my hair got in the way when I was working, but I liked it too much to have it cut short. Along with my blue eyes, I thought it was my best feature.

"Have some," Tish insisted, pushing the plate toward me.

I shook my head. "No, thanks. I'm good." I took another drink.

"Kathleen, you drink too much and eat too little," she said with a frown.

I snorted, my eyebrows climbing. "Yes, Mom," I teased.

Tish didn't smile back. "I'm your friend and I'm worried about you."

"I'm fine," I dismissed. To appease her, I picked up a fry and took a bite.

She hesitated. "You know, maybe you could talk to someone. I have this lady I see every once in a while—"

"No, thanks," I interrupted, taking another swig.

"But it may help . . ."

Tish stopped talking at the look I gave her. She heaved a sigh and ate another cheese fry.

I couldn't be mad at her, not really. She cared about me and was just trying to help. Once upon a time, I'd have probably said the same thing. Come to think of it, I actually had given the same advice, in what felt like a lifetime ago. And the recipient had reacted the same way I had.

Why the fuck would I want to do that?

"It's just a breakup," I said, feeling bad now that she was worrying about me. "Everybody goes through them." I shrugged and finished off my beer, tossing the bottle into the trash with a loud clank.

"It's just . . ."

She paused and I raised my eyebrows.

"Just what?" I asked.

"You're . . . different now," she said, looking slightly abashed. "Harder, I guess. Colder. And I just really hate to see you that way."

Her words stung. I couldn't disagree with her, but it wasn't something I could fix right now. I needed an emotional distance from everyone, including myself.

"I'm sorry," I said quietly. "I don't mean to be. I just can't—"

"I know," she said, reaching out to rest a hand on my arm. "I know you need to be in this place for now, just don't let yourself stay there, okay? I miss the old Kathleen."

I gave Tish a weak smile, but inwardly I wondered if the old Kathleen was gone for good.

"Rough night, eh, ladies?"

I turned to see that Scott had grabbed his own beer. He leaned against the bar behind me, glad to be done with his bartending shift.

"Good tips, though," I said, stepping away from Tish.

Scott turned the volume up on the television, sipping his beer while he watched the news. A familiar name froze me in my tracks.

". . . gubernatorial candidate Blane Kirk is back in Indy tonight for a fund-raiser downtown after ten days on campaign stops throughout the state."

I felt as though someone had sucker punched me. My hands turned to ice. I couldn't take a deep breath. Even so, I couldn't stop myself from turning to look.

Blane.

I'd avoided all newspapers and the television for three months. This was the first time I'd seen his face since that awful day in March. The day he'd accused me of sleeping with his brother, the day he broke off our engagement.

If I'd thought the passage of time would ease the blow when I saw his image again, I was very, very wrong.

I avidly drank in the news footage, which showed Blane shaking hands with people in a crowd, the sunlight making his dark-blond hair shine like gold. He had on a loosely knotted tie and a white shirt with the cuffs rolled back. His smile was gleaming white, dimpled, and perfect. A politician at his best. I noticed his smile still didn't reach his eyes, but then again, it rarely did.

The scene changed, showing Blane now in a tuxedo entering the Grand Plaza downtown. A woman was with him, his hand on her lower back. I watched, unable to tear my eyes away, as she turned and the camera caught her face.

Charlotte Page.

Dressed in a long gown of deep bronze, she exuded elegance and sensuality. Her hair was long and nearly black, her skin a warm olive. I'd once likened her to Penélope Cruz and I could see the description was still apt. A fellow lawyer in the firm, together she and Blane made a stunning pair.

I couldn't breathe.

"I've . . . uh . . . I've got to go," I stammered, making a frantic grab for my purse under the bar.

"Yeah, sure, I'll close up," Tish said.

She frowned at Scott, but he didn't see, since he was still watching TV. I couldn't blame him. I'd told only Tish the sordid details of my breakup with Blane.

"Thanks." I managed a grateful smile before beating a hasty retreat outside. I heard Scott calling a belated good-bye to me as the door swung closed.

Once I reached my car, I just leaned against it, bracing my arms on the warm metal.

Just breathe.

I drove on autopilot, replaying the images of Blane in my head. It made my chest hurt and my stomach turn into knots. I regretted even the small bite of French fry I'd eaten as nausea clawed my throat.

I thought by now it would have been easier to see him with someone else.

It wasn't.

Tigger met me at the door. My two-story apartment building was in a section of Indy where police sirens were a nightly occurrence, but I hadn't had any problems since I'd lived there. At least, no problems that were because of the neighborhood.

I changed into a more comfortable pair of shorts and a tank, opening the windows to give my AC, and my electric bill, a break. Light filtered in from the streetlamps, so I didn't bother turning on any lights in the apartment. I poured myself a vodka tonic and curled up on the couch, absently petting Tigger as I stared into space.

It was late, but I knew if I went to bed, I wouldn't sleep. And even if I did, I'd probably be plagued by nightmares. The ordeal I'd endured a few months ago at the hands of human traffickers had left mental scars, though physically I was fine. So I didn't sleep a whole lot.

My stomach churned and I resolutely took another drink. I did not want to puke. I hated throwing up.

I thought about what Tish had said and wondered when, if ever, I'd feel like myself again. Normal. When I didn't dread each new day as something to get through. When I'd look forward to waking up. When the ice inside me would melt.

I was angry with Blane, that much was true. He had believed his uncle's lies instead of me, his fiancée. He hadn't trusted me.

But I was devastated, too. Blane had devastated me, and part of me hated him for that, even as I ached to see him, talk to him. The newscast tonight had been bittersweet to watch.

I finished my drink in one long gulp, pushing Tigger aside as I got on the floor and started doing sit-ups. When the liquor didn't work to quiet my brain, I exercised, trying to make myself as exhausted as I possibly could. Sit-ups and push-ups when it was dark outside, running when it wasn't.

I was in great shape. I wish I cared.

Running always made me think of Kade. Kade Dennon. Ex–FBI agent. Assassin-for-hire. Blane's half brother. I hadn't heard from him in months, not since the night he'd kissed me and told me I should be with him, not Blane.

I hadn't counted on how much I'd miss having him in my life.

I glanced at my cell phone as I lay panting on the floor, my abdominal muscles screaming at me. Blane and Kade were still listed in my contacts. I should get rid of them, and I would. Just not tonight.

A warm breeze flowed through the open window, bringing with it the familiar scent of a summer's night. At the moment, no sirens wailed and I could hear the occasional car pass by. I wondered what Blane was doing, and if it included Charlotte.

~

Sunlight streaming through the window and a marmalade lump of feline woke me Saturday morning. I'd fallen asleep on the floor and now my back ached. Tigger used my stomach as a pillow, his clawless paws kneading my flesh.

"Give it a rest," I grumbled as I sat up. He complained about the loss of his pillow and followed me into the kitchen, where I started the coffeemaker. I went for a run and showered before bolting down some caffeine. I had homework to do and had agreed to meet Clarice for lunch today.

A few hours later, I was winding my way behind a hostess as she led me through a local restaurant to the patio tables outside. I was glad of that. I'd be able to leave my sunglasses on. Lack of sleep left a toll that makeup couldn't always cover.

Clarice had already arrived and was waiting for me. She stood to give me a hug. She wore a long, flowing skirt, a sleeveless top, and sandals.

"So good to see you!" she said.

"You, too." My smile was genuine. I'd missed seeing and talking to her every day.

"You look great," she added as we sat down.

"Thanks. So do you."

And she did look fantastic. Being in love agreed with her. She was a mother of two who'd been divorced for some years. Right before Valentine's Day, the high-school science teacher she'd been dating had proposed.

"So how is Jack?" I asked, scooting my chair into the shade of the umbrella. I'd worn a spaghetti-strap sundress today and I didn't want my arms or shoulders to get burned.

"Jack's great, kids are good, too," she replied. "They're so excited for the wedding."

"Just them?" I teased.

She grinned. "Okay, me, too."

We laughed. "Two weeks," I said, "and you'll be Mrs. Jack Bryant."

"I know. I can't wait."

Clarice looked so happy it practically radiated from her. It was wonderful to see and I was so glad she'd found someone who made her feel that way. She certainly deserved it.

We paused to order when the waitress came by. Clarice joined me indulging in a cold glass of chardonnay.

"Your dress fitting is Thursday afternoon," she said. "Can you make it?"

I was one of her bridesmaids. "Sure," I said.

We chatted for a while about the wedding plans and where she and Jack were going on their honeymoon—Hawaii. We ate our salads and drank our wine and it felt nice and normal to be having lunch with a girlfriend.

"So," Clarice said after we'd exhausted the topic of her impending nuptials. "How are you doing, really?"

I stiffened. Clarice and I always refrained from talking about Blane or the breakup. I refused to let her. Since she was his secretary, I didn't want to put her in a bad position, and I didn't want to be tempted to quiz her about Blane. I'd told her he'd broken off the engagement and that was all.

My smile was forced. "I'm fine. Just takes some time, you know?"

"I know, but I worry about you," she said. "You've lost weight, it seems you hardly eat anymore. I mean don't get me wrong, you look great, but I can tell you're unhappy. It's written all over you."

"Well, I can't say I recommend the breakup diet," I admitted. "But I'll be fine. I just . . . want to move on." I paused. "It certainly seems he has."

I could hear the bitterness in my voice and knew I shouldn't have said that. I didn't want to know, didn't want to hear about Blane. But I also really did, and after seeing him on TV last night, I couldn't help hoping Clarice would tell me something, even though I knew it would hurt and I'd regret hearing it.

She hesitated. Then carefully she said, "I don't know about that."

My breath seemed to freeze in my lungs. "What do you mean?"

"He's not the same, at all. I mean, yeah, he's dating other women, but it's like it was before. Blane's always been real professional at the office, but he was happy with you. I could see it. Now, I never see him crack a smile or a joke.

He's just constantly on the move, pushing himself. He never slows down."

I swallowed and readjusted my sunglasses while I digested this. I knew what Clarice meant about it being "like it was before." Blane had been a playboy for years, always a different woman on his arm. The time he'd spent with me was the longest I think he'd been with someone in quite a while.

"Well, I'm sure he'll be fine," I said stiffly. "So he and Charlotte . . . ?"

I left the question dangling.

Clarice's lips thinned. "Yeah, she's managed to weasel her way in."

I frowned. "I thought you liked her."

"I did, when she wasn't trying to be Blane's shadow."

"What do you mean?"

"She's always there, always wanting to help him or something. Like last night. His uncle insisted he take a date to that fund-raiser. Well, wouldn't you know, Charlotte just happened to be available, so he didn't have to show up without one." Clarice's disdain was clear. "I mean, she couldn't be more obvious if she tried, but I think Blane is completely oblivious."

Clarice's mention of Blane's great-uncle had me clenching my fists in anger. I hated the man. A powerful politician from Massachusetts, Senator Robert Keaston had been re-elected so many times it was now a mere formality.

Keaston had wanted me to break up with Blane, had tried to bribe me to do so. When that hadn't worked and Blane and I got engaged, Keaston had lied to Blane about Kade and me having an affair. It made me furious that not only was Blane still listening to his uncle, but apparently

Keaston was being as meddlesome as ever and Blane was just letting him.

"What about you?" she asked. "Are you seeing anyone?"

I shook my head. "No. I don't want that right now. I'm not ready."

The idea was ludicrous to me. I was still in love with Blane, no matter how much he'd hurt me. I couldn't just turn that off like a light switch.

Clarice studied the remaining wine in her glass as she asked her next question with deliberate casualness. "Have you talked to Kade lately?"

She knew that Kade and Blane were half brothers, though most people did not. Both Blane and Kade chose to keep it that way.

"No. Why?"

She looked up at me. "Because neither has Blane. I mean, I know they used to talk several times a week. Kade would call the office, or Blane would have me get him on the phone, but as far as I know, they haven't spoken since you and Blane broke up."

My stomach sank into knots as guilt rose like nausea. It was my fault they weren't speaking. I had come between them. Even after Blane had accused me of sleeping with Kade, I'd hoped Kade could talk some sense into him. Even if Blane didn't believe Kade's denials, I thought he'd forgive him. They were brothers, after all, and history had proven them to be extremely loyal to each other. I was just the girl-friend, and as Blane had proven time and time again, girl-friends were replaceable. Brothers were not.

I couldn't eat another bite of my salad and just sipped my wine as Clarice changed the subject, sensing my distress.

I nodded and smiled, but didn't hear ten percent of what she said, my thoughts in a jumble.

Should I try to call Kade? Figure out what was going on between him and Blane? My heart leapt at the thought of talking to him again, wanting it so bad it was like a physical need. God, I missed him.

But no, I shouldn't get involved. I was the cause of their estrangement. I certainly wasn't going to be the one who could fix it.

I was leaving the restaurant after reassuring Clarice I'd be at the fitting on Thursday when I saw him.

A man was loitering near one of the storefronts lining the street. He appeared to be window-shopping, but every few seconds, he'd glance my way. Before my training with Kade, I would never have noticed. But Kade had made me practice until I reflexively took stock of my surroundings.

Pretending I didn't see him, I got in my car and started the engine. I fiddled with my hair while I watched him in the rearview mirror. He hurried to get into a blue sedan.

I drove a circuitous route home, always keeping an eye on the sedan, which stayed at least three or four cars behind me at all times. I had no idea who he was or why he was following me, and I certainly didn't want to lead him to my house. I mulled over what to do until an opportunity presented itself.

The stoplight ahead was green, so I slowed down. It turned yellow as I drew near, then red just as I hit the line. I gunned it, shooting through the intersection and barely missing the cars crossing the opposite direction. Tires squealed and I heard someone honk, then I was through. A glance in the mirror showed that the sedan was stuck behind three cars at the light. I drove quickly to leave him behind, glad to have lost him.

Weird.

I spent the afternoon studying and doing homework before heading in to work. I tried not to dwell on the things Clarice had said, but it was futile. Blane with other women. Blane becoming close with Charlotte. Blane and Kade not speaking.

I was even more despondent than usual. But I didn't cry. I hadn't cried since the night Alisha had come over and I'd told her everything. Since then, I'd carried on. I worked, I signed up for classes, and I started attending once the summer session began. I did my laundry, cleaned my apartment, and did all the things one did that said I was living my life.

And I tried to pretend it wasn't a lie.

I was nearly at The Drop when I saw the blue sedan again.

He was trailing me like he had earlier, three cars behind. How the hell had he found me?

He must know where I live.

A shiver of fear went through me, but I quickly shrugged it off.

How dare he follow me? Try to scare me? The bastard.

I parked a couple of blocks from The Drop and grabbed my purse. Locking the car door, I started walking, taking the back way in between the buildings. It was light—the sun wouldn't set for a few hours—but the shadows were thick in the alleyways.

Pausing, I opened my purse and took out a compact. As I pretended to powder my nose, I watched in the mirror. Sure enough, the same guy had gotten out of the car and was following me on foot. I took quick measure of him. He was about five eleven, maybe a hundred eighty pounds. Not huge, but not small either.

I snapped my compact closed and resumed walking. My hand remained inside my purse.

Turning a corner, I slipped into the shadows, and waited. When he stepped into view, he was only a foot from me and he had a gun pointed at his chest.

"Who are you and why are you following me?" I asked. The gun was steady in my two-handed grip.

"Whoa, take it easy," he said, putting his hands up.

"Answer the questions," I demanded.

"Listen, lady, I don't know what you're talking about—"

I cocked the hammer back on the gun.

"All right, all right!" he said in alarm. "I'm just doing a job, okay?"

"You're supposed to scare me? Hurt me? Kill me?" I asked. It wouldn't be the first time, which probably explained my utter lack of shock.

"No, I swear! None of that!"

"Then what?"

The guy swallowed, his eyes on my gun. "This wasn't supposed to be a dangerous job," he muttered.

"Tell me!"

"Fine! I was just supposed to follow you, keep an eye on you, make sure nothing happened to you," he said. "Though it looks like you can take care of yourself well enough," he added in an irritated undertone.

"Who hired you?" I asked, trying to process his claim that he supposedly wasn't following me to hurt me, but to . . . protect me. Why?

He pressed his lips together, refusing to answer.

I lowered my gun to point it at his knee.

"You like your knees?" I threatened.

Sweat broke out on his forehead and he swallowed heavily. "Fine," he said. "Blane Kirk hired me, okay? Now can you put the gun down? Please?"

I reeled, the name dropping like a load of bricks on my consciousness. Confusion and shock were followed quickly by rage.

Lowering the gun, I got in the guy's face.

"You tell your boss," I spat, "to leave me the fuck alone. If he sends someone else to follow me, he'll regret it and so will they."

I left him standing in the alley while I walked quickly to The Drop, my hands shaking uncontrollably as I put the gun back in my purse. When I reached work, I locked myself in a bathroom stall.

My heart was pounding and tears wet my lashes as I tried to hold them back. I breathed, closed my eyes, and tried to get a grip.

Why would Blane have someone follow me? It didn't make any sense. Was he afraid I was going to go to the press about the relationship we'd had? Leak all the sordid details? There were plenty of women who could do that. Or if the guy had been telling the truth, that he was supposed to make sure nothing happened to me, then why would I be in danger?

I couldn't concentrate on any of this, my emotions still overruling my logic. Blane still thought of me—albeit in his usual heavy-handed, controlling way. It was pathetic how much of an impact that made on me. *I* was pathetic. How embarrassing.

God, I needed a drink.

I escaped the bathroom and clocked in. We were already busy and I had little time to do more than throw a quick hello to Scott and Tish. However, I did find time to toss back a shot of bourbon, to steady myself.

A group of four college guys came in at some point during the night, setting up at a table close to the bar. They wore casual clothes that I could tell were expensive brands, which meant they had money. I told Scott I'd take the table and headed over there.

They were cute and funny, and I flirted shamelessly as I delivered their drinks. Working for tips required its own kind of skill. I used to be friendly but keep my distance. Then a stripper I'd met a few months ago had given me some good advice.

You've got assets. Use them to your advantage. Men are fools for a nice set of boobs.

I'd taken it to heart, and my tips had improved. While the uniform Romeo made us wear irritated me, it showed off an impressive display of cleavage. And judging by the college boys' lingering stares as they got more inebriated, showing extra skin worked. If I was lucky, I'd get twenty bucks off that table tonight, maybe more if they got drunk enough.

Scott and I had a good rhythm when we worked together, and he was fun. He teased me mercilessly, making me laugh. I could almost push the whole incident with the man Blane had hired to the back of my mind.

But not completely, which was why I didn't turn them down when the college guys wanted me to do a round of shots with them. Business was slowing as one o'clock neared, so I didn't feel guilty leaving Scott behind the bar while I hung out with two remaining guys. The others were out on the dance floor with girls they'd picked up.

"So, Kathleen," one of them said—Bill or Brian, something with a B. "You busy after work?" He'd slung his arm around my waist as I stood next to their high-top table.

I tipped back the shot in my hand, the whiskey burning a fiery path down my throat, and tried to concentrate on what he'd said.

"Sorry," I said. "Gotta get home tonight. Maybe some other time."

I smiled to soften the rejection. Just because I wanted to relieve them of some of their cash didn't mean I wanted a date, even if he was a good-looking guy.

"We could have a real good time," he insisted. His hand drifted down to my ass.

"Just the three of us," the other guy chimed in. I wanted to say his name was Trey.

I looked at him in surprise and he laughed. "Betcha never done that before, right?"

If I'd expected Bill/Brian to object, I was disappointed. He seemed all for the idea. He'd gripped my waist and tugged me back between his thighs so I faced Trey, who'd scooted his stool closer.

"You're fuckin' hot, Kathleen," Bill/Brian said in my ear. "We'll take good care of you. Don't you worry."

I swallowed hard, trying to fight the rising panic in my chest just as Trey leaned over and kissed me. My hands automatically came up to push him away, but they were caught and held by the guy behind me.

Well, fuck. There goes my tip, I thought sourly.

I jerked my head back hard, cracking Bill/Brian in the face. He yelped and let me go. I quickly slipped out from between the two men.

"I'm not into that," I said calmly from a couple feet away.

Bill/Brian was cupping his nose with his hand.

Trey spoke first. "Sorry there, Kathleen. We meant no harm."

I eyed him suspiciously, but he seemed sincere, for a drunk guy.

"Yeah, sorry," Bill/Brian said, his voice muffled from behind his hand. "The way you were acting . . . well, we obviously got the wrong idea there."

I nodded and headed back to the bar. So I was such an obviously easy lay that a couple of college guys assumed I would be into a threesome one-night stand?

I poured myself a drink.

"Those guys get out of hand?" Scott asked, sidling up next to me.

I shook my head. "Nothing I can't handle."

He nodded and Tish handed him an order to fill.

By the time I'd restocked the bar and begun cleanup, the table of guys had gone. They left me fifty bucks, which I supposed was their way of saying sorry. Whatever. It was much better than I thought I'd get after nailing that guy in the face.

Scott and Tish left after I assured them I'd close up.

"You sure?" Tish asked as she grabbed her purse.

"No worries," I said. "See you Monday."

When I was alone, I locked the front door and turned off all the lights but the ones that shone directly down on the bar. I was keyed up, despite the drinks I'd had tonight. The incident with the college guys bothered me and I still couldn't get Blane out of my head.

Maybe I should've gone home with Trey and Bill. Or Brian. Or whatever his name had been.

With a sigh, I eased myself onto a barstool and took a swig of the beer in my hand. I rested my head in one hand, my elbow braced on the bar. My other hand toyed with the beer bottle. I wasn't in a hurry to get home.

Jeff, the cook at The Drop, had made me a hamburger earlier, and glowered at me until I'd taken a few bites. Jeff was a bald Army guy with tattoos up and down his arms. Romeo was terrified of him, though he'd always been nice to me. He was a man of few words, content to cook and smoke his cigarettes, usually at the same time. He'd taken a particular interest in making me eat lately, which was sweet of him.

I was lucky, I told myself. I had great friends who cared about me. And I was being cruel to them by making them worry. I just needed to get over it already. People broke up, got divorced, and died all the time. I was not the first to experience heartbreak.

A prickling on the back of my neck had me looking over my shoulder at the expanse of windows lining the walls. I couldn't see out, could only see my reflection in the opaque glass as it reflected the dim light from the bar.

Dismissing the sensation, I finished off the beer and tossed it. Time to go home.

The streets were quiet and empty at this hour. I walked slowly to my car. I loved summer nights when the heat of the day had passed and the warm darkness covered everything like a welcoming blanket. It had rained earlier, leaving the air smelling fresh and clean. I paused to look at the moon peeking from behind clouds. Bright and full, it was a good reminder that life goes on, that each day would get just a tiny bit easier until one day I'd wake up and not think about Blane at all.

My keys slipped out of my lax fingers, hitting the ground with the clink of metal against concrete. I grumbled a curse at my clumsiness and bent down.

A gunshot shattered the silence, and I cried out in alarm. The glass of the car window exploded above me and I instinctively crouched down, covering my head with my arm as the shards rained on me.

I scrabbled inside my purse, searching for my gun. Adrenaline coursed through my body. I heard the sound of gunfire again, but this time from another direction. Someone was shooting back, and it wasn't me.

Tires squealed and more gunshots rang out. I stayed down, not wanting to get in the cross fire of whatever I'd managed to land in the middle of. Gangs maybe—who knew? Just my luck, though.

When it was quiet again, save for the pounding of the blood in my ears, I gradually uncovered my head. A tickle on my face had me swiping my cheek, my hand coming away bloody. A piece of glass must have cut me. Great.

My knees were scraped from the concrete and I winced as I got to my feet. I glanced around to be sure the shooters were gone, wondering if I should call the cops. Then the breath left my lungs in a rush.

A man had stepped out of the shadows mere feet from me, a still-smoking gun in the hand at his side.

His familiar features made me swallow hard before I said, "So, I guess you were just in the neighborhood."

Here ends the first chapter of
Out of Turn.

Check Tiffany's website—www.TiffanyASnow.com—for more information on *The Kathleen Turner Series.*

ACKNOWLEDGMENTS

Thank you to Leslie, for your daily book reports. You're such an encouragement to me!

Thank you, Tracy, for taking the time and the fine-tooth comb to this. As always, your input was invaluable.

To my family, thank you for your patience and encouragement throughout the process of writing. Your support and enthusiasm have meant the world to me. I love you.

Thank you to Eleni and everyone at Montlake for your hard work on the release of *Turning Point*. I'm very grateful to you.

Lastly, I'm constantly amazed at the strength and perseverance of many of my friends, women who make the hard choices and sometimes must take the difficult path on the road to their own happiness and self-fulfillment. Their stories, how they have met and overcome the trials in their lives, have humbled me.

Whether it be cheating husbands, loveless marriages, motherhood and single motherhood, a burning desire to achieve the career of their dreams, or just the day-to-day living of their lives, my friends have amazed me with their strength in the face of life's challenges, humor in spite of life's disappointments, and love for each other no matter what, in good times and bad.

So to Nicole, Ronda, Stephanie, Paige, and Lisa, thank you for sharing your life, love, stories, and friendship with me. You inspire me, and in turn, Kathleen.